PRAISE FOR *THE PAL*

CU00829078

"*The Pale Flesh of Wood* is a nuanced literary novel about a family's intricate struggles with their legacies."

—*Foreword Clarion Reviews*

"Tucker has my favorite kind of gift on the page: she creates real deal intimacy between her characters and her audience. This is a family saga that showcases so many different people, and yet I knew and loved them all."

—Joshua Mohr, author of *Model Citizen*

"A beautifully written kaleidoscopic novel that explores the roots of depression, the long shadow of grief, and the healing power of time."

—Stephanie Reents, author of *The Kissing List*

"*The Pale Flesh of Wood* is epic and intimate all at once, both sweeping and deep. As its title suggests, this novel sees beneath the surface of things, taps the lifeblood pulsing inside families and communities and the natural world. Elizabeth A. Tucker has crafted a masterpiece—I can't wait to see what this gifted author will write next!"

—Gayle Brandeis, author of *Drawing Breath: Essays on Writing, the Body, and Loss*

"It is no exaggeration to say I made friends with many of the richly drawn characters in this novel, which is both lyrical and precise in its choices, and quintessentially Californian. Three generations of Hawkins-folk, charismatic, troubled, tenacious, straight-backed, not unlike the oak at the center of the story—they got under my skin in the best possible ways and remain there. *The Pale Flesh of Wood* is a well-wrought, complex and deeply satisfying debut."

—Pam Houston, author of *Deep Creek, Finding Hope In The High Country*

THE
PALE
FLESH
OF
WOOD

THE PALE FLESH OF WOOD

A Novel

ELIZABETH A. TUCKER

SHE WRITES PRESS

Copyright © 2025 Elizabeth A. Tucker

All rights reserved. No part of this publication may be reproduced, distributed, or transmitted in any form or by any means, including photocopying, recording, digital scanning, or other electronic or mechanical methods, without the prior written permission of the publisher, except in the case of brief quotations embodied in critical reviews and certain other noncommercial uses permitted by copyright law. For permission requests, please address She Writes Press.

Published 2025
Printed in the United States of America
Print ISBN: 978-1-64742-834-1
E-ISBN: 978-1-64742-835-8
Library of Congress Control Number: 2024916255

For information, address:
She Writes Press
1569 Solano Ave #546
Berkeley, CA 94707

Interior Design by Tabitha Lahr

She Writes Press is a division of SparkPoint Studio, LLC.

Company and/or product names that are trade names, logos, trademarks, and/or registered trademarks of third parties are the property of their respective owners and are used in this book for purposes of identification and information only under the Fair Use Doctrine.

THIS IS A WORK OF FICTION. Names, characters, places, and incidents either are the product of the author's imagination or are used fictitiously. Any resemblance to actual persons, living or dead, is entirely coincidental.

NO AI TRAINING: Without in any way limiting the author's [and publisher's] exclusive rights under copyright, any use of this publication to "train" generative artificial intelligence (AI) technologies to generate text is expressly prohibited. The author reserves all rights to license uses of this work for generative AI training and development of machine learning language models.

For Sadie, Joachim, and Matthew, my three glorious, dynamic, and natural wonders—the magnitude of all that is you registers deep and forever within my core.

And for my mother, who gave me life and taught me how to live.

The tree is more than first a seed, then a stem, then a living trunk, and then dead timber. The tree is a slow, enduring force straining to win the sky.

—Antoine de Saint-Exupéry

CONTENTS

BOOK I

(1931–1956)

CHAPTER ONE

RELIEF PATTERNS—JUNE 1953

"She's a real beauty, isn't she?" Lyla's father slapped the old oak tree as though he were spanking the hindquarters of a prized Thoroughbred.

But Lyla didn't answer. She stood underneath the enormous tree, eyeing it, wondering how in the world she'd crawl out along the branch to tie off the rope for their swing. Sure, the branch seemed sturdy enough with its thick muscular arm reaching high and wide over the grassy hill. Still, it was a good fifteen feet off the ground, and she'd never climbed that high before, not even when her cousin Robert scrambled up there last summer, calling her a scaredy-cat when she refused to follow him. But that was last year when she was six. She'd climbed plenty since then.

"What do you say, birdpie? You ready to hang our swing or what?" Lyla's father heaved an acorn out into the dried, yellowed grass. "Or you just gonna stand there all day thinking about it?"

Lyla bit her lip. What would happen if she lost her balance? What if her father got distracted like when she'd jumped off the back of the couch last week? He was supposed to catch her but had reached over to grab his drink instead and let Lyla tumble to the floor. Her right ankle still throbbed a bit.

On the opposite side of the trunk was another branch—equally strong, equally thick—but it was too close to the ground. Her father would never go for that one; he'd claim it was for *sissies*, a word that bit like a splinter stuck under her skin.

The California live oak stood just beyond her grandparents' back fence like a giant, like Gulliver in the land of Lilliput, its arms stretched wide and ready to scoop up little children and steal them away. Winter or summer, spring or fall, with or without its leaves, the tree commanded center stage of the Hawkinses' property, as if everything—the structure of the house, the perimeter of the sun-beaten gray fence, and the rolling hills beyond—were all being held together by the tree's roots. Under this tree, Lyla's family took their annual Christmas photograph or gathered beneath its branches for summer picnics when Grandmother Caroline declared it was too hot to eat inside. And four feet underneath was the very spot where poor old Jefferson, the favorite of their family presidential dogs, was buried after he succumbed to old age.

Even from inside the house, the plate glass windows framed the tree like a work of art, drawing one's eye to the foreground so the mind had no choice but to blur the rest. The surrounding landscape with its golden hills and deep vales became nothing more than a mere backdrop. Years later, when Lyla's therapist would encourage her to draw a picture about the day her father left them, all she'd remember to sketch would be the tree. She wouldn't include the hills at all.

"Earth to Lyla." Her father fiddled with the dials of an imaginary walkie-talkie. He even made the fuzzy, crackling sounds of a radio slipping in and out of range. "Zzzzz, come in, Lyla. Zzzzz, do you copy?"

Lyla pulled her own pretend two-way from the pocket of her red jumper. "I hear you loud and clear, Daddy, but I think we should go find another tree. This one's no good."

"No good?" her father roared. "Why, this is the perfect tree, Lyla, and you damn well know it." Her father was no longer speaking into his pretend radio; he was staring right into her, which made Lyla's face burn hot and her stomach grow cold. His eyes narrowed. "Listen, sweetheart. You know I've been itching to hang a swing in this tree ever since I was your age, and your grandmother just gave us the go-ahead. We can't back out now." He turned his pretend radio back on as he stared up into the canopy. "This tree will do just fine. Over and out."

Lyla took several steps away from the tree to see what it was her father saw. What made him so darn certain this was the only one, that no other tree around the property would do? But standing back, looking at how the canopy slightly listed over to one side, Lyla suddenly thought of the old-fashioned hat the family cajoled her grandmother to wear when they dressed up like pioneers at the state fair. Lyla let out a small burbling laugh remembering her grandmother, seated at the center of the Hawkins family and staring dour-faced into the camera with that ridiculous hat flopped over her head while her two grown sons stood on either side—one hand on their empty rifles, the other on their mother's stone-stiff shoulders. When the cameraman held up his fingers and counted to three, *poof* went the bright white flash in the phony saloon, but Lyla's grandmother didn't say cheese. She didn't even smile. Yet that old-timey photograph was living proof her grandmother could be convinced to do things against her better judgment.

"It was my damned tree," Caroline would say years later as she and Lyla stared out the kitchen window one dawn. "Your father had no right to do what he did out there."

And it was true. No matter how many times Lyla's father told stories about how he'd climbed the tree out back of his childhood home, how many times he'd hidden behind it while playing hide-and-seek with his brother or avoiding the belt from his mother, how many times he'd snuck out back with his father's cigarettes, smoking jig after jig behind the enormous trunk, or even the time he'd kissed his first girlfriend under the wide canopy one September afternoon, it was still *her* tree.

―――――――――――

"Oh, for Pete's sake," Caroline had relented earlier that morning when Lyla's father pressed his mother into finally letting him hang a swing in the tree. Why she gave in, nobody knew. She just did. Just like that. *Poof.*

"Good Lord. Go ahead and put one up, if you want one so bad. See if I care." She flung her sudsy hands out of the dishwater as she rinsed the last of the breakfast dishes. Bubbles flew up and drifted around the kitchen. "But I don't want anyone to come in here boo-hooing because they got hurt, do you hear me?"

"You won't hear a peep." Lyla's father tossed his dish towel onto the back of the chair where it hung like wet hair. He kissed his mother on the cheek and burst out of the kitchen, bright-eyed with equal measure of happiness and disbelief. It was the same look he wore after Bobby Thomson hit his famous three-run homer, settling the 1951 pennant race—when Lyla's father turned off the television and sauntered over to the bar to fix himself a drink as though he were the one responsible for the Giants' ninth-inning victory that day.

―――――――――――

Lyla turned her pretend radio back on. "All right, Daddy. I'll do it."

Her father kicked himself away from the tree where he'd been leaning against the trunk, his arms folded across his chest, his hat dipped over his eyes as though he had fallen asleep while waiting for Lyla to make up her mind.

"If you honestly think it's the best one," she said. "Over and out."

Her father spat out a long blade of grass. "Hot diggity dog! I knew you'd come around, Lyla." He winked. "You always do." He grabbed the rope off the ground and slung it over his shoulder as he stared up at the underskirt of the tree. "Sometimes we just need a little time to warm up to an idea, right?"

"Righty-o," Lyla agreed, all puffed up inside, warmed by the idea that she helped the smile grow bright in her father's eyes. "But at least I didn't take as long as you-know-who." Lyla cocked her head in the direction of the house.

"Boy, I'll say." Lyla's father stole a glance to the kitchen window where his mother was already preparing lunch. "Heck, I'd be an old man if you'd waited any longer."

Lyla's father peeled a piece of bark off the trunk and broke it in two. "Here," he said, handing half to Lyla, keeping the other for himself. He slipped his eyes closed and ran the peeled bark under his nose like a fine cigar. A dreamy sort of look spread across his face.

"Lyla?"

"Yes, Daddy."

"I have something to tell you, a confession, actually."

"A confession?"

"Yeah, but you gotta promise you won't run in there and tell your mother. Okay?"

Lyla felt the insides of her stomach tug apart. She didn't like being asked to keep secrets from her mother, but she didn't want to see her father's smile turn upside down like it did sometimes. "Okay, Daddy. I promise." Lyla crossed her heart and hoped to die.

"Okay, well. You know I served over in Italy, right?"

"Course I do. You've only told me like a million times."

"Well—" He paused, inhaling the smell of his oak piece. "When I was over there doing what we had to do, it was the smell of this tree I missed most."

"More than Mama?" Lyla took a small, careful whiff of her bark slice.

"Oh, your mother smells awful nice, and boy did I miss the *feel* of her during the war. But she doesn't smell like this old tree. Nothing comes even close."

And there, under the oak's wide canopy that June morning, Lyla's father told her about the time he'd written to Lyla's mother, asking her to send him a piece of bark, a bit small enough to fit into the breast pocket of his fatigues so he could pull it out from time to time and smell home.

"I needed something to remind me of what I was over there fighting for."

"Did she?" Lyla rubbed her thumb along the soft, mealy underside of the bark chip as though it were a rabbit's foot. Waiting for her father to answer, she weighed it in her hands. Heavier than a kestrel feather, lighter than an obsidian arrowhead—both of which she'd found while exploring the back hills the week before and had kept hidden in the shoebox of special things she kept tucked under her bed.

"Nah." Her father bit into his bark slice, tucking a chunk of the oaky rind under his lower lip like a plug of chewing tobacco. "Somewhere along the line, my letter got lost and that was that." The dream in his eyes slipped away.

"Didn't you write to her again?"

"Nope." Her father reached over and picked a stray eyelash off Lyla's cheek and held it under the sunlight. "Here, make a wish."

Lyla pinched her eyes shut and tried to think of something to wish for. But on that morning, she came up short; she couldn't think of anything at all she wanted.

Lyla opened her eyes. "Got one," she fibbed, and let her father blow the eyelash from his fingers where it trailed off like a dandelion puff. "So, what did you do?" Lyla pressed.

"What did I do? Why, the simplest thing of all, sweetheart. I learned how to manufacture the smell of the tree from memory."

"From memory?"

"Yes." Her father smiled, tapping the side of his head. "You can do a lot with memory. Trust me."

Her father went on to tell her about how he'd sit in those dirty foxholes night after night, concentrating on nothing else but the color and the smell of the tree. How he'd been able to fool himself into smelling past the rot of feet, past the stench of urine, past the lingering haze of sulfur from a recently fired howitzer.

"I'd concentrate as hard as I could until I could finally smell home." He turned to Lyla with a look—not quite a smile, but something awfully close to it—and then in a whisper, he said, "God, I hated it over there." His teeth clenched, and the three creases in his forehead tightened.

Lyla hated how those clouds could suddenly take over the look in her father's eyes like that. This time she took a deep whiff of her bark piece. She couldn't quite smell what he'd described, but she didn't doubt him either. She slipped the small flake into the pocket of her jumper, determined to try again later that night at home after her mother tucked her into bed.

"God, what I wouldn't have done to be back here"—Lyla's father pressed his pointer finger in between her eyebrows and whispered, "*Bang!*—instead of shooting strangers in the tight spaces between their eyes. You know what I mean?"

Lyla flinched. But before she could say she didn't like it when he pretended to shoot her in the head like that, he spit his piece of bark out into the grass and walked underneath the branch, measuring his steps to the point where Lyla would crawl out and hang their swing. His knuckles grew bone white as he clutched the rope, but his eyes were back to clear bright blue when he turned to her. "God, I can't believe she finally said yes."

Just then, Lyla heard the living room door slide open. Her mother walked outside with Baby Daniel in her arms, waving out to them before leaning over and giving Lyla's grandfather, who had been sitting on the back porch reading the newspaper, a kiss on the cheek. Lyla watched Pops fold his paper and snub out his cigarette. He took Lyla's baby brother into his arms, kissing Daniel on the red sprouts of hair, red like Mama's. Pops then picked his newspaper up and began reading to Daniel. Although Lyla couldn't hear what he was saying, she figured he was reviewing the pitching stats from last week's games. Pops loved baseball, almost as much as he loved sailing. Maybe even more.

Lyla turned back to her father. "If Grandmother Caroline always said no, why didn't you just go ask Pops? He lets me do anything."

"Are you kidding?" Lyla's father burst into laughter. "You know how it works around here. If your grandmother says no, then Pops, God bless him, knows when to keep his trap shut. Anyhow, who knows what goes on inside that head of your grandmother's. I sure don't. Never have." He twirled his finger by the side of his head and made googly eyes, which made Lyla laugh. "Well, you'd better scoot on up there and tie off the rope, before she comes out and changes her mind. What do you say?"

Lyla chewed the inside of her cheek, a habit her grandmother swore she'd break, if it was the last thing on earth she'd do.

"Can't you do it?" Lyla finally asked. But she knew the answer. There was no way her father could climb up there with his bad knee and all. When they'd been rooting around the garage earlier for a rope, he'd told her she'd have to be the one to climb the tree. Inside the garage, Lyla readily agreed. But now, standing underneath the wide canopy, seeing how high the branch actually reached out, she wasn't so sure.

"Oh, come on, Lyla," he said, more patient than she'd expected. "It's not so bad. All you have to do is shimmy yourself out to there." Her father pointed to the middle of the branch. "And tie her off. Easy as pie."

But Lyla was no longer staring at the branch. She squinted through the gaps in the leaves, into the relief patterns made by the foliage against the new summer sky. It wasn't what was there—the intertwining branches, the small-cupped leaves, the tiny acorns holding tight as buttons to the branchlets—but what was not. The shape and darkness of the leaves against the summer sky reminded her of the woodblock print that had hung over her parents' bed but had fallen from the wall during a small earthquake a few months before. The painting, cracked and cockeyed in its frame, remained leaning against the wall next to their dresser.

"What if the branch breaks?" Lyla knew she was pressing her luck.

"That branch!" Her father let out a riotous laugh, a roar so loud it shocked Lyla, just like when her cousin Robert dragged his feet on the carpet and snuck up from behind to touch her arm. "You've got to be kidding. There's not a snowball's chance in hell *that* branch could break. Why, it could hold the weight of a grown man. Easy."

Lyla's face pinched; she crossed her arms. She hated it when her father made her feel so dumb. Sometimes she even wished he wouldn't joke around at all, that he could just be a *normal* dad, like her uncle David. Someone serious. The next time her father blew one of her lashes away, Lyla swore she'd wish for him to stop making her feel stupid.

"Oh, come here, silly goose." Lyla's father got down on his good knee and opened his arms. "Give your old man a hug, will ya?" When Lyla refused, he pulled her toward him, holding Lyla's face close to his. They remained still for a few quiet seconds—their matching blue eyes a mere inch from one another. Her father rubbed the tip of his nose to hers. Lyla couldn't help but let a smile slip out when her father made her stand so close to him like that. His hot breath felt funny on her cheeks.

"I wouldn't do anything to hurt you, Lyla. You know that, don't you?"

"I do, but . . ."

"But what?" He slipped the rope off his shoulder and arranged it around Lyla's neck. "You think I'd let you fall?" He began squaring the line, so it lay over Lyla's shoulders in just the same way he'd straightened the epaulets on Uncle David's winter uniform before he walked down the aisle at his wedding to Aunt Dianna.

Lyla's father liked order; he liked things just so.

"Is that what you think?" he asked.

Lyla didn't answer.

"Well, for the record, I'd never let that happen. Not in a million years." He lifted her chin. "And even if you did fall, I'd be right here to catch you. Pinky promise." Her father held out his pinky finger, but Lyla didn't hook her finger to his.

She did trust her father, but still, he had turned his back when she'd thought he was going to catch her from the couch, leaving her to lie on the floor and watch him sip his drink instead.

"Can't we just put it up on that one?" Lyla pointed to the lower branch, the one her father had to duck under.

"We could, but that pretty skirt of yours will be dragging in the dirt if we do." Her father propped his hands on his thigh and puffed out a horse's snort as he pushed back to his feet. "Plus, if we use that one"—he pointed to the higher branch—"I can really send you flying. You'd like that, wouldn't you?"

"Sure, but—" Lyla paused.

"But what? Jesus, Lyla, do you want a baby swing? Is that it?" The way her father squished his face when he said the word *baby* made it sound like a bad word, like *Kraut* or *Wop*.

"I'm not a baby!" Lyla snipped, feeling the red flush in her cheeks.

Lyla's father bent over and laid his hands on her shoulders. She watched his Adam's apple bob up and down before he spoke again. "I didn't say *you* were a baby. I just asked if you wanted a baby-girl swing. That's all. Geez." He then walked around the base of the tree, kicking the kinks out of his bad knee, and when he came around the other side, he was smiling again. "But I'm happy to hang it on that branch, if it's what you really want?" He gave another quick punt to his knee. "Your choice, sweetheart."

Lyla could feel her father losing patience. He might even call it quits if she didn't hurry up and do what he asked.

"It's just—" Lyla's shoulders buckled under the heft of the rope that now felt like it weighed a hundred pounds.

Before she could finish her thought, her father got back down on his good knee. He was smiling his nice smile again, the one he wore when he bent over her bed and gave her butterfly kisses on the cheek in the morning before school. "Listen, Lyla. I know you're scared. I can see it clear as day. But you're going to be fine. Here," he said, wrapping her arms around his chest. "Pretend I'm that branch and give me a great big squeeze."

Lyla hugged her father close and tight. He always smelled of wind and vanilla on Sundays after they had gone to church.

"Come on! Is that all you got?" he teased, sputtering out a small breath.

Lyla tightened her grip and squeezed harder.

"That's my girl. Now, when you climb out along the branch, just pretend you are hugging me, and you'll be just fine."

"You won't move?"

"Not a single, solitary inch."

Lyla held out her little finger first this time. "Pinky promise?"

Her father smiled and hooked his little finger around hers.

Together they counted, "One, two, three," before letting their hands fly apart like birds. No one in the Hawkinses' house ever broke a pinky promise. Never ever.

Lyla turned to face the thick trunk. "Okay, Daddy. Lift me up."

Lyla's father grabbed hold of her under the armpits and raised her into the neck of the tree. She took a moment to hold on and catch her breath. Out in the distance, the dry golden grasses ran along the backs of the rounded hills, making soft rustling sounds like an animal sneaking around. Lyla's stomach tightened; her right leg began to jackhammer.

Below, her father circled the base of the tree, whistling as he fingered the loose change in his front pockets like worry beads.

You said you wouldn't move an inch, Lyla wanted to remind him.

The branch seemed to stretch out for eternity.

"It's too far, Daddy. I want to come down."

Her father stopped whistling and looked up at her as though Lyla had asked for something ridiculous, like a monkey for a pet. He didn't say a word, but just went around the tree again. This time, he had folded his hands into his armpits and started clucking like a chicken.

"Bwaaaack, bwaaaack!" he clucked with the high, throaty cackle of a hen celebrating the laying of an egg.

"Daddy!" Lyla's face reddened.

"Oh, come on, Lyla. I was just having a little fun. You know that."

He flashed that easy smile of his, the one Grandmother Caroline insisted was the *Smile of God*.

Lyla's leg jackhammered harder on the branch. She was pretty sure God wouldn't be clucking around in the dirt like a chicken. But still, she couldn't back down now. She glanced over at Pops who was playing peek-a-boo with her baby brother. A heat surged through her, watching how her grandfather was doting on Daniel. She took a breath and finally found the courage to lower herself onto the branch, bellying her way out, inch by slow inch, scraping the insides of her knees along the rough bark.

If earthworms could climb this high, Lyla thought—refusing to look at the ground or her father—*they'd certainly make faster progress*. She had the end of the rope clenched tight in her teeth. She could even taste the salt and iron trapped in the fibers of Pops's old boat line. It tasted like blood.

"Okay, birdpie, that's far enough," her father instructed. "Stop right there and tie her off."

Lyla drew in a long breath; she tightened her thighs around the branch and sat up, straddling the thick limb like she was riding a horse. She slid the rope off her neck and rested the coil over the broad back of the woody limb. Feeling steadier, she uncoiled the end of the line and marveled at how small her father looked as he stood on the ground below. Why, he looked like an ordinary man, instead of a giraffe!

"Okay, shorty, now what?" Lyla teased.

"Shorty?" Her father reached up and took a light swat at her feet. He missed. "Who are you calling shorty?" He took a few steps back and attempted a running layup, trying again to tap her shoe. "Heck, I wasn't the center of our basketball team because of my good looks, I'll have you know."

Lyla scrunched up her legs each time her father jumped and then dangled them back down in a teasing way when he missed. "Can't get me, short stuff."

"Oh, is that so?" Again, her father jumped. But this time when Lyla drew her legs up, she bobbled over to one side of the branch.

"Careful now." Her father threw his hands out to catch her. "I can't have you falling before we've even hung our swing. Not with your mother watching."

But Lyla's mother wasn't watching; she never had time to watch her now that Baby Daniel was born. Her mother was resting on the lounge chair with her big black sunglasses covering her eyes. Her skirt was folded up over her knees, and she held the insides of her arms out to the sun as though she were asleep at the beach, tanning herself. Pops was oohing and aahing over her baby brother just like he used to do when he clowned around with Lyla. Once Baby Daniel came into the world, Pops no longer bounced Lyla on his knees, singing, "*This is how the horsey goes.*" Now that she was older, he liked to play catch with her instead, insisting one day she'd pitch for the Giants. "You'll be the first female to pitch in the majors. Mark my word," he'd say every time Lyla stood on the mound that Pops had fashioned at the edge of the lawn.

Sometimes Lyla wished she was still small enough for Pops to bounce her on his knee.

Sometimes she even wished Daniel was never born.

———

"Earth to Lyla. Come in Lyla." Her father was again talking into his pretend radio.

Lyla steadied her eyes and held the end of the line out in front of her like reins. "What now, Daddy?"

"You know what to do. Go ahead and wrap the end in your right hand around the branch a couple of times, then tie your bowline, just like we practiced."

Lyla payed out several feet of the rope and wrapped the end around the branch. But when it came time to tie a bowline, her mind went blank. The knot she'd tied hundreds of times before on Pops's sailboat became a mystery now that she was fifteen feet above the ground.

She made a small loop in the line but forgot what she was sup-posed to do with the other end. No sooner could she tie her own shoe up there than tie a stupid bowline. She shimmied more line around the branch. But because her hands were trembling, she accidentally knocked off the bulk of rope, where it dropped to the ground like a fat python, missing her father's head by inches.

"For Christ's sake, Lyla!" Her father threw his hands up over his head.

Lyla's face grew hotter. Tears began to well up. She tried to choke them down, certain her father would get after her for *crying like a little girl*, but she couldn't make them stop. The tears dribbled down her cheeks as she looked out to the dry grasses that minutes ago had rustled in the wind but now stood in a watery pool of gold.

"I want to get down!" She spoke more firmly this time, wiping the tears out of her eyes. "I don't want to do this anymore."

"Come on, Lyla." He snorted. His eyes flared. "You can't quit now. Just pull the damn rope back up and start over. Jesus, it's not the end of the world."

"No, Daddy. I can't. I won't."

"Yes, Lyla. You can. You will." Her father jabbed a finger at her. "Don't be a quitter. Hawkins men don't quit. You hear me?"

Hawkins men? I'm not even a boy, Lyla wanted to bark at her father, just like her mother did when she had to remind him that Lyla wasn't their son. Daniel was. *Don't push her so hard, Charles*, Lyla once heard her mother say while they were getting ready for a dinner party before Daniel was born. *I'll give you a son, I promise.* Fourteen months later, she did.

"It's okay, sweetheart," her father said, his voice once again calm. "Everything feels different when you're up there. Believe me, I know. Remember, the rabbit just goes around the tree and back into its hole. You can do this, Lyla. I know you can."

Lyla tightened her thighs into the saddle of the branch, the rough bark leaving tiny impressions on her pale skin like a cow brand. Hand over hand, she hauled the rope back up and listened to her father as he talked her through the knot—in and out and around and through, until she successfully tightened the bowline to the tree. She even tied two half hitches before lowering the other end back down.

"That's my girl." Her father stood on his tippy toes and grabbed hold of the rope, pulling the other end to the ground. "I knew you could do it, Ace!"

Lyla scooted backward along the branch, faster and more confident now. This time, when she stood in the neck of the tree, she wasn't even hanging on. "Look, Daddy. No hands." She waved her arms around.

"Lyla! Be careful up there, or I'll have to sleep on the couch for a week."

"You got that right, mister." Lyla's mother was no longer asleep on the lounge chair; she had magically appeared out of nowhere and was leaning up against the back fence with the movie camera in her hands. Lyla had no idea how long she had been standing there, filming the two of them.

"Lunch is ready, by the way," she announced. The lens was pointed directly at Lyla, but she was clearly talking to Charles. "And you'd better hurry or you won't hear the end of it. Your mother is in quite a dither this morning."

"Wait, Mama! Watch this." Lyla blew a long black strand of hair—black like her father's—out of her eyes. "Ready, Daddy?" she asked, preparing to jump.

"Not yet, Lyla. Give me a second." Her father was tugging on the line, making sure the knot was secure.

But Lyla had already started counting. "One, two—"

On three, her father rushed over with outstretched arms as Lyla leapt into the air like a flying squirrel, weightless in her success. He caught Lyla tight around the rib cage and, for a moment, her breath was blown clean out of her chest. Her father hugged her tight and kissed her good and hard on the cheek. And because it was Sunday, the tight little bristles of his beard didn't scratch her like they did on Saturday nights.

"I did it, Mama! I climbed up there and tied the bowline! Just like Daddy showed me. Right, Daddy?"

"You got that right." Lyla's father turned to the camera as he carried Lyla step-by-giant-step toward Lyla's mother. "You should have seen her, Louise. She climbed up there like an old pro. Not a lick of hesitation. Right, sweetheart?"

Hugging her father tight around his neck, Lyla could feel the wild heartbeat swallowed up in his chest.

She didn't bother to correct him.

But she didn't deny what he said either.

She just let his slippery words drift off into the dry golden hills, carried by the wind like one of her eyelashes, because she knew she'd done right by her father, the only thing that mattered on that cloudless June day.

CHAPTER TWO

THE THINGS WE IMAGINE—

SEPTEMBER 1931

"Stop!" Mother barked underneath the tree one September day. "You're squeezing too tight!"

My arms, thin as cattails, stretched around the trunk of Mother's unforgiving waist. But I did not stop. I would not let go.

Stop did not mean *no*.

Stop did not mean *let go*.

Stop meant *hold on tighter than ever before*.

"Charles Dean Hawkins, that is enough! You are hurting me," Mother said with a slap. "I said no and that is that."

My cheek stung, pink with her handprint, and I fell to the ground amongst the scattered acorns and waxy oak leaves recently rinsed from the great tree.

Her tree.

The tree that begged for a swing.

But I refused to get up.

You see, I rather liked it down there; earth to back, back to earth.

But Mother didn't care for it one bit. I could see it in her eyes, those cold wolf-blue eyes. She hovered over me, tight-faced, red-lipped, and told me in no uncertain terms to get up, to stop acting the fool.

"You should be ashamed of yourself," she snapped. Tiny bits of spittle flew from her tight, dry lips. "Now, get up before your father sees you acting like this."

"This?" I asked. I wasn't trying to annoy her.

"Yes, like a pill."

But she said so much more with those eyes. I've always heard Mother's eyes loud and clear, like thunder two clicks away. *Such a stupid, selfish boy*, she said with those cold blue eyes before she turned and marched back to the house, her long white hair, down for once, loose and flapping in the wind. *Just you wait.*

And I did.

Wait.

With Mother gone, I fell asleep under the enormous tree, only to wake hours later with the sun nearly finished for the day.

The disappearing light turned purple with cold; my mouth flamed orange with hot hurt.

"Mama," I called out.

But of course, she couldn't hear me. I hardly ever called her Mama. She hated such casual addresses, preferring Mother instead. *Mama*, she claimed, *was for hayseeds.*

———

There, in the new night sky, Venus was the first to shine.

Then Jupiter.

The slivered moon had already begun to chase the sun to the other side of the globe, to the shores of Japan. And back at the house, I could see Mother float from room to room, popping lights on one at a time. She glided and soared through the house, as though her feet never touched the ground. As if the wind was always at her back.

She eventually made her way to the kitchen where she stood at the sink, probably stone-faced and peeling potatoes.

I fought the urge to wave. I knew she couldn't see me. Or didn't want to. I started to push myself up, but something inside my ear began to wrestle around, tickling down the length of the canal. Whatever it was must have nestled deep inside while I had fallen asleep and then burrowed into the darkness of Mother's words.

Stop. You're hurting me. Let go, you stupid, foolish child.

I tried to tease the tickling thing out of my ear with my fingertip, but it was buried too deep inside.

"Come on out, you silly ol' thing. You don't belong in there." I tilted my head and yanked at my earlobe like when I tried to get pool water out of my ears. A little gray pill bug—curled in a tight ball—fell out and rolled across the dirt like a BB on the loose. When it came to a stop, the roly-poly didn't move. It just lay there in its protective ball, refusing to unfold, unwilling to open up and crawl back home to where it belonged.

I poked at the little guy with a small stick, jabbing at its shell. "Open up!" I ordered.

Seconds later, it did.

Plate by armored plate, the bug stretched to life. Fourteen squirming legs broke free. Its antennae skimmed the dirt as it trundled away. Who knew where it was going? But I too wished I could curl up tight in a ball, then roll away from Mother's disappointed eyes.

Her unforgiving words.

And all the rest.

I snuck a peek back to the kitchen. My chest grew cold as I watched Mother still standing at the sink, waiting for me. I wasn't ready to go back in. I wasn't ready to face her and those awful cold eyes. So I lay back down and imagined my flattened body had been fossilized to shale like the trilobite I'd recently found out in the hillsides, the fossil that Pops told me had been caught and frozen in the simple act of crawling along the ocean floor, the fossil that now sat on my bedside table next to my magnifying glass.

Above me, the great tree, *her* tree, towered. Moonlight gushed through her oval leaves. I lay there, patient, envisioning my very own fossilization process taking permanent hold.

I knew I was being ridiculous. Mother had said so. Many times, with those icy eyes.

I turned over and spied the roly-poly inching farther away.

"Hey!" I called. "Come back." I held out my hand, inviting him to crawl aboard. But he simply climbed up and over my finger before scuttling down a small hole in the earth. I crawled over and poked my twig into the hole, fishing around, and pulled it back out, examining the end like my father would when he'd check the oil levels in Mother's Buick.

My stick came up empty and dry.

"Fine," I said. "Have it your way, stupid." I threw the twig far out into the grass, wishing I'd brought my magnifying glass with me instead. I'd have held the glass inches over its body, letting the blue-cold rays of moonlight zap it to death.

We did that sometimes, my brother and me. We burned all sorts of things with our magnifying glasses—ants, bugs, leaves, our homework—but only when Mother wasn't looking, and only in the daytime under the hot eye of the sun.

I thought about sneaking into the house and grabbing the magnifying glass.

But then I'd have to walk past her.

I'd have to say I am sorry.

I'd have to stand by the sink and wash my mouth out with the soap she saved for punishment, that awful green dried cake of soap she kept under the sink and mixed with just a little bit of water.

Mother used to only wash my mouth out when I said something wrong, like *bugger* or *twit*. Then she started doing it all the time, like when I'd forget to pick up the burned-out caps from my toy gun off the back porch. Or when I left my dirty socks on the bedroom floor. Or when I'd leave the toilet seat up.

But seeing Mother in the window—her jaw tight in dinner preparation—I knew better than to go inside, so I stared up into the wild hair of her tree, ready for her arms to reach out and pluck me off the ground by my shirt collar and march me inside.

But everything remained still.

I looked up into the night sky. There was not a single whistle of a bird. Not a rush of wind.

No moonlit clouds covered the sky, or I would have searched for animals—an elephant, a rabbit, a crocodile eating a pig. But the night was clear and dotted with a mash of stars.

I blurred my eyes and searched through the patterns of foliage against the purple sky, looking for connected configurations like the inkblots Mother's doctor made me stare at for hours on end. I had given Mother a scare, once, by charging out of her bedroom with her red lipstick painted across my face and chest, hollering like a warrior going into battle. I even grabbed a kitchen knife and held it to my temple, as though I'd scalp myself alive. I was just playing a game—cowboys and Indians—but Mother didn't see it that way.

She said I was mad as a hatter.

She said I needed to see someone.

I see people all the time now.

In the tiny stream of stilled moonlight, I felt something else, not in my ear but stuck to my skin, hidden in the small space between my turtleneck and hairline. I ran my finger over a small oval leaf, wet with sweat and stuck to my neck like a bandage.

Underneath was a thick, hardened mass.

I gnashed my teeth, pretending I had been in battle, a soldier hit by enemy fire.

"Man down! Man down!" I could barely get the words out. But nobody came to my rescue—David was at baseball practice, Pops was at work, and Mother was still doing her thing, floating around the dining table, setting out the place mats, polishing smudges on the utensils with her hot breath.

I peeled the leaf off my neck and fiddled for an imaginary bullet shell with my fingernail. I bit my lip and fixed myself for the pain, bracing for emergency field surgery. I reached over and stuck a couple of acorns between my molars. I bit down hard and dug my dirty fingernail deeper into the wound.

And what should I find?

I had not been hit by enemy fire.

I was not at war.

While I had been asleep, dreaming of burning life, a caterpillar had crawled onto my neck and taken up quiet residence where it formed a hard-shelled chrysalis.

I had become a garden! A strange and wonderful garth.

I spat the acorns out like shrapnel. My teeth had left deep marks in their woody shells. I coughed hard, so hard, nausea washed over me.

I did *that* sometimes at the pool too—coughed until I threw up. I never meant to do it; it just happened.

But Mother never believed me. She'd grab my towel and tell me it was time to go. She'd say I was a faker.

And when we'd get home, she'd grab that awful green cake of soap and run it under the sink until I was cleaned of my sassafras.

⎯⎯⎯

But out here, I could cough to my heart's content.

Cough, cough, cough.

Cough, cough, cough.

Again and again I'd hack, until a painted lady flew out of my mouth, because I could do that sometimes too—make something from nothing. I was practiced in the art of imaginary play, much to Mother's disliking, even though Dr. West assured her I'd grow out of it one day.

The lady fluttered around in the wibbly-wobbly way they do when butterflies first put wings to flight. Up and down and around amongst the belief patterns I had made in the leaves against the sky.

It was a thing of beauty, really.

It was magic.

And just before she flew away, the orange-and-black flutterby with her pure white eyes hovered over me. She told me in the nicest way possible—in the same sing-songy voice of my first-grade teacher—to get up.

"It's time to go home, Charles," she said in a fluted voice. "You can't stay out here forever. Your mother is waiting."

And so I did.

I got up and brushed the dirt off my jeans, and I walked to the house with my mouth open, ready for Mother's brittle green bar of soap to be warmed under the tap.

CHAPTER THREE

MAYDAY, MAYDAY—JUNE 1953

After lunch, Lyla's father rolled one of Pops's old truck tires out of his parents' garage, promising he'd take Lyla on one of his fantastic tire rides down the driveway before they rolled it out back to the tree to be hung on the rope.

He stood in the hot sun with his white undershirt untucked. A fresh cigarette dangled from his lips. "You ready for the ride of your life, birdpie?"

Lyla was ready, but before she hopped inside the tire well, she watched her father study the trajectory of how he would send her down the driveway. It wasn't steep; in fact, the driveway was nearly flat. But once the tire got going, her father claimed, "Why, it could go on forever and ever."

He eyed the street in a dreamy sort of way, then chuckled.

"You should have seen how I used to launch your uncle David back when he was your age." He shielded his eyes from the sun and stared down the street, and possibly, Lyla thought, all the way into his childhood. Lyla loved when her father told tales of back when he and Uncle David were kids, especially when they did things against their mother's approval.

"Once, I got him going so fast, my brother cruised all the way down to the stop sign and kept on going. I had to run fast as hell to catch him before he hooked left and rolled down into town." Lyla's father paused for a bit. "It was a total hoot, but that didn't stop Mother from giving us the belt after Mrs. Marshall ratted us out. We were grounded for two whole weeks."

Lyla's father wagged his hands at the side of his head like donkey ears at the old Marshall house on the corner, as though Mrs. Marshall was still in there spying on them, even though she had been moved into an old folks' home years ago. Now, a plastic pink flamingo stood on the lawn, something Lyla's grandmother found cheap, claiming it was yet another sign the neighborhood was *going to pot*.

"Anyhow." Lyla's father slapped the worn treads of the tire. "Hop in and I'll take you for the ride of your life, sweetheart." He took a drag on his cigarette and blew the smoke out from both sides of his mouth.

Lyla turned back to the house where the front curtains were drawn to keep the afternoon sun off her grandmother's furniture. "What if Mom sees us?" The last time Lyla's father was itching to take Lyla and her cousins for a ride in one of Pops's truck tires, her mother waddled out of the house eight months pregnant and stopped them dead in their tracks.

"Charles? What in the world are you thinking? They could get hurt," she'd said.

Later, her cousins Steven and Robert taunted Lyla, mimicking the way her mother held her bulging stomach and chastised Lyla's father. *Charles, that's dangerous. Charles, they could get hurt.* Lyla told her cousins to shut their traps, even though she also hated how her mother sometimes wrecked their fun just like Grandmother Caroline.

Holding the tire upright, Lyla's father leaned over and said, "Well, what your mother doesn't know won't hurt her, now will it? Plus"— her father removed his cigarette from his mouth and kissed Lyla on top of her sunburnt nose—"I'm your father, and I get a say in what we do sometimes, don't I?"

"Sure you do, but—" Lyla didn't always like it when her father stuck her in positions like this. She felt pulled upon like a Thanksgiving turkey wishbone.

"Never mind," Lyla said, seeing the impatience blooming in her father's eyes—like when she'd pump him full of questions just as he got home from work, when all he wanted to do was *sit down on the couch and watch a baseball game and relax for Pete's sake.*

Lyla slid herself inside the tire and braced her hands against the rubber well as her father wrangled it into position.

Lyla leaned her head out. "Don't push me too fast, though. Okay, Daddy?"

But her father didn't seem to hear her. He took one more drag on his cigarette and told her to hold on.

He jogged the tire out a bit. The world rolled slowly end over end.

"Daddy?" Lyla shouted louder this time from inside the dark wheel well. "Did you hear me? Not too fast. Stay right next to me."

The tire stopped with a jerk, making Lyla bump her head in the rubber well. Her father tossed his cigarette onto the driveway and snubbed it out with the toe of his shoe. He leaned over the rim so his big bright smile loomed mere inches from her face. "I'm going to stay right next to you, Lyla. But you're going to need a little speed or you'll just flop over. And that, my friend, is a one-way ticket for you to get scraped up and for me to get a good old-fashioned tongue-lashing." He rolled the tire back to the top of the driveway. "Okay?"

Lyla pushed her hands harder into the tire well and clenched her teeth. She was excited. But she had the same butterflies flying around in her stomach like when she and her father rode the Big Dipper at the Santa Cruz Boardwalk. It all felt terribly thrilling, if a bit terrifying. "Okay, but don't let me go through the stop sign like Uncle David. Promise?"

"Scout's honor." Her father righted the tire into position. "Now hold on."

And she did. Lyla braced as her father ran the tire down the length of the driveway.

The sky and ground began to rotate in quick succession, gaining speed, spinning faster and faster until everything became a wild blur.

Lyla heard the slap of her father's footsteps on the concrete as he chased after her. He let out a bunch of loud hoots. Lyla whooped back. Not her pleaser whoop, but a real honest-to-goodness whoop-a-doo! The two of them hooted and yawped like a couple of starlings calling out to one another across a river valley.

As she gained speed, Lyla squeezed her eyes shut. Her father was right, this *was* the most thrilling ride in the world and worth the tug of disappointment should her mother catch them. Around and around she twirled, until the tire swerved too far to the left and hit her grandmother's rosebushes.

"Daddy!" Lyla half hooted, half screamed as the tire took a wobbly turn to the right, rolling clear across the driveway and colliding into the side of her grandmother's royal-blue Buick. The tire flung back and flopped on its side with a hard thump. Lyla's knees and elbows stung as they scraped against the concrete driveway.

The butterflies had vanished and Lyla wanted to cry as she shimmied out of the tire, waiting for her father to pick her up.

One Mississippi, two Mississippi, three Mississippi, she counted.

But he didn't come over, not even after a full ten Mississippis. He just stood up the driveway in the hot, bright sun with that stupid, apologetic smile on his face. A pair of wide wet stains of sweat soaked through the armpits of his undershirt. He lit another cigarette and shrugged his shoulders. "Whoopsie poopsie!"

"Daddy?" Lyla yelled at her father. But it was not a question. It was an accusation. The *how could you* part had yet to make its way past her lips and perhaps never would. She knew better. Her father wore criticism like a too-tight collared shirt. Just last week when Grandmother Caroline accused him of not spending enough time at their house ever since Baby Daniel was born, he slammed the phone down in the cradle and immediately fixed himself a drink, shaking the ice in his empty glass before he fixed another.

———

Eventually, her father walked down the driveway toward her, wearing that dumb *Who, me?* smile of his and smoking his cigarette, not bothering to ask if she were hurt, which she was. But it wasn't the tiny pebbles of asphalt stuck in the red scrapes on her knees that stung, or the awful ache in her wrist. It was a different kind of hurt. It was the kind of hurt that got trapped sometimes in her chest and burned.

She wanted to scream at him for letting the tire get away like that. For not staying right by her side like he promised. Yet words of blame or betrayal hadn't the courage to spill out of her seven-year-old mouth.

So Lyla just sat where she was, picking the bits of grit and gravel out of her knees. From behind, she could hear her father tiptoe up before he kissed her on the top of her head. And when she refused to respond, he tickled her under the armpits.

"Stop it." Lyla stiffened her shoulders. "It's not funny."

"Oh, come on, Lyla. I didn't mean for you to get hurt. You know that? The tire just took an unexpected turn, that's all. Not my fault."

"Go away." She clenched her jaw, forcing back the tears. "Leave me alone." But even as she said it, she knew her father could never do such a thing. Asking him to leave her alone was like telling a bird to stop flying—to give up its wings for legs.

"Leave you alone? Ha!" He grabbed Lyla under the armpits and lifted her high above his head and began running around the front yard, making out-of-control airplane sounds. "Mayday, mayday," he cried, dodging the objects blocking his way—the fallen tire, the rosebushes lining the driveway, her grandmother's big blue Buick. Lyla tried her darnedest to stuff her growing smile inside, but she couldn't. And by the time he had put her down again, she was laughing so hard, she'd forgotten she was ever hurt at all.

"Again, again," Lyla begged her father in the same way he'd pleaded with his own mother for permission earlier that morning to hang their tire swing.

But this time it was his turn not to respond.

He spat into the palm of his hand and tried to rub the scuff mark off the door of his mother's new car. When the blemish just became more pronounced in the polish of his spit, her father snuck a peek back at the front window of the house to where the curtains remained drawn.

"Come on, birdpie," he said as he pulled his handkerchief out of his pocket and wiped the rivulets of sweat running down his neck. He heaved the tire back onto its worn threads. "Help me push this thing around back, so we can hang it up before it gets too late."

"Okay, Daddy." Lyla brushed off her knees and positioned herself between her father and the tire and helped him push it up and around the side of her grandparents' house. They marched in unison, step-by-sturdy-step. Lyla's father broke into one of his old military songs, the one he sang whenever they went hiking in Point Reyes, whenever he tried to keep Lyla from falling too far behind.

Left my wife and forty-nine kids
On the verge of starvation
Without any bread
Did I do right? Right. Right. Left. Right.
Right by my country
I had a good job.
And I left. Left. Left. Right. Left.

Synchronizing her steps, Lyla stomped hard to the left when the song called for it, then hard to the right. They marched past Lyla's mother who stood at the back fence, once again filming, as if she'd been waiting for the two of them all along.

"About time," Lyla's mother called out from behind the camera. "I was beginning to wonder whether you'd given up."

Lyla and her father didn't miss a beat. They saluted the camera as they rolled the tire past. *"Did I do right?"* Lyla sang louder than her father.

Just then, the tire rolled back onto her toes. But Lyla knew better than to complain. She was on film.

"Right, right. Right, left, right." Lyla stomped her foot harder than before, kicking the pain out of her squished toes that were curled inside her too-small saddle shoes.

When they reached the tree, Lyla's father rested the tire against the trunk.

"So. What do you think, Mama?" Lyla watched her father walk over and turn the camera so that the lens was focused squarely on him, on his handsome face, on his bright, wide smile. He kissed the lens, then turned back to the tree.

"Is this not the perfect place to spend our days, or what?" Lyla's father grabbed hold of the rope and looped the line through the tire. Lyla rushed over to help, but her father put out his hand. "Step back, sweetheart; it's rather heavy. And I don't want you to get hurt." Which Lyla thought a strange thing to say now that her mother was watching. Her knees still stung from scraping them after falling out of the tire onto the driveway.

Lyla stepped back and watched as her father, hand over hand, ratcheted the tire up to the right height. He tied her off and stepped back to admire how it hung in the air.

"Ladies, I think I have just died and gone to heaven," he said as he pushed the rim with the tips of his fingers, sending the tire on its first empty ride on that bright June afternoon.

Lyla rushed over and stopped the tire. "My turn," she said, reaching for the swing, but again, her father held her off.

"Not so fast, squirt," he said.

"But Daddy?"

"But Daddy, nothing. I've got to make sure she's going to hold first. I can't have this slipping from the rope, now can I?"

"No, I suppose not."

"That's my girl. Just give me a second, and then I'll give you a ride," he said as he climbed onto the rim and bounced, a bit tentative at first, then harder and harder still, making sure the knot was indeed secure. When he jumped off, he turned to Lyla's mother, who had the camera trained right on him. He walked up close to the lens, smiled bright, and declared it was fit for the weight of a man. "Easy."

"Okay, Lyla," he said, bending over and touching his nose to hers. Lyla could smell the bitter scent of bourbon on his breath. "Now it's your turn. Are you ready for the ride of your life?"

"Ready, Daddy!" Lyla threw her arms up in the air, letting her father lift her into the tire.

"Okay, then, let's do this thing."

Sitting on the rim of the tire, Lyla straightened her red jumper and pumped her legs. The butterflies that had been in her stomach earlier that day were now calmed. She leaned backward. Upside-down, she waved to her mother. "Look, Mama. No hands."

"Lyla!" Her mother poked her head out from behind the camera and told her in no uncertain terms she was not to joke around. "Or you," she warned Lyla's father. "Do you hear me, Charles?"

"She's fine, Louise. No need to worry." Lyla's father pulled the tire back and peered at her. "Let's do this thing. Hold on." He danced his black eyebrows at Lyla. Up and down, up and down.

Lyla wiggled her own eyebrows back at her father. "Roger, Daddy," she confirmed. "I'm holding." Lyla drew a deep breath and held it, waiting for her father to let her go. He didn't—at least not right away. He held Lyla high over his head and waited.

And waited.

And waited.

Lyla let out the rush of air from her lungs. "I said I'm ready, Daddy."

And with that, he let her go.

He pushed her hard and high over the dry Northern California hill, so hard and so high Lyla swore she could see all the way to the Pacific Ocean. To the Farallon Islands, even. With each push, she flew over the dropping angle of the hill below; her skirt blew open.

Her stomach dropped each time her bottom lifted off the rim of the tire.

"Please, Charles. Be careful," Lyla's mother warned from behind the lens. The camera was still rolling.

"She's fine, Louise. Plus, I'm right here to catch her if anything happens. Right, bird?"

"Righty-o," Lyla said with a wide smile as she swung back and forth over the hill, fixing her gaze on the small notch in the mountains to the west—a geologic cut her father had once claimed was "carved by the cruelty of wind and eroded by the eventuality of time." Her father talked all smarty-pants like that sometimes when he wore his serious face. When he read to Lyla at night about rocks and minerals, the formation of the Earth, or the forces of nature. Her father had long fancied himself an amateur geologist, wishing that was what he had become after the war instead of an assistant manager at his father's lumberyard.

But what had he meant, exactly, when he talked in that strange way? About the cruelties of nature and erosion of time? Lyla never really knew.

She just took her father at his word.

And there, on that hot June day, Lyla did just that—believed in her father, that he'd be there to catch her. Swinging to and fro, Lyla found herself gazing at that singular gap in the mountain across the way where she could see past the pain her father had caused her that day. Beyond the bark's impressions on her thighs as she clung to the branch in the morning, past the scrapes, the bloody knees, and skinned elbows as she fell out of the tire, even past the sickening feeling of being forced to climb the tree in the first place. But not far enough ahead to see what he would eventually do to himself. To all of them.

CHAPTER FOUR

PANORAMIC HIGHWAY—

NOVEMBER 1954

The day after Thanksgiving, Lyla's father pressed for one last drive to the coast before the fall heat wave ended and the weather turned for good.

"Won't be long 'til we're stuck driving around with the bloody top on." He swatted his newspaper against the edge of the breakfast table as though he were killing a fly. "What do you say, ladies? Who's in?"

Lyla bolted out of her chair. "Me, Daddy! I'm in. I want to go."

Lyla's mother gathered the breakfast dishes and placed them in the sink. "You two should go," she said, insisting she ought to stay home and get things ready before the new baby arrived.

The new baby wasn't due until Easter, and even that felt too soon.

But Lyla knew it wasn't the dishes or the unfinished baby blanket keeping her mother back. It was the wind. She despised it more than anything, always searching for an excuse to get out of those weekend drives in the convertible.

Lyla's father was different, though. He loved the wind. It was when he felt most alive, he'd confided in Lyla one still evening as he stood over the barbecue, flipping a hunk of meat over the hot coals when there wasn't a breath of wind to be found.

"Come on, Mom. It's so nice out. See?" Lyla pointed out the kitchen window to where the last bits of the Indian summer sunlight poured through the gaps between the redwood trees that stood tall as soldiers around their Craftsman-style house.

Lyla's father tiptoed up from behind Lyla's mother and put his hands on her swelling stomach, kissing her on the neck. "Yeah, Louise. Don't be such a party pooper. We can go lay on the beach after and get some ice cream. Come on, it'll be fun." He slipped his hand inside her bathrobe and began rubbing small circles over her pale bare skin. "Abracadabra Kalamazoo," he whispered. "I grant you three wishes. But only three."

Lyla's mother placed her hands upon his, holding him still. "My wish is for the two of you to go on without me," she said. "I'll just hold you back. Plus, I am meeting your mother later this afternoon to plan Pops's surprise birthday party. You know better than anyone that I couldn't dream of canceling on her this late. I'd never hear the end of it."

"True, but—" Her father paused.

"But nothing," she interrupted. "I'm not going, and that's all there is to it."

Lyla's parents stood for a long, quiet moment at the kitchen sink—her father's face curled into her mother's neck, her mother's head rested on his shoulder. They swayed back and forth like a couple of swans, the floorboards creaking as they shifted their weight from one foot to the other. Lyla's mother then whispered something in his ear, making his hands jump off her stomach as though he'd touched hot coals.

"Go on." She turned the hot water tap and slid the dishes into the basin.

"Are you sure? We don't have to go. We can stay home, and I can tackle any Honey Do projects you like." Her father slipped his hands into his front pockets, looking at the sunlight outside.

Across the kitchen, Lyla fiddled with the arms of her sweater tied over her shoulders, wondering what in the heck her mother had

whispered. Her mother had had two miscarriages already, not to mention what happened to Baby Daniel, so Lyla suspected her mother was
just trying to prevent her father from doing something, anything, to
mess up *this* pregnancy.

"I'm fine." Lyla's mother turned and swatted a dish towel, shooing
the two of them to go. "Plus, you'll have more fun without me."

Not a truer word could be said. Lyla loved her mother something
awful, but she wasn't *fun* fun. Not like her father. Her father was the
king of fun. Everybody thought so.

"All right, then, if you insist." Turning to Lyla, he clapped his
hands and rubbed them together. "Looks like it's just you and me,
sweetheart. Why don't you go grab our mitts, a ball, and meet me in
the car in five minutes. I'll even let you drive if you like."

Which Lyla did. She liked it a whole lot when her father let her
sit on his lap and steer his big yellow car down to the end of the street.
She felt grown-up, even if her feet were nowhere close to touching
the pedals.

Lyla's mother turned and slapped Lyla's father with the dish
towel. "Over my dead body, Charles," she said. "Not on the mountain
highway. Promise me that at least. No funny stuff, okay?"

Lyla's father solemnly swore. "No funny stuff. Scout's honor,"
he promised, saluting Lyla's mother with two claps of his heels.
But behind his back, Lyla could see her father cross his fingers. His
definition of *funny* never quite matched Louise's.

As they pulled out of the driveway, Lyla's father gave three quick
taps to the horn. They both blew air kisses to Lyla's mother on
the front porch, tightening the belt of her light blue robe around
the small bump in her stomach. She blew an air kiss back before
going inside.

Once they were off, Lyla settled into the back seat with her
books and two stuffed animals, but as soon as her father rounded

ELIZABETH A. TUCKER

the corner, he pulled over and put the car in neutral. He pumped the gas pedal several times so the engine roared. In the rearview mirror, his caterpillar eyebrows bounced up and down with each goose of the gas.

"Well, are you going to come up here and keep your old man company or what?" He patted the empty passenger seat where her mother usually sat bundled up in a sweater, her bright red hair wrapped in a scarf, even when it was warm out.

But Lyla didn't move. Her mother made them promise no funny stuff. After having read the front passenger seat was considered *the death seat*, Lyla's mother always insisted Lyla was to sit in the back all by herself, even though there was plenty of room up front for the three of them, even though Janet Jenkins was allowed to sit up front with her parents on the way to church.

Even though when Baby Daniel was still alive, Lyla's mother had always held him in her lap, which wasn't fair at all.

"Well?" Her father rattled his glass, breaking up the ice in his smoke-colored drink. He took a sip and ran his tongue across his teeth. He put the glass on the dash. "Let's see if you can keep her straight this time. Let's see if we can keep the glass from tipping."

"What about Mom?"

"Mom said no highway. Mom said no mountains. Right?"

"Right!"

"Well, is this the highway?"

"Nope."

"Then we're all right."

And with that, Lyla crawled over the front seat and sat on her father's lap. She gripped the wheel as he put the car in drive. They started down the street, steady and slow at first.

"That's a good girl."

Lyla kept the car smack dab in the middle of the road.

"Look at you, Ly. You already drive like an old pro. I can just close my eyes and go to sleep." Her father put his hands behind his head and pretended to snore.

38

But then Lyla steered a little too far left, then right, down the empty street, making big, wide serpentines.

"Whoa!" He grabbed the wheel, putting his hands over hers, and together they weaved his big yellow convertible from one side of the street to the other, making the drink in his glass slosh back and forth ever so slightly. When they got to town, he pulled over at the corner market and told Lyla to hop over to the passenger seat.

"I'll only be a minute. I just need to grab a little something first. Then we'll be all set."

As her father opened the market door, the bell jingled. From where Lyla sat, she could hear the owner of the store greet him with a big, loud hello. "Charles! How are you this fine morning?" the man said, just as the door slid closed. Lyla loved how everybody in town greeted her father. Her mother often said he was like the mayor, which—along with his good looks and that big bright smile—had gotten him out of a speeding ticket or two.

Lyla lay back with her head on the headrest and felt the glory of the sun warm her face. She could already taste the peppermint ice cream she'd order when they got to the beach; maybe she'd even order a double scoop with toppings! Lyla loved days like this because her father always let her eat dessert before lunch . . . if they ate the lunch Lyla's mother packed at all.

She folded her hands behind her head and put her feet on the dash, swiping her new tennis shoes back and forth like windshield wipers. She was glad her mother decided to stay home. When it was just the two of them, they could goof around all day long. No chores. No errands. Just gobs and gobs of fun.

Her father returned minutes later with a small paper bag and a big smile.

"All set. Now let's go have some proper fun. Shall we?"

As Lyla's father merged onto the highway and started up the mountainside, he turned on the radio and flipped the dial until he found what he was looking for. "Spooky Boogie" breezed in over the airwaves. "Oh yeah," he said, and turned up the volume. He pressed down harder on the gas, sending a rush of hot air over the windshield.

"Feel that, Lyla?" her father turned and yelled over the thump of Charles Mingus's double bass. He ran a hand through his wild black hair. "Now, *that's* what I'm talking about."

She did feel *that*, but *that* stung. The loose strands from her ponytail had a way of breaking free and whipping her cheeks, making her wince like she had from the sting of her mother's slap just after Daniel died, when Lyla had said she wished he was never born in the first place. How he had ruined everything.

Yet those lashes of hair against her cheeks will be the kind of pain Lyla will crave after her father leaves them. As a teenager, she will stand on top of Mt. Tamalpais on the wildest and windiest of days. She will face the cold Pacific Ocean and let the strands of her hair—black like her father's—whip against her cheeks. The wind will swallow her screams. And once—really, it will only be once—she'll take a razor blade to her cheekbone. She'll stand in front of the bathroom mirror and watch the blood drip down her face. Her mother will knock on the bathroom door and jiggle the handle. "Lyla, honey? Are you okay?" she'll ask from the hallway in that faraway voice. Then, "Sweetheart? Please." Her mother will quietly beg for a response. But Lyla will not answer, not right away. She will listen to her mother's footsteps as she pads her way back to her bedroom. With the dribbles of blood reaching the corner of her lips, Lyla will be frozen in anger because her mother didn't try hard enough to comfort her, didn't demand she come out. That she simply walked away. Lyla will curse her mother as she takes a stiff washcloth to her cuts and rubs hard. It will sting something fierce, but Lyla will wish it was the only kind of pain she'd have to endure—nothing but a couple of thin slices to the cheek.

Lyla gathered her hair in her hand as her father pressed the gas and they zipped up the narrow two-lane highway toward the mountaintop.

"Yep, that's what it's all about, all right," he repeated. "Don't you think?" Her father took his eyes momentarily off the road as he fished for a piece of ice from his glass. The car veered slightly into the opposite lane.

"Daddy." Lyla grabbed for her father's leg.

Her father righted the car and said with a smile, "Whoopsie poopsie!" He had his lips pursed just like Lyla's grandmother when she disapproved of something they had done, even something small like forgetting to put their napkins on their laps at the dinner table.

Lyla puckered her lips too and wagged her finger at her father. "You keep your eyes on the road, mister! Do you hear me? No funny business, remember?" Lyla mocked her mother, then reached over and snuck a chunk of ice from her father's glass and popped it in her mouth, sucking the bitter coat of bourbon. The taste was strong and hot and made her shudder. She leaned over the side of the car and spat the ice out into the wind. "That's disgusting." She wiped her mouth.

"Says you." Her father took another long sip; his Adam's apple bobbed up and down in his throat like a yo-yo. "Why, I think it tastes just like heaven."

If that's true, Lyla thought, *I want no part of it.* "I'll stick with milk, thanks," she said as she got up on her knees and lifted her hands over the windshield, fighting the force of the wind against them.

"One Mississippi, two Mississippi." She counted to a full ten Mississippis before they came to a dogleg on the highway. Lyla flopped back down. The yellow sign warned them to slow down to fifteen miles per hour, but the needle on the speedometer pointed to a clean thirty-five. Lyla held her breath as her father steered the car up the two tight curves in the road, right, left, and then right again, their bodies flung back and forth like rag dolls. Her father reached for the bag that sat between them, and on the backside of the next turn, he whistled when he swerved a little too far.

"Well, that was close," he cheered.

But Lyla knew it wasn't close enough, almost never was. Whether it was betting all he had on a late-night card game with Pops or Uncle

David, or heeling the family sailboat over as far as it could go, he liked to push the limits. He liked to give it all he had, all the time.

"That's just who I am, Louise," he'd barked one night after they had tucked Lyla in, after he'd tickled Lyla's feet, riling her up just before bedtime, after Lyla's mother urged him not to. "You knew that when you married me." From her bedroom, Lyla could hear the sucking sound of the stopper being yanked off the decanter as her father poured himself a nightcap and her mother walked to their bedroom without another word.

⸻

"Again, again," Lyla egged her father on.

"Okay, but first"—he handed her the paper bag—"would you be a lamb and pour me two more fingers?"

Despite their earlier promise of no funny stuff, Lyla set the glass on the dashboard and removed the bottle from the bag. She held out her two small fingers horizontally and poured.

"Oh, what the heck. Make it three. Why not?" He pressed a little harder on the gas pedal.

Lyla twisted the cap back on the small bottle and handed the drink to her father.

"Just like you ordered," she said as the car whooshed up the Panoramic Highway toward the crest.

As her father took a sip, Lyla reached for her lap belt but decided against it, letting it slip back into place without him noticing.

On the straightaway, her father handed Lyla his drink. "Hold on," he said as he inched up the leather seat so he was almost standing. He kept his foot steady on the gas and threw his hands over the windshield. The car crested the mountaintop. His hair whipped in the wind and a bright smile spread across his face. "What a view!" he shouted over the rush of the wind. He was steering the car with his knees. Waving his hands high in the air, he carved up the beat in quick 4/4 time as though he were conducting a roadside symphony.

Lyla did the same.

Together, they conducted their orchestra to the Pacific Ocean down below that stretched out for thousands of miles. Ribbons of swell rolled toward shore, and in the distance, the Farallon Islands popped out of the ocean like witches' caps.

"Look, Daddy." Lyla pointed. "They're so close. I can almost touch them."

"I see." He turned to yell, and just then, the wheel slipped in her father's grip. The car swerved and flung Lyla into her seat. She quickly buckled her lap belt as her father eased off the gas.

"Now, Chaaaarrrles." Lyla shook her finger again at her father. "I told you no funny business."

But her father didn't laugh. He just snapped his fingers and held out his hand, waiting for Lyla to hand him his drink. He took a sip, and then another, and handed the emptied glass to Lyla.

"Hold on, girl. Steady now," he said, as though he were taming a wild filly. Her father wasn't talking to a horse or to Lyla. He was talking to his car—*his girl*, his beautiful, shiny yellow convertible that he'd bought just the year before with his Christmas bonus.

As her father eased the gas pedal toward the floor, Lyla clutched the door handle.

"Don't worry, birdpie," he said. "I've got this in the bag."

On the next straightaway, he leaned back in his seat and pushed the pedal all the way to the floor. The car surged along the highway; the wind slapped her hair against her cheeks, harder than before. Lyla's stomach tightened. She wanted to tell him to slow down a little, but she held her tongue.

Her father knew what he was doing. He always did.

Beyond the shiny hood of the car, the road was empty—nothing but a long gray stretch of asphalt and blurring yellow lines. The ocean was still miles away. Her father released his hands from the wheel, one at a time, and again steered with the insides of his knobby knees.

"That's a good girl," he said over the thunder of the engine and a new song on the radio that Lyla didn't recognize.

Lyla held tight to the door handle.

It all felt a bit dangerous, but it felt like something else too. Electric. She let out a quiet, unexpected *wahoo* as they sailed down the highway toward a sharp bend in the road. This really was fun, far more fun than if her mother had joined and they had to basically crawl down the highway so as to keep her hair from tearing loose from her scarf.

But he was going awfully fast.

The closer they got to the next bend, the more certain she was that her father would lower his hands and grab the wheel. But he didn't. He kept his foot planted on the gas.

"Daddy? I think—" Lyla gulped, now wishing he'd slow down as the tires screeched a little. But she didn't know what else to say, what she could do to get him to stop, not the way her mother could. Her knuckles whitened as she clung to the door handle. Her mother would have placed one hand on her father's thigh, and that would have been that. He'd lift his foot off the gas and grab the wheel like she had tapped a reflex hammer to his knee. Like when she'd held his hands still earlier that morning as he rubbed her bare stomach.

"Daddy!" Lyla yelled, and grabbed her father's leg.

"I told you, Louise," her father said. Lyla winced, but before she could correct him, he said, "I've got this." And just before they hit the sharp turn, he grabbed the wheel and lifted his foot off the gas. "Here we go!" he howled, banking his girl into the turn.

Lyla bit her cheek. Her stomach felt cold and stiff as cement as the car came out of its tight hug of the turn. The tires screeched along the pavement.

As they rounded the next bend, a car appeared racing up the hill toward them in the oncoming lane. In their lane! It was passing an old clunker of a truck chugging its way up the highway.

Lyla's father slammed the brakes, sending his girl into a fishtail. They skidded from one side of the road to the other, crisscrossing the two-lane highway, nearly sailing off the cliff's edge on one side or careening into the mountainside on the other. If Lyla had time to turn around, she would have seen smoke rising off the pavement and the two rubber streaks following after them like long black snakes. But she didn't turn around.

There wasn't enough time.

Plus, she was too focused on what was dead ahead.

In those close few seconds that their cars hurtled toward one another, time slowed impossibly down. Sight and sound inched at a fraction of real time.

Each pump of blood echoed through the hollows of her eardrums.

Every band of the November light slid to a crawl.

Each bat of her eyelashes took days.

Each note on the radio stretched for infinity.

It was like watching one of her father's home movies on the *slowest-possible-setting*, so slow, she was able to see the other convertible was filled with a bunch of high school football players and their girlfriends, coming home from a big game. Cheerleaders sat on the back headrests with their feet locked over the shoulders of the players.

"Two, four, six, eight. Who do we appreciate?" they cried, rattling their red-and-white pom-poms in the air, oblivious to what was happening.

Even in the wild blur of it all, Lyla could make out the tiny red ribbons tied to the girls' sun-bleached hair and the black streaks smeared under the football players' eyes, making them look like a bunch of smiling raccoons.

Lyla's father yanked his girl hard to the right, steering her into a turnout on the side of the road. He slammed the brake pedal to the floor, and they skidded to a stop in the mashed-up gravel, mere inches from the craggy shoulder of the mountainside.

And just like that—like flicking a switch—time sped up and returned to normal.

Lyla spun around. Through the settling dust, she saw the two other vehicles continue up the hill, horns blowing at each other. The girls kept on cheering for their boys, not once turning around to

45

appreciate how close they had come to crashing, or worse, sliding over the side of the road.

"Goddamn it!" Her father hurled his empty glass against the mountainside where it exploded against the rocky wall in a hot bright flash and a million little pieces. He flung open the car door and stormed around the hood.

Still shiny.

Still in one piece.

He began pulling at the roots of his wild, disheveled hair and thumping at his chest with his fists, grunting and groaning like a trapped orangutan. "Goddamn it. Goddamn it," he repeated over and over, palming the silver hood ornament as though he were trying to break it loose.

Still sitting in the front seat, Lyla didn't unfasten her lap belt. She just flipped off the radio, and everything went silent. Her stomach no longer felt like thick, heavy concrete but like a pair of birds were trapped inside, flapping around. She hated when those birds got stuck inside her stomach like that. They made her want to be sick. She pulled her lap belt tighter, hoping the pressure would calm the birds' wings from whirling around and around.

"Daddy?" Lyla said quietly, but she didn't get out of the car to make him stop acting this way.

What in the world could she say? What could she do? After all, she was the one who had egged him on, hadn't she? She was the one who sat in her mother's seat and told him to go faster.

Again, again, she had cried as they zoomed up the highway.

She had encouraged the funny business.

So Lyla just sat there while her father rocked back and forth on the hood, thumping his chest, wishing she had never agreed to go for a drive in the first place, wishing, for the very first time, the new baby had already been born so he would have wanted to stay home instead.

Her father suddenly jumped off the hood and got down on his hands and knees. Lyla peeked over to see if he too had those pesky birds in his stomach. If they were making him sick like the time, the only time, she had seen her father and Uncle David fight. When they began hollering at one another about the war and what it was all for, her father was so drunk, he eventually threw up in the bathroom and tore the toilet paper holder out of the wall.

But that wasn't it at all. Her father was not getting sick. He was on all fours, strangely running his thumb along the dark ribbons of the rocks, studying the thick bed of sediment tucked into the side of the mountain.

"Well, I'll be a monkey's uncle." Her father suddenly roared with laughter. He pried a piece of rock about the size of a notecard from the wall. He held it in his hands. "Will you take a look at this?" He got up and walked over to Lyla's side of the car. He was smiling again, as if nothing had happened, neither the near miss nor his strange animal outburst. "Check this out, Ly."

But Lyla sat right where she was, flipping the metal ashtray in the door handle.

Up. Down.

Up. Down.

Up. Down.

She didn't want to look at him and see him try to make light of what had just happened. It wasn't funny. Not one single bit.

Her father reached over the window and held the rock closer to her.

"Here."

She refused to take it.

"Come on, sweetheart. Don't be such a party pooper. I'm trying to show you something special here." Her father's voice was a strange mix of a plea and an admonishment. He placed the rock on her lap. "Just take a look."

Lyla eventually picked up the small slab and wiped away the layer of dirt, fingering the clean, fractured patterns on the bottom of the rock, not at all understanding what the big deal was.

"No, silly goose. The other side."

Lyla's father flipped the rock over in her hands. There, embedded in the surface, was a fossil of a fish—its small pale ribs, the fan of its bony tail, the hole where its eye once was, all perfectly preserved.

"So?" Lyla said.

"So!" Lyla's father pulled her chin up so she had to look at him. His eyes had that strange bit of confusion in them like in the days following Daniel's death. "This, sweetheart, is a very special piece of rock. It's sedimentary."

And when Lyla still didn't respond, he carried on with another one of his stupid geology lectures like they hadn't almost died five minutes ago.

"This here was once part of the seafloor, and long ago, there was a whole lot of pressure. Water was squeezed out and the grains of the ocean's floor were cemented together, trapping plants and burying animals in the sediments. Sediments, like this one, hardened into rock, and all the dead animals hardened into fossils. So, this rock"—Lyla's father ran his finger over its surface reverently—"this very special rock has been pushed up this mountainside for well over a million years, Lyla, taking the little fishy for a ride until it popped out right here for us to find! Can you believe it?"

Little fishy? Lyla wanted to scream, wondering why he was talking in that stupid, sing-songy voice. In the same dumb way he used to talk to Baby Daniel when he bounced him on his knee, trying to coax a smile out of her brother.

Who cares about this stupid rock? We almost died! She wanted to cry.

But she didn't. He'd get angry if she started crying. He'd call her a sissy, so she kept her mouth shut and vowed she'd never go on one of his dumb adventures without her mother ever again.

"Not many people appreciate the importance of such things, Lyla." Her father tapped his fingernail on the head of the fossil. "Not even your mother. Geology is not just the study of rocks, sweetheart, but the investigation of how they change over time. Finding fossils like this gives us clues about the Earth's history. Anyhow, you should take this and put it in that shoebox of yours, the one you keep under your bed. Don't let anybody have it; don't let them even look at it. It will be our special thing. Okay?"

Lyla rubbed her thumb along the strange rock, clearing the rest of the dirt off the fossilized creature. How did he know about her secret collection box? She'd never shown it to anybody before. And she didn't want to keep a stupid piece of rock in it, even if it was a fossil.

Lyla almost threw the rock over the car, almost told him, *No thanks, let's just go home*. But then she saw the worry lines creep up her father's forehead like they had the night before they threw Baby Daniel's ashes into the ocean, when he sat out on the back deck, spinning the small ceramic urn in the palms of his enormous hands as though he were trying to warm them, or trying to bring Daniel back to life.

If she were in a playful mood, she'd have looked up at her father and said, *Whatever peels your banana*. But she wasn't feeling the least bit jokey. She wanted nothing more than to go home. Lyla opened the glove compartment and shoved the fossilized rock on top of her father's road maps, vowing she'd sneak out back and throw it over the fence when she got home. *Let him study the history of that!*

Lyla leaned back and kicked the glove box shut.

"I know, Lyla. Those guys had no idea what they were doing. That was really scary." Her father walked back around the car, tapping the hood with the butt of his uninjured fist. But when he climbed back in the front seat, he didn't turn the ignition. He just sat there, running his hands along the leather steering wheel. "They had no bloody idea what they were doing. They were just taking a joy ride up the mountain, like that fish."

He started the engine and put the shifter in reverse. But before he pulled out, he turned to Lyla and grabbed her shoulder, trying to pull her close. She didn't move. Her seat belt was fastened.

"I'm sorry, Lyla," he finally offered. Her father's apology trickled out quietly, something just beyond a strangle of a whisper. "I shouldn't have been so foolish too. Not with you in the car. I was just trying to have some fun. You know?"

"It's okay, Daddy," she finally said, even if it wasn't.

They made it to the beach around three in the afternoon. After a quiet sack lunch, Lyla and her father grabbed their gloves and tossed a baseball back and forth. Her father didn't sit in his usual squat, punching his glove and sending the 1-3 signal for Lyla to fire one over the make-believe plate made of seaweed. Nor did he correct her four-seam grip between pitches. They just threw the baseball to each other without a word, listening to the waves crash against the shore. Their black hair was messy and wild. Lyla's cheeks turned pink from the sun.

When they finally sat down in the warm sand, Lyla looked out at the ocean. She could still see all the way out to the Farallons, their craggy cliffs jutting up from the sea and into the bright November air.

"Look at Noonday Rock, Daddy." Lyla finally broke the silence. "It's so close, I can almost touch it." She reached out her arm and wiggled her fingers at the islands like she had earlier in the car.

"You're right, sweetheart." The furrow lines between her father's brows relaxed as he smiled. "It's the clearest I think I've ever seen." He put his hands to his eyes like he was looking through a pair of binoculars. "Heck, I can even make out the cap of guano on Noonday. Looks like vanilla frosting."

"Gross, Daddy," Lyla said, knowing he couldn't really see the bird poop from that far away. But still, she liked that her father was back. That he was smiling for real, after all that had happened earlier that day.

For the remainder of the afternoon, they sat and watched the waves crash against the shore. It started to cool down near sunset, and because Lyla had forgotten her sweater in the car, she scooted up close to her father and leaned into him.

The November heat wave was officially over.

Lyla's father put his arm around her. "It'd be best if your mother didn't find out about what happened back there. She doesn't need anything else to worry about."

"About what?" Lyla wasn't trying to be cheeky; she just wasn't sure if he was talking about how they almost crashed the car or how he threw his bourbon glass against the rock wall and started bashing around like a monkey.

Or maybe it was when he'd let her suck the bourbon off the cube of ice.

Or maybe it was all of it.

Lyla was shivering now. She wanted to go home, but her father didn't seem to notice she was cold. He was scratching at his arms like he had just been attacked by a swarm of mosquitos.

"That's my girl." He leaned over and nudged her shoulder. "We don't need your mother worrying any more than she already does, now do we?"

Lyla took handfuls of warm sand and started covering her legs, remembering how cold and grainy Baby Daniel felt when she threw his ashes out into the wind and how her mother went home afterward and locked herself in their bedroom and didn't come out for two whole weeks, no matter how many times Lyla had called to her underneath the doorway, pleading for her mother to emerge and hug her. And then one day, she did. Lyla found her mother showered and dressed and sitting in the living room with her needlepoint in her lap. Every single picture of Daniel had been taken off the walls.

"Bury me, Daddy." Lyla lay in the sand.

And he did.

Pile upon warm pile of sand, Lyla's father buried her to her neck. The heat and heaviness of the sand felt safe and secure, like the lead blanket the dentist laid over her chest last week when he took X-rays of her teeth.

Lyla's father leaned over and gave her a butterfly kiss on the cheek with his eyelashes. It tickled, but she held perfectly still under the blanket of sand.

"Don't worry, Daddy," Lyla said. "I won't say anything."

"Thanks, Ly. I knew I could count on you." Her father lay down beside her and reached for Lyla's hand underneath the sand. When he found it, he laced his fingers around hers and squeezed.

"So close," her father whispered, his voice thin and reedy. He tried to speak again, but something strange grabbed hold of his voice, something that caught the normal easy flow of words from his mouth like a fish hooked on a lure.

Lyla wiggled her arms and legs free from the sand and sat up. But she didn't look over at her father. She didn't want to see him cry. But then again, she didn't want to *not* see him cry either. She was still a bit sore at him for all that had happened that day. Staring at the black witch's cap of Noonday Rock, she also felt her face burn a little at the thought of her mother getting pregnant again so soon after Baby Daniel had died.

As far as Lyla was concerned, it was all too close. Every last bit of it.

CHAPTER FIVE

MADE IN ITALY—FEBRUARY 1955

L yla knew better than to be eavesdropping, but there was something in her father's voice, an unexpected heat that pricked her ears like a dog's and lured her up the hallway.

"Jesus, Mother!" he roared. "Have you heard a goddamned word we've said?" Then, just as suddenly as his anger boomed out of the kitchen, it rumbled off into the distance, leaving Lyla to count the quiet seconds between outbursts.

One Mississippi. Two Mississippi. She nearly got through three full Mississippis before he went at it again.

"It's not like Dad left us much of a choice here."

The way her father nipped the back end off the word *choice*, Lyla knew he was talking through clenched teeth, sounding just like Pops when he'd had unpleasant news to report. *Well, gang, it looks like the Giants don't stand a chance this year.* The two of them, father and son, sucked bad news behind their teeth as though they were better off swallowing it.

Lyla inched closer to the kitchen door when a loose floorboard groaned underneath her feet. She stopped and stood still as a scarecrow. What *choice* was her father even talking about?

Usually after church, choices in the Hawkinses' house amounted to who wanted gin and tonics or iced tea before lunch while the kids *eenie meenie miney moed* over the BLT sandwiches or who was stuck with tuna salad. Sometimes the grown-ups would sit around and debate who ought to be the starting pitcher in next week's game or what Eisenhower had better accomplish in his second term *if he knew what was good for him.* They would relax in the living room, mulling over anything and everything but that day's sermon.

But not this Sunday.

This Sunday, the grown-ups had all marched into Grandmother Caroline's kitchen after church, where they huddled up like a drift of pigs to a sow and started bickering. They didn't even bother to tell the kids to go outside before they shut the door. They didn't even pour a round of drinks.

"So, tell me, Mister Big Shot," Lyla's grandmother scoffed. "What is it you've got planned, then? Huh?"

Lyla hated how her grandmother had started calling her father Mister Big Shot ever since Pops had died, and how she practically spat the nickname at him. Pops would never have allowed her to talk like that. But Pops was no longer here; he was out in the ocean with Baby Daniel.

"What are you even suggesting?" her grandmother continued.

"What I'm saying, *dear Mother*, is"—Lyla could tell her father was about to lose it again—"you have to sell the house."

"Oh, don't be ridiculous."

Lyla winced as her grandmother slapped the kitchen table. "Have you lost your mind? I'm not selling this house." The kitchen went quiet for a moment. "Good Lord. What would your father say if he heard you talking like this?" Lyla's insides snapped at the mention of her grandfather.

"What would *he* say?" Lyla's father let out a harsh laugh—not one of those funny *ha-has* but more like a horse's snort. "Why, I'd say, 'Thanks a lot, old man. You really pulled the wool over our eyes with the state of the yard's books.'" He was talking about the lumberyard

that Pops had owned for as long as Lyla knew, and where her father
worked while finishing up his physical science degree at the university. Now that Pops was gone, her father was in charge of the yard,
something even Lyla knew was not what he wanted. What her father
really wanted was to work for the United States Geological Service.
But that all seemed to be slipping away.

"It was my home too, you know." Lyla's father's voice softened.
"It's where I grew up. And now—"

Even from the hallway, Lyla heard the crack in her father's voice
like he was about to start crying. He was doing that more now and
she didn't like it. Out of the blue, his eyes would water up, and when
Lyla would catch him, he'd swipe the tears away, calling them *happy
tears*. But Lyla knew it wasn't always true. He wasn't as happy as he
used to be, not since Baby Daniel left in the middle of the night. And
now Pops.

"And now," her father continued, more sharply this time like snap-
ping a twig, "all those memories, gone. Poof."

"Oh, for heaven's sake, Charles." Her grandmother scraped
her chair back from the table. "That is enough. My word, listen
to you. *Help, help. The sky is falling. The sky is falling.*" She mocked
Lyla's father in a shrill voice, her Sunday heels click-clacking across
the kitchen floor like a typewriter. "Good Lord, you sound like a
little girl."

"Mom!" It was Uncle David who spoke this time. "This isn't easy
for any of us. Charles is just trying to help. We all are."

"Well, I don't need help, thank you very much. Your brother's the
one who needs help. My God, just listen to him."

Lyla could hear her grandmother turn the faucet on, where water
blasted into the bottom of the aluminum teakettle. "I swear, Charles."
The tap turned off. "Something's been wrong with you ever since you
came home."

"Jesus, Mom!" Again, Uncle David tried to intervene.

And again, Lyla's grandmother wouldn't let it go, and Pops wasn't
there to hold her arm.

"Well, it's true. Look at him. I mean, really, Charles. Was it really all that bad over there? Your brother fought in the war too, but he didn't come home and start *boo-hooing* all the time."

Lyla then heard the flick of the gas on the stove. "Your father was so ashamed. He could hardly walk to his Elks' club meetings near the end."

"Caroline, please!" Lyla's mother spoke up. "You have no idea what it was like for him."

"Oh, I have an idea all right. Do you want to hear what I think?"

"Not particularly," Louise said. Lyla imagined her mother, closing her eyes for three whole seconds, counting, before she opened them again, something she taught Lyla to do when Lyla had the urge to blurt out something she'd regret later. "But I suppose we don't have a choice."

"What I think is Mister Big Shot over there is cracking at the seams, and you, all of you—you just walk around here, pretending everything's okay. But it's not. Ever since Charles came home, he's been nuttier than a fruitcake."

"Gee, thanks, Mom." Lyla heard her father's resigned sigh drift out underneath the kitchen door. "You really know how to hit a guy when he's down."

"Morris was my husband. And now, here I am, all alone. Have you ever thought about how *I* might be feeling? Huh? You aren't the only one who is hurting, I'll have you know."

And with that, the grown-ups all stopped talking and began milling about instead, opening and closing the refrigerator and clearing dry throats while the teakettle hissed under the heat of Caroline's accusation. Even Lyla's cousins in the other room stopped horsing around.

Standing there, it took everything Lyla had not to barge into the kitchen and yell at her grandmother. *There's nothing wrong with my father. There is something wrong with you, you old bat!* But Lyla knew better; she'd be in a heap of trouble if she were caught in the hallway eavesdropping. She might even get the belt. Not by her father, of course, but her grandmother. Lyla's father would never lay a hand on her, but he wouldn't be pleased. And that was worse than one of Caroline's belts to the backside. So Lyla stood as still as she could outside the kitchen door as the grandfather clock marked the long silence of the Hawkinses' household—the weight of the pendulum swung back and forth.

Tick-tock. Tick-tock.

"I hate you," Lyla whispered. Her grandmother should have died first, not Pops. Pops was the nice one. He used to wake Lyla up in the middle of the night when she would sleep over, holding two bowls of ice cream. They'd eat under the stars, and he'd boast he was the luckiest grandfather in the world. Pops made everybody feel good.

The clock struck noon. Lyla flinched as the first gong thundered through the quiet house. She had to escape before somebody came out of the kitchen and caught her. On the next gong, she carefully timed her steps so each song of the clock swallowed the groans of the floorboards. On the final bell, Lyla ran onto the living room carpet, jumped onto her grandmother's silk sateen couch, and waited.

And breathed.

And when nobody came out of the kitchen, she exhaled and let her heartbeat settle while she looked around the room.

The living room—filled with her grandmother's antique knick-knacks and art books—was heavily accented in blue-and-white upholstery and usually off-limits to the grandchildren unless it was Christmas or Easter Sunday. Even then, they had to remove their shoes and sit quietly.

Lyla sat still, realizing she'd never been alone in her grandmother's formal living room before. She was about to get up, but the porcelain doll on her grandmother's side table caught her eye. Dressed in a light blue pinafore, the smiling doll held a parasol over her matching bonnet. In her other hand, the figurine held the leash to a sheltie dog at her side. The doll—with her long, loose curls and real horsehair eyelashes—was in many ways unremarkable. Except for one.

Nobody was allowed to touch her. Even the mere act of looking at the doll felt forbidden.

It was Cousin Robert who had first told her about why the doll was so special.

It was the single souvenir Lyla's father had brought home from the war.

"Can you believe it?" Robert had said. "Nothing but a stupid doll for Grandmother Caroline. Your mom got nothing. Geez, what a flop. Heck," he continued, "when the Jerries surrendered, my dad brought home loads of gifts for my mom. But then again, my dad didn't go AWOL."

"Shut your mouth, blockhead. My father fought just as hard as anyone."

"Running off isn't the same as fighting, dummy."

"He didn't run off. He got hurt. That's all."

"Not the way I heard it."

"Well, you heard wrong. My dad killed plenty, so hush your mouth before I hush it for you."

Now, Lyla leaned over to get a closer look. Something must make the doll special. But just then, she heard the kitchen door thrown open. Lyla curled into a ball and held her breath.

"God, she can be so damn stubborn sometimes," Lyla heard her father say, sifting change in his front pockets as he walked toward the front door. Ever since Pops had passed, Lyla's mother said he *fingered the change in his trousers like a full-time job.*

"Yeah," Uncle David said as they stood in the entryway, "but that pigheadedness is what got us through high school English. Remember, how she had us rewrite those darn papers until she gave them her stamp of approval?"

"Yeah, but—"

"Don't worry, she'll come around. Trust me."

"Still, I'm gonna lose my mind in there. She's always after me for one thing or another. I feel like when I was a kid; I can never do anything right."

"She makes me feel that way sometimes too," David offered. "Just so you know."

"Hardly. You're the one who can do no wrong. And lucky for you, you're in law school and didn't get stuck with the yard. Somehow, I didn't get that choice. Thanks for that, Dad." Lyla imagined he was talking up to the acoustic ceiling tiles like Pops was listening down on him.

"Well, like you said back there, Mom doesn't have a lot of choices," David continued, his voice growing quieter. "But while she was blowing her steam, I got an idea on how we can keep her here and not have her move in with either of us."

"Jesus, can you imagine?" Lyla's father said. It wasn't really a question.

"Yeah, I can. Which is why I have a plan. Just leave it to me, big brother." Lyla heard a clap of palm to back. "Now go on and enjoy a quick smoke. I'll handle her."

The front door opened and closed.

A pair of footsteps drew closer.

Lyla held her breath.

"Hey, Lyla, what are you doing in here?" Uncle David stood at the edge of the hallway and the living room.

"Nothing." Lyla sat upright. She looked around the room, trying to fix her gaze on anything but her uncle. Her skin burned hot, and she hoped her cheeks weren't red.

"Well, your grandmother would have a fit if she found you in here. She's in a pretty foul mood."

Lyla took a shallow breath and remained where she was, tapping her toe against the underside of the coffee table.

"Go on and play with the rest of the gang." Uncle David hooked his thumb in the direction of the family room where Robert had Steven in a headlock and Margaret sat at the miniature table, playing Chinese checkers against her one-eyed Raggedy Ann doll.

"Do I have to?" Lyla wasn't in the mood to play with her cousins, especially after Robert had teased her about catching her pick *the crumbs* out of her nose during Sunday school. Lyla chewed on the inside of her cheek.

David sat next to Lyla on the couch. "Hey, what's with the long face?" Her uncle pushed out his lower lip, mimicking Lyla. "Is Robert being a pest again?"

"It's not funny," she said.

"I'm sorry, Ly."

"It's all right. I just—" Lyla paused. Sometimes she hated how grown-up time on Sundays got in the way of having fun with her father or Pops.

"Just what?" Her uncle slid his dress shirt up over his wrist and checked his watch.

"What's going on in there? Why is she being so mean?"

"Ahh, that." David bit his lip and looked away from Lyla. "Nothing for you to worry about. We've just got some things to sort out with Pops gone."

"Like what?"

"Grown-up stuff, Lyla. That's all. But it will be fine in the end. Don't you worry." He slapped his knee and started to get up.

Even if Lyla hadn't been eavesdropping, she would have known her uncle was walking around the edges of the truth. He had a look about him, just like her father when he was fibbing, like when she'd asked him if he was Santa Claus and he snapped off the light and kissed her good night, calling her a *silly gooseneck*.

"I hate what she said about Daddy," Lyla finally blurted out. She immediately knew she shouldn't have said anything.

"Lyla?" Her uncle's eyes narrowed. "What did you hear, exactly?"

"Nothing." Lyla picked at a loose thread on the hem of her Sunday skirt. Her father once teased her, saying she was the *world's worst fibber* because of her *nervous eyes*, telling her she looked like Old Mr. Johnson when he passed around the collection plate at church.

Her uncle sat down beside her on the couch and lifted her chin. "Look at me. What did you hear, exactly?"

Lyla's eyes started to water. "I hate her."

"No, Lyla, you don't hate her," her uncle said, laughing. "Your grandmother says a lot of things she doesn't mean. Trust me. Your dad and I have heaps more experience with your grandmother than you do. It'll blow over. It always does."

"But why is she so mean to my dad?" Lyla wiped her nose. "She's so—"

"Cuckoo?" Her uncle twirled his finger beside his head, stuck out his tongue, and fell back into the couch cushions, bringing a quick smile to Lyla's face.

Leaning back, her uncle stared up at the ceiling. "It's just who she is. Been that way all our lives—a little hot to the touch, if you know what I mean." Uncle David pretended to put his finger to a flame and then jerked it away, blowing on his finger.

Again, Lyla laughed. She loved how both her uncle and father were able to make her smile, even when she didn't want to.

"She's still upset about Pops. We all are. Nothing more to it."

"Promise?"

"Cross my heart and hope to die," her uncle said, and kissed her forehead. "Now, go on and find something else to do before your grandmother catches us and we're both in trouble." Her uncle slapped his knee again and stood up.

"But?" Lyla asked, not wanting him to go. Just then, the front door opened and closed, and Lyla could hear the slow, steady beat of her father's footsteps as he walked back into the kitchen.

"But nothing." There was a little more strength in her uncle's voice. "I said, go on." He turned and disappeared back into the kitchen where the grown-ups had begun grumbling again.

Lyla walked over to the family room where Robert was sitting on Steven's chest.

"Say uncle, dummkopf." Robert dangled a yo-yo of spit over his little brother's face. "Come on, say it."

"Get off me!" Steven tried to buck his brother.

Lyla sighed. Nothing good would come of playing with her cousins. Not today. She tiptoed back into the living room where the doll smiled at her, as if singing, *Come play with me instead!* Lyla reached over and picked her up. She actually touched her! The porcelain felt cool in her hands.

Lyla knew, good and well, she should have put the doll back down on the side table. But she couldn't help herself. She wanted to get a better look, to inspect the doll from head to toe.

To see what made her so darn special.

To see why her father had brought it home to his mother and not Lyla's.

The doll did have lovely, delicate features: round cheeks brushed with glaze, small rosebud lips, milk-white skin. Every inch of her was smooth and fine.

"And fake," Lyla whispered to the doll.

It wasn't the clarity of the doll's skin that bothered Lyla so much but how the doll looked back at her; it wore the same self-satisfied smile her grandmother wore whenever she bragged about her sons in public, which was quite different than how she looked at Lyla's father at home. *My little kings*, her grandmother would boast to just about everybody, even though both Uncle David and Lyla's father were a good half-foot taller than Grandmother Caroline—no small woman herself, standing just under six feet.

"I hate you," Lyla whispered again. And she *did*. She loathed everything that made the doll so precious: her polished black shoes, her long blonde curls, her dress-up clothes that never got dirty, her wide-brimmed hat, and that useless umbrella! But most of all, she hated her smug smile. "You're just like her." Lyla squeezed the doll tight around the waist. "And I hate everything about you."

"But why?" A voice filled the room, so sweet and pure, as though the word *hate* was unfathomable. "What did I do?"

Lyla snapped her head around the room. "Who's there?"

Nobody answered.

"Robert?" Lyla reached behind the couch and pulled at the curtain, sure as daylight Robert was hiding back there. But when she heard him in the other room, calling his brother all sorts of dirty names in German—*der Penner, das Arschloch, der Scheisskerl*, little souvenirs Uncle David had brought home from the war—her heart began to gallop so fast she thought it might break free from her skinny chest.

Lyla brought the smiling doll up to her face. "Was that you?" Lyla tightened her grip on the doll. "Did you say something?"

The doll batted her horsehair eyelashes. "I merely asked why on earth you could hate me? You don't even know me. Why, I'm just a doll, for heaven's sake."

A wild fizz rushed up Lyla's neck. "You can talk?"

The doll batted her eyelashes again.

"Why haven't you ever said anything before?"

The doll refused to answer.

"Who are you?"

Lyla squeezed her glazed bodice. "Come on. Say something else."

The doll smiled.

"At least tell me your name?"

Silence.

"What?" Lyla whispered. "Do you think you are better than everybody else? Is that it?"

"Why, no." The doll sprung back to life. "That seems terribly nonsensical, if you ask me."

Lyla nearly dropped the doll, stunned into momentary silence as she grappled with how a porcelain doll with painted-on lips could talk, let alone use the word *nonsensical*.

"Have you always been able to talk?" Lyla asked.

Again, the doll refused to answer.

Lyla tapped the doll's forehead. "Hello, anybody in there?"

Silence.

"Can you hear me?"

"Sure, I can hear you," a voice finally answered. But it wasn't the doll. Her five-year-old cousin Margaret stood at the threshold of the living room with a quizzical look on her face. "Who in the world are you talking to?" she asked, swinging her Raggedy Ann by one red braid.

"Nobody." Lyla stuffed the doll in the folds of her skirt and flopped over, pretending to tie her shoe.

"Well, it sure didn't sound like nobody." Margaret walked into the hall bathroom, dragging poor little Raggedy Ann behind her.

Lyla was about to let Margaret in on the secret, but she knew better. The last time she'd trusted her cousin with a piece of hush-hush—when Lyla had lied about washing her hands before supper—Margaret blabbed to her brothers. The boys, in turn, refused to wash their hands, insisting if Lyla didn't have to, they didn't have to either! It took Grandmother Caroline no time at all to storm into the dining room and march Lyla to the kitchen sink and rinse her mouth out with a dry cake of green soap.

Lyla removed the doll from the folds of her skirt. Refusing to wash one's hands before supper was one thing, but getting caught holding her grandmother's favorite doll, claiming it could talk—forget it! She might as well dig her own grave.

"Psst," Lyla whispered to the doll. "Can you still hear me?"

"Yes," Margaret's voice whispered back from underneath the bathroom door, "I can hear you loud and clear."

"I'm not talking to you, Margaret."

"Well." Margaret threw open the door and shut off the light. "They sure don't seem interested in talking to you." Margaret put Raggedy Ann on her hip and walked back to the family room where her brothers were still torturing one another.

"Are you okay, miss?" Lyla asked when the coast was clear.

Again, the doll remained silent.

"Hey, I have an idea. Do you want to go outside?" Lyla faced the doll toward the backyard. "I can take you for a ride on my swing, if you'd like!"

Still, the doll refused to come back to life.

"Hello? I asked you a question." Lyla tugged at the doll's hair. The doll's eyelashes closed. Lyla shook the doll awake, and the girl's eyes popped open.

"I just don't understand a word you are saying, Charles." Grandmother Caroline's uneven voice took Lyla by surprise. "Just cut through all the damn gobbledygook and say what you mean, for Christ's sake."

"I'm saying, you might even have to get a job." Lyla could hear her father's patience being tapped in the way he served up the next sentence, how it wrapped around the first like a tetherball winding around a pole. "I don't see any way around it. Dad didn't leave you a whole hell of a lot."

"Oh, don't be ridiculous." Her grandmother's laugh was mulish. "Hawkins women don't work." She enunciated *work* like she had discovered a piece of dog poop in her front rosebushes. But it was true, the thought of her grandmother working was ridiculous. Lyla didn't know of many women who *had* to work. Some volunteered at the hospital or at the library, but nobody *worked* worked, least of all, Caroline Hawkins.

"Well. It's either that or sell the house and move in with one of us, or—" Lyla held her breath. What did her father mean? Sell the house that had always been at the center of their family gatherings? And live with Lyla and her parents half the time and Uncle David and Aunt Dianna the other half?

"Oh, right. That'd be the day. There's not a snowball's chance in hell I'd sell this house." Lyla heard the slam of the kettle on the stove so hard it woke Baby Samuel, who Lyla knew had been under the kitchen table, napping in his sleeping basket. He started to cry.

"Shh, darling," Aunt Dianna cooed. Lyla imagined her aunt had picked him up and rubbed his tiny nose to hers. Sometimes Lyla would ask her mother to do this to her when she was tucking her in at night. But ever since Daniel had died in his sleep and her mother had another miscarriage, Lyla was told she was *too old for such silly games.*

"Don't worry, handsome." Aunt Dianna tried to hush the crying baby. "Everything's going to be okay."

"I beg your pardon, Miss Know-It-All?" Grandmother Caroline roared. "Your father-in-law has just passed, and you have the nerve to say everything is going to be okay. Well, I'll tell you what, everything is most certainly *not* okay. You must be as blind as Charles is a crybaby. Nothing is okay in this house." Just then, the kitchen door flew open, and Caroline rushed out.

"Wait, Mom, I've got another idea." Uncle David pressed after her. "A way to keep the house."

Lyla stiffened. She tucked the doll in the elastic waistband of her underpants and pulled her sweater over the top of her skirt and sat there. They couldn't see her from where they stood. But if she walked three steps toward the living room, it would be curtains for her! Thankfully, her grandmother went down the hallway toward her bedroom, grumbling something under her breath.

Uncle David lagged behind a few paces. "Mom, stop. What if you just sold off a part of the property? Keep the house, but sell the second lot?"

"Stop. Please."

Lyla could still hear the two of them as they stood down the hall outside her grandparents' bedroom at the far end of the house.

"Mom, I know you are upset, but—"

"But nothing, David. So help me God, I won't hear another word. Your father and I—"

"Mom, listen."

The back bedroom door slammed shut. Her uncle stood outside and knocked.

"Mom, please. Let me in. You have to be realistic here. We all do."

Lyla held her breath and began counting. But after forty-five full Mississippis, Uncle David gave up and walked back to the kitchen.

"Well, that went about as well as expected," Lyla heard her uncle say as the kitchen door swung back in place.

This was Lyla's chance. She bolted upright. Her heart was ready to tear out of her chest. She walked over and carefully slid open the living room's glass door to the backyard.

"Where are you going?" Margaret called from behind her.

Lyla drew in a long, deep breath as she watched Margaret's

reflection in the glass. Lyla didn't turn around. She couldn't. Wouldn't. The doll might pop out of her waistband and fall to the floor.

"None of your business."

"Can I come?"

In the reflection, Margaret was bouncing Raggedy Ann on her hip, just the way Lyla's mother used to walk around the house with Baby Daniel on hers, dancing and singing to him after his long afternoon naps.

"No."

"Why not?" Margaret shifted Raggedy Ann to her other hip and began bouncing the doll again.

"Because I said so. That's why." Lyla stepped out of the house and slipped the door closed. She trotted across the lawn in the bright sunshine, cupping the foot of the doll so it wouldn't fall to the ground and break. The porcelain felt cold against her hot, criminal skin. When she reached the back fence, she scrambled through the slats and hid behind the trunk of the old oak tree. She stole a peek over at the house where she saw her father's back as he leaned against the kitchen counter and Uncle David opening the refrigerator, likely gathering the makings for a sandwich. Her mother's and Aunt Dianna's heads sat motionless at the table. Lyla pulled the doll out and set her on the ground, dusting the little bits of dirt off her black porcelain shoes.

"What do you think now, miss?" Lyla couldn't contain the smile spreading across her face. "Isn't this a whole lot better than being stuck inside all the time?" Lyla rocked the doll back and forth, making the doll's eyelashes open and close.

Clearly, the girl agreed.

Clearly, they could be friends after all.

"So, what do you want to do?"

The doll didn't utter a word.

"Wait, what did you say?" Lyla held the doll's rosebud lips to her ear as though she were listening for the whispers of waves from a seashell. "You want to go for a ride on my tire swing?" Lyla rocked the doll so the girl couldn't help but blink in agreement. "Well, all right, then."

Lyla snuck another peek at the house, making sure Margaret hadn't followed her outside. But Margaret was sitting in the window seat of the family room rocking Raggedy Ann to sleep.

"Let's do it, then. You'll love it." Lyla propped the doll in the rubber well so the smiling girl peeked over the rim of the tire.

"Okay, now hold on good and tight." Lyla nudged the tire with the tips of her fingers, swaying it back and forth, a few inches at a time.

"How's that? You want to go higher, you say?"

The smiling doll blinked at Lyla as the tire rocked back and forth.

"Super." Lyla pushed harder this time, sending the tire out over the hill. The tops of the fuzzy foxtails swooshed underneath.

"Whoopsie doo," Lyla squealed, sounding just like her father.

On the next pass, the doll toppled over in the rubber well, still happy, still smiling as she always had.

Lyla jerked the tire to a stop. "Hey, what are you doing in there, silly? You can't lie down. You have to sit up to see where you are going. Here!" Lyla reached in and propped the doll back up. "Is that better?" she asked.

But before the doll could answer, Lyla hoisted the tire up as far as she could and held it above her head. "Ready?" she asked, but she didn't let go of the swing, not right away. Over and over, Lyla pretended to drop the tire.

"When's it going to happen?" Lyla teased.

"Now?" Lyla joked. "Or now?" And when the doll least expected it, Lyla let go and shoved the tire as hard as she could.

The doll's eyes batted closed as she swung back, opening again as the tire raced forward.

"Watch out!" Lyla ran toward the doll, flailing her arms and dodging underneath the swinging tire. "This is a game my dad and I call Underdog!" Lyla turned around and pushed the tire again. "Have you ever played it before?"

The doll remained silent; she just sat there, soaring back and forth on the bright February day, blinking her china doll eyes as though she were in on the game.

"Hold on!" Lyla yelled.

Lyla flung the tire harder than before, so hard the tire wobbled up in the air and the doll tumbled out. Lyla held her breath as the bemused doll and her little dog sailed through the air and hit the ground with a thud.

"Oh Lordy, no." Lyla rushed over to where the figurine landed. Just then, the tire swung back and knocked Lyla to the ground where she lay disoriented on her back as the tire swung back and forth until it came to a stop. Her head throbbed. Her eyes blurred as she saw two arms of the branch, instead of one, that held her swing.

Next to her, the doll lay on her back, smiling and unbroken. Lyla even thought she might have heard her laughing.

"It's not funny!" Lyla rubbed her head, and when her vision cleared, she barked, "What do you have to say for yourself, young lady?"

The doll lay under the tree, grinning up at the canopy with that stupid smile.

"Are you broken?" Lyla rolled over and brushed the dirt off the girl's rosebud cheeks. Lyla's head throbbed, and a trickle of warm blood dripped down from her skinned knee.

"Hey," Lyla prodded. "I asked you a question. The least you could do is answer me. A polite yes or no would do." Lyla sat up and dabbed at her blood, then swiped it on the doll's creamy cheeks. "There. That's what you get."

When, again, the doll shunned her, Lyla smeared more blood on the doll's lips, across her dress, along her forehead, so the doll looked less like a well-bred country girl taking her dog for a stroll and more like a female warrior ready for battle.

"So, you *do* think you're better than everybody." Lyla stood the doll upright, circling the girl and her stupid dog in a ring of acorns. She picked up a handful of dirt and threw it at the doll. "Witch! Devil's magic! Burn her!" she cried.

The doll stood in the circle of acorns and stared off into the distance.

"Jesus Christ, are you even listening to a word I'm saying?" Lyla cussed. She even sucked the Lord's name behind her teeth.

"What's wrong with you anyway? You idiot blockhead." Lyla grabbed the doll and was about to throw her out over the hill when she noticed an inscription on the unglazed foot of the doll.

Made in Italy.

"Made in Italy? Hey, my dad fought in Italy. Did you know that?"

The doll didn't breathe a word.

"He's a war hero, and he's the bravest man I know," Lyla declared. "There's nothing my father couldn't do."

"What?" Lyla held the doll close to her face. When the girl's horsehair lashes closed, Lyla dipped her back so that her black eyes popped. "You're brave too?" Lyla questioned, eye to eye. "Is that so?" The doll hadn't said a word, but none of that mattered. Lyla had a fresh idea.

Lyla looked up the tree to the branch reaching out far and wide.

"You think you can climb up there?" Lyla pointed the doll up to the thick branch, but the doll's eyes closed again. Lyla pried them open. "Look."

Lyla jumped up and placed the soiled doll in the neck of the tree before hoisting herself up. Again, Lyla glanced over at the house. She wished her father could see she was no longer afraid to climb so high. Heck, she could scramble five branches up if she wanted!

"Okay, Miss Priss. Let's go." Lyla straddled the branch and began scooting out. "Oh, don't you worry," she told the doll. "I've done this plenty." Which was, of course, a bald-faced lie, but at least she didn't have nervous eyes when she said that.

Finding more courage, Lyla leaned the doll over to get a good look at the ground. "So high, right?"

Silence.

"What? Cat's got your tongue?"

The doll refused to answer again.

"Hey, anybody home?" Lyla pinched the doll's arm, the same way her grandmother would when Lyla walked into the house without taking off her shoes.

"Fine, have it your way." Lyla nudged the doll farther along the branch. "Go on. Take your silly old dog for a walk."

Lyla leaned forward and pushed the doll nearly out of arm's reach. Slipping off-balance, she toppled to the side and clung to the branch by her legs.

"Help!" Lyla flailed her arms in the air like upside-down windmills. "Please," Lyla begged, locking eyes with the doll.

"Help you? Why on earth should I help you after the way you treated me?" The doll popped back to life. She batted her eyes and smiled. "I'm quite fine where I am, thank you very much."

Hanging upside down, Lyla couldn't believe it. The doll leaned over the branch and winked at her. She actually winked!

"I knew you'd come back. I just knew it." Excited, Lyla was suddenly unconcerned with falling. She swung back up and hoisted herself into the saddle of the tree. She scooted closer. "Did you ever talk to my dad? Did he ever tell you what it was like over there? In Italy, I mean?"

Lyla got too close to the doll's smiling lips as she listened for an answer. And in the process of doing so, she accidentally knocked the doll off the branch. The porcelain girl fell to the ground and broke clear in two. Her head rolled away and settled in the dirt face up.

Even beheaded, the doll wore the same idiotic smile.

"God Almighty," Lyla choked, sounding just like Grandmother Caroline when Elvis Presley had the nerve to sing "Heartbreak Hotel" on the Ed Sullivan show last week.

There would be no explaining how her grandmother's prized doll had broken in two or what the doll had been doing outside in the first place. There would be no running to her father for assurance, no collapsing in his arms or crying heavy sobs of an apology like when she had broken his car window with an overthrown baseball.

She was done for.

Lyla quickly swung over the side of the branch and hung. About to drop, she realized she was so much higher up than when she hung from the monkey bars at school. She tried to muscle herself back up, but she didn't have the strength. She lost her grip and dropped to the ground, sending an electric shock up her spine.

"Miss, I am so sorry." Lyla crawled over to the doll, ignoring her own injuries—the scratches on her skinned knees, the bloody elbow, and now the sprain in her wrist that would only later start to hurt.

"I didn't mean to. I promise." Lyla cupped the detached head in her hands as though she was carrying a fragile robin's egg back to its nest. She spat in her hand and tried to clean the dried blood off the doll's face, her lips, her dress.

"I am so sorry," she repeated, but not sorry enough to do the right thing—to march into the house and apologize for what she had done.

She could explain away the cuts and scrapes and the tear in her skirt, but she couldn't hand over the doll, now broken in two. Not in a million years. Lyla looked over to the house and back to the doll.

There was only one possible solution.

She needed to hide the evidence.

Lyla dropped to her knees and began mining the soft earth with her fingernails like a backhoe. She was good at digging graves. Just last year, she had buried her pet hamster, and the years before that she laid to rest many goldfish, despite her father's insistence she just flush the dead down the toilet.

But *this*? *This* was different. *This* was a grave for something she had killed with her own bare hands!

"You'll be okay." Lyla laid the girl into the makeshift grave. "I promise, you'll be fine down here." Lyla wiped the dirt off the doll's lips. But it was those eyes. They just wouldn't stop smiling, so Lyla grabbed a fistful of dirt and threw it over the doll's face and began praying.

"Our Father, who art in heaven. Hallowed be thy name." Lyla recited the Lord's Prayer as she knelt beside the grave. "And lead us not into temptation but deliver us from evil. For thine is the kingdom, the power, and the glory forever." Lyla paused, forgetting what came next. "Or however it goes." Lyla got up and scattered a few acorns, camouflaging the fresh grave.

She dusted off her skirt and was about to walk back to the house when she saw her father standing on the back porch. He was smoking a cigarette. How long he had been standing there, Lyla had no idea. She sucked in a deep breath and ran back to the house. Not into her father's arms, crying, or apologizing, or asking him to forgive her. Instead, she blew right past him and threw open the sliding glass door.

"Lyla May?" he asked. "What's going on?"

But Lyla didn't answer.

"Lyla?" he called after her again. "Birdpie?"

Lyla ran straight into the bathroom. She lifted up the toilet seat and threw up all the badness that was trapped inside her. She heard his footsteps in the hallway.

"Lyla, honey, are you okay?" Her father knocked on the door.

"Go away," she said, and threw up again, trying to get rid of the cold, awful grip in her stomach.

In the end, it was Lyla's mother who carried her out to the car and laid her in the front seat. She combed Lyla's hair with her fingernails, calling Lyla her miracle girl, a name she only seemed to resume calling Lyla after Baby Daniel was gone.

Her mother never asked what had happened or why Lyla had dried blood on her knees. Instead, she leaned over and rubbed Lyla's nose with her own and whispered, "Why don't you crawl into our bed when we get home?"

Lyla felt both safe and sickened lying in her mother's lap. Solace only felt true and whole when it wasn't mucked up by a lie or doing wrong by her father, who sat in the driver's seat, not saying a word.

He turned the key in the ignition and pulled out of his parents' driveway. He didn't look at Lyla but instead kept his eyes on the road ahead, gripping the steering wheel as though it could get away from him. Nobody asked a single question or recapped the day like they usually did after a visit to Caroline's house. Instead, they all listened to Lyla's mother hum an old Irish waltz Lyla loved so much. And by the time they pulled into their driveway, Lyla was nearly asleep.

In the fuzz of her awareness and the dull throb of her head, Lyla heard her mother and father talking outside the car.

"No. I'll take her in. You go and relax for a bit. I've got her." Lyla's mother lifted her out of the front seat and carried her to their bed. Still humming her tune, she tended to Lyla's cuts and bruised wrist, and gave her half an aspirin for the dull ache that stretched from temple to temple.

It didn't take long for Lyla's grandmother to call, and another fight ensued.

"I have no idea what you are talking about," Lyla's father said into the telephone in the hallway. "Hell, Mother, I don't know. Maybe one of the boys took it."

Again, Lyla felt that naughty bird trapped in her stomach, banging around the cage of her ribs, unable to wend its way out.

And then silence—the same agitated silence as after her grandmother said her father wasn't right in the head, the same nasty quiet as when the doll refused to speak.

"Goddamn it, Mother. I said that's enough." Lyla's father talked through tight teeth. "We've all had a long day. You should get some sleep."

Lyla heard him slip the phone into its cradle, followed by his heavy footsteps as he made his way toward their bedroom. He didn't come in and rub Lyla on the forehead or tuck her hair behind her ears like he usually did. He didn't lean over and give her butterfly kisses on her cheek. He didn't poke fun at his mother.

He stood in the doorway instead—his broad hands holding onto the doorframe as though he were keeping it from collapsing. Lyla had always been told the doorway was the safest place to be in an earthquake, yet it looked like her father might just pull the frame down on himself.

Lyla considered confessing but couldn't. She didn't want to see her father go berserk like he had that day when he almost crashed his car up on Mt. Tam.

"That was your grandmother," he said.

Lyla locked eyes with her father. She neither blinked nor looked down at the book in her lap nor got up and made an excuse that she needed to go to the bathroom. She just sat up against the headboard and stared at her father, holding her gaze as steady as she could. *One Mississippi. Two Mississippi*, Lyla counted. *Three Mississippi. Four. Five Mississippi. Six.* Lyla refused to let her nervous eyes wander around. It wasn't until she had reached nine Mississippi's that she saw the terrible look of surrender in her father's eyes.

She despised seeing her father that way.

She hated that she had won.

Had her father simply asked—*What were you doing with the doll, Lyla?*—she would have told him everything. She would have confessed it all to him, even the eavesdropping and hating her grandmother for what she said about him.

But her father didn't ask. He didn't mine her for the truth. He didn't yell or punish her. Or any of that. He just let her silence speak for itself. He sighed and turned, fingering the change in his trousers as he walked back down the hallway. Lyla sat there with the book open in her lap, listening to the jangle of all those nickels and dimes being replaced by the sounds of ice tinkling in a glass and the familiar pop of the decanter.

CHAPTER SIX

NO MEANS HOLD ON TIGHTER

THAN BEFORE—SEPTEMBER 1956

How does one find the courage to walk out to a tree—to the very spot where a mother once stood like a sultan, with her massive robes billowing like white sheets drying in the pre-war September wind, her hair wild with anger?

How do you walk out to a tree where you were once accused of being ridiculous?

A stupid, selfish boy. Get up, Charles. Go inside before your father sees you like this. Just you wait.

And you did wait.

For decades.

And here you find yourself again, your hands clasped tight around Mother's thick, unbreakable waist. The rough bark tears up the white insides of your arms. Of course, you remain frightened of what she will say, what she will think.

You are no longer a little boy.

You are a man.

And this time, you solemnly swear, so help you God, you will not let go.

No still does not mean *no*.

No means *hold on tighter than ever before*.

Handcuffed around her trunk, you toss the key across the dried-up earth where it hopscotches from one brittle leaf to another, finding home far out of your reach.

You hold her waist tight, swearing you will never let go.

She will be the one to eat her words. She will be the one to come out back and find you. Not the other way around.

Too tight, you hear her say again. Then, *Let go!*

But you will not be played the fool. Mother isn't out here.

Not yet anyway. The echo of her voice has only been caught in the nighttime wind as it rinses far-gone leaves and unwanted acorns out of her hair. Hard-capped nuts bounce to the ground like gumdrops.

This time, she cannot slap your hands away. Or clap you to attention.

You are stronger now.

Stronger than her.

Stronger than Father ever was.

Your arms are thick as Paul Bunyan's. Why, you feel like you could fell this tree with your own bare hands should you wish. But that is not your wish to make.

Your arms hook around Mother's waist, and you wait.

Days pass, and yet still she cannot break free. You hold on bitter in the fight.

No does not mean *let go*.

No means *hold on tighter than before*.

Just ask the termites who break down her heavy bark in quiet, studious labor. The wind catches fine dust and carries it up, up and away through Mother's wild hair. The termites could have warned you.

You must be patient.

You will work hard to stay here to the very end.

Then she will come for you.

Your knees start to buckle. But you fight to stand up. You will not give up. You will carry on like the team of soldier ants near your feet, the vast army lugging large pieces of bark on their small backs. You move your aching feet so the diligent fellows can carry their heavy loads without you standing in the way. They have no clue what you're doing or who you are. Or why you stand there handcuffed to the trunk. As far as the soldiers are concerned, you are just part of the damned tree.

And they are right. You become one with the trunk, grafted to her. At some point, you can no longer stand.

Your legs begin to crumple.

You hang by the bones of your torn wrists.

Your knees barely touch the ground.

The handcuffs dig deep into your thinning skin, so deep your wrists begin to bleed. Trickles of blood roll down your arms like tiny mercury balls suddenly free from the confines of their glass thermometer.

The weight of Mother's words still hangs in the air of quiet desperation. Not the too tight ones or the stupid ones, but the others. Those that cut you deep to the bone.

How could you do such a thing? You should be ashamed of yourself! She had handed you a letter with the foreign script stamped across the front. *What in the world were you thinking?*

Then with her slap. *You stupid fool.*

Hanging by your thinned wrists, you spy the key sitting atop an oak leaf, like a fork on a picnic napkin, as though its sole purpose is to keep the wind from blowing the leaf away. You envy the tiny metal key for days—weeks, even—until your wrists are almost small enough to fit through the handcuffs themselves. But even if you could wriggle free, you wouldn't.

You had vowed to never again leave her alone in the darkness.

She is your mother, and she needs you to stay right where you are. To not move from the base of her, where she will eventually find you and set you free.

CHAPTER SEVEN

MAGNETIC ROTATIONS—

OCTOBER 1956

Caroline's hands shook as she reached for the water glass on the bedside table. She sat up and caught her breath. Her heart galloped in her tight, frightened chest.

It's just a nightmare, she told herself, the same ridiculous dream that had been tripping up her sleep ever since she was a little girl, ever since her father coaxed her into camping along the shores of Mattawamkeag, where a legendary twenty-four-foot serpentlike monster was rumored to live at the bottom of the deep, dark lake.

Every single night of that trip, the same thing happened. She'd wake, hearing a crackle out in the woods. When the sound drew closer, she shined her flashlight up through the canvas tent. And there, my goodness, she would have sworn on the Holy Bible, was Ole Molly hovering and growling overhead. Its tongue lashed out, ready to eat her.

"You were only dreaming," her father had said the very first night Ole Molly slithered into her dreams. He peeled the flashlight out of her grip and told her to go back to sleep. "Things always look better in the light of day, trust me," he promised. "Now, shut your eyes."

As if.

As if she could simply shut her eyes with Ole Molly out there!

Caroline was seven years old at the time, but from that trip forward, she vowed she'd never sleep under the stars again. And if there was one thing Caroline Anne Hawkins, back then Caroline Anne St. Croix, was known for, it was being true to her word. She never so much as slept on someone's living room couch, let alone pitched a tent outdoors. Camping was for other kinds of people—people who ate cold cuts.

Forty-four years later, it took Caroline a few disorienting seconds in the darkness of her bedroom to catch her breath and convince herself: (1) Mattawamkeag Molly was just a myth, (2) she was not a child about to be eaten by *that thing* but a grown woman, for heaven's sake! and (3) it was four thirty in the morning in California, three thousand miles from the shores of Lake Mattawamkeag tucked in the backwoods of Maine.

Caroline propped the pillows behind her back and allowed her eyes to adjust. Her room was in order: the chair tucked under the vanity, the closet doors properly shut, her slippers by the bedside, the drapes closed. Nothing was amiss. She smoothed out the bedspread. All was as it should be. She took a small sip from her water glass, which had the unfortunate effect of aggravating the tickle in the back of her throat, the same dry cough she'd had for three weeks now. Try as she might, the tickle made her spit the water across her lap.

"Good Lord, Caroline!" She grabbed a tissue and dabbed up the mess on her chin, then the bedspread. "What in the world is the matter with you?" She leaned back against the headboard and massaged her throat, as though she were trying to coax a dog to swallow a pill.

Next door, the neighbor's Rottweiler had started barking.

"For the love of Pete," she said to the window. "Will you just shut up, for once?"

She had had enough of that stupid dog whining night after night and fantasized about slipping something under the fence, maybe a little rat poison or, at the very least, a sleeping aid to keep the damn animal from barking all bloody night. Caroline despised that dog almost as much as she hated having neighbors. The Petersons, over on the right, were nice enough, both elementary school teachers, always bringing over a pie at Thanksgiving or offering to take her trash bins out to the street when it was raining. But still, they were neighbors, and Caroline didn't like people living so close, bringing over baked goods as some sort of peace offering or sending their sons over to con her into buying raffle tickets. She didn't like people in her business. And as for the neighbors to the left, they were numbskulls; their ill-behaved dog, worse.

Caroline had lived in her house for nearly three decades. She and Morris had bought the property with the intent of raising their boys close enough to the town square so they could bike to school but far enough away to give them all a real sense of peace. But not now. After her sons conned her into selling off the adjacent lots, she had the nice but nosy Petersons on one side and those numbskulls to the left, flanking her property and blocking her view of what used to be *her* fields. She could even see those half-wits brushing their teeth at night in their underwear, for Christ's sake! And that stupid dog. It yowled all night lately.

"Oh, put a cork in it!" Caroline barked back as she picked up the clock from the bedside table. She listened to the second hand tick-tock around the clock face with the same relentlessness of that idiotic dog.

Tick-tock, bark, bark. Tick-tock, bark, bark. The two of them never gave up.

Caroline thought about marching over in her bathrobe and ringing the neighbor's doorbell, shoving the clock in their sleepy faces. *It's four thirty in the bloody morning!* Or better yet, throwing the clock over the fence and beaning the dog square on the block of its head.

But of course, she didn't.

Retribution was for hayseeds.

Retribution was for people who ate sliced bologna by a campfire.

So, she lay back down and tried closing her eyes. But that too was of no use. Morning was just around the corner, and there wasn't a cat's chance in hell she was going back to sleep.

"Well, I'm up now, thank you very much," Caroline said, ripping the comforter away. She slipped her bathrobe over her shoulder and slid her feet into her bedroom slippers, padding her way to the kitchen to refill her water glass. Caroline Hawkins had long believed that water coming out of the bathroom tap tasted vastly different from the water flowing from the kitchen. Water from the bathroom sink was too closely associated with toilet water and, therefore, undrinkable. And anybody who thought otherwise needed a proper education in wastewater treatment.

Standing in front of the kitchen window, Caroline wagged her finger under the tap, waiting for the water to get cold enough to kill her cough for good, waiting—almost willing—for a hint of morning to replace the hopelessness of another interrupted night.

Nothing good ever happens in the middle of the night, she knew good and well as one finger rubbed the deep pockmark on her cheekbone, one of the last remaining scars from that stupid camping trip when her father pitched their tent on a spider mound.

Caroline drifted into the not-forgotten visions of the giant reptilian monster still swimming in her head—how she had lain awake in the middle of the night all those years ago, convinced it was the tip of Molly's tongue licking her.

"Daddy." Caroline poked her father awake again. "Something's licking me."

Her father was not amused. He rolled over, not even bothering to turn the lantern on.

"You're just having a nightmare, Caroline. Now, go back to sleep and don't wake me 'til the first light of day. Do you hear me?" He turned over and was snoring again in seconds. But the next morning, Caroline woke with a rash of painful blisters all over her face.

"Well, wouldn't you know," her father said, as he pulled the tent stakes up and found a mess of spiders swarming underneath. Not once did he even acknowledge the raft of bites dotting Caroline's face. He simply picked up the still-erected tent, shook it out, carried it to the car, and packed it away. On the long, silent drive home, as Caroline scratched her face, making the bites bleed, her father finally spoke.

"Well, Carol Bean. Let me give you a little piece of advice that will help you for the rest of your life." Without taking his eyes off the road, he handed her his white handkerchief with his initials stitched in the corner and said, "Sometimes you eat the bear. And sometimes the bear eats you. The next time we go camping, we'll do better."

As if.

As if there would be a next time!

***

Staring into the dark over four long decades later, Caroline remembered wanting to tell her father the next time he wanted to go camping, he'd be going alone. He could be the one to get eaten. But of course, she didn't. In the St. Croix household, insolence was as acceptable as dog droppings on their front lawn. So she sat in the back seat, quietly blotting her angry spider bites with her father's no longer bright, no longer white handkerchief.

Caroline filled her water glass and shut the faucet off.

The dog went at it again, running up and down the fence line and barking its brains out, as though it were Paul Revere warning the Patriots *you know who* was coming.

"There's nobody out there, you idiot!" Caroline took a long sip, then another. This was precisely one of those unpleasant times her father had warned her about all those years ago—a time when she was most definitely *not* eating the bear.

Outside, the backyard began to emerge, slow and sure in the predawn gray light. Caroline leaned over the kitchen sink and rubbed the sleeve of her robe against the window, urging daybreak to come quicker. She knew she was being silly, but she had a luncheon in San Francisco that afternoon, and such invitations didn't happen every day.

Gradually, the faint outline of the hills appeared, the silhouette of the old oak tree with its enormous crown, the framework of the back fence, the dish towels she'd left hanging on the line. She realized she'd never witnessed such a slow break of dawn before. But then again, she wasn't accustomed to being up milling about at this hour. Usually, she stayed in bed and read, and cursed the neighbor's dog 'til the sunshine popped.

It was remarkable, beautiful really, watching life slowly materialize in this fashion, like waving a Polaroid to witness objects crop up out of the dark.

Caroline pinched her eyes. She thought maybe she saw something move in the oak tree. She squinted to narrow her focus, but it was still too dark; the black shadows had yet to release their final grip on the night. She refilled her glass and swirled the water around in a backward current and took another long sip. Then—and dear Lord, it was only a matter of seconds—she looked back up, and with just enough light grinding away at the fringes of night, she saw something was, indeed, up in her tree.

"What on earth?" Caroline leaned closer to the window, her mind trying to play catch-up to her eyes. Her hot breath fogged the glass.

"Oh, fiddlesticks!" Again, she wiped the window with the sleeve of her bathrobe, making small blurry swirls on the glass. Still, she couldn't make out what was in her tree. But it was something, all right. She marched around the kitchen counter and threw open the sliding glass door.

"Who's there?" Caroline called out into the cold October air. She listened for the breaking of twigs or the grunts of the wild boars that sometimes rooted around her property. Caroline almost never strayed far from the house in the dark, having always left the job of chasing pigs off her property to the men in her life.

But she lived alone now, and it was up to her to chase away whatever was out there.

"Shoo!" she yelled.

But nothing moved. Not so much as a peep. Everything remained dead still. Even the dog next door had finally shut its trap.

There was another creak coming from the direction of the tree.

And that was when Caroline saw a figure swaying on the rope of her granddaughter's old tire swing. There wasn't so much as a breath of wind, but she could make out the body in a slow circle like the deliberate second hand of her bedside clock.

It must be some sort of sick joke. Halloween was just a few days away; her pumpkin had already been smashed to pieces on the street, and somebody had the nerve to spray *Free Broom Rides Here* in shaving cream on her driveway.

"Who's out there?" she cried.

Again, no response.

In her bedroom slippers Caroline shuffled out to the edge of the cold cement porch to get a better look. It must have been those darn boys down the street playing a nasty prank on her, having slung a dummy of old clothes in her tree like a scarecrow.

"You take that down right now, or I'll call the police." Caroline was sure those damn neighbor kids were out there spying on her. She couldn't see them, but she could feel their delinquent eyes tracking her every move as they hid in the bushes.

She grabbed the neck of her robe. "You have no right to be back there. Do you hear me? This is my property."

But nobody came out. Nobody made a peep.

Another small crackle from the branch, groaning with the weight of the swaying dummy. "One, two," she counted out to the hooligans. The toes of her slippers curled over the edge of the porch.

"Three."

And when nobody came out, she yelled out in the dark, "All right, that does it!"

But just before she turned back into the house to pick up the phone and dial the police, the night lightened into a softer shade of gray, and she saw everything clear and true—the tire on the ground, the shoes on pointe like a ballet dancer, and the back of her son's black hair as his body *tick-tocked* around the earth and faced her.

Caroline dropped her water glass, and it shattered across the cement porch like a broken snow globe. Lifting the hem of her bathrobe, Caroline bolted across the cold, dewy lawn toward the tree.

"Charles! Get down from there, right now," she screamed at her grown son, as though he were still just a child and had climbed on a countertop and was putting his hand in the stove's blue flame.

"Charles! Charles!" she hollered, as she tried to scramble through the slats of the back fence but was caught by a wonky nail that grabbed her bathrobe. "Stop. Let go of me." She fought, pulling against the nail. Her bathrobe tore loose from her shoulder, exposing her naked, sagging breast to the break of day. "I said, let go!"

Caroline finally broke free and ran headlong to the tree with a long gash in her bathrobe, the robe she would, hours from now, throw into the garbage when she would try to rid herself from any evidence, any connection to that morning.

"Charles!" she screamed again.

Next door, the porch light came on and the Rottweiler began to bark. The neighbor stood in his boxer shorts and whistled, commanding the dog to hush. Or maybe the neighbor was whistling at her for once, telling *her* to shut up. But none of this would she ever know. Because in the fresh face of dawn—as her son's body, dressed in his old winter service uniform, twirled around the magnetic clock of the Earth—Caroline neither saw the light go on nor did she hear the yelp of the dog as it was yanked by the collar and brought indoors.

All Caroline knew to do—all she had the strength for—was to climb up onto the tire and grab hold of her son around the knees, stopping his body from its slow, grotesque rotations away from her and back again.

CHAPTER EIGHT

FAULT LINES—NOVEMBER 1956

Even before Lyla's father died, things started to go missing. At first, it was small ordinary items: her father's cuff links, a pack of cigarettes, one of his drill bits. Then it was the keys to his car, a favorite fishing lure, his bowling shoes. And once, he lost his pocketbook. He walked through the front door, patting his coat pockets, swearing he'd been pickpocketed. Later that afternoon, Manny called from the lumberyard, reporting he'd found the missing wallet. It was sitting on the shelf tucked between the quarter rounds and spackling putty.

"I'll be damned." Lyla's father turned around with a weak shrug of the shoulders and drove back to the yard. It took him hours to return that day, and when he did, he sat at the dinner table with a blank stare as he moved his peas around his plate—this way, then that way—never really eating.

And one time, after finishing some last-minute holiday shopping, he forgot where he'd parked the car. He walked up and down each row of the mall's parking lot, searching in the dark for hours.

Next, it was her father's knock 'em dead charm that disappeared, the one Lyla's mother swore could disarm just about everyone he met, even Lyla's Sunday school teacher who smiled as sincerely as a crocodile. It used to be that when they had friends over, Lyla's father would open the front door with a joke and a drink at the ready. At some point, though, he started opening the door with only his drink in hand. Then he stopped opening the door altogether, leaving Lyla or her mother to greet their dinner guests while he sat in the living room and watched the television.

And just last summer, he even lost his desire to poke fun at Grandmother Caroline whenever she had her back turned, something Lyla could count on like the sun rising at dawn. Her father instead started staring out his childhood kitchen window as though he were searching for something.

Then it was Lyla's mother's quiet reassurance—*Everything's okay, Lyla*—that vanished.

Then it was her father.

He slipped away from Lyla in the middle of the night.

And now, it was Grandmother Caroline's formal manners that had gone AWOL, which was the last thing in the world Lyla would have ever expected. Her grandmother was a stickler for etiquette, especially when it came to hosting visitors. It had only been a month since the funeral, but when Lyla and her mother showed up unannounced that morning, Caroline glared at the two of them like they were a couple of strangers standing on the doorstep asking for money.

"What do you want?" she barked.

Lyla's mother removed her sunglasses and gripped them in her hands. "We just came by to check in. You know, to see if you needed anything."

"Oh, for heaven's sake, Louise. What in the world could I possibly need from *you* of all people?"

Lyla's mother drew in a breath and put a hand on Lyla's shoulder. "We brought you some banana bread."

Lyla held out the tinfoil-wrapped loaf she had baked earlier, expecting Caroline to snatch it out of her hands. Her grandmother did that sometimes, grabbed things from her grandchildren as if they were a bunch of imbeciles who'd drop whatever they were asked to help carry in from the car.

Caroline remained in the doorway with a sickened look. She didn't receive the bread, graciously or otherwise. She didn't even offer a polite *thank you*. Instead, she gathered the folds of her sweater at the neck and stared at the loaf in Lyla's hands as if Lyla were presenting something she'd dug up in the backyard.

"Would it be all right if we came in, even for just a few minutes?" Lyla's mother pressed. "We should talk."

"About what?" Caroline snorted. "What on earth is there to say?"

"Caroline, please!" Lyla's mother snapped, and then quietly added, "This isn't easy for any of us."

As far as Lyla was concerned, nothing could be closer to the truth. Now that her father was gone, nothing was easy anymore. Their life felt like a giant puzzle made from pieces in the same shape and color. Nothing obviously fit together.

Lyla's grandmother finally stepped back and allowed them in, her hand clutched tight at the collar of her sweater as though it were snowing outside. Before she closed the front door, she looked over at the big yellow convertible parked in the driveway and shook her head. The canvas top was buttoned up.

Lyla watched her grandmother let out a quiet puff of air as she closed the front door. Maybe she thought this was all just a bad dream, that Lyla's father would suddenly pop out of the trunk and yell, *Gotcha!* But Lyla knew better. She'd thrown him into the Pacific Ocean, making him disappear for good.

In the darkened hallway, Lyla and her mother waited for Caroline to invite them to come sit in the living room. But she didn't. They all just stood in awkward silence—Lyla holding the warm loaf of bread, her mother gripping her sunglasses as though she might break them in half, and Lyla's grandmother smoothing out the pleats in her Sunday skirt. Lyla hadn't seen her grandmother at church that day, yet she dressed as though she had attended, heels and all.

"May we?" Lyla's mother finally asked.

"May we what?"

"Come in and sit down for a moment? Would that be okay?"

"I wasn't expecting company. I don't have anything to offer."

Lyla peered into the house, unprepared for the state of her grandmother's living room. Normally, her grandmother kept everything dusted and polished. Lyla's father used to tease his mother about the way she kept her house in constant order. "What, is the president coming to dinner?" he'd joke when he'd flop on the couch and put his feet up on the coffee table.

But now, the drapes were drawn. Vases of old flowers and brown water had yet to be cleaned up and put away. Dried-up petals were scattered on the coffee table.

The loaf of bread in Lyla's hands suddenly weighed about a hundred pounds. She hadn't been back to her grandmother's house since the funeral, which felt like a lifetime ago. In a way it was, and she wanted nothing more than to hand the bread over and hightail it out of there.

Lyla started for the kitchen to put the loaf on the counter, but her grandmother put out her hand and stopped her, like a crossing guard. "Best if you go wait out back," she said. "Your mother and I apparently need to talk."

Lyla turned to her mother with a *There's not a chance I'm going out there* look.

But before her mother could come to her rescue, Caroline stood there frowning at Lyla's bare legs below her Sunday school skirt. "Too dirty," she said, then added, "filthy."

Lyla clenched her teeth. It was always something different—her unkempt hair, the dirt or length of her fingernails, the way Lyla hunched at the table.

Sit up straight, Lyla. Heaven knows you don't want to look like a hobo when you sit at a dinner table.

Lyla rocked back on her heels to see what was so offensive this time. A chain of green-and-yellow bruises rode up her shins, bruises from when she'd tripped on the prayer bench the Sunday of her father's service.

Lyla bit her lip waiting for her mother to intervene, but she didn't. She just stood in the dark entryway, fidgeting with the thin belt around her waist, straightening it one way and then the other.

Through her nostrils, Caroline let out an exasperated breath. "Wait here," she said, and snatched the loaf of bread out of Lyla's hands. "I'll make you some lunch and you can sit outside while your mother tells me what is so important, she needed to come over unannounced like this."

"I'm not hungry—" Lyla started to protest when her grandmother turned and drifted down the long hallway to the kitchen, leaving Lyla and her mother alone in the stale air.

Lyla glanced at the part in the drapes. "I'm not going outside by myself," she whispered to her mother. "It's too cold."

"I'm sure we won't be long. Please, just do as you're asked, sweetheart." Her mother started rummaging through her purse.

"I won't do it," Lyla insisted.

"Lyla! Please." Her mother found what she was looking for. She opened a little green prescription bottle and shook a tiny white pill into the palm of her hand, then slid it onto her tongue. She closed her eyes and swallowed.

"But what if I have to use the bathroom?"

"Lyla May Hawkins, stop arguing with me!" Her mother snapped her purse shut and rubbed her neck. "I am not asking you. I am *telling* you to do as you're told." Lyla's mother closed her eyes, and her throat muscles tensed as if she were trying to swallow a walnut whole.

"Can't I just go to the car and read?"

"Honestly, Lyla. I—"

Just then, Caroline came out of the kitchen with a white paper plate filled with a peanut butter sandwich and apple slices. In her other hand was a glass of milk.

"Sure, okay. Yes, why don't you do that." Louise leaned over and kissed the top of Lyla's head. "And when we're done here, I'll take you to Howard's for a cherry soda." Her mother's voice and eyes softened. "And then maybe we can go to the movies. How does that sound?"

Lyla grabbed her lunch and started for the front door, but Caroline had already walked over and pulled the cord to the drapes and slid the glass door open to the backyard. "We won't be but a few minutes." Lyla bit the inside of her cheek and walked to the sliding glass door. Her body stiffened as her grandmother lay a bony hand on her shoulder and ushered her out back. "Plus, it's such a pleasant day out. I hadn't realized until now. Much nicer than in here." Her grandmother stared at Lyla's mother and slid the door closed. Then locked it.

Through the plate glass door, Lyla's mother mouthed the word *sorry*, but Lyla turned her back without mouthing *it's okay* back.

Lyla sat on the edge of the cement porch and swore that after today, she'd never come back here. Not in a million years. She put down the glass of milk and paper plate. She wasn't hungry or thirsty.

She was cold.

She was angry.

And she was scared.

She hadn't stepped foot in her grandmother's backyard since the memorial. But at least then, Lyla had had her cousins to be with— though nobody dared go to the back fence or anywhere near the tree. Nobody seemed to so much as look at it. They all just sat on the patio furniture in a circle, kicking the red rubber ball back and forth among them, not knowing what to say or what else to do.

Sitting there, Lyla refused to look at the tree. She hoped it would suddenly combust and burn to the ground. And secretly, she hoped her grandmother would too.

"Too dirty," Lyla mumbled in a mocking tone, pursing her lips like her grandmother.

Under the bright November sun, Lyla closed one eye. With her index finger, she began tracing the rounded hills out beyond her grandmother's property. She used to imagine the hills were the graves of giants—fat-bellied ogres buried on their backs, their plump stomachs pushing the earth toward the sky. Her father had laughed at her when she described this and tried to explain how seismological activity had formed these hills eons ago, long before Lyla was born. Lyla thought he was just trying to sound clever, using all those big words: *lithographic stress, alluvial fans, ablation zones.* Her father did that sometimes, talked all fancy-pants.

"One, two, three." Lyla traced the giants' bellies. But then she heard her father's voice. *Now come on, birdpie, you're too old to believe in giants, aren't you?*

Lyla stopped. Her eyes darted over to the tree as if her father were leaning against the trunk with his hat perched back on the crown of his head and a piece of grass stuck in his teeth. She shielded her eyes from the sun.

"Daddy?"

But Lyla knew better. Her father wasn't out there.

The tree stood alone behind the back fence as it always had. Except now, her tire swing was gone.

Lyla's stomach tightened. She forced her concentration back to the hills, keeping a steady count—*four, five, six*—still believing her father's explanations of plate tectonics and magnification factors too fantastic. It was a good deal easier to believe in a world of buried mythological creatures than something as far-fetched as ground displacement, slip planes, fault lines, and all the rest. Plus, she couldn't pronounce half the stuff he'd said.

Lyla lowered her hand and opened both eyes.

"See, Daddy, there's twelve giants out there." Then in a louder voice: "I said TWELVE! DID YOU HEAR ME?"

But of course, her father wasn't around to call her a *silly gooseneck* or bore her with explanations of continental drifts and seismic uplift—though she would give just about anything to hear him explain it one more time. Maybe she'd even listen.

Lyla picked up her peanut butter and honey sandwich and took a big bite. "That's twelve big ugly giants to your stupid seismological mumbo jumbo," she said, chewing her sandwich with her mouth open.

And try as she might not to look at the tree, Lyla found herself eyeing it like a criminal who stole her father away.

"How could you?" Lyla asked as a thick glob of peanut butter and bread cemented together inside her chest. She tried to swallow, tried to force the lump down, but it was stuck.

Her chest began to burn. Her eyes watered.

Lyla squeezed her eyes and rubbed her neck, trying to garner enough saliva to coax the bulge down. But the thickness in her chest burned, and it became hard to breathe. Lyla suddenly wondered if this was it. If this was what death felt like—burning-hot coals inside one's chest? If that was what her father had felt at the end?

Her heartbeat quickened; the blood pulsed and pumped in her head. She suddenly felt dizzy. Lyla turned to the house. What if her mother found her out here slumped over on the porch? *It'd serve her right*, Lyla thought, then quickly reached for her glass of milk. She took a tiny sip and squeezed her eyes again as the cold milk coaxed the lump down. When it finally passed and she could breathe again, Lyla burst into tears. She got up and walked over to the sliding door and rested her fist against the glass. She was just about to bang on the door and scream, *Let me in!* But then she saw the way the two of them sat across from one another, stiff and silent as porcelain figurines.

Lyla tapped on the glass. Her mother looked up.

"I want to go, Mama," she begged.

But her mother didn't get up. She held a finger to her lips and mouthed, *One more minute.*

Lyla shook her head, her eyes still watering. The phantom pressure in her chest still stung. "No. I want to go home. Now!"

Her mother closed her eyes and dropped her head, and when she opened them again, she too was crying—not the small tears that slid down her cheeks when they watched a sad movie together but with the wet, quiet eyes of someone who'd seen a ghost. It was the same look her mother had worn right before she locked herself in her bedroom for four whole days after Lyla's father died, when she cried and cried. And screamed. And threw something heavy against the wall.

THE PALE FLESH OF WOOD

Lyla sat outside the bedroom, listening to her mother's hard grief just like when Baby Daniel died. She knocked on the door every so often to see if her mother needed anything, but she never responded. Lyla began sleeping in the hallway, fending for herself at mealtimes, and waiting for her mother to emerge. And then on the fifth day, she did. She came out one morning with her hair brushed and lips wet with fresh lipstick and told Lyla to hurry up. She was late for school.

———

Lyla didn't want to be responsible for her mother locking herself in a room like that again. She dropped her fist from the glass and sat back down.

And waited.

She stretched her legs out in front of her, staring at the parched white skin on her kneecaps and the bruises skipping up her shins. She picked up her glass and blew into the plastic straw. A raft of tiny bubbles frothed at the surface of the milk. She blew again, creating more bubbles, all the while staring at the film on her knees, the bruises on her shins. The magnitude of her grandmother's words began to register. *Too dirty.*

She blew.

More bubbles grew.

Filthy.

Bubbles popped, one by one.

Go outside.

She blew again and ran her palm down the length of her bony legs just to the edge of her bobby socks.

Too dirty.

She ran her hand back up again, stopping short of her kneecaps.

Too dirty. Filthy. Go outside.

Again, Lyla blew bubbles and ran her hand down her shin. The hair against her palm reminded her of when she ran her hand along her father's jawline that one Christmas vacation when he tried to let his beard grow. One way, the wisps felt smooth, delicate even. But when she rubbed the opposite direction, the hairs prickled her fingertips. *Too dirty. Filthy. Go outside.*

She cupped her hands over her kneecaps, hoping the chalky film would magically disappear. But when she lifted her hand and peeked underneath, no such luck. She brushed at the film. It remained. She then licked her pinky finger and swiped her kneecap. And just like that, *poof,* the white film vanished. Her skin glistened in the streak of spit.

She put the glass of milk down, the straw still in her mouth, and rushed back to the sliding glass door, to tell her grandmother the good news. *I'm not dirty! I just have dry skin!*

Lyla cupped her hands around her eyes and peered through the glass. The straw hung off her lips like one of her father's cigarettes.

"Red rover, red rover, let me on over," she sang, her knuckles resting on the glass, ready to knock. "In. Inside."

When neither of the women turned, Lyla reached for the door handle. But something stopped her. Her mother was no longer quietly crying but shaking. The sharp heel of her shoe bore up and down, leaving a small round depression in the carpet. The teacup and saucer in her lap quivered.

"Mama?"

Across the room, Lyla's grandmother sat perfectly still. Her long skirt splayed out over her quiet knees and down to the carpet like one of the alluvial fans her father had told Lyla about. Her feet were crossed at the ankles, static.

Lyla became too afraid to knock any louder and startle them.

"Oh, Daddy," Lyla whispered. Her hot breath left a sweaty cloud on the sliding glass door.

She wiped her fog of breath off the glass, wishing her Daddy would come back. He could always be counted on to make his mother and Lyla's laugh when they didn't see eye to eye. He could always make the sun shine. And there in the cleaned glass, her father did! He came back! His picture sat on the mantle—so handsome in his winter service uniform, dark obsidian hair, and those deep, vast ocean eyes. Next to his picture was a smaller photograph. It was a picture of Lyla's mother and grandmother taken just last year—their hardened smiles caught in the flash.

Her father had coaxed them into their smiles. *Come on now, ladies. Just pretend I'm standing here naked, wearing nothing but my socks,* he had said just before he snapped the picture. Lyla loved that about her father. How he could make his mother smile, even when she didn't want to.

Lyla looked back to the picture of her father, who seemed to be smiling right at her. She removed the straw from her mouth, pretending to smoke it like she was a movie star. She took a couple of long puffs and blew her hot breath against the glass, walking up and down in front of the sliding glass door as though she was wearing high heels, a long dress, and a fancy shawl. She stopped and posed, trying to get their attention and lighten the mood. She tapped the ashes off of her fake cigarette and took another long drag, trying her best to look like Marlene Dietrich in the movie *Angel in Paris.*

"Have you ever been a stranger in a strange city?" Lyla said in her most sultry adult voice, delivering the line she and her father had often recited.

But they didn't hear her. They didn't even see her.

Lyla's mother reached back into her purse and opened up the green bottle. She slid another pill onto her tongue. Her foot kept jackhammering away while her grandmother refused to move an inch. An unsettling line seemed to have cracked open between the two of them.

"Oh, what's the point?" Lyla threw her straw to the ground and pushed at the glass.

Her reflection pushed back.

She stuck out her tongue.

Her reflection did as well.

"Copycat." Lyla turned, not willing to let her reflection have the final say. She sat back down and picked up the glass of milk, now warm from the midday sun.

It didn't matter, though. Nothing did anymore.

Her father was gone, and everything once good about her life had gone with him. Now she was stuck with her mother who walked around like a ghost, taking those pills from the little green bottle, and her grandmother who Lyla tried to avoid like Medusa.

She drained the glass, not bothering to wipe off her milk mustache. She let it sit there above her upper lip. Her stone-stiff grandmother would not approve, but Lyla could give two hoots.

The mustache felt dirty. But dirty in a good way.

She put the glass down, determined to wear the dried mustache until her mother came out and told her it was time to go home. Even then, she wouldn't wipe it off. She'd walk straight through her grandmother's house, wearing the mustache proudly above her lip. She'd wear it as she climbed into the back seat of her mother's car. And she'd wear it all the way home. She'd wear it to bed. Heck, she'd even wear it the following morning at breakfast if it lasted that long.

Lyla swore she wouldn't wash her face until the mustache disappeared all on its own.

Before then, Lyla would sit quietly on the porch, waiting for her mother to come out and take her to Howard's for the cherry soda she was promised. She'd skip the movies, though. She didn't want her mother to feel like she could "fun" her way out of this mess. Lyla wanted her mother to feel the same burn of rejection she had felt on days when Lyla needed her.

Lyla sat back down on the porch and closed one eye, avoiding the tug of her gaze to the tree that stood at the epicenter of it all. She held her arm, and with her index finger began retracing the graves of all the giants buried in the hills—the soft mounds of the earth that remained right where they were, as full and bulging as always.

BOOK II

(1957–1967)

CHAPTER NINE

SUNDAY NIGHT MOVIES—

1957–1962

One Sunday night, Lyla and her mother start a new tradition. They stay home and watch old home movies projected on the living room wall—reels of silent 8mm footage that didn't seem to add up to much of anything when Lyla's parents filmed them. But now, these movies seem to be all they have left. Watching their former selves in black and white will be a ritual that will last for many years—until one day they stop.

Side by side, Lyla and her mother sit on the carpet with their backs against the couch. They hold hands underneath the woolen blanket draped over their legs. Lyla's mother reminds her of how her father *accidentally* brought the blanket home after an anniversary trip to Big Sur, the very trip that brought them Baby Daniel. Over the next few years, they all learned to love this blanket as though it were part of the family, like a pet. Because it still smells of her father's Old Spice aftershave, Lyla forbids her mother to put it in the laundry machine for fear her father's scent will be washed away. Lyla is not ready for that yet. She is ten years old and has only just thrown grainy bits of him over the side of the boat.

This first night, her mother unpacks the projector and sets it up on the coffee table.

Lyla holds her breath and begins counting, *One Mississippi, two Mississippi*, like when they'd drive through the rainbow tunnel coming home from San Francisco. Counting Mississippis, Lyla prepares herself to see her father again.

Lyla's mother fiddles with the projector, but she is taking forever. At twenty-eight Mississippis, Lyla's face turns red. Her lungs want to explode.

"Hurry up!" Lyla manages to squeak out, then steals a sip of air and continues counting. *Twenty-nine, thirty.*

"I'm trying, honey. You have to be patient."

But patience, Lyla begins to believe, might send her to the grave. She sneaks another breath.

Lyla's mother removes the first movie, *July 1946*, from its aluminum canister and lines the sprocket holes of the film onto the teeth of the projector. Lyla's father had not taught them how to do this. There are many things he failed to tell them before he left. But this, threading the film projector, wasn't even on the radar.

"Do you even know what you're doing?" Lyla gives up holding her breath. She doesn't mean to hurt her mother's feelings, but Lyla has never seen her do anything remotely handy. That was Daddy's job.

"Oh, give me a break, Miss Debbie Doubter. How hard can it be?" Her mother flips the metal switch to the *on* position, but she's forgotten one important step. She's failed to lower the roller arm to secure the filmstrip in place. The movie immediately bunches up onto itself and jams the machine.

"See!" A weight starts building in Lyla's chest again.

Her mother snaps the projector off and tries to unravel the mess, but it's useless. The filmstrip has jumbled into a giant knot. She leans over and tears at the film with her teeth. Her mother looks like an animal when she does this, like the tiger at the San Francisco Zoo at feeding time. The filmstrip tears free, and Lyla's mother peels the tail out of the machine. She holds the tangled ball in her hands, then tries to balance it on her nose, clapping her hands and barking like a seal. The filmstrip ball falls to the floor.

"What are you doing?" Lyla asks.

"I was just trying to have a little fun. Geez, Louise. Get it? Geez, Louise." Her mother snorts with laughter, pointing to herself. She takes a sip from her wine glass, still giggling.

Lyla rolls her eyes, and her mother rolls her eyes back, before getting up. "Well, here's looking at you, kid," she says, as she chucks that portion of their lives into the wastebasket.

Watching this, Lyla makes a promise to herself. She will sneak into the living room after her mother goes to bed and retrieve the discarded film, swearing she will be the one to tape their lives back together. She will hide the gnarled filmstrip in the shoebox underneath her bed, along with a host of other things that remind her of her father—his old dog tags, a signed baseball from when the Giants moved to San Francisco, the old fish fossil he guilted her into keeping on that drive to the beach when they almost crashed, the American kestrel feather she had taped to the back of an obsidian arrowhead, a collection of newspaper clippings about his days on the high school basketball team.

His return from the war.

His obituary.

Louise pulls the instruction manual out of the projector box and reads the directions, cover to cover, before she attempts to thread the machine again. It takes hours, a whole bottle of wine later. But this time, when she lowers the roller arm and flicks the switch, the movie starts at its new beginning.

"See, Lyla!" Her mother is giddy with her small triumph. "Have a little faith, will you," she jokes, as though Lyla should have never questioned her know-how.

I do have faith, Lyla almost protests but doesn't, because right then her father pops onto the living room wall.

"Daddy!" Lyla screams. "Look, Mama. There he is!" Lyla waves to her father.

"Yes, sweetheart. There he is!" Lyla's mother holds her hand to her mouth.

On film, Lyla's father is sitting on the edge of the bed with his camera turned toward himself. His smile is wide and bright. He talks to the camera, but because it is a silent movie, Lyla can only guess what he says. She is certain he is telling her he loves her because of the happy wetness in his eyes. He then blows a kiss to the camera as though he somehow knew they'd be watching this movie without him one day.

Together, Lyla and her mother sit on the living room floor and watch the footage wobble as he turns the camera back around and focuses the lens on baby Lyla, who is asleep on her mother's chest.

"Look, and there's baby me!" Lyla squeals.

"It is. You in all your glory, miracle girl." Under the blanket, Louise squeezes Lyla's kneecap. Lyla likes it when her mother reminds her that she's a miracle, how her birth defied all odds, especially with that sneaky umbilical cord wrapped around her neck like a python.

"I was so small," Lyla says.

"Yes, sweetheart, you were. Your tiny head used to fit right in Daddy's palm like a grapefruit." Her mother holds out her hand, palm up, showing how he'd cup Lyla's infant head. "You weighed almost nothing. Just a little bird sitting in a nest. And now look at you!"

Lyla is mesmerized by watching her baby self—every yawn, every blink of the eye, each bubble of spit that escapes her newborn lips. Frame by frame, nothing more seems to unfold than Lyla's silent breathing. But she's utterly captivated. On film, Lyla's eyelids flutter like the wings of a hummingbird, resisting sleep, something she does for the rest of her life. Like her mother, Lyla will never be a good sleeper.

Clip after clip, baby Lyla grows before their very eyes; her nose rounds, her cheeks start to fill out in a sort of time-lapse photography.

"My goodness." Her mother sighs. "It's hard to believe you're the same girl." She reaches back under the blanket and pulls Lyla's hand out, measuring their hands. "It won't be long until yours are bigger than mine."

Lyla doubts this. The tips of her fingers only reach her mother's first knuckle.

"My hands will never be like yours, Mama," Lyla says. Her eyes remain dead ahead on the living room wall. "They're just stupid piggy stubs."

Her mother doesn't disavow Lyla of her mistaken belief. She doesn't remind Lyla she possesses half of the Hawkinses' genes—a family of giants—so she has no choice but to tower over her one day. Instead, her mother tucks Lyla's hand back under the blanket and squeezes it between the knobs of her knees. It hurts when she does this, but Lyla can't pull it away. Her mother's grip is too tight.

Teased by the image of her father cast upon the living room wall, Lyla tries with all her might to remember how it used to be back when he was still alive. It's not hard; he's only been gone for six months.

Her chest tightens. For a hot second, she feels like she might need to get up and run to her bedroom.

But she doesn't.

She can't move.

She is paralyzed by all she sees.

And all that she will never see again.

Lyla closes her eyes and pretends—even if just for a moment—her father is not gone; he is still here, quietly standing in the corner, mixing a drink at the bar and watching his girls watch one of his movies.

But when Lyla opens her eyes and turns to the corner of the room, her father is not there. He is not mixing a drink and running commentary on their lives. He is now just a two-dimensional ghost caught on film.

"Daddy?" This is all Lyla manages to ask. She doesn't yet question why he did what he did. That will all come much later.

Next to Lyla, her mother draws in a long, deep breath through her nose and exhales slowly out of her mouth, as though Dr. Ramsey is holding a stethoscope to her back. Her eyes are squeezed shut. Lyla's mother is not crying, but she's stopped watching the movie.

Lyla pinches her eyelids shut again too, wanting to see what her mother sees behind closed eyes.

In the darkness, Lyla hears the thrum of the film as it rolls through a small part of their lives.

In the darkness, she listens to the gallop of her heartbeat.

And then, just like that, the film is swallowed up and spat out onto the take-up reel.

"Oh, Lyla." Her mother throws off the blanket and gets up. "I don't think I can ever do that again."

But she does.

Months later, Lyla's mother hauls the projector back down from the attic with a second film canister tucked under her chin. *February 1947.* Lyla doesn't know why her mother changed her mind, but she is glad she did. She misses her father something terrible, and Lyla guesses her mother does too.

This time, Louise double-checks her work before she turns off the lights and crawls back to where Lyla sits against the couch, painting her toenails in a rainbow of Revlon colors.

Blue, then red, then orange, then green, finally a dash of purple on her little piggies.

A wad of toilet paper snakes between her toes.

It doesn't take long before Lyla looks up and sees something in the movie she shouldn't.

Silly, Daddy! He'd put the camera down on its side but had forgotten to turn the camera to the *off* position. Together, Lyla and her mother lean their heads over and watch the film sideways. On the wall, they watch him strip off his clothes until he is down to nothing but his boxer shorts and climbs into bed next to Lyla's mother. Lyla doesn't realize baby her is nestled and hidden on the other side of the bed in a fortress of pillows.

"Are you touching tongues?" Lyla's face flushes while the two lovebirds are kissing on film. "Gross. Why would you want to do that?" Lyla focuses her sights on the sheets instead. They look even whiter on film. They look impossibly bright.

Her mother doesn't think to seize the moment and begin the early stages of sex-education talks with Lyla. Louise's head is still tilted to one side. "Gosh, do you remember how absent-minded he could be?" she asks. "It's a miracle he even remembered our birthdays."

Lyla licks her finger and cleans a smudge of polish off her big toe like she's seen her mother do a million times before, trying not to focus on all their yucky kissing. And when her parents finally do stop, baby Lyla reappears on film.

Like magic.

Abracadabra Kalamazoo.

Lyla's father picks up baby Lyla from the side of the bed and places her in the empty dresser drawer on the floor. Despite what Grandmother Caroline maintained, Louise tells Lyla the top drawer of the dresser makes a fine crib.

"It's where you slept best," her mother says. "In your little nest."

It was the same nest where Baby Daniel slept, before he decided to sleep forever.

In the movie, Lyla's father climbs back in bed and pulls the sheets over their heads. They begin to wrestle around. Lyla doesn't know what they are doing, exactly, but this time she keeps her eyes glued on the wall. "What are you doing under there?"

Her mother yanks the blanket up and over Lyla's ten-year-old eyes. "This is too much. You shouldn't be watching this at your age," she says. But her mother doesn't get up and turn off the projector.

Behind the blanket curtain, Lyla feels her mother's muscles tense. Her breathing deepens.

Her body leans forward as if she's ready to crawl across the living room carpet and back into the film itself.

Lyla steals a peek around the blanket just as one of her mother's legs kicks free from the sheets in the movie.

"No, Lyla." Her mother tugs the blanket back up in front of Lyla's eyes. "This is definitely too much for a girl your age."

Lyla feels her mother getting ready to reach over and turn off the projector. But from behind the blanket, Lyla grabs her mother's arm. "Wait," Lyla says, because the funny game her parents were playing in the movie is apparently over.

Lyla pulls down the blanket. Her mother's muscles relax.

In the movie, Lyla's mother is now sitting up in the bed; she leans against the headboard with a grin on her face. She clutches the top sheet over her chest. Her red hair—which isn't really red in the black-and-white movie—spills over her pale shoulders. Lyla realizes she hasn't seen her mother smile like that in a long time now.

"Look how beautiful you were," Lyla says. Then quickly adds, "Are."

Lyla's father buries his face into a fistful of her mother's long hair; the shock of red against the bright white sheet seemingly bleeds through the monochrome of the film. Lyla's father always loved Louise's hair, declaring it to be the most decadent thing in the world.

Sitting there waving a magazine over her toes, Lyla wishes she had inherited the color of her mother's hair, not the black of his.

"You have the best hair in the world. You're like a shampoo model." Lyla reaches over and twirls a finger around a lock of her mother's hair, but Louise doesn't say thank you or hug Lyla. She simply stares at herself on film.

"Oh, Lyla, your father was something else."

It was true. Her father was something else. There was nobody like him in the whole wide world.

When the movie ends, Lyla's mother doesn't reach over and flick the projector off. She just picks up her wine glass and rubs her index finger around the rim. They sit and stare at the blank wall, listening to the film slap against the reel, a continuous *thwack, thwack, thwack* in the otherwise quiet room.

Finally, Lyla's mother puts down her glass and crawls over to the machine, turning it off.

"I have a confession to make," she says, busying herself with packing the film into its canister. She tells Lyla about how she had cut a lock of her hair and laid it across Charles's lips before she had him cremated so that, together in the oven, her hair and his body would disintegrate into one grainy mass.

Lyla is stone silent.

When her mother finally turns around, Lyla doesn't so much as look up. She rests her chin on her knees as she stares at the long middle toes she inherited from her father, trying to make sense of what her mother has just revealed.

It sounds too much like a fairy tale.

Lyla unravels the twisted-up toilet paper from between her freshly painted toes. She strains both to remember *and* to forget the day they took his ashes out on the sailboat. It's hard to do both at the same time because memory—she has only just begun to learn—can be stronger than the will to forget. It's like pulling the dried wishbone from a Thanksgiving turkey. The memory bone always seems to snap off larger.

With the blanket draped over her lap, Lyla dredges up that November day when they went out on the boat.

Lyla remembers holding tight to the rails as her uncle David steered the boat up and over the incoming swells. They were bundled in their thickest sweaters, as it was cold that day—so cold, Lyla didn't want to let go of the rail, but she finally did. She took a handful of gritty clumps from the box Grandmother Caroline held out to her.

"Go ahead, Lyla. It's all right," her grandmother urged. "Let him go."

And so, Lyla did. In the wind, she let her father's bone and skin and hair sift through her fingers like sand, unaware she was scattering a piece of her mother too.

Lyla clenches her teeth. Her eyes begin to water; she's suddenly angry at her mother and her stupid confession.

"I knew you'd rather be with him than me!" Lyla throws the wad of toilet paper at her mother. She storms to her room and slams the door. In the dark, she buries her head in her pillow.

How could her mother not have thought she would have liked to burn a piece of her with her father too?

There is a light knock on the door.

"Go away!" Lyla yells.

And her mother does. She turns and walks away without a word.

Hearing her mother's disappearing footsteps, Lyla is relieved, even if a small part snaps inside her—like that wishbone. Left alone in her room, Lyla is stuck with the small end, wishing her mother hadn't so readily done what she had asked.

———————

Things are different now that Lyla is thirteen and in the eighth grade.

Her mother can thread the machine like an old pro. She's read the instruction manual about a million times now—something Lyla's father would've never done. He always threw instructions straight into the trash, retrieving them only after instinct failed him.

Because Lyla is a teenager, her mother tells her she's old enough to set up the projector, that it will be her job from now on. Louise hands her the film canister—*February 1948*. She shows Lyla how to set the movie on the front mount, how the tail of the filmstrip attaches to the take-up reel. They do it together, slow and methodical, always reciting the instructions step-by-step as if they were disarming a land mine.

"Voilà!" Her mother beams. "Well done, my miracle girl."

Lyla feels successful, though she's not exactly sure the reason her mother is proud. Was it because Lyla was able to follow her mother's instructions so carefully? Or was it because her mother was the one who taught her how to do something for once, not her father?

Maybe, Lyla finally settles on, it's a little of both.

She doesn't really care, though, because when she flicks the switch, her father is there on the wall, smiling, playing a game of peek-a-boo with toddler Lyla.

Lyla rushes over and sits down. She pulls the blanket up over her legs.

Her mother doesn't move. She remains standing in front of the projector with her big fat head blocking Lyla's view.

"Hey, move over," Lyla says. Still, her mother doesn't budge—she just stands there with her shadow cast upon the wall. Lyla tells her mother that she makes a better door than a window. And this makes her mother laugh.

"Oops, sorry, sweetheart." Louise ducks out of the way and steals back to where Lyla sits, holding the edge of the blanket up for her mother to climb in.

"Thanks," Louise whispers, as though there are other moviegoers in the room.

"No problem, blockhead," Lyla whispers back.

"Blockhead?" Her mother nudges Lyla in the ribs.

"Shh." Lyla rests her finger on her lips because on the white wall, her father is smiling hard as he plays his game with toddler Lyla. He puts his handkerchief on top of his head and sticks out his tongue. Her father is about to cry.

His eyes give him away; they always do.

"Oh, God, there he goes again," her mother teases.

The *again* part trips Lyla up. The hint of exasperation in her mother's voice stings like a paper cut.

A small army of tears spills down her father's unshaven cheeks. He looks right into the camera.

"So damn beautiful," Lyla *sees* him say. She has become a good lip reader by now.

He is talking about her mother. How could he not be? He is looking right at Louise who is holding the camera. Yet the longer that time slips by between their Sunday night screenings, Lyla starts to question to whom he is referring when he utters that last word, *beautiful.* Little bubbles of doubt surface.

"Was he talking about me or you?" Lyla asks.

"You, of course, miracle girl. You were everything to him. His baby girl!" Her mother confides in her now that Lyla is older, a full-fledged teenager being assigned essays on weighty subjects in school: the Great Depression, Hitler's rise to power, and all the history that came in between.

Lyla doesn't quite know what to make of her mother's distanced tone. Logic has always told her if this were true—that if *she* was everything to her father—he would still be here today. That he would have never left her in the way he did.

"Time is a funny thing, Lyla," her mother slurs as she pours another helping of wine. "Enjoy it while you can."

But like the many drowned-out words her mother has begun to utter when they sit and watch these movies on Sunday nights, Lyla has no clear idea what she is talking about.

Lyla is another couple of years older now. Old enough to earn her driver's permit. Old enough to see things differently and hear what is *not* said in the silent films.

Because these movies bear witness to only the best parts of their lives, Lyla begins to play detective, searching for clues that led to her father's decision. She scours the movies, hunting for glimpses of when it all began. But she can't find a damn thing because her father was a good magician. Same goes with Baby Daniel. Just like Lyla's father, Daniel fooled them into thinking they had it all, until one day they didn't.

One Sunday night, Lyla's mother brings a new film down from the attic. She tosses the canister over in Lyla's direction like a metal Frisbee. "Here, catch."

Why her mother is being so cavalier—throwing their movies around like this—Lyla doesn't understand. The flying object is heavy and nearly knocks the wind out of her as she traps it against her ribs.

"What are we watching tonight?" Lyla flips the canister right side up.

April 1954 is taped to the outside of the tin.

"More of the same," her mother says with a tight voice, as though she's trying to swallow a raw oyster.

But her mother is wrong. It's not more of the same. Her mother has never brought this canister down from the attic before.

This is the year of Baby Daniel.

"Are you sure?" Lyla asks.

"Yes." Her mother reaches into her sweater's pocket and pops something in her mouth—a Tic-Tac, Lyla figures—and swallows.

When Lyla turns out the lights and flicks the switch, Baby Daniel appears on the living room wall, the very same wall that used to house his newborn pictures until the day Lyla's mother took them down, the day she was determined to eradicate any evidence of him around the house.

Lyla throws the blanket off and reaches over to turn off the machine. She suddenly doesn't want her mother to be reminded of Daniel and have her go into another one of her funks.

But this time, her mother stops Lyla from turning off the movie.

"No, sweetheart." Louise grabs Lyla's elbow. "I can do this now. I promise."

"Really?" Lyla asks, because she is not at all convinced. In all these years, they have not talked about Baby Daniel. They try never to say his name. His life on this planet seems like a fleeting dream by now. Yet there he is across the room: fat, red-faced, and alive.

Lyla sits back and snuggles up to her mother, fearing she will crawl into her bed and not come out for days. They have been through all that before, too many times now. Plus, Lyla doesn't want to have to call Grandmother Caroline and make her come over and sit in the passenger seat and teach Lyla how to drive to school, to tennis practice, and all the rest.

Life is so much better when it is just Lyla and her mother, even when it isn't.

"I'll be fine," Louise says.

Lyla looks at her mother as if her mother has been captured by aliens.

"I said, I promise." Her mother crosses her heart. The tone in her voice is too crisp, like she's bitten off the end of a carrot.

"Okay, but just give me the word and I'll turn it off. I'll throw the movie into the trash."

"Thank you, sweetheart. You are always so good to be looking out for me like you do, like you're the mother. Not the other way around."

In the movie, they watch Daniel crawl away from Louise. Lyla's father has left a trail of broken-up Gerber cookies on the floor, coaxing Baby Daniel to crawl toward him. That *cheater, cheater, pumpkin eater!*

Daniel scoots closer and closer, palming the pieces into his mouth; gummy crumbs stick to his chubby face.

"No," Louise mutters quietly as the film rolls on.

In her periphery, Lyla can see her mother's hands curl into tight balls.

"The chunks are too big. He'll choke," she says, as if Daniel were still alive. "Don't you see? He could have killed him." Her voice is thin, biting.

Lyla does see, and she wonders when exactly that combination of anxiety and accusation took up permanent residence in her mother's voice. As though Daniel's death was somehow her father's fault.

Behind the camera, Lyla sees her father's big hand toss another cookie on the floor. Even though the sound of the film is silent, Lyla imagines what her mother was saying back then:

Charles! I'm serious. He could choke, and that is not something we want caught on film.

Funny, though, it wasn't the cookie, or a fall out of his high chair, or sticking his finger in a socket, or any of the other billion things her mother worried about.

He died while sleeping.

Poof. Just like that.

One day he was here.

One morning he was gone, like a visitor.

───────

On film, little girl Lyla runs in front of the camera and grabs the uneaten chunks from the floor. Daniel immediately starts crying. His old-man face bunches up.

If there's one thing Lyla remembers to this day about Daniel, it is how he cried all the time, for hours on end. Lyla's mother usually calmed him, but sometimes only Lyla's father could make him stop. He'd take Daniel for a walk around the block at all hours of the night and soothe him back to sleep.

Watching these movies reminds Lyla how angry she'd been when her mother came into the room one night while her father was reading the end of *Treasure Island* to Lyla and handed Daniel over to Lyla's father, telling him it was his turn.

And once, when her father took his *little king* into his arms and walked him outside, Lyla wished Daniel was never born, that it was still only the three of them and no intruders.

In the movie, red-faced Daniel reaches for more cookie chunks, but seven-year-old Lyla pushes him over and slaps his hand.

Watching her younger self on the living room wall, Lyla's heart grows a bit cold and tight like it's been stuffed into a small frozen anchovy tin. She had only meant to protect Daniel at the time, she is sure of it. She'd only been trying to stop him from choking but pushed him a little too hard. He falls onto his back. His arms and legs flail above him like one of those baby turtles unable to right itself. Daniel wails harder than ever before.

On film, Lyla's mother sweeps in for the rescue and picks up crying Daniel, holding him tight.

"Lyla May!" She is certain her mother barked back then. On film, her mother's face is pinched. Those three wrinkles on her forehead appear—the ones Lyla calls her *mad creases*. On film, Lyla begins to cry too.

"Come on, Louise." Lyla wants to believe it's what her father had said. "She's only trying to help." Because it was Daddy who always came to Lyla's rescue.

The film suddenly goes black.

Lyla's mother has turned off the projector. The film has rolled to a warbled stop, and whatever her mother was about to say or do is swallowed up on the take-up reel.

"How about some ice cream?" Louise asks, her voice a little too perky.

"Um. Sure, okay," Lyla says, suspicious of what else happened in that moment of such fierce protection—Louise of Daniel, Charles of Lyla. So, when her mother returns from the kitchen holding out two bowls of Rocky Road, Lyla finds the courage to ask, "Did you love Daniel more than me?"

"Oh, sweetheart. That is a terrible thing to wonder about."

But here is the thing.

Her mother never answers the question. She simply flips the projector back on and sits down, this time a tad farther from Lyla. The blanket stretches tight. Lyla is a lefty, and their elbows always bonk whenever she sits to her mother's right. But at this moment, Lyla doesn't believe her dominant arm is the cause for her mother sitting farther away.

"Lordy, Lordy," Louise whispers when the film continues, and they watch Daniel latch to Louise's breast with such ferocious hunger.

Lyla can barely watch. It looks too painful. She puts down her bowl, suddenly not very hungry.

"Will I have to do that someday?" she asks.

"Only if you want to." Lyla's mother can't take her eyes off Daniel. He bites down harder than before, and Lyla sees her mother wince.

"No, thanks," Lyla says. "I'd rather own goats."

Lyla's mother laughs so hard, chocolate snorts from her nose.

But Lyla is not kidding. She is fifteen. She has kissed two boys, smoked one cigarette, and already decided she will never be a mother. She is convinced it would hurt too much.

One Sunday night, Lyla's mother doesn't bring any film canisters down from the attic. It is October 1961, the fifth anniversary of when Charles left them.

When Lyla asks her mother if she should go grab the projector, her mother says no, then reminds Lyla of what day it is.

"I'm sorry, Mama. I forgot."

Lyla's mother smiles weakly and tells her that it is a good thing to forget. It's important to prune back such things. "Like deadheading the rosebush out front; it's good for us."

Lyla thinks this is an odd thing to say. Deadheading won't bring her father back.

Instead of watching a movie that night, they sit with their backs against the sofa, their heads resting between their knees as though they are Olympic athletes trying to recover oxygen after an impossible feat of athleticism. But Lyla and her mother are not athletes; they are just two people in the midst of a head rush, trying to keep themselves from passing out on the floor.

"I hate you," Lyla whispers.

"Lyla May!" Louise barks.

But Lyla is not talking to her mother; she is talking to her father, the one they are supposed to be deadheading. It is the first time Lyla has ever said such a thing to her father. She's said *I hate you* plenty to her mother's face by now because she is deep in her teenage years, and the words have become as familiar a taste in her mouth as toothpaste.

"How could he be so selfish?" Lyla's voice cracks. "How could he have done that?" Lyla's face sinks down into the dark folds of the blanket. She cannot smell her father anymore; his scent has been washed away.

"Oh, honey." Louise rubs quiet circles on Lyla's back.

Lyla doesn't realize how good it feels when she does this until her mother stops—not just this one Sunday night, but when she stops comforting Lyla altogether.

After her father's death, time seems stuck in geological mode, inching along at glacial speeds, never moving fast enough so they can move on. Questions about her father's decision harbor deep inside Lyla, questions that are only answered in the brief seconds when Lyla is asleep, dreaming of him.

One night, Lyla kneels by her mother's bed. She shakes her awake.

"Lyla?" Louise bolts up and reaches for her glasses. "Are you okay? What's happened?"

"Daddy came for a visit in my sleep. He told me he missed me. That he made a mistake." Lyla tells her mother how he started describing that night, what drove him to do it. But just as soon as he was about to whisper his confession, Lyla woke to Fillmore's barking. Fillmore is their dopey golden retriever that Lyla and her mother adopted soon after Charles died, believing a dog could help fill the absence.

"I tried to fall back asleep, to bring Daddy back. I wanted to hear what he had to say."

But it is useless. Lyla is no magician with a host of tricks up her sleeve. She is just a teenage girl wanting her father more than ever before.

"He was right there, Mama. I swear I could feel him sitting on the bed next to me. I could smell his Old Spice."

Louise pulls back the covers, inviting Lyla to crawl into her bed. Lyla has not slept in her mother's bed in a long time now. Years ago, Louise told Lyla she needed to learn to sleep on her own, that Lyla was too old to come in every time she had a nightmare. But tonight, her mother taps the empty space on the mattress. "Come here, sweetheart."

Lyla rests her head on her mother's warm shoulder, and Louise admits she's had that very same dream nearly every night since he left. Her mother's breath smells like stale butter, but Lyla doesn't move away.

"Maybe," Louise suggests, still half asleep, "maybe together, we can make him come back in our dreams. Maybe we just need to work as a team."

They haven't worked as a team for some time now, especially since Lyla's mother started dating Al, a man who is thick as a brick. A man who builds houses. A man who goes off on fishing trips with his buddies. A man Lyla takes to calling The Ape.

Lyla feels warmed by what her mother suggests, that they can be a two-person team again, a pitcher and catcher, a quarterback and wide receiver. Lyla snuggles up to her mother, and they curl up like earthworms. They press their eyes tight, hoping for the impossible, that they can somehow miraculously make him reappear. They count to ten and open their eyes, but Charles is nowhere to be found, and they concede that it is impossible. He can only come back to life when he is cast upon their living room wall on Sunday nights or in the clouds of their dreams.

"Oh, phooey." Louise turns on her side, away from Lyla. "Better luck next time."

Lyla gets up and goes back to her own room.

"When's The Ape coming home?" Lyla asks one Sunday night, though she knows her mother hates it when she calls her second husband by that name. But that is what Al is to Lyla. A thick, hairy buffoon. He will never be Lyla's *dad*.

"Please, Lyla. He's a good guy. Can't you just be nice?"

"All right, all right. I'm just kidding," Lyla says. Then she asks, "Wanna watch a movie tonight?" They haven't watched their old home movies in a long time now, not since the wedding.

Louise stops slicing the onions for dinner. She looks at the clock on the kitchen wall. Lyla imagines her mother is calculating the time between when Al left to go bowling and when he is due home. Lyla believes her mother feels she must only watch these movies in secret. Louise hasn't ever admitted this, but Lyla can read more than lips.

"Okay, let's do it." Her mother rips off her apron and flicks off the stove. She chases Lyla up to the attic; they are giddy as thieves on the lam. But as they rummage around for the old suitcase of movies, Lyla finally asks something she has wondered all along.

"Was it me?" She moves a heavy box of books out of the way. "Was it my fault? Because of my swing?"

"What was that, darling?" Her mother pretends not to have heard Lyla.

"You heard me."

Still, her mother doesn't answer. She just keeps searching around for the old suitcase of movies.

They catch eyes for a millisecond.

And there it is! Lyla sees the look in her mother's eyes. She is sure of it. Lyla is convinced she sees a look of blame because she was the one who hung the rope for the swing. She has seen it in Grandmother Caroline's eyes too.

"I asked you a simple question. Was it my fault?"

And when her mother again fails to respond, Lyla shoves her father's old golf clubs to the side.

She wills her mother to come over, to hold her, to correct her, to comfort her, but she doesn't. Her mother just keeps moving those stupid boxes around and around, looking for the dusty suitcase of movies.

"It's got to be around here somewhere." Her mother pushes things back and forth, kicking up dust.

Lyla wants to ask if her mother is deaf, but then Louise says with a cheeky tone, "There you are, you little devil!" She heaves a box off the suitcase.

"Whatever," Lyla says. She can't even look at her mother. She storms back downstairs and grabs a Coke out of the refrigerator and drains it. She stands looking out the window, at the silhouettes of redwood trees, barely feeling the cold of the glass against the heat of her palms.

Later, when the two of them stand like strangers in the kitchen, Lyla asks her mother why she didn't bother to answer her. "Did you even hear me? Don't you even care?"

"Oh, my miracle girl." Her mother grabs Lyla's hand. "Follow me," she says, and leads Lyla to the living room. She sits Lyla down on the couch and pulls her into her lap. Her mother rakes her fingernails through Lyla's long black hair. Goose bumps wash over Lyla like when her father used to push her on the swing. Lying in her mother's lap, Lyla can still feel the thrill of her body lifting off the tire, weightless, even if just for a second in time. Maybe her father felt the same sense of weightlessness when he kicked himself from the downed tire and into the darkness.

Lyla suddenly wants to throw up.

"It's best just to think of the good times," her mother says, combing the knots out of Lyla's hair, one by one. "God, you look so much like him." Her mother rubs her thumb along Lyla's cheek, but Lyla has begun to wonder if that's a good thing or bad. Maybe if she didn't look so much like him, her mother wouldn't look like she's seen a ghost every time Lyla walks through the front door.

Suddenly, the two of them snap to attention. All this time they've been staring at one another—straddling good times and bad—the projector has been trying to grab hold of the filmstrip. The loose end whacks against itself, over and over.

Louise lifts Lyla's head off her lap and crawls over to the projector. She flicks the machine off. The slap of the film comes to a stop, then raw silence.

There will be the same absence of sound after Louise slaps Lyla's face a couple of months from now, a night when Lyla will come home drunk and accuse Louise of being the one who drove her father away. Lyla will have no evidence for it, of course, but she will be tired of shouldering the blame for her father's great disappearing act. She will run away that night, far away from her mother, but not far enough to go missing. She will head right to her grandmother's.

But that will be many months from now.

For now, they are knee-deep in muck.

"Are you sure you want to do this?" Louise asks, and crawls back to Lyla. "Maybe we should call it a night."

But Lyla shakes her head. She needs to watch his movies. She'd watch them all in one night if she could. She needs to witness everything again, back-to-back.

"I never want to forget him." Lyla sighs. She shrugs the blanket off her legs and gets up to restart the film from the beginning. It is the summer of 1953, the day Lyla climbed the oak tree and hung the rope for the swing. She needs to see this particular movie again; she needs to search for clues hidden in her father's eyes that she may have missed in all these years.

When the camera shows seven-year-old Lyla in the tree, Louise is the one to bolt. She gets up and runs straight to the hall bathroom and dry heaves over and over again.

Through the crack left open in the door, Lyla sees her mother attempt to pull herself together. She hunches over the tiny sink in the corner of the hall bath, the sink that is big enough for her mother's hands, but nothing more. There is something ludicrous in the way her mother stands over the itty-bitty porcelain bowl, seemingly made for dolls.

Lyla's mother looks enormous over that sink.

But she also looks like something else.

She looks old.

Louise braces her hands against the mirror, like a boxer about to climb into the ring. She looks ready to pick a fight. Lyla doesn't know with whom she wants to fight exactly. She should run over and drag her mother out of the bathroom before she does something terrible. But Lyla can't move; she's too afraid to interfere.

But that's not all—there is something else.

Lyla wants her mother to see what Lyla has been witnessing for some time now. She wants her mother to stop pretending that all is hunky-dory now that she is remarried.

Her mother slaps the mirror with the flat of her hand. Over and over, she whacks the glass, and Lyla starts to worry that the mirror might break.

But then, in a seesaw of fury, something changes again.

Her mother begins to feverishly pluck out a few white hairs that have started to sprout in her part. She yanks and flicks each white hair into the sink. She pulls out a few more and washes them down the drain.

Lyla can then see it coming. Her mother is about to cry. She balls her fists against the mirror. Her jaw tightens. Somewhere along the line, her mother had stopped crying in front of Lyla, believing it to be a sign of weakness.

And over the years, her mother has taught Lyla to feel that way too—to feel bad about herself when tears begin to roll, like crying is a fatal flaw.

"Mom?" Lyla calls to the bathroom.

But Louise kicks the door shut.

When her mother doesn't come out for a long time, Lyla eventually switches off the projector and turns out the lights. She goes to her room to read.

Later that night, Louise waltzes into Lyla's bedroom with a bowl of popcorn. She pretends nothing has happened, oddly cheerful even as she throws Lyla's dirty laundry off the bed.

"Well, at least I didn't burn it this time," she says, grabbing a handful of popcorn.

Lyla takes the bowl and cradles it in her lap, shoving handfuls into her mouth as though she hasn't eaten in days.

"It's perfect," Lyla says, taking a sip of water. Her mother has remembered to shake the garlic salt and red pepper flakes on top, just the way Lyla's father liked it—with a touch of heat.

At one point, they reach their hands into the bowl at the exact same time. Their fingers touch.

"Sorry," they say in unison.

"No, I'm sorry." Louise chuckles.

"No, no, I'm sorry." Lyla giggles.

Sorry, laugh. *Sorry*, snort. *Sorry, sorry, sorry*; they keep reaching in the bowl, touching hands, yanking them out, apologizing, and laughing until Lyla wants to pee her pants.

Finally, Louise grabs hold of Lyla's hand and they measure their hands to each other. They begin their goofy little game of *Who is the mother? Who is the daughter?* They hold their hands out, admiring the beauty of their skin, and ask these silly questions as though it isn't completely obvious. They learn to laugh at this joke for decades, before Lyla's hands start to age faster than her mother's from too many summers spent working as a lifeguard in the hot California sun.

At one point, it will be almost impossible to tell the difference.

What they don't see in these movies are all the weddings they attend over the years—Cousins Robert's and Margaret's. Even Louise's marriage to Al goes undocumented. Lyla once never thought it possible, a second marriage, not with the weight of her father's love still pressing down upon her mother. When Louise finally summons the courage to ask for Lyla's permission, she tells Lyla, "He's a good guy. I promise. He will take care of us."

Seeing the hope in her mother's eyes, Lyla vows to see him that way too, as a good guy who will take care of her mother when Lyla moves out.

When Lyla asks if Cousin Steven should record the ceremony, Louise instantly refuses.

"God, no," her mother says like a reflex hammer to the knee. She insists nobody even takes so much as a photograph.

When her mother introduced The Ape to the family, only Uncle David gave Al his full blessing. He clapped Al on the back like an old war buddy and took him out front for a smoke.

At the wedding, Uncle David ends up drinking too much and gives a hearty, teary-eyed toast to his *new brother*. He then orders too many rounds of drinks, which nobody but he ends up drinking. He slaps glass after glass on the bar and calls people all sorts of sour names for refusing to drink with him. Uncle David winds up passing out in the hotel lobby bathroom. It is The Ape who takes care of David; he drags him out of the bathroom, puts him in a cab, and sends him home while everybody else sticks around, dancing awkwardly under the too-bright lights before they clean up and go home.

Thankfully, Grandmother Caroline is saved from all the fuss. She had declined the wedding invitation and is spared the pain of bearing witness to her remaining son's disgrace.

Unlike Lyla's father, The Ape is small and thick, built like a tank. He is not much taller than Lyla's mother, but he is sturdy enough to endure her brief episodes of depression and anxiety, and Lyla and her mother's growing feuds in the last years of high school.

The Ape has a tattoo on his right bicep—an anchor with a number below it. The number is not Al's naval identifier but the total number of American men killed in the Pacific during his tour. It's a reminder of what was at stake.

"You have no idea what it was like over there, ladies," he lectures one night at the dinner table, clearly unaware that Lyla's father had gone AWOL.

Lyla's mother doesn't correct him; she tries never to speak about Charles when Al is around. In fact, Louise begins to avoid the subject of Charles altogether. Then one night, Lyla catches her mother rubbing her finger along the blue tattoo ink bleeding along Al's bicep. The Ape doesn't seem to notice when Louise does this, but Lyla wonders if her mother is thinking of Charles.

In Lyla's worst moments, she accuses her mother of being a traitor; she accuses her of trying to steal glimpses of her father on The Ape's arm.

"Why did you even marry Al in the first place, if you keep thinking about Dad?"

"Because I hated being so alone," Louise says one night, despite the fact that Lyla still lives under the same roof.

"Thanks a lot." Lyla grabs the car keys. She doesn't agree to come home at midnight like her mother asks.

Instead, Lyla tells her she might not even come home at all.

One Sunday night, The Ape returns home earlier than expected. He smells of cigarettes and beer. Lyla and her mother are not sitting on the floor, as normal, but they are on the couch, Lyla at one end, Louise at the other. The blanket is nowhere to be found.

Lyla suspects her mother has thrown it away.

Lyla is reading while her mother watches the movie about the summer they spent nearly every weekend out on Pops's boat when Lyla was a little girl. In the movie, the wind catches hold of her mother's bright red hair as they take a late-season sail to the Farallon Islands.

The Ape leans over the back of the couch and lets out a guttural catcall.

"Hubba, hubba," he says.

Lyla is surprised her mother doesn't jump up and turn the movie off. She just sits there watching the living room wall while Al gives her a sloppy, drunken kiss.

"Get a room," Lyla says, not even looking up from her book.

"Oh, come on. Look at her—your mother looks like a movie star," The Ape says, seemingly unfazed that Louise is watching herself with Charles.

How Al did that, Lyla never knew. At first, she believed he was just plain stupid, well . . . an ape. But then, somewhere along the line, the notion that he is *a good guy* began to seep in.

Sitting at the far end of the couch, Lyla watches her mother gather the neck of her sweater, as if the wind is blowing over the rails and straight into their living room.

Present-day Louise looks down at her hands.

"God, they look just awful," Louise says, seemingly alarmed at how the onset of rheumatoid arthritis has started to wreak havoc on her grip. Clenching and unclenching her fingers, she concedes her hands are working against her. Lyla first noticed the problem two years ago when Louise began having trouble threading the film on the reels.

Now, Lyla is the one who must thread the projector, even though she's over it.

And at some point, Louise becomes over it too. She leaves the films tucked away in the attic where they dwell next to the rest of Charles's belongings, all the stuff that she could never throw away: his old clothing, his enormous shoes, his first baseball mitt, the letters he wrote home from the war.

One Friday afternoon, Lyla comes home early from tennis practice.

"Mom?" Lyla yells, setting her racquet down on the kitchen counter. "You here?" Lyla opens the refrigerator, looking for something to eat. She grabs an apple, pours a glass of milk, and wanders through the house, calling for her mother.

"Hello?" Lyla pokes her head into one room and then the next, eventually climbing the attic stairs after hearing a creak above the living room.

Halfway up, she sees her mother sitting on the suitcase of the films. She is holding one of Charles's old sweaters out in front of her, talking to it as though he is standing right there, listening intently to what she has to say.

Lyla sits on the stairs, and through the spindles of the railing, she spies on her mother. Lyla sips her milk but doesn't dare bite the apple.

Louise wraps the sleeves of Charles's sweater around her shoulders, arranging the arms so they hug her. She begins to sway in the dusty afternoon attic light, dancing with the empty sweater, and humming her favorite Irish lullaby.

Lyla is about to laugh out loud and poke fun at her mother, but then she watches her do something unspeakable. Her mother lies down on the attic floor with Charles's old sweater on top of her. She begins to writhe around, moaning, crying out, kicking her legs as though she is making love to him like in that movie Lyla watched with her mother all those years ago, when Louise hid Lyla's eyes with the blanket, telling her she was too young to see such a thing.

Lyla is frozen, sickened by what is happening. She doesn't want to watch this anymore. But she doesn't want to get up and have her mother catch her either. She knows better than to call out her name, to scream at her, or ask her what in the hell she is doing. Because Lyla doesn't want to see her mother shoot up from the floor, hiding Daddy's sweater behind her as she fumbles around for an excuse.

No daughter needs to see that.

No daughter needs to catch her mother in the act of doing something so bizarre.

Lyla finally gets up and quietly tiptoes back down the stairs with her uneaten apple and the glass of milk, leaving her mother alone, wrapped in the arms of her father's empty sweater.

CHAPTER TEN

GREAT EXPECTATIONS—

OCTOBER 1963

For as long as Louise could remember, Lyla had always brought a book to dinner. When she was small and still wore footed pajamas, her daughter would plunk an armful of picture books onto the table, then line her stuffed animals around her place mat as though she planned to read her entire library collection to them over dinner.

My little bookworm, Louise would apologize to whomever they'd be dining with. But Louise wasn't really sorry. Her daughter was adorable—with that fierce concentration on Lyla's face as if she were working out the loss function of a complex statistical problem, not poking her way through *Goodnight Moon*.

But now that she was seventeen, Louise no longer found her daughter's habit of reading at the dinner table all that endearing. In fact, she found it rude and wished she'd never encouraged such a custom in the first place. But that horse had left the barn years ago; there was no calling it back now.

"How was your day, sweetheart?" Louise placed a platter of roasted pork loin in the center of the table. "Any news on your essay?"

Lyla didn't respond. She didn't even look up. Her nose was buried deep into Charles Dickens's *Great Expectations*, which Louise could swear Lyla had read like *a million* times by now. Louise herself was not one to spend time with a book cover to cover, let alone inhabit the same damn story multiple times.

"Gosh, I'm dying to hear how you did after all the work you put in. That was a real grade-A effort, if you ask me." Louise peeled off her apron, grabbed her half-drained wine glass along with the bottle, and sat down. She picked up the serving fork and plopped a slice of pork onto Al's plate, then scooped up roasted root vegetables. But Al waved her off; he was not a vegetable kind of guy, root or otherwise. Instead, he eyed the bowlful of her mashed potatoes, so Louise dumped the parsnips, turnips, and shallots onto her plate and slapped a pile of potatoes onto his.

"Oh, I forgot to tell you," Louise blurted out. "I ran into Judy Morrison yesterday. She said Ruth will be going to the University of Washington next year and was given a full ride! Isn't that exciting?"

Lyla turned the page in her book.

"Whatever happened with the two of you, anyhow?" Louise took a quick sip of wine. "You were such good friends. But now I don't hear a word."

Still, Lyla didn't look up.

Louise sat back and took another sip. She kicked Al under the table, giving him the *See what I have to put up with?* look. But she knew Al was well aware. Louise had been hammering on about Lyla's teenage apathy just about every night as they brushed their teeth before bed.

But this?

This was different.

This was Lyla making a point.

Earlier that afternoon, Lyla had started out the door to wish her boyfriend good luck before the big homecoming game. But Louise had said no. On Monday, she had insisted they all have dinner together at least one night this week. It was now Friday, and she was putting her foot down. "You promised," Louise reminded Lyla, who threw the keys on the table and stormed into her bedroom, telling Louise for the umpteenth time she was *the worst mother on the planet*. To which Louise responded as she opened a bottle of wine, "Well, it takes two to tango."

Now Louise picked up her knife and tapped her wine glass as if she were about to give a wedding toast. *Tink, tink, tink*, she tapped and—in her best Etta James impersonation—began to sing, "At last, my love, dinner has come along. My lonely days of eating without you are gone!"

Louise snorted. So did Al, who tried not to spit out the mouthful of mashed potatoes he'd squirreled away in his cheeks.

But across the table, nothing. Not so much as a razzing about Louise's inability to carry a tune.

Louise clanked her knife a touch harder this time. "Lyla, honey, it's time to put the book down." Her voice was a mix of sing-songy drunk and rising irritation.

Lyla licked her finger and turned another page.

"Earth to Lyla. Come in, Lyla. Can you hear me?" Louise barked. Sometimes it took a sharp rise in her voice, a shout even, to get Lyla's attention.

But when Lyla refused again to acknowledge her, Louise slapped her knife on the table, making the bowl of Jell-O salad jiggle. "Lyla May Hawkins! Sit up and eat!"

Lyla's head popped over the top of her book. She glanced at Louise and then to Al, who sat back, eyeing the two of them like he was watching the US Open.

"What do you want?" Lyla snipped.

"What does she want?" Al's eyes grew dark. "You darn well know what your mother wants, Lyla. You don't have to be such a brat."

Normally in situations such as this, Al's opinions were as welcome as burnt toast. But tonight, Louise appreciated Al's involvement. Tonight, she needed backup. Tonight, she felt like throttling Lyla.

Al wiped his mouth with his napkin. "You heard your mother. Put the book down and eat." He reached over and grabbed a handful of iceberg lettuce with his bare hand and plopped the pile onto Lyla's plate. "Pick up your fork."

Louise sat back with a slight smile. *Well okay, then*, she thought, admiring how easily Al took the bull by the horns. She could feel the muscles in her throat loosen, her chest expand. Her jaw relax.

"Your mother made a real nice meal here," Al continued. He smacked the side of the salad dressing bottle, drowning his lettuce in Thousand Island. He slid the bottle across the table to Lyla. "The least you could do is show a little gratitude."

Lyla marked the page in her book with her thumb. She sat up in her chair. With a feigned look of innocence, she smiled and said, "Well, gee whiz, Dad. No need to get your boxers in a wad. I already told her, I'm not hungry." Lyla opened her book back up and began reading again.

Al drew in a deep breath and mouthed something across the table, something Louise couldn't quite make out. It looked like he'd said *that little shit* as he stabbed a hunk of lettuce and stuffed it into his mouth. But Louise must have been mistaken. Al was not one to swear. Cursing was her territory.

"Honest to Pete, Lyla." Louise took over. "You've made your point. Just have a little something before you go. That's all I ask." She got up and carried an ear of corn in the tongs to Lyla's place setting, but Lyla threw an elbow in the way.

"Oh, come off it, Lyla." Louise grabbed Lyla's arm and dropped the ear of corn onto the empty white plate. "The corn is from Acevedo's." Louise returned to her seat. She could feel the familiar hot buzz rising up her chest, the fuzz in her head as she drained her glass of wine. She grabbed the bottle and poured the remainder into her glass. "Remember how we used to walk over to Tony's stand when you were little? We'd buy a whole big bagful, shucking so many ears the two of us couldn't possibly eat in one sitting. Remember that?"

That little bit of nostalgia seemed to be just the thing to spark Lyla. Her daughter placed her book face down and looked over at Louise with what Louise thought was a return of her daughter's long-ago good nature, her go-alongness. The heat in Louise's chest dissipated.

But Lyla began miming in made-up sign language and shouting, "ARE YOU DEAF? I ALREADY TOLD YOU, I AM NOT HUNGRY!"

And that was it. Blood rushed to Louise's head. She snatched the book from Lyla and tossed it onto the kitchen counter, where it happened to land on the rim of the roasting pan, sending both the book and the pan crashing to the floor.

Fillmore jumped out from under the table and yelped as though his tail had just been stepped on; he sidled up to Louise for comfort.

"Mom!" Lyla yelled. "What the hell is wrong with you?"

But this time it was Louise who refused to respond. She grabbed Fillmore by his collar and brought his face close to hers. "Shh, it's okay, buddy." She heard her shushing slur out of her mouth a little wibbly-wobbly in her drunkenness and hoped nobody noticed. She leaned over and stroked Fillmore's graying muzzle. "It's just a stupid book. That's all."

"Stupid book?" The ropey veins tightened in Lyla's neck. Her face turned red. "That was Dad's book. He gave it to me. And now look at what you've done."

The book lay on the tile floor in a pile of grease and pork chunks.

"Oh well. Easy come, easy go." Louise cut off a row of corn and let Fillmore eat out of her hands, even though corn made the dog a little gassy. She'd have hell to pay later, but she couldn't help herself; she was warmed by how Fillmore smiled up at her, how he did everything Louise asked. How reliably he stayed by her side no matter what. "At least you'll eat when it's dinnertime, won't you, buddy? Unlike some people around here." When Fillmore finished the first handful, she shaved off another row and fed him.

"Mom, stop it! You know that corn isn't good for him. He's going to need to go out all night."

"Oh, you'll be fine, won't you, buddy?" Louise bent over and kissed Fillmore's cold black nose. "Yes, you're such a good, good boy. Just us two Musketeers, right, buddy?"

Fillmore wagged his tail and hopped from foot to foot, begging for more with those sweet black eyes.

"Oh, what the hell. Have a field day." Louise handed Fillmore her half-eaten corn cob, which he took underneath the table and started gnawing like it was a bone.

"Mom, seriously. Have you lost your mind? You can't give Fillmore the whole ear. He could get really sick."

"Oh, says who?" Louise reached over and grabbed another ear for herself. She dug in, working her way meticulously left to right. When she finished each row, she'd inspect the cob before rolling it over, and dug in again. Louise was not one of those who chewed at her corn haphazardly. Charles used to say she excavated each kernel like a tooth extraction. Louise glanced over at Al, who looked like he was about to interject, and gave him another look. This one said, *Back off.*

"Says the vet," Lyla said. "Remember?"

Louise didn't remember. She found all that veterinary gobbledy-gook talk a bit suffering.

"Dr. Koch said it's the leading cause of death in dogs; you could kill him." Lyla grabbed a slice of pork from the platter and got down on her hands and knees. Under the table, she traded the hunk of meat for the half-eaten corn cob.

"Oh, he'll be fine." Louise took another sip from her glass, now avoiding Al's eyes. "I swear that vet is such a worrywart. God, I might just need to go up to Santa Rosa and find another one," Louise went on as Lyla crawled out from underneath the table. She watched her daughter put the slobbered-up cob on her plate.

"What is wrong with you tonight?" Lyla asked. "Why are you acting so weird?"

"What's wrong with me? Tonight?" Louise took a sip. Wine dribbled down her chin. She wiped it with the back of her hand. "Oh, I don't know. Gee whiz, Lyla. I just thought we'd have a nice family dinner, here; some light conversation, you know, like, 'Hey, Mom, how was your day?' Not all this"—Louise whirled her cob around the table and nearly knocked her wine glass over—"all this crap."

"Crap?"

"Oh, stop it, young lady—you know what I'm talking about. You ignoring me, then suddenly pretending to give two licks about Fillmore. He's *my* dog. Not yours. You gave up on him long ago."

And sometimes I wish I could do the same with you, Louise almost blurted out but then looked over at Al, who shook his head and gave her the *Don't go there* look.

Sometimes Louise couldn't help herself.

Sometimes she pressed her foot on the gas pedal, steering what was supposed to be a good time to bad. Both her husbands had told her in different ways that she needed to know when to let go of the wheel and ease off the gas. Just throw up her hands and let things coast.

"And sometimes I wish I could give up on you too," she muttered just under her breath. It felt good to be a bit honest with how she felt.

"What did you say?" Lyla pressed.

"Okay, that's enough." Al folded his napkin and put it on the table. "Now, both of you are being pigheaded. Just cut it out. Okay?"

"No, Al," Lyla said. "I want to hear what Mom said. Go on, Mother dear. What did you want to tell me exactly?"

"Nothing." Louise picked a husk of corn out of her teeth and put it on her plate. "I just wanted to talk, that's all."

"Oh, that's what you want!" Lyla let out a fake laugh. "Why didn't you just say so?

Hmmm . . . okay, let me think here." Lyla rubbed at her chin. "Let's see. What shall we talk about? Oh, wait. I've got it." Lyla smiled. Her eyes sparkled in the way they did when she used to be able to name all the United States presidents in under a minute.

"So, Mom? What did you do today? Lie on the couch all afternoon with another one of your famous headaches and have a bottle of wine? Or did you have two bottles already?"

And that was it.

Louise chucked her half-eaten ear of corn cob across the table where it flew like a football and smacked Lyla on the cheekbone.

Butter sprayed everywhere and Fillmore again leaped out from underneath the table, yelping. He retrieved the thrown cob and began gnawing it beside Louise's feet.

"What the hell is wrong with you?" Lyla held her cheek. She reached for her glass, dipped her napkin in the water, and dabbed the butter out of her eye. "You are such a freak!"

"Oh my God, Lyla—" The hot buzz vanished, and instantly a moment of clarity took its place. She stared at the red welt growing on her daughter's cheek. She raced over to the freezer. She cracked the ice tray and started wrapping a couple of cubes in the dish towel. "I didn't mean to, honey. I don't know what came over me."

Al scooted his chair back and got up to leave.

"Al, wait?" Louise begged.

But Al told her he had had enough. He got up and walked out of the kitchen, leaving his dirty dishes for Louise to clean up.

Lyla got up from the table too.

"Wait. Lyla, honey." Louise tried holding the ice to Lyla's cheek, but Lyla pushed her back.

"Get away from me."

"Lyla, please. Stop. I didn't mean to. It just—" Louise paused as she held the ice-filled dish towel. Her chest tightened, and the small black pepper flakes she had told the optometrist about began swirling around in her eyes. She was finding it hard to breathe, so she put the dish towel on the table and sat down.

"It what?" Lyla cried. "Slipped?"

"No. No. It—" Louise could only manage small sips of air. Everything suddenly felt so heavy and disorienting. The pepper flakes eddied around, making her blink repeatedly. She held out her arms and tried envisioning herself lying on her back in the desert, feeling each ray of sunshine warm through the center of her, like she had been taught to do years ago during her month at the Dhamma Mahavana Meditation Center in the Sierra foothills after Charles had died.

"What are you doing?" Lyla asked.

"Hold on a minute." Louise counted to twenty-five, feeling each inhale fill her stomach, then disappear. The tension relaxed. Steady breaths expanded her chest. And when Louise finally opened her eyes, the pepper flakes were gone.

"Oh, Lyla. It wasn't supposed to be this way," Louise finally said, grabbing a napkin and folding it. "It was supposed to be different. It was supposed to be—" She paused, uncertain of what it was supposed to be. "Oh, I don't know." Louise looked around the kitchen, staring at the mess: the half-eaten plates, the piles of potatoes and vegetables left untouched, the roasting pan that had fallen on the floor. Lyla's book that now sat in congealed grease.

The butter that clung to her daughter's eyelash like a dewdrop. The welt on Lyla's cheekbone.

"Not this," Louise said.

"No, you got that right." Lyla shook her head. Something shifted in her daughter's voice and in her eyes, like she was looking at her reflection down a well. She touched her cheek. "No. I suppose it wasn't, but here we are, funny enough."

Lyla walked over to where Louise sat hunched over at the table. She put both hands on Louise's shoulders and gave her a quick squeeze. Louise looked up into her daughter's eyes and smiled slightly, half expecting Lyla to give her a kiss on the cheek.

"Well, don't worry," Lyla whispered into Louise's ear. "I won't tell anybody. Not even Dr. Schmidt. He wouldn't believe me anyhow."

Lyla grabbed a dinner roll, took a bite, and walked out of the kitchen. "I mean, really, who does something like that?" she asked, the edge now back in her voice. "Who throws a corn cob at their daughter?"

"Lyla, please," Louise begged. "Wait."

But Lyla waved her off. "Lyla's going down to the game," she said, using third person in that way that drove Louise nuts. When Lyla reached her room, she shut the door quietly.

Louise sat at the table as though the wind had been knocked out of her. From the living room, she could hear David Attenborough's voice on the television as he narrated another one of those nature shows that Al was hooked on.

Just outside, the rain began to spit against the window.

And under the table, Fillmore chewed away at the corn cob.

Louise finally pushed her chair back and got down on all fours. She stroked Fillmore's coat. "Come on, buddy, give it here," she whispered, and slid the cob out of his teeth.

Fillmore didn't fight her. He simply let go.

"That's a good boy," she said, and crawled back out from under the table. Louise walked over to the sink and threw the cob in the trash. She slid on her yellow rubber gloves and turned the faucet on.

As the water filled the basin, Louise bent over and picked up the hard-backed book; a layer of gelatinous fat now covered the cloth cover and gold foil–stamped inlay. She tossed the book into the rubbish bin and was about to scrape her half-eaten dinner on top of it but quickly decided against it.

There was something about the book that tugged at Louise. A souvenir of her late husband given to her little girl years ago.

She pulled the book out of the trash and held it in front of her, wondering why he'd given it to Lyla or what the fuss was all about. How could Lyla bear to read this book so many times? What new things could she possibly discover after pouring over the pages time and time again? Louise had never read this—or any of Dickens's work for that matter—not even in high school.

"*Great Expectations*, huh," she said, placing the book on the countertop. She wetted the edge of her sponge under the faucet. Standing there with Fillmore at her feet and the rain pelting the window, Louise began to clean the congealed grease out of the gold foil inlay like she was an archaeologist, vowing that cover to cover, she'd clean the book so it shone again like new. She'd stay up all night if she had to, surprising Lyla with her efforts.

Her olive branch.

And then.

Maybe then, she'd give it a read.

Maybe then, it could be a story she and Lyla could share.

CHAPTER ELEVEN

HOMECOMING—OCTOBER 1963

Louise peeled off her yellow rubber gloves and hung them over the faucet to dry. Out the window, a dark mass of clouds billowed and rain drummed against the glass. The wind grew and swirled, rinsing the sycamore trees nearly clean of all their leaves. Though they were still a week away from turning back the clocks, Louise could feel the time change, the steady slide toward winter.

She looked down at Lyla's book that lay on the countertop—its covers spread like angel wings. Louise picked up her old toothbrush and dental pick and continued mining the congealed fat out of the gold foil title, *Great Expectations*. Next, she'd use Al's shoe-shining brush to buff the leather cover. She'd make the old book come back to life if it was the last thing on earth she'd do.

The rain pelted harder and Louise perked up a bit. Maybe it'd begin to pour so hard, they'd cancel the game and Lyla would stay home.

Maybe then, Louise could show Lyla all the work she'd put into cleaning the book, her efforts to make amends.

Maybe then, they could laugh at the ridiculousness of it all:

The silent treatments.

The stupid, made-up sign language.

The slamming of doors.

The throwing of corn.

Maybe then, they could sit on the couch and tease out how things steered so far off course between the two of them. And how they might veer back to some sort of normalcy.

Maybe it was time to call a *do-over.*

Yes, that was it! Louise wiped the fat off the dental pick with the dish towel. When Lyla came out of her room, Louise would call her into the kitchen, singing, *"Do-over!"*

It was a game they'd played when Lyla was younger, when they both needed to hit the reset button after some stupid spat. They used to run to their rooms, count to thirty, and walk out with pillowcases over their heads, arms stretched wide, searching, until they finally bumped into one another.

Do-overs had always resulted in a fit of giggles.

And hugs.

And a flood of apologies.

Do-overs made things right again!

Louise was just about to clear her throat and sing, *"Do-over,"* when she heard Lyla emerge from her bedroom. She came into the kitchen, wearing another one of Kyle's huge red football sweatshirts. Louise stifled a groan. Lyla looked ridiculous wearing her boyfriend's oversized clothes: his varsity jackets, his plaid pajamas, his huge T-shirts. She practically swam in Kyle's clothes, and Lyla was no small gal herself.

"Oh, hi, honey. I was thinking—" Louise turned and flung the dish towel over the book, to conceal her surprise. Her gift.

But Lyla wasn't paying attention; she had grabbed Louise's purse off the counter and was rifling through its contents.

"Can I help you with something?" Louise took off her apron and folded it.

"The keys?"

"Keys?" Louise asked.

"The little metal things you need to start cars?" Lyla mimicked turning a pretend car key. "You know. Vroom, vroom."

"You're still going?"

"Of course. Did you think I would stay home after that?" Lyla pulled out a bunch of crinkled receipts, a pack of Certs, Louise's wallet.

"Won't the game be canceled?" The clouds were so dark it was beginning to look like nightfall. "It's going to really start pouring. The forecast is even calling for some flooding and potential mudslides."

"Are you kidding?" Lyla looked up from Louise's purse. "It's the homecoming game."

"Oh, right." Louise twirled her finger into the air. "Homecoming. Whoop-de-do." Louise loathed how the whole town celebrated the homecoming game like it was the most important day of the year. Red-and-white banners had been hanging for weeks from every store window, every conceivable lamppost. Grown men and women, even those without children enrolled in the school district, paraded around town, wearing cherry-red sweatshirts with the letter "F" painted on their cheeks like it was V-Day or something.

"You know—" Louise tried to sound more upbeat than she felt. A headache had already started to stretch between her temples. "What if you and I stayed home? We could watch our old movies together. I could paint your toenails, do your hair. I could even make our special popcorn! Like old times!" She could feel the fake smile cementing across her face, the tug-of-war between the left side of her head and the right.

"Stay home?" Lyla looked at Louise like she was speaking Tagalog. Lyla snapped her gum and unzipped a pouch inside Louise's purse. "I think we've had enough corn for the night, don't you think?" She popped another bubble.

"Oh, Lyla." The smile on Louise's face dissipated. "I'm sorry. I really am."

Lyla grabbed a twenty-dollar bill out of Louise's purse and stuck it into her back pocket. She hadn't even bothered to ask.

Louise was about to press her when Lyla asked again, "So, where are the keys?"

"Can't you walk?"

"Hello, it's raining. Remember?"

The look on Lyla's face matched how Louise felt. Exasperated.

"Over there." Louise sighed and pointed to the far side of the counter where her key ring sat on top of a bunch of magazines, junk mail, and to-do lists. "But you'll need to be careful. The brakes sound worse than ever. I have an appointment with the garage next Thursday." She tried to sound casual and indifferent. "Promise you will be gentle. Okay?"

"Roger." Lyla turned to leave.

"And be careful driving, the roads will be slick with the rain. Okay?" Lyla didn't answer. "Okay?"

"Okay." Lyla twirled the car keys around her index finger and walked down the hall.

"And Lyla?" Louise paused, though she had no idea what else she could say. She suddenly just wanted to give her daughter a big fat hug. "Wait, come here for a second." Lyla turned and Louise held out her arms and walked toward Lyla with a wide smile, accidentally kicking Fillmore's water bowl. The water sloshed onto the kitchen floor. But she still kept her arms open and plowed toward Lyla.

But Lyla did not open her arms and walk toward her mother. She just stood there and looked at Louise as though Louise had just walked out of the house naked. "What are you doing?"

Louise dropped her hands and jammed them in her pockets. "Sorry. Nothing." She looked up at the clock above Lyla's head. "Well, I guess go have fun. And wish Kyle good luck." She hated how her voice had a pleading tone to it.

"Later." Lyla turned and jingled the keys over her shoulder as she walked out the door. From the back, her daughter looked so much like Charles.

Tall, broad-shouldered. Confident.

"Later, alligator," Louise replied, again with that stupid, insufferable rising, begging sound in her voice. "And be home by midnight, okay?"

But Lyla had already thrown the front door shut.

"Lyla, sweetheart? Wait." Louise rushed toward the front door, her clogs clip-clopping along the hardwood floors like a draft horse. She grabbed her coat off the rack and flung the door open, but Lyla had already revved the engine and peeled out of the driveway.

"I love you!" Louise said, watching the dry patch of the pavement where the car had been parked now fill with raindrops. A gust of wind blew over the mountaintop and flushed her sycamore tree of its final few leaves. "I really, really do. I love you, Lyla." Her voice returned to a more comfortable steady and solid tone.

Louise stood on the front porch, wondering why it was so hard for the two of them to just admit it—they loved each other, despite all that they had been through. Why couldn't they just say it out loud to each other's face—*I love you! I love you! I love you!* They were mother and daughter, not presidential opponents, for Christ's sake. Yet somehow, words of love, of admiration, of respect seemed to get stuck inside them like tar.

"I'll be right back," Louise called to Al, who was sitting on the couch, drinking a beer, enjoying his show.

She put on her coat and ran to the mailbox in the light rain. From the driveway, Louise could hear songs of celebration from the high school football field a few blocks down. Cheers swirled above the redwood tops like red-tailed hawks caught in a thermal. Up and up and up the referees' whistles and the cheerleaders' cheers took flight. *Gooooooo Falcons!*

Even as Louise opened the mailbox, the cries of *Push 'em back, way back* grew louder, as though the goading cheers and responsive roars of the crowd were emanating from inside the box itself.

God, it was going to be a long night. She threw the lid closed. Homecoming never ended with the final score. The parties went on all night, sometimes to dawn. As a teenager, she'd never been one who took part in those booster club activities and dances: the decorating of floats, the parades, the nominating of kings and queens. She had been a loner in high school, an outsider, even though she had been born and raised in her hometown, a small island community tucked up in the far northwest corner of the country.

In the drizzling rain, Louise covered her head with the mail and ran back to the house. Fillmore greeted her at the front door with his leash dangling in his mouth. "Not now, buddy." Louise shook the wetness out of her hair and hung her coat on the rack. She bent over to brush Fillmore's graying coat. "Maybe later, huh?"

Fillmore dropped the leash at her feet and followed Louise to the living room. Even Fillmore knew *later* meant tomorrow.

Louise threw the mail on the coffee table and flopped down next to Al, resting her legs across his lap. She wiggled her toes, and good ol' Al, dutiful Al, grabbed her feet and began massaging. His eyes remained glued to the television.

God, how she loved the way Al could work the kinks out of her feet with those hands of his. Why, he could squeeze the air out of a tennis ball if he wanted.

"Jesus," Louise moaned, and picked up the old copy of *Life* magazine that she'd accidentally taken home from her doctor's office the week before. "I swear to God, Al. You're a magician."

Al slid her socks off and kissed her toes one at a time. "If you like this, I could show you so much more." He smiled. "Follow me to the bedroom, young lady, and I could turn you into a mother for a second time."

"Oh, right," she said. As if that was what she needed! A second kid to make her go prematurely gray. "No, thanks." Louise snorted. "I'm barely keeping up as is."

As she flipped the pages, she noticed that the magazine seemed terribly out of date. Louise turned to the front cover and read aloud, "October 21, 1957? Well, no wonder."

"Huh?" Al stopped massaging. "What's that?"

"This magazine! It's from '57! I thought something seemed awfully peculiar about it. Look at the length of this woman's skirt." She held out the magazine to Al, but he had his eyes back on the television set.

"Oh, whatever," she said, flipping through the thin, well-worn pages until she settled on an old feature piece about Sputnik that warned Americans how the Soviets were spying on them. How they were reporting their every move.

"Well, have at it." Louise snickered at the idea of being under constant surveillance, that she had something worth spying on.

She continued reading, merrily tapping her toes against Al's thigh in time with the ceremonial beat of the high school marching band down at the game, the whumping bass drums in concert with the fluttering trumpets and the deep reverberations of the big brass sousaphones. The sound was triumphant. A great gust of wind shook their windows, making Louise throw the magazine up in the air as if a car had just barreled into the side of the house. A giant torrent of rain fell from the sky.

Fillmore ran to the windowsill and barked.

"Geez, woman. It's just the wind." Al lifted her feet off his lap and got up to turn off the television. "Anyhow, I'm going to bed. Join me?"

"So soon?" Louise looked at her watch. It wasn't even eight o'clock.

"I have to get up early, hon. Meeting the guys at four thirty a.m. sharp. Remember?"

"Oh, right." Louise rolled her eyes. Louise wasn't a fan of when Al went duck hunting with his buddies, how he waltzed back through the front door with that tired but satisfied look on his face as he held a couple of dead ones on a string, as though Louise should be proud of him like he was the great provider.

"You go ahead. I'm not at all tired. I think I'll stay up and read for a while."

"Okay, hon, but don't stay up too late. Lyla will come home when she's good and ready. Sitting on the couch won't make that happen any quicker." Al patted his leg. "Come on, Fill. Let's go take a leak."

Hours later, Louise woke on the couch with the magazine spread across her chest and her head splitting apart. A new bolt of pain zinged behind her right eye. She blew her hair out of her face and brought her watch close. It was eleven thirty and dead quiet, except for the water dripping from the gutter and the rhythmic *tap, tap, tap* of Fillmore's tail against the couch next to her as he farted his dog farts—the ones that could make Louise's eyes water.

"Holy smokes, Fill." She sat up. "Come on, buddy. Let's go outside."

Louise slipped on her shoes and walked Fillmore through the kitchen to the back porch, stopping briefly to uncap the prescription bottle she had tucked in the pocket of her sweater. She tapped a little white pill into her palm and put it on her tongue, anticipating that silky feeling of her headache drifting away and her muscles releasing all their tension.

She thought about what happened earlier—how stupid she'd acted and how the pain in her temples had grown in her sleep. Because she felt like she'd been hit with an anvil, Louise tapped out another pill into her hand, bent over the sink, sipped a bit of water straight from under the tap.

And swallowed.

It was misting now. Hard to even call it rain. Louise pushed the screen door open to let Fillmore out, but the dog just stood by her side. He looked up at her with those lonely black eyes.

"Come on, buddy," she said with a little push on his backside. "Better now than later." Fillmore ambled out and started sniffing around the back fence.

Louise hugged her sweater close to her chest, hoping Lyla would have the good sense to come home before the rain started again. And if she was still up, Louise promised herself she wouldn't check Lyla's breath. Nothing good would come of it. Louise could still feel the weight of the corn cob in her hand before she winged it across the table earlier that evening. They both needed a good night's sleep, and they could start again in the morning.

Louise's headache eased as she stood on the porch. A warm

deliciousness rushed through her like butter greasing the inside of her skull, instantly replacing the pain. She was feeling so much more clearheaded now and vowed she'd wake up early and surprise Lyla with those pumpkin chocolate chip muffins she used to bake when Lyla was young. She would bring them on a tray to Lyla's bed with a cup of orange juice and a soft-boiled egg. She'd hold the warm muffin under Lyla's nose and watch her daughter's eyes flutter awake.

The clouds above began to break apart. A few bright stars shone through. Overhead, a small blink of light jogged across the gap in the clouds, then disappeared. She wondered if Sputnik was whizzing around, spying down. She had no idea if the Russian satellite was still up there. And when the light reappeared on the other side of the cloud, Louise threw open her sweater, lifted her top, and shook her bare breasts at the night sky.

"What do you think of them apples?" she joked, jiggling her bare chest at the stars. It felt good to be a little zany, far away from the roll of Lyla's critical eyes. She was tired of having to be so damn serious all the time. "Have at it, boys!" She danced, the welcome warm rush still pulsing through her body.

Fillmore ran across the yard and bounded onto the porch, nearly knocking Louise over as he bolted past her and into the house. "Fillmore!" Louise yanked her sweater closed, clutching it at the collar.

Twigs snapped in her neighbor's yard. Her body flushed with an untenable heat.

"Hello?" she asked, embarrassed that her neighbors might have seen her dancing around on the back porch like a total nut job.

That was all she needed now—to have the Richards gossiping about her.

The Richards had already heard enough of her and Lyla's yelling matches of late.

"Dave? Linda?" she called.

Nobody answered, and Louise hoped to God it was just a raccoon that startled Fillmore, not Dave sitting out on his lawn chair, smoking a cigarette, and having a good laugh.

Even as Louise climbed into bed, she knew there wasn't a chance she could fall asleep. She opened her magazine and picked up where she'd left off.

They are watching you, the article warned.

"Well, at least somebody is." Louise stifled a small giggle. Neither Al nor Fillmore stirred; the two of them remained fast asleep—one lay in the bed next to her snoring like an animal, the other sprawled out on the floor, farting like an old man.

She turned the page.

It is Americans' patriotic duty to help track Sputnik, the article claimed, suggesting that every US citizen should go outside and listen for the distinctive *beep, beep, beep* of the Russian satellite.

If detected, the observer should note the time of day and location and report their findings to NASA immediately.

"Good Lord." Louise laughed out loud this time. "When the United States government needs my help, we're all sunk."

Al rolled over. "What was that, hon?"

"Oh, nothing." Louise tossed the magazine on the floor. "Go back to sleep. I'm sorry I woke you. I'll stop making so much noise." And by the time Louise turned off the light, Al had his arm flopped over her side and was already snoring again.

In the dark, she watched the minute hand tick along: 11:55, 11:56, 11:57.

Worry crept back in, replacing the exquisite swirl that had rinsed away her headache. She shouldn't have given Lyla permission to take the car. That was a stupid thing to do with the brakes acting the way they were. She should have insisted on dropping Lyla off at the game in Al's car.

Louise tried not to stir. She didn't want to wake Al again. Plus, she was trying to keep an ear out for the unmistakable sign—not the *beep, beep, beep* of Sputnik's radio but the quiet creep of Lyla's return, the pull of the front door as it clicked into place and the soft moan of the floorboards. Lying in bed, Louise would track Lyla's progress as her daughter tiptoed to her room.

But there was only the swish of rainwater as cars drove up the street.

By 1:00 a.m., only a few cars drove past.

And by 1:30, just one automobile made its way up the narrow, winding street.

Louise knew Al was right. Lyla would be home when she got home, and there was nothing she could do to make her arrival happen any sooner. She closed her eyes and tried to fool herself to sleep. But she knew it was useless.

She finally peeled the comforter off and padded out of the room toward the kitchen. She peeked inside Lyla's room just to make sure Lyla hadn't snuck in earlier while Louise had been brushing her teeth.

From the doorway, Louise stood still and listened for sounds of her daughter, just as she had when she stood over Lyla's crib, listening for her soft baby breath in the middle of the night. But Lyla's bed was too far away, and it was too dark to see properly. Louise crept closer, letting her eyes adjust. It was then that she saw the outline of Lyla's body under the crumpled covers.

"Oh, thank goodness," Louise whispered. She quietly pulled the covers back to kiss Lyla on the cheek, but her daughter was not fast asleep. Instead, Louise found a pile of Lyla's clothing arranged under the covers, making the heap look like a sleeping body.

Louise pulled a volleyball out of the sweatshirt's hood and threw it on the floor.

"You little fink." Louise swept the clothes off the mattress. She started to remake the bed but then decided against it. She pulled the top sheet down and short-sheeted the bed instead, just as her brother had taught her to do when they were kids, when together they'd team up and pull all sorts of pranks on their mother.

Louise then folded the bedspread and pulled down a corner, just to let Lyla know Louise had not been played the fool. And on her way out, Louise turned and punted the volleyball to the far side of the room. She had only meant to give it a light tap against the wall, but the volleyball struck the glass vase on the windowsill. The vase, filled with hundreds of marbles, crashed to the floor. Marbles ricocheted around the room like the scurrying of rats.

"Oh, Jesus." Louise slapped a hand over her mouth. The vase was an heirloom, not from her side of the family but from Charles's, passed down the Hawkinses' line for four generations. Lyla's great-grandfather had handed it to her grandfather with a hundred marbles in it. Lyla's grandfather then gave it to her father with another hundred. And just before he died, Charles had given it to Lyla. It was said that when the vase reached five hundred marbles, the recipient would have good luck.

How in the world was Louise going to explain this? That she had spoiled her daughter's good fortune?

Louise dropped to her hands and knees and started gathering the loose marbles into the circle of her arms. "Fuck me," she said. She knew she needed to clean up the broken glass and hide the marbles in her own closet before Lyla got home.

In the morning, she'd go and buy a new vase, an identical one. She'd fill it back up and sneak it back onto the windowsill as if nothing had happened. She'd done that once with one of Lyla's pet hamsters that had died while Lyla was away at summer camp, when Louise forgot to fill the water container. She went to several pet stores until she found one that fooled her daughter into believing it was the same old hamster. The same old Billy. Louise could be clever that way.

After removing the bigger shards of glass from the floor, she crawled under the bed to reach for the few stray marbles that had rolled underneath next to a discarded pair of underwear. She scooted back out from under the bed with the underwear in hand, but when she sat up, she realized they were not Lyla's. They were men's underwear, white Fruit of the Looms, waistband size 32.

"What in the world?" Louise held the boxer shorts out in front of her like a dead animal. "Lyla May!" she said. Then, "Kyle!" She threw the underpants across the room, then swept her hand into the pile of marbles, scattering them back across the carpet. She didn't care a whit about the stupid Hawkinses' tradition. It was all a bunch of nonsense.

"This is your own damn doing, Lyla. Not mine," she said, before getting up and turning out the light. Had it been Lyla's head in that sweatshirt and not that damn volleyball, none of this would have happened.

The rain started back up again. Outside, a pair of headlights lit up the street. Louise leaned over the kitchen sink to get a better look, but the car zoomed past. It was two thirty in the morning.

"She has no idea what she's going to face when she gets home," Louise said aloud, standing tall as she looked out into the darkness. "I swear, I'll ground her for two months. Three, if she gives me any lip." She closed her eyes and massaged her temples, trying to push against the headache that was trying to worm its way back in.

But then Louise wondered, *What if Lyla has been in an accident? What if she's stuck in a ditch?*

"Oh, Fillmore." Louise reached down and petted her old boy, trying to erase the awful scenarios that jammed up in her mind, one after another:

Lyla standing with her hands on the hood of a police car.

Lyla standing alone on the side of the road with shards of glass poking out of her face.

Lyla trapped in the crumpled-up car after sliding off the mountainside.

Lyla bound and gagged, kicking the inside of a stranger's trunk.

Louise almost picked up the phone to dial the police, but then she thought of the underwear under Lyla's bed and the simulated body under the comforter. Lyla was neither in a ditch nor in somebody's trunk. She and Kyle were probably off necking somewhere.

The rain drummed harder.

But still. What if?

Louise tried to busy herself from the worry by pulling out all the dish towels from the drawer and refolding them, organizing the silverware, collecting all the loose rubber bands in the junk drawer and putting them in a baggie, but in the end she decided it was best to wait out the night in Lyla's room, so as not to bother Al before he got up. Maybe she'd even finally fall asleep.

"Come on, Fill," she said, leading the dog into Lyla's messy room. She sat on Lyla's bed and ran her hand over her daughter's flowered pillowcase. Fillmore lay on the floor next to her. The rain pelted the windows even harder now; oceans of water poured from the sky. There was no way Lyla could drive in this.

And that was it. Louise couldn't stand the worry any longer. She picked up the phone and started to dial 911. But again, in the seesaw of emotions, she stopped herself. Seeing the piles of clothes that Lyla had hidden in her bed, Louise placed her finger on the switch hook.

This was no accident.

The clock glowed 3:15 in bright green numbers. She took a breath and steeled herself to wait another forty-five minutes before she made the call—but not a minute more.

And just like that, the fury of rain lightened to a drizzle again.

Louise set the receiver into its cradle, and as if on cue, her car pulled into the driveway. The headlights were dimmed; the engine was cut. Louise watched as her car coasted down the driveway to a quiet stop.

"Clever girl." Louise smiled, relieved.

Through the window, Louise saw that Lyla didn't get out immediately. She just sat in the driver's seat with her hands on the wheel and Kyle next to her, still wearing his football jersey. They weren't fighting. They weren't even talking. They just sat there, staring at the house as though they were parked at a drive-in movie.

Two minutes went by.

Five.

Seven.

Louise almost got up to go see if something was wrong, to see if Kyle had hurt her in some way, but then the driver's side door flew open, and Lyla stumbled out of the car. She stumbled around the front, leaning on the hood to steady herself.

"Oh, God," Louise said. "Here we go again." She shook her head as she watched Lyla rummage clumsily through the pockets of her jacket. Lyla stuck a piece of gum in her mouth and waved to Kyle, who climbed out of the passenger seat and teetered over to Lyla.

"Lord. Not you too," Louise said, watching Kyle whisper something into Lyla's ear just before he kissed her, long and hard. Louise probably should have looked away, or at the very least, closed her eyes, but she couldn't help herself. She had never seen her daughter, her baby girl, being kissed like that. Or Kyle being so forward. He'd always been such a sweet kid, but did he really just stick his tongue in her daughter's mouth? And reach inside Lyla's coat, inside her blouse, and start fumbling around, practically mauling her?

Louise bolted off the bed and nearly banged on the window—*Get your bloody hands off my daughter!* But before she could intervene, Lyla stumbled back and gave Kyle a playful slap on the cheek. She grabbed him by the jersey, put her finger to her lips, and together they tiptoed to the house like a pair of feckless cartoon burglars.

Louise would have loved to throw open the window and call out to them, *You needn't be so quiet; I'm wide awake, thank you very much.* But she didn't. She sat back down on the edge of the bed and watched her daughter push her way through the hedge to the bedroom window.

It was then, standing just a few feet away, that Louise saw what a mess her daughter was: her hair was matted against her head like a wet dog; her mascara dripped from her eyes. Behind her, Kyle stood underneath the eaves, his hands crammed in his armpits.

Lyla tested the window, but the sash had swollen and was stuck with the rain. Lyla *tap-tap-tapped* at the frame; still, it wouldn't budge. She furrowed her brows and bit her lip, just as Charles would do when tackling their taxes or trying to assemble one of Lyla's presents late on

Christmas Eve. The two of them, father and daughter, were problem solvers. Just give them enough time.

"God, Lyla. You're just like him."

Lyla turned to Kyle and said something.

Kyle shook his head.

What are you up to, young lady? Louise wondered. Then, *You are not sneaking him into the house? My house?*

But that was exactly what Lyla was doing, and Louise darn well knew it.

Her daughter pointed to the ground as though she were chastising a dog for making a mess.

Again, Kyle shook his head to say, *No way.*

Lyla grabbed her boyfriend by the collar and yanked him down to his hands and knees. She then climbed on his back and, standing oh so much taller now, leaned into the window and gave a good push.

The window flew open.

"Voilà!" Lyla whispered.

"Voilà!" Louise snapped back.

Lyla banged her head on the window frame. "Ouch. Fuck." She rubbed her forehead and squinted in the dark. "Mom? What are you doing up?"

"What do you think I'm doing? It's three thirty in the morning. I've been worried sick."

"Well, I'm fine." Lyla flung herself over the windowsill and tumbled to the floor—onto some remaining shards of glass and loose marbles.

"What the hell is going on here! What have you been doing in my room?" Lyla pushed herself up by her elbows and examined her hands. Little shards poked out of her palm.

"I had a little accident. Here, let me see." Louise felt a strange flush take over her like she wanted to take Lyla's hands and not pull the shards out but press one deeper into her daughter's palms.

"A little accident?" Lyla held out her hands. "You call this a little accident? I've got glass in my goddamned hands."

"Are you okay in there, Lyla?" Kyle poked his wet head through the window.

Louise snapped on the bedside lamp.

"Oh. Hi, Mrs. Hawkins," he said as though he were dropping Lyla off from school in the middle of the afternoon.

"Kyle."

Lyla began to pick the small bits of glass out of her hands. "What are you even doing in here, setting a trap for me?"

"Oh, don't be ridiculous. A trap." Louise snorted.

Kyle started to climb through the window, but Louise held out her hand.

"No, Kyle. We'll see you in the morning."

"Oh, okay," he said as he fumbled his way back out.

"And watch the hydrangeas," Louise warned him. "They don't like being pushed around."

"Okay, yeah. Sorry about that, Mrs. Hawkins. Night."

"Kyle, wait!" Lyla yelled up at the window. "Mom, he can't walk home. It's raining."

"I noticed." Louise stared at Lyla as she sat on the floor.

"He'll get wet."

Louise let out a riotous laugh. "I think it's a little too late for that. Good night, Kyle."

"Night, Mrs. Hawkins."

Lyla stumbled to her feet, holding her hands out like a child catching snow for the first time. Little bits of blood dotted her palms. "Wait, Kyle. I'll drive you home."

"Oh, no, you don't, missy. You are not getting back in my car. You're done."

"Mom." Lyla laughed. "You're being ridiculous. I'm fine."

"You *are not* fine, Lyla. Look at you."

Lyla wiped her nose with her sleeve. "I was just trying to come home quietly. I was trying not to wake you since you're always blaming me for ruining your sleep. And then there's glass all over my floor. It's like you wanted me to get hurt."

"Stop, Lyla." Louise could feel the heat rising up her chest, flushing her cheeks with anger. A new headache began to thrum inside her skull. "Oh, Lyla." Louise bent over and yanked her daughter into her arms. "What on earth has happened to you?"

But Lyla shrugged her off. "Get your hands off me." Lyla grabbed hold of the bedspread and tried to pull herself up, looking so much like Charles did those last few months before he left them.

Desperate. Sad. Angry. Drunk.

"Please, Lyla." Louise found herself begging. "I want to help. I know that things have been difficult. I don't blame you."

"Blame? Who said anything about blame?"

"I meant hard. I think we can all agree this has all been so fucking hard."

Lyla laughed. "What do you know about hard? All you do is sit around all day and take those little pills that Dr. Schmidt gives you."

"What are you talking about?" Louise's cheeks reddened like she was the one caught and in trouble now.

"You think I don't know about them? Shoebox, upper left side of the closet. Do you even know what they are? Or what they're doing to you?"

Louise swatted her hand in the air. "They're for my—" She paused. "Oh, never mind. You wouldn't understand."

"No. You're right. I don't understand. I have no clue. You haven't exactly given me a road map."

Louise clasped her hands and held them to her chest; she no longer wanted to hurt her daughter. "I know I haven't always been the best mother. But I *do* love you." She grabbed Lyla by the shoulders, trying to shake some sense into her. "I really do. You know that, don't you?"

Lyla jerked away from her. "No, Mom. Actually, I don't. I'm no expert here, but aren't you supposed to protect the ones you love? You know, make sure they are safe, not hurl things at them at the dinner table. Or leave glass on their bedroom floor?" Lyla scoffed. "I mean, who acts like this? Huh, Al? What kind of parent does this?"

Louise snapped her head over to the doorway where Al now

stood, wearing nothing but his boxers. His short, compact body was solid and sturdy. A brick.

Al didn't say anything. He didn't even look at Louise. He walked over and helped Lyla to her feet. "Come on," he said. "Let's get you cleaned up before things get any worse."

Louise stood up. "No, Al. I'll do it. You go back to bed. She's my daughter."

"Despite what said *daughter* wishes," Lyla mumbled under her breath.

"What did you say to me?" Louise hollered. She had always loathed the smugness of people talking in the third person. All those Christmas newsletters she received from friends and relatives summing up their yearlong accomplishments with such phony objective reporting. Those third person voices went straight into the trash.

Louise drew in a long, deep breath. "Just stop it."

"Stop what?" Lyla yelled.

"You know I don't like it when you talk like that."

"Well, guess what? I honestly don't give a crap anymore. And here's a news flash," Lyla cried, tiny dots of blood and glass littering her forearms. "Despite what you claim, I don't even love you. I'm just stuck here until I graduate. Then I'm outta here."

Louise stormed to her daughter and slapped Lyla hard across the face, so hard it knocked her daughter to the floor. "Don't you ever say such a thing!" Louise screamed, standing over her daughter, her hand held high and ready for another slap. "I'm your mother, goddamn it. And I love you. Do you hear me?"

Al reached for Louise's hand. He pulled her tight to his chest.

"Get your hands off me, Al!" she screamed as she tried to break free, but Al's thick arms were too strong.

Lyla was crying now. Louise's hand had branded her cheek. Blood trickled out of her nostril.

Louise had actually given her daughter a bloody nose! Again, she tried to wrestle out of Al's grasp, but he kept her to his chest. "Let go of me!" she screamed again.

Al slowly let her go. Louise reached for Lyla, but Lyla threw her hands over her head as if Louise were a wild grizzly on the attack.

"Get away from me!" Lyla screamed, her head now buried between her knees.

Louise froze. "Oh, Lyla. I didn't mean to. I—" She paused. "Lyla, please. I'm sorry."

"Just leave me alone," Lyla said, letting Al help her to her feet.

"Come on, Lyla," Al said. "I've got you." And he did. He truly had her.

Stunned, Louise just sat there. She could do nothing but watch her daughter lean against Al as he guided Lyla to the bathroom.

"Al. Lyla. Please!" Louise begged.

Al turned. His eyes were not filled with reproach, nor with anger. They were the eyes of someone who was taking control, the eyes of the cleanup man. "It's okay, Louise. I've got this."

From Lyla's bedroom, Louise could hear the sink being filled and the silence of two people forced to live with each other and having nothing to say. Louise imagined Lyla sitting on the countertop, her head leaned back while she pinched the bridge of her nose, while Al sat on the toilet in his boxers and his reading glasses, plucking slivers of glass out of her hand and dropping them in the sink, bit by bit. She then heard Lyla tell Al that she needed some space. She needed to clear her head. She needed to get out of there.

Exhausted, Louise sat down on Lyla's bed and held her daughter's pillow on her lap. Her headache had all but disappeared. She stared at the mess on the floor—the scattered pile of clothes, the volleyball, and the drips of blood on the floor leading out of the room like breadcrumbs.

She bent over, picked up the pile of clothes, and started the thankless job of folding them like she'd always done. She tucked one of Lyla's shirts under her chin and folded the sleeves back one at a time. She smoothed out the shirttail and folded it up into a nice, neat package and put it on the bed beside her.

Next, she picked up a pair of jeans and folded them too.

Hadn't she been a good mother?

She picked up Lyla's T-shirts, a pair of pajamas.

Hadn't she been the one to nurse Lyla at all hours of the night when she was a baby? Hadn't she held Lyla's hair back when she was sick with the stomach flu? Helped her with her homework? And for God's sake, all those Halloween costumes she sewed! And Girl Scouts? She'd never wanted to be a troop leader, but oh, she did it all right.

And all those tears! Louise matched up a pair of her daughter's socks.

Who was the one to rub Lyla's back and sing her to sleep, night after night, when Charles had left them?

Louise had tried. Had *really, really* tried to do things right, hadn't she? But it was never good enough.

Or maybe Lyla was right all along. Maybe there was no road map. Maybe Louise had never been good enough, capable enough, to shield Lyla from the world of hurt after Charles did what he did. Maybe that was never supposed to be her job description.

Louise reached for Lyla's varsity tennis sweatshirt and smoothed it out in her lap. She felt something in the front pocket. Something small.

Something wrapped in foil like a square of chocolate.

A Trojan condom.

Louise held it in front of her.

One lubricated rolled rubber prophylactic with special receptacle end, the small plain wrapper read.

Louise rubbed the packaging with her thumb, feeling the rib of the rolled-up condom inside. It had been a long time since she'd held a condom, let alone felt the hunger of ripping one open with her teeth in the heat of the moment.

Isn't Lyla too young to have sex? Louise wondered. She looked down at the clothes on the floor, the underwear under the bed, the open window.

She got up and remade Lyla's bed, wondering if this was something they did often when she and Al were fast asleep.

Or whether this would have been their first time.

She picked up Lyla's pillow and held it to her nose, smelling Lyla's shampoo.

The conditioner.

The do-over she had hoped for that night.

Louise slipped the pillowcase off and placed it over her head. Listening to Lyla and Al mumbling in the bathroom, Louise counted to thirty, stood up, and walked around Lyla's bedroom with her arms stretched out.

"*Do-over*," she sang quietly as she scooted around the bed, making her way to Lyla's bathroom where she hoped to make amends. She bumped against the bedpost as she felt her way in the dark.

"*Do-over!*" she continued to sing. Just then, she stepped on a stray piece of glass. She clenched her teeth and, hopping on one foot, was about to holler a string of obscenities when she heard something. Not in the bathroom.

But outside.

In the dark.

The unmistakable crunching of pebbles underfoot.

"Lyla? Al?" Louise yanked the pillowcase off her head. She blew the stray hairs out of her face and let her eyes adjust.

Silence.

She was just about to close the window when she saw a small orange glow at the top of the driveway where Kyle stood, smoking a cigarette. She meekly waved to him, wondering why he hadn't gone home—had he been waiting to sneak back in or what?

But Kyle did not wave back.

She almost called out, *Wait, Kyle! Come back. I'll take you home.* But something stopped her; she watched him throw his cigarette to the ground, turn, and walk his way home. His white-and-red jersey— number 22—with his name stitched on his back, disappeared into the night.

Standing there, holding the pillowcase and feeling the prick of glass stuck in her foot, Louise felt sorry for Kyle. He was just a teenage boy who wanted to celebrate his big win after the homecoming game. He just wanted to have a good time. But instead, he had come back to this.

Louise reached up and closed the window, then hobbled over to Lyla's bed and slid the pillowcase back onto the pillow. She fluffed it and placed it against the headboard. She unwrapped the condom and laid it on top.

Maybe after they all got some sleep, they could talk about what happened.

They could talk about every last bit of it.

CHAPTER TWELVE

REVERSE FAULTS—OCTOBER 1963

Caroline was sitting in the kitchen when she heard the light rap on the glass door, as if a starling were pecking at its reflection. But Caroline wasn't fooled. It was too early for the morning call of birds; it wasn't even dawn. And though she couldn't see out into the dark, Caroline knew who stood outside. Her daughter-in-law had already called to say Lyla had run away.

"Oh, for heaven's sake, Louise, she didn't run away. She's seventeen and has her driver's license." Caroline propped a pillow behind her back. "You had a scrap, that's all."

But the long silence on the other end confirmed what Caroline suspected. It was more than a petty quarrel; it was probably their worst yet, and Caroline knew good and well not to say *I told you so*. Whiffs of blame had been circling around those two like condors over carrion for years. Accusations so ripe, you could smell them.

"It was more than a little scrap, Caroline. It was just awful. She said I was the *one*. That it was my—" Louise stopped. She sat on the other end of the line. Her heavy sigh snaked its way through the receiver like the hot breath of a crank caller.

"Speak up, Louise. I can't hear you."

"Before she took the car, she screamed back at the house that it was all my fault, everything that had happened to us," Louise whispered. "That I was the one who drove Charles to do what he did. That she couldn't blame him. Jesus, the whole neighborhood must have heard her."

Caroline reached over and pulled the chain to the bedside lamp. On the nightstand sat a photograph of her two beautiful sons taken under the oak tree, the first Christmas after her boys returned from the war. Dressed in their winter service uniforms, Charles had an arm draped over his brother's shoulder. And he was wearing that damned cheeky smile. The *Smile of God*, she always claimed. It fit her firstborn so well. And when it didn't, she still pretended it did.

"Well, you can hardly say you didn't see this coming." Caroline ran a finger along the top of the silver frame.

"What?"

"The blame game. It was just a matter of time with that girl. You knew that. But really, it's just a case of a teenager placing blame on the ones they love. That's all."

"Still, it hurts." Louise sighed.

"Of course, it does. She's a teenager. They're built to hurt." Caroline turned the frame slightly away so her firstborn was no longer smiling at her. "It'll pass. Trust me."

Caroline smoothed the creases out of the bedspread that lay over her lap. Her long, skinny legs nearly reached the end of the bed frame. Now was not the time to remind Louise how many times Charles had caused her pain when he was a teenager—all the joyrides in their only car; the late-night pranks with his buddies; the time his best friend tackled him to the ground when Charles stood on the rail of the Golden Gate Bridge, preparing for the ultimate of swan dives. She had been through it all.

"I do trust you, but—" Louise paused. "Hold on a minute."

On the other end of the line, Caroline heard a screen door open. She figured Louise was slipping outside so as to not wake up Al. How that ape could sleep through any of this, Caroline had no idea, but she was glad he wasn't up trying to take control of the situation as though it were some kind of military operation. None of this was any of that addlepate's business anyhow. It was enough he had the nerve to be sleeping in her son's bed.

"I'm afraid of losing her, Caroline. What if she—"

Louise again failed to finish her thought, so Caroline tapped the mouthpiece as though the connection were lost. "Hello? Hello?"

"I'm still here." Louise was back. "But what if she does it too?"

"Oh, just stop it, right now." Caroline sat up straighter. "There's no need to make more of it than it is, Louise. She came home drunk. That's all. End of story."

Truth be told, that wasn't the end of the story. There never would be an end to the story, but Caroline was sick of her daughter-in-law's constant fretting: *What if she does it too? What if she can't help it? What if it's genetic?* As if the perversity of taking one's life were something Caroline had passed on to her son.

"But . . ."

"But nothing, Louise. It's not hereditary if that is what you want to hear. He made a foolish mistake, that's all."

Up until that very moment, Caroline had reserved outright criticism of her son and what he did to be spoken only to her bathroom mirror. Pulling the teeth of her comb through her bright white hair, she always tried to untangle *who he was* from *what he did*, and the unanswerable question of *why*.

Even in the days following his death, Caroline wouldn't believe the evidence. She'd insisted Charles had been murdered.

"There is no way my son would do that to himself," she'd told the sheriff that October morning after she found him hanging in the tree. She'd even written a lengthy letter to the local newspaper defending her son, reminding those who subscribed to the *Index-Tribune* that he was, above all, a war hero and he should be remembered that way. But the editor refused to publish the letter.

Everybody knew the truth. He was no war hero. He was just an ordinary man who, like all other ordinary men, received an honorable obituary in the paper.

"I hit her," Louise finally confessed. "I gave her a bloody nose, for Christ's sake. God, she can make me so angry sometimes. But I've never hit her before. I swear, Caroline. I don't know what came over me."

Oh, I know what came over you, all right, Caroline wanted to offer. She'd thought about giving her granddaughter a firm hand for some time now.

"I'm surprised it took you this long. Lyla's been practically begging for you to stand up and say enough is enough."

"No, Caroline. You're wrong. No one deserves to be treated like that. I should have been a better listener, a better mother."

"Well, you got her attention now."

"Oh, Caroline. I feel just awful about the whole thing."

"Of course, you feel awful, Louise. Kids are experts at making mothers feel terrible. They never outgrow it."

"What do I do?" Louise's softening voice started to quiver.

"Not a darn thing. I'll handle it. Just go to sleep and I'll call you in the morning."

"Tell her I love her. Tell her I'm sorry. Tell her to come home."

The rat-a-tat-tats of Louise's *tell her this, tell her that* got on Caroline's very last nerve.

"I said, I'll handle it." Caroline placed the receiver back in its cradle before Louise could say another word.

Leaning over, she straightened the picture of her boys so Charles was facing her again.

"Good Lord, Charles." She traced her finger over his once-bright smile. "Look what you've done." Caroline sighed and rubbed the sleep out of her eyes, preparing for what was to come. She slipped her feet into her slippers and made her bed. "All right, Lyla. Let's see what you got," she said as she padded her way to the bathroom.

Standing in front of the mirror, Caroline pulled her wide shoulders back, her neck long and straight. At six feet, two inches, Caroline had a strange combination of looks, which inspired both awe and a touch of fear, a reaction she'd grown accustomed to over the years. As a child, she'd always been much taller than the other kids in the schoolyard, making her look older and a good deal more imposing. And her long neck never helped her cause, that's for sure. Kids used to tease her, "Quick! Run! It's a Carolosaurus!" They'd scatter to all ends of the playground and stare at her from the monkey bars or the top of the slide as she walked to the swings by herself.

Even now, people seemed to give her a strange, wide berth whenever she walked into a room. Why, just last week as she approached the cosmetics counter at I. Magnin's, two saleswomen suddenly dispersed, pretending to be busy, leaving a less-attentive saleswoman to wait on her. As Caroline made her purchases, she caught sight of the other two women staring at her over by the perfumes, whispering. Caroline grew so perturbed that on the way out of the department store, she waved her receipt at them, reminding the numbskulls that their rudeness had cost them a healthy commission.

"It's not your fault," Caroline said to the mirror, rehearsing the line she'd tell Lyla. "It had nothing to do with us. He just came home a different man after the war. Plain and simple. Get over it."

Caroline dragged the teeth of her comb through the tangles in her straight white hair. Yet no matter how hard she yanked and repeated the refrain, knots remained inside her.

His suicide was hers—and always would be.

"There was nothing I could have done. Don't you understand?" she snapped, and despite the fact that it was four forty-five in the morning, she pulled out her Rouge Dior lipstick and colored her lips.

"I did the best I could." Caroline folded a square of tissue in half, pressed it between her lips, threw the used tissue in the toilet bowl, and flushed it down. She stood taller and took a deep breath.

"It's showtime," Caroline said to her reflection, and snapped off the light.

———————

At the kitchen sink, Caroline filled the tea kettle as she searched for the glow of Lyla's headlights in the dark.

Waiting for the water to boil, she sat down at the kitchen table and rubbed her hands along the wood like a Ouija board, steeling herself for all the inevitable boo-hoos. The screaming. The fist pounding. It was all to come, sure as the daylight that would follow.

Caroline traced the small fissure that ran down the surface of the table, the crevice in the wood that, over the years, trapped old food in its shallow cleft; she removed the bits of long-ago meals with the tip of a butter knife. The crack never widened or deepened; it stayed exactly the same as the day she and Morris purchased it in Sebastopol so long ago—their first big purchase after they had married.

Something that would hold up over the years.

Initially, Morris had pushed for a more modern design, something less weathered, believing that was what Caroline would want too. But she had surprised him that day, and herself for that matter. She wanted a table with some age already bred in. In all other matters, Caroline despised country-ware because it looked cheap, but she knew the kitchen table would get a great deal of use. Even then—before she had children of her own—she knew it would become the family's central meeting place, and she didn't want to witness a clean, new purchase go bad with years of wear and tear. "No," she said to Morris that day in the furniture store. "Let's get this one over here."

The farm table was about seven feet long and over four feet wide and took up most of the space in their otherwise small kitchen. But it was all so worth it, every single inch of it. Her two sons had grown up at this very table. It was where they had done their homework, where they ate dinner every night at exactly six o'clock, and where her boys glued and painted hundreds of model airplanes over squares of newspaper. As teenagers, the two boys would play blackjack, betting small sums or heavy chores. Sometimes they'd arm wrestle on it when their arms were no bigger than spaghetti noodles. And it was at this table where they gathered for family meetings, where her sons talked about their intentions of marriage, and where they signed their enlistment papers.

And it was at this table that Caroline opened the telegram:

The Secretary of War desires me to express his deep regret that your son, Private Charles Dean Hawkins, has been reported missing in action since 28 September in the Apennine Mountains, Italy. If further details or other information is received, you will be promptly notified.

After reading the telegram over and over again, Caroline had barely left that table until one day, three weeks later, when she received a second telegram:

Despite what you may have heard, I am alive and well!! Missing home. Not to worry. Love, Charles

After receiving the second note—having examined and scrutinized the double exclamation marks—Caroline folded the two telegrams into the pocket of her sweater and walked outside into the bright Northern California sunshine for the first time in nearly a month, feeling the warmth of light and life on her face.

"Come on, Lyla!" Caroline said in the dark kitchen, knowing good and well that her granddaughter would make her way straight to this table like a moth to light. Instinct would trump all reason. "We don't have all night here."

Just then, the headlights shone up and over the roofline, illuminating the backyard, and for the briefest of moments, the top of the enormous oak tree was lit like a candle.

Moments later, a light rap on the glass slider.

Caroline got up and unlocked the door, and though she had been prepared for this near-dawn arrival, the sudden appearance of Lyla's face butting up against the window—her hot breath fogging the glass—startled her.

"Good grief." Caroline grabbed the collar of her bathrobe as Lyla slid open the door. "You scared the daylights out of me."

Lyla stood there, her mascara smeared, her black hair wet and frizzy from the rain. A small strip of white gauze was wrapped around her left arm, and several bandages were on the palms of her hands.

Jesus, Mary, and Joseph, Caroline thought. *Louise wasn't kidding; she is a mess.*

"You're up?" Lyla asked.

"Of course, I'm up." Caroline turned off the kettle and set it on a trivet with the instant coffee. She poured herself a cup, eyeing Lyla. "What'd you expect? That you'd just tiptoe in here and fall asleep in the spare room like nothing happened?"

Lyla fidgeted with the keys in her hand. "So, I take it Mom called."

"Of course, she called. She was worried about you. She's your mother."

"Whatever that's worth," Lyla mumbled.

Caroline slammed her hand down on the table, sending the coffee in her cup sloshing back and forth. "You will not, young lady, walk into my house and talk under your breath like that. Do you hear me?"

Lyla didn't answer; she began chewing on the inside of her cheek, something she had been doing all her life.

"And good Lord. Stop that."

"What?"

"That!" Caroline vigorously chomped her teeth up and down like those wind-up teeth her boys used to play with at the dentist's office, those stupid teeth that they sent nibbling along the receptionist's desk as she was trying to schedule their next cleaning.

"It's disgusting."

"Sorry?" Lyla rolled her eyes.

"Sorry won't cut it, Lyla. Not this time." Caroline pointed to the chair at the opposite side of the table and scooped two spoonfuls of Folgers Instant Coffee crystals into the second cup. "Now, sit down."

"Can't we just talk in the morning?" Lyla's broad shoulders sagged. "I'm tired."

"It *is* morning." Caroline jutted her chin in the direction of the clock that hung over the sink. "Or hadn't you noticed?"

"You know what I mean." Lyla pulled a chair out from the table. She sat down, rested her head against the back of the headrest, and blew a giant gum bubble. It popped against her face.

Caroline fought the urge to get up and yank the girl by the shoulders and show her how to sit up properly, to sit like a lady and cross her feet at the ankles, and, for God's sweet sake, stop it with the gum, already. She looked like a cow chewing cud. But Caroline bit her tongue.

She poured hot water into the second cup and stirred. "Here, this ought to sober you up."

"God, you sound just like Mom."

"I'm warning you, Lyla May." Caroline mimed the zipping of her mouth shut. "I'm in no mood for your back talk. Got it?"

"Well, I'm just saying. In this family, it's hardly a federal offense."

Caroline slapped the table again. "You are not in a position of *saying* a goddamned word, do you understand me?"

Lyla sank deeper into the chair and crossed her arms. She blew her bangs out of her eyes, as if she had learned the obnoxious teenager bit from the movies.

But Caroline wasn't easily intimidated. She drummed her fingers on the table and waited for Lyla to say something. Out in the hallway, the pendulum of the grandfather clock swung back and forth.

Back and forth.

So, it's a waiting game, then. Caroline crossed her ankles, folded her hands on the edge of the table, and watched her granddaughter clean the gunk out of her fingernails with the tip of the car key.

Lyla finally looked up and tossed a strand of wet hair out of her eyes. "What?"

"What were you doing all night?"

"We were at the beach." Lyla snapped her gum again. "It's not my fault it started to rain."

"Well, the least you could've done was wipe that ridiculous makeup off your face before coming over. You look like a clown." Caroline got up to refill the kettle and leaned against the counter. "Good Lord, Lyla. What would your father think?"

"Of what?"

"Of all this," Caroline said, waving her arms around in the air. "Of all of this ridiculous nonsense." She tightened the belt of her robe around her waist and walked back over. She sat down and drew her fingernail along the crack in the table.

"I don't know what you are talking about," Lyla said, wildly waving her arms around too, mimicking Caroline. "I don't even know what *this* is."

Caroline closed her eyes and pinched her thigh, trying to prevent herself from lunging across the tabletop and slapping Lyla like her mother had done. "God, you look just like him when he'd come home drunk."

"No, I don't." Lyla shook her head. "I don't look anything like him." The look on her granddaughter's face changed suddenly from insolence to . . . sadness?

"And I hate that you and Mom always say that."

"What?"

"That I look just like him."

"I'm sorry, Lyla." Caroline wasn't used to apologizing. An unsettling wave of emotion rushed through her, disorienting her for a moment. She'd always believed that to look like Charles was a good thing. "I just thought—"

"Thought what? That I love being reminded about how much I look like Dad? Well, I don't. And here's a news flash." Lyla gazed upward as though she were reading from the bright lights of a marquee and shouted, "I hate being reminded of him all the time. He's dead to me!"

"Lyla May!"

"Don't *Lyla May* me." Her granddaughter sat up straight and leaned toward Caroline. "Don't you think I see how you and Mom look at me, always sneaking a peek to see if he is in here? Well, he's not." Lyla pressed at her chest with her thumb. "It's me in here, not him. Me!"

Caroline reached her hand across the table, but Lyla wouldn't take it. "Lyla, honey. I'm sorry." The sharpness of Lyla's accusation and the resulting apologies that toppled out of her threw Caroline terribly off-balance. "It's awful what he did, but everything is going to be okay. You are just full of teenage hormones. They're wreaking havoc on you," Caroline weakly offered.

"But don't you see? It's not okay. It never was." Lyla's tone calmed down. "I just want to forget him. I almost have, you know. And if you all would just—" Lyla wiped her nose with her sleeve. "Just . . . just give it a rest, and maybe we could move on. We can just forget he ever existed, once and for all."

Lyla's suggestion knocked Caroline back into her chair. Her elbow hit her cup, and hot coffee spilled across the kitchen floor. "That is impossible, Lyla. I forbid it!" Caroline didn't bother to bend over and clean up the mess. "You can never forget him. He's your father!"

"Not anymore." Lyla paused, before adding, "Al's the man of the house now."

"Shame on you. Al's not your father. Charles is."

"Was."

"What did you say to me?" Caroline could feel her jaw stiffen even more.

"I said, 'was.' Past tense. He *was* my father."

In the wake of this pronouncement, the two of them fell silent. Caroline doubted such a passive verb could ever adequately describe the man she knew her son to be.

Was a father.

Was a husband.

Was a brother.

Was a son.

Outside, dawn began to overtake the night. It wasn't light yet, not by a long shot. But it was only a matter of time before gray morning light gave slow shape to all that was out back.

"Mom once asked me to call him Dad." Lyla's voice broke the hush between them.

"Who?" Caroline turned her gaze from the window to her granddaughter.

"Al. She said it would make him feel better. She said it was hard for him to be in the position he married into, that he was trying his best."

"Oh, that's ridiculous. Al's not your father. He's your mother's second husband, and he'll never measure up to Charles. Not in a million years."

Out the window, Caroline could just make out the round heads of the sunflowers leaning over the fence, as if they were nosy neighbors failing to mind their own business.

"Your mother has every right to worry about you, Lyla." Caroline quickly turned the conversation away from the man who'd replaced her son.

"She has a heck of a way of showing it." Lyla laughed. "Did she tell you that she hit me? Or did she conveniently leave that part out when she called?" Lyla pulled a crumpled ball of blood-soaked tissue out of her purse and held it out to Caroline as evidence. "I mean, who knew Mom had it in her?"

"She didn't hit you, Lyla. She slapped you. There's a big difference."

"She gave me a bloody nose!" Lyla tossed the tissue across the table.

"Mothers can be protective." Caroline grabbed the wastebasket from underneath the sink. She held out the metal can, but Lyla didn't seem to care what Caroline was asking her to do. Caroline cleared her throat, but still Lyla sat in her chair.

"I'd call it something other than protective. She's totally losing it. Last week I caught her lying on the attic floor with one of Dad's old sweaters wrapped around her. She was talking to it. She was lying on the floor with it as though—" Lyla paused.

"As though what?"

"I don't know, like she was having sex with it. God, it was so weird."

"Oh, that's ridiculous, Lyla. She did no such thing." Caroline stared at the bloody tissue. She couldn't quite imagine her daughter-in-law hiding in the attic with one of Charles's sweaters draped over her doing such a thing. "She's still hurting, Lyla. She misses him terribly. We all do."

"But who does that? I mean, you don't go around the house doing things like that. Talking to Dad? Like he's still here?" Lyla swallowed as though she might get sick, as though she had asked a question that she really didn't want to know the answer to.

"Oh, Lyla. You can't imagine what it's like to lose a son," Caroline blurted out, but the minute she said it, she wished she could take it back.

"Oh, really? I can't imagine what it's like? Are you kidding me? Every day, I look in the mirror, and I see Dad staring back." Lyla closed her eyes. "Sometimes I don't even know who's standing there. Me or him." Lyla's eyes popped open. "And *I* have no idea how hard it is? Give me a fucking break."

"Lyla May!" Caroline snapped. "You use that language one more time and I'll wash your mouth out with soap." Realizing how ridiculous that sounded, she calmly added, "It's hard for everybody. But we have to move on. You know that."

"Right. Move on. Okey-dokey." Lyla ticked off an imaginary to-do list in the air. "Forgive Dad. Check. Move on. Check. Live a normal life. Check. Done, easy as pie."

"I didn't say it was easy, Lyla. But you can't do this to your mother. And for heaven's sake, you can't do this to yourself."

"What am *I* doing? What about what *Mom* is doing to *me*?" She held out her bandaged hands to Caroline.

Out the sliding glass door, the black stain of night was nearly gone; everything out back—the fence line, the hills near and far, the old oak tree—started to materialize like ghosts walking into the pale morning light.

"I just don't think I can take it anymore," Lyla said. She looked out the window. "I'm so tired of it all. I'm sick of living with her."

"Well, you can't just leave your mother in the middle of the night and not tell her where you are going." Caroline was still holding out the trash can like an offering basket at church.

"What was I to do?" Lyla turned around. She grabbed the tissue. Instead of throwing it into the trash, Lyla unraveled it and licked a clean edge to wipe the black smudges underneath her eyes.

"She had no idea where you'd gone."

"Oh, I think she had a pretty good idea." Lyla laughed. "You were sitting right here waiting for me, weren't you?" Lyla pulled the compact from her purse and held it up to her face. "Jesus. You're right. I do look horrible." Lyla spat on the tissue and rubbed harder at the mascara, but the black smudges just grew longer and wider, making her look like she had two black eyes.

"Oh, forget it." Lyla finally threw the tissue but missed the trash can. "It's useless."

Caroline leaned over, picked up the tissue with the sleeves of her bathrobe like it was a dead mouse, and disposed of it, once and for all. She jammed the trash can back in place between the disposal and the dishwashing liquid.

"Nope. No shame in that at all." Caroline slammed the cabinet door closed. "Just give up, just like your father." She leaned against the kitchen sink and watched the silhouette of the oak tree finally take shape in the dawn light, the thick muscle of the branch that once held the entirety of her son's weight. She felt a small well of tears gather.

She clenched her teeth, fighting them back. She would not cry in front of Lyla.

Lyla walked up next to her and leaned against the kitchen sink too. Together, they stared out at the tree.

"Did you know?" Lyla finally asked.

"Know what?"

"That he'd do it. That he would leave us like that?"

"Oh, Lyla. How could I have known such a thing?"

Just then, a spit of sunlight hit the crown of the tree.

"I hate what he did to you, Lyla," Caroline finally confessed. "It was an unforgivable thing to do, to all of us. But mostly to you. His daughter. He loved you so much. I can't imagine what he was thinking." It was the first time Caroline had ever uttered anything remotely unfavorable or disapproving to Lyla about Charles since his death. She had kept all those concerns zipped tight.

Caroline grabbed the bullnose of the countertop to steady herself. "Oh my God, what was wrong with him?" Her voice cracked.

Lyla looked at Caroline with wet, pleading eyes. "Caroline?"

"I am sorry, Lyla." Her grandmother clenched her teeth and regained her stiff composure. "He was a good man, your father," she said with adamancy. "He just made a mistake. That's all. A stupid mistake. He didn't mean to do what he did. I'm certain of it."

Lyla placed her hand over the top of Caroline's as morning sunlight poured down the slope of the hills, illuminating everything after the good autumnal rain. There was no stopping daybreak now.

The sun lit up the oak tree broadside; the yellow light slid down the length of the tree.

"I hate him for what he did to me," Lyla confessed.

Caroline felt momentarily blinded.

"No, Lyla. You don't hate him. His decision had nothing to do with you. You're just upset. That's all."

"Of course, I'm upset." Lyla scoffed. "Wouldn't you be upset if you had to think about it all the time? Every time I come here and I have to look at that stupid tree? He forced me to climb up there and hang that rope." Lyla paused. "I never even wanted that swing in the first place. That was his idea."

"You're remembering things all wrong, Lyla. You were just a little girl."

"You weren't there!" Lyla snapped. "He called me a chicken when I was too scared to climb out on that branch. Can you believe it? My little legs were shaking up on that branch, and down below he was calling me a chicken. Do you know how that made me feel? God, he was such a bully."

"Stop it, Lyla." Caroline fidgeted with the neck of her robe.

"No. You stop! My therapist says I am allowed to say these things. Why? Because they happened to me. Not you. Not Mom. But me. So please stop trying to tell me what I can and cannot feel."

The sun shone along the branch where the pale flesh of wood had been polished clean by the old rope that once held the swing.

They stared at the tree.

"Your father could have had anything he wanted," Caroline said, remembering her grown son smiling the morning he'd caught the bus to Sacramento and then on to Camp Shelby, Mississippi, for basic training. "That war did something awful to him. You have no idea."

"Uncle David fought in that war too," Lyla whispered. "But he didn't hang himself. Nobody's making excuses for him."

"Nobody's making excuses, Lyla."

"Call it what you want."

The backyard was fully lit now, everything brilliant and clear— the green of the grass shone even brighter after last night's rain. The sky was a deep, bright blue, perhaps bluer than Caroline had ever seen before.

"Don't you remember all those sweet times, Lyla? All the fun we used to have. The Easter egg hunts, the picnics, the trips on the boat. That should count for something, shouldn't it?"

Lyla looked out the window. "I don't know. I am starting to wonder if we had any good times at all."

"Oh, but we did."

"But really, who cares about fun? This"—Lyla stepped back from the sink, her arms suddenly windmilling around—"is not very much fun. This is not what I call a good time." Lyla let out a wholly unexpected and exaggerated laugh. "Ha, ha, ha." Lyla's head rocked back and forth like she was walking through a carnival fun house. "Ha, ha, ha. Fun, see? I am having so much fun." A wide fake grin was plastered across Lyla's face.

Caroline had no idea what to do. She put her hands out. "Stop it, Lyla. It's not funny."

Lyla dropped her hands and turned her back to the window, the smile now gone. "How can you stand to even look at it? Why didn't you have it removed?"

Caroline looked at her granddaughter. She couldn't answer her at first.

Yes, how could she stand to look at the tree after what her son did up there? Certainly, the thought of cutting the tree down had crisscrossed Caroline's thoughts many times over the years. But she always landed on the same question: What then? Try and forget about what he did out there? Impossible.

The tree stood magnificent in the morning light.

"It wouldn't change a damn thing." Caroline tucked one of Lyla's curls behind her ear. "What he did out there can't be simply removed. We can't just cut the tree down, put the stump in a grinder, and wipe our hands, Lyla. Don't you see? The tree has to stay. It's a part of us."

Just then, Caroline swore she saw something out of the corner of her eye: a young boy darted across the backyard and hid behind the tree. *Her* tree. At first, Caroline thought it was the neighbor boy retrieving his soccer ball. He did that sometimes, hopped the fence into her backyard to chase down his ball and then ran away. He was always rather quick about it, which Caroline appreciated, but today the boy, who wasn't her neighbor but someone else, somebody strangely familiar—wasn't looking for a ball. From behind the tree, this new neighborhood boy wrapped his arms and legs around the thick waist of the trunk and began to shimmy up the tree.

Caroline banged on the window. "Get down." She knocked the glass even harder, but the boy kept climbing. She threw open the window and yelled out to him, "You aren't supposed to be up there. You'll get hurt. Get down, right now!"

"What are you doing?" Lyla grabbed Caroline's arm. "Who are you talking to?"

"That boy. He's . . ." But when Caroline looked back at the tree, the boy was gone. He had disappeared just as quickly as he had arrived.

"He was climbing my tree—" Caroline paused and watched the horror trapped in her granddaughter's eyes. Caroline looked back out the window with a hot surge of shame. "Oh dear, I think I'm just a little tired."

Cool morning air slid through the open window. Somewhere in the treetops, the songs of the thrushes began—the hopeful whistles of the male, and the warbled response of the female. They would go on and on like that through the morning—calling out to one another— like it was any other start to the day.

"Do you think he knew he was going to do it?" Lyla pressed. "Do you think, even way back then when we hung the rope for the swing, he knew what he was asking me to do?"

Caroline didn't respond. How could she? She took a dish towel and began wiping the tiny spiderwebs that had accumulated on the window screen. She wrapped the dish towel around her index finger and began scrubbing the four corners of the window screen in the neat geometric way that was so natural for her.

Lyla stood still as Caroline moved to the sink, washing the tiles underneath the windowsill, rubbing at the already sparkling-clean grout, working her way from left to right and back again.

"It wasn't your fault, Lyla," Caroline finally said, "if that is what you are asking." Caroline ran the dish towel under the tap and wrung it out, squeezing the dirty water into the sink. "It was me." Caroline gasped as she said it. She'd never admitted this before, not even to herself. She flattened the wrung-out dish towel on the countertop to let it dry. In the silence that took hold of the kitchen that morning, Caroline traced her finger up and around the tiles.

"What?" Lyla pulled her grandmother by the shoulders. "What did you just say?"

"I mean . . . it wasn't the war. It wasn't your mother. And it most certainly wasn't you, Lyla. It was my fault," Caroline said, more firmly this time. It was so strange to hear the words spoken out loud. But she went on, trying to find clarity in what she had long ago suspected. "If anyone is to blame, it's me."

"You?" Lyla looked at Caroline as if she'd just walked out of a dark movie theater and straight into the hot sunshine.

"I was too hard on him." Caroline held Lyla's cheeks in the palms of her hands and saw the confusion in her granddaughter's eyes. "Oh, Lyla. Of course, you'd never considered that *I* might be to blame. How could you? I worked so hard to distance myself from what happened that night, always placing the heavy blanket of guilt on others. On you, even. I am so sorry, Lyla. I should have said something years ago. I just didn't know how."

"What do you mean?" Lyla asked, her voice a boil of confusion. "You knew he'd do it?"

"No, of course not, Lyla."

Caroline let go of Lyla's face and took another dish towel out of the drawer. She began cleaning the long, shiny neck of the kitchen tap, leaning into the stainless-steel spout like she was brushing the hair on the side of a horse. "It was a stupid idea, to let him hang that swing. But you know your father. He somehow always got whatever he wanted in the end."

Caroline's eyes were fixed on the tree. "But I should have never said yes. I should have never let you climb up there and hang that rope. Look what it's done to you. What it's done to all of us."

"Why did you?" Lyla was crying quietly now. "Why did you let him talk you into it?"

"Yes, why did I? Now, that certainly is the million-dollar question, isn't it?" Caroline paused and smiled. She was actually smiling at the three-hundred-year-old oak, the tree thick with resilience as it stood on the edge of the slope, its wide canopy bending, inch by inch, over to the side from generations of wind blowing from the coast.

"I don't know. I figured he had grown out of it. Not of wanting the swing part, but—"

"Grown out of what?"

Even Caroline had no plan for what she was about to say. Everything just started pouring out of her, fast and sure like water from the tap.

"God, I used to tell Charles and David that I didn't want to have to look at an ugly tire swing every day. But now, I wish that was all I had to look at."

Caroline froze, clinging to the kitchen counter, barely able to breathe. It wasn't a heart attack, that much she knew. The muscle of her heart felt just fine, stronger than ever, but she couldn't move. Leaning over the sink, she began hyperventilating, then coughing. Her vision was disoriented and cloudy. "Oh, God," she said quietly.

"Caroline?" Lyla grabbed a chair and eased her down. "Wait here, I'm going to call Dr. Halderman."

But Caroline seized Lyla's arm. "No," she said. Her breath was easing back. Lyla's strong, handsome face came back into view. "I'll be fine. It happens sometimes. You don't need to worry."

"What do you mean, it happens sometimes? What does the doctor say?"

"He doesn't know."

"What do you mean, he doesn't know!" Lyla's voice cracked with alarm, something Caroline had only heard happen once before when she'd had to coax Lyla to throw her father's ashes over the side of the boat after she'd grabbed a handful of Charles but refused to let him go.

"How could you have not told the doctor about this?" Lyla went on. "This could be serious."

"It'll pass. Just give me a second."

The belt on Caroline's bathrobe had come loose around her waist, and the robe fell off to either side of her lap, exposing the thick varicose vein that ran up her left leg. She grabbed the fold of the robe and covered herself. She had always been very careful to hide that vein, always wearing long skirts or slacks to cover the monstrous bulge that grew out of her pregnancy with her firstborn. When Charles used to ask about it as a boy, running his finger along the red-and-purple vein, she'd slap his hand away and tell him that it was his fault. *You were such a beast when you came out.* She, of course, was talking about his size, not his temperament, but now she realized she never bothered to clarify what she'd meant.

Lyla began rubbing Caroline's back. "Are you going to be okay?"

"No, Lyla, it's not going to be okay." Caroline took in a deep gasp of air.

"Wait here. I'm going to call him."

"No. No, not that." Caroline grabbed at Lyla's still-damp jeans. "Don't you see? It was there all along. I never did anything about it. I just pretended I could muscle my way through it, but the signs were always there. It was all my fault. I should have done more." Caroline started crying now. She hadn't cried in decades.

Lyla kneeled in front of Caroline; she placed her hands onto her knees. "What do you mean, signs?"

"Oh, you know, small things at first." Caroline wiped her nose. "The way he would play in the sandbox as a boy. When the other kids wanted his shovel or his bucket, he'd refuse. He'd hold onto the tools so close to his chest and walk away, sitting by himself on the grass, clinging to the shovel like it was the Bible for Pete's sake. Or the way he'd crumple up his homework and throw it across the kitchen when he couldn't figure out a simple math problem, or how he'd throw his bat at the umpire when he struck out and then sit in his dark room, refusing to come out for dinner.

"And once, he and a few boys were out back playing cowboys and Indians," Caroline continued. "He must have been eight or so. One of the neighbor kids, Jimmy O'Neill, who was a little bit older than my boys and always assigned the parts, told Charles he was going to be an Indian that day. He was trying to be fair. Three cowboys to three

Indians. But Charles didn't want to be an Indian. So, do you know what your father did?"

Lyla looked at Caroline.

"Your father locked himself in my bedroom. When he emerged, he had taken off his shirt and had streaks of my red lipstick tattooing his bare chest, his face, his arms. He ran through the house, howling like a warrior going into battle. He grabbed a kitchen knife and ran into the backyard, where he climbed the fence and straddled it like he was riding a horse. He held the knife to his head, claiming he'd scalp himself. I watched the whole thing myself, standing right here at this very sink. I can still see it—the way the knife glinted in the sun, the way he bared his teeth at everybody, the way his eyes shone wet. But you know what I did?"

Caroline picked a thread off her bathrobe.

"Not a goddamned thing. I just stood right here at the sink, peeling the skin off the potatoes. All the boys giggled and hooted, cheering Charles on, believing it was all part of the game. But I knew it was something else. Yet I didn't do a damn thing. I just kept right on doing whatever it was I thought that needed to be done, except the one thing that mattered most. He needed help, Lyla."

Caroline got up, but she wasn't feeling any better.

"I tried to take him to somebody once," Caroline finally admitted. "But I thought it was all just a bunch of nonsense, all that gobbledygook, staring at pictures, forcing Charles to see something he didn't. I thought it was just a phase, and I could shake Charles out of his darker moods with a firm hand."

"Oh my God. I had no idea." Lyla sat as still as a robin's egg.

"It *was* my fault," Caroline said again. "I tried to ignore it. And I just turned my back."

Later that morning when Lyla went to take a shower, Caroline walked outside, letting the sun warm her face. Still in her bathrobe, she dragged the old wicker chair across the yard and placed it under the canopy of the oak tree. She sat underneath, rocking back and forth, looking up at the branch where the rope had worn through the bark, leaving a clean groove.

Whether it was because she had been staring at the sun that poured through the foliage or simply because she was tired, the muscles of her eyelids began to twitch. She rubbed her eyes and opened them again.

And there he was—the boy.

Her boy.

Young Charles was sitting on the branch above her, his legs dangling on either side as if he were riding a horse bareback. He was no more than ten years old. She knew because that was the year he got a black eye from a baseball to the cheek. Nearly half his face was taken up with a smack of black and blue, yet the young, bright smile on her son's face was as wide as it was true, as if there were no better place for him to be than up in the tree looking down on her. As if there were no other place he belonged.

"Come on. Climb with me, Mother," the boy said, patting the broad back of the branch. "You won't believe what you can see from up here."

But Caroline couldn't climb the tree. She couldn't even climb a ladder to change a light bulb anymore. Her vertigo had gotten the best of her.

"I can't, honey, but I'll be right here." Caroline rocked back and forth, watching young Charles up on that branch. She marveled at the sight of him. Her heart was warm and her jaw, for the first time in as long as she could remember, unclenched and fully relaxed.

Charles kicked his legs in the air. "Giddy-up," he said, and then turned so his back was to Caroline as he faded off into the hills.

Caroline watched her son's shadow dim as he got farther and farther away, slow and sure as day bleeds into night. "No, Charles. Don't go," she cried.

But Charles didn't turn back. He didn't even say goodbye.

"Charles, sweetheart. Wait!" Caroline grabbed an acorn from the dirt and threw it up at the vanishing boy, trying to get her small boy to turn around, trying to make him stay with her just a little while longer. "Charles, please!" she hollered, as though she could still force him to do what she wanted. "Get back here, right this instant. Do you hear me?"

But the boy disappeared, leaving Caroline alone underneath the tree. Her body fell back into the chair; all the strength that she had summoned over the years had suddenly vanished.

"Dear God." Caroline let the tears again cloud what she saw. "Forgive me, sweetheart. Forgive me, my bright boy. Come back," she begged, trying to sear his boyhood image on the branch, forcing him to return even for just the remainder of the morning. "I need you."

But she knew there was no chance for him to stay.

There was no chance for the boy to ever return that morning, because he had never been there to begin with.

CHAPTER THIRTEEN

DISPLACEMENT THEORY

AND THE NIGHT SKY—

AUGUST 1965–NOVEMBER 1966

"Come on. Don't you dare quit on me now." Lyla pumped the gas pedal as she turned the key from the *off* position to the *on*. Off. On. Off. On. The engine refused to turn over.

Instead, it screeched with each turn of the key—a noise so abrasive it startled the elderly man standing at the pump in front of her. He actually let go of the pump handle and put his hands over his ears as though air raid sirens had just gone off.

After the sixth or seventh try, the man turned around and shook his fist, yelling something at Lyla that she couldn't hear.

Sorry, she mouthed, and hesitantly turned the key again. She was a little embarrassed to keep at it, but what was she supposed to do? Sit out here all day? Wherever *here* was.

Again, she goosed the gas pedal.

Again, the car whined, and a thin stream of steam started to seep out from under the hood.

"No. No. No. This can't be happening." Lyla finally pulled the key out of the ignition and sat back in the driver's seat.

Just yesterday, she had filled the coolant before she crossed the Nevada state line into Utah, where the station attendant—who had to be eighty-five years old and had no teeth—filled up her radiator and pointed to a couple of buzzards feeding off something on the side of the highway. Their red beaks dug into the dead meat.

"Dinnertime," the attendant said with a gummy laugh, then slammed her hood back in place.

Lyla had watched the birds, thinking it was lucky she hadn't taken her mother's clunker out to college, or she too might be stuck sitting on the side of the road, cooking in the hot sun. Lyla's mother had been hurt when she refused her offer to take the family car to Chicago.

"That thing? Are you kidding me? I'd rather ride my bike," Lyla had said, and continued to scan the classifieds.

Lyla was going to do this on her own. Buy a car and get herself out to college. She didn't need her mother's help. Or worse, to feel indebted. The next week, she bought her very first car, a green 1960 Chevy Impala, and packed her belongings in the trunk.

On the morning she left, Lyla had rolled down her window and held her mother's hand. "Don't worry, Mom. I've got this," Lyla had said, even if she wasn't totally sure of her decision to go live in the Midwest. All Lyla knew was that she wanted to get out of the house, out of California altogether. She wanted a new place to call home, and the University of Chicago was the first to accept her, even if her mother thought it too far and too cold in the winters, and had told Lyla she wasn't meant for that kind of cold, that she would be sorry for leaving all this beautiful sunshine. As if the warmth of the sun was what mattered most.

"Well, drive safe, sweetheart." Her mother handed her a map that highlighted Lyla's entire route to Chicago, rest stops and all. "And don't take any wooden nickels."

Lyla rolled her eyes at her mother's old joke—the one her mother told even when Lyla was simply going to the market to pick up some milk. Lyla honked her horn as she pulled out of the driveway, but when she rounded the corner, she shoved the map in the glove box.

Lyla blasted the radio with the windows rolled down, her black hair going wild in the wind. Just before turning onto Highway 80, as highlighted on her mother's map, she continued south on Highway 101, over the Golden Gate Bridge to San Francisco. She had over a week until orientation, and she wanted to say goodbye to some old high school friends before she left California. Lyla had only meant to spend the night, but things got a little out of hand, as they sometimes did with her friends. She ended up spending the weekend at an old Victorian that was crammed full of a raft of roommates and visitors and strangers, some smoking peyote, others dancing naked on the roof or reading poetry, or just plain sleeping to the buzzing sounds of the city. One night, as she lay on the tar paper rooftop near dawn with a pile of warm bodies around her, Lyla almost decided to quit the idea of going to college altogether. How easy it would be to just stay and smoke pot and make love to anyone and everyone. To slip into the city and disappear. And not tell her mother. Or her grandmother.

In the loose, dreamy haze of her high, Lyla slowly traced the faint outline of Orion in the night sky, just as her father had done with her over a decade ago, when she'd lie on his chest and they'd connect the hallmark stars of the mighty giant in the sky, her hand in his. Together, their fingers would trail the stars of the huntsman's club, his belt, and his sword. Her father had taught her the myth of Orion. How it came to pass that Zeus had placed Orion up in the sky and how Oenopion had blinded the huntsman for violating his daughter.

"Violating?" Lyla had asked as a little girl.

"You know. Not being very nice. Hurting someone."

Little Lyla had blanched at the thought.

"Why would somebody do that? On purpose?" At that point, intentional harm was as foreign to her as mung beans.

Her father had gone on to tell her that Orion ultimately recovered his sight but boasted about having the strength to fell every animal that came before him. How invincible he thought he was. "But in the end, it was just the sting of an itty-bitty scorpion that killed him."

It was all so fantastic, especially when her father would suddenly stand up in a start and slay the air with his pretend sword as he told Orion's story, killing imaginary beasts large and small.

But now, without her father's finger guiding her and in her altered state, Lyla had to reach far, far back into her memory bank to recite the brightest stars that formed the distinctive hourglass pattern in the sky.

"Rigel, Betelgeuse, Bellatrix, and Saiph." Her lazy finger traced the stars but suddenly stopped when she saw something moving steadily across the night sky. It was neither a meteor shower nor the tail of a lone comet, but a collection of stars literally driving across the sky above.

Lyla rubbed her tired, drugged eyes as the starry outline of her Chevy Impala came into focus. Lying on the rooftop, she could see it as clear as day. Her car—with its hardtop and space-age tailfins, its enormous steering wheel and the knobs on the radio—slowly drove west to east. A gathering of small stars lined the way like lights on a landing strip. In Lyla's hallucination, her smiling mother was right there, chasing after Lyla, waving goodbye with a sack lunch in one hand and a map in the other.

"Jeannie, wake up." Lyla leaned over to her best friend, who was sprawled naked next to her. "Take a look at this."

Jeannie's eyelids roused only halfway, but under the heavy weight of drugs and deep sleep, she rolled back over and began snoring again, her face covered with imprints of the pebbled rooftop.

"Wake up." Lyla poked her friend, but Jeannie was already dead asleep in the arms of a stranger who lay next to her, who was wearing nothing but a puka shell necklace and a flower stuck in his long auburn hair.

"Oh, forget it." Lyla rolled back over, but when she looked up, her car was gone. She kicked Jeannie's heavy leg off of her and sat up. Lyla knew she was seeing things, knew she should just lie back down and sleep it off. But she didn't. In a rush, Lyla gathered her clothes in her arms, stole her way downstairs, and ran out the front door with little more than her underwear on. She found her car parked blocks away. She leaned against its door and stuffed her cold legs into her jeans, one clumsy foot at a time, not minding the city bus that rolled by. She only cared about sticking to the plan. Chicago was calling. She had seen it in the stars.

That was nearly three days ago now, and now here she was out in the middle of nowhere. Lyla blew her bangs out of her eyes, trying to figure out which was worse—the steam spilling out of the hood, the intolerable sound of the engine, or the fact that she'd have to call her mother and admit that she hadn't made it to Chicago, that she had gotten a little waylaid. None of it was particularly promising, especially being stuck out here amongst the dry, sun-beaten landscape and grasslands that seemed to stretch on forever.

"Oh, for Christ's sake." Lyla put the key back in the ignition and waited for the old man at the pump in front of her to get back into his car. When he drove away, she'd give it another go. Until then, she rested her chin on the steering wheel. Behind the station was a ridge of long, craggy cliffs with big white letters painted on the red rock face.

PB.

Lyla dug deep into her memory of fourth-grade geography, when they had to memorize all fifty states and their capitals, state flowers, and mottos. But with Wyoming, she drew a blank. "PB, PB?" she repeated.

She leaned over and pulled the map out of the glove box, the one her mother had given her with highlighted stars marking where she should stop for the night and smiley faces where she should enjoy lunch or dinner. Circling the city of Chicago were hand-drawn concentric rings with electric-bolted arrows pointing toward the University of Chicago.

Lyla unfolded the map, a bit thankful her mother had such little faith in her.

She ran her finger along Highway 80, searching for a Wyoming town with the initials *PB*, and just then, there was a knock on her window. Outside, the service attendant was mouthing something behind the glass. His eyes darted to the back seat—perhaps expecting somebody to be sleeping back there—then to the front passenger seat, until, at last, his bright, welcoming brown eyes settled upon her. He cranked at an invisible window handle.

"Sorry." Lyla rolled down her window. Hot Wyoming wind rushed in. "What were you trying to say?"

"I think your starter relay has gone bad. No doubt, your car has overheated, but I think the bigger problem is your starter. Here, try her again."

Lyla knew the engine wouldn't turn over, but the attendant was kind of cute and had the eager smile of those adorable baby caimans she'd seen on that nature show, the one she watched with Al just before she left. And those eyes! They were the eyes of milk chocolate. God, the thought of it made her mouth water. What she'd give for a sliver of chocolate right about now! It had been hours since she last ate.

Lyla turned the key and gave a single pump to the gas pedal. But the engine did nothing more now than make a pathetic *wah, wah, wah* sound before it cut out completely.

"Or"—the attendant wiped his hands on a greasy rag and smiled—"it could just be a dead battery. But I'll bet a month's wages, it's the starter. Did you hear how she fought to kick over like a broken horse before she gave out? Sometimes it's just best to shoot her, if you know what I mean." The attendant stuffed his work rag into the back pocket of his overalls and smiled that sweet smile of his.

"Excuse me?" Lyla wasn't about to kill her car.

"Here, let me tell you what I'm going to do."

He spat a wad of something over his shoulder. Tobacco? Phlegm? Lyla refused to look.

"First, I'll try to jump her, and if that doesn't do the job, I'll throw in some coolant and check the starter on Monday."

"Monday?" Lyla looked at her watch. She was supposed to check into her dormitory by Sunday evening.

"I'll need to order the part. Should only take a week. Then we can get her all fixed up and send you on your way."

"A week?" Lyla repeated. It wasn't really a question. Across the street, a tumbleweed rolled down the highway. He couldn't be serious. A week in this place?

"'Til then, California, I suppose you'll be making our little town home for a while."

Lyla blurted out a laugh. She didn't mean to sound smart, but really? Other than the garage, there wasn't anything in sight, not even a general store, let alone a town.

"Don't worry." The attendant smiled and spat again. "You haven't gotten to the turnoff quite yet. Pine Bluffs is still a mile down the highway." He jutted out his chin in the general direction of *town*.

"Oh, okay." Lyla was relieved. There would be no way to explain it to her mother when she called home. *Hey, Mom, guess what? I didn't make it to one of your asterisks. I decided to camp out in Wyoming instead.* Plus, Lyla would run out of money soon. She needed to get to Chicago where her grandmother had already wired her first semester's room and board and a little spending money. Collect on arrival. It was her grandmother's way of making sure Lyla did what she said she'd do.

"Come on. Let's push her over there, so I can take a quick peek under the hood." The attendant unexpectedly leaned in through her car window and grabbed the steering column shifter.

Lyla leaned back as he put the car in neutral. He smelled like two-day-old sweat.

"Okay, go ahead and take your foot off the brake," he instructed.

As he tested the steering wheel, Lyla noticed a pale scar running down from the back of his right ear before it hooked left and continued down the side of his neck. She almost reached out to touch it, when he said, "Okay, now just steer her like normal." He ran around the back of the car and yelled, "Nothing fancy! Just straight on over to the garage."

Lyla released the brake and steered her car, feeling a bit silly, and a little guilty, as she sat behind the wheel while he was out there in the heat of the day, pushing her slowly across the asphalt. That was, until he yelled, "And don't hit anything, will ya?"

Lyla wanted to lean out the window and tell him that she had just driven all the way from California by herself, *thank you very much.* But then, remembering how his eyes had darted around her car to see if she had a traveling companion, she thought it best not to let him know that she was going at it alone. When she got out of the car, she'd lie and say she was meeting her fiancé in Chicago. They were moving into their new home.

"Okay, now throw her in park," he instructed as she steered into the mouth of the garage. "You know, the one with the *P.*" He smiled.

Lyla closed her eyes and sucked in her breath. *Just 'til Monday,* she said to herself. Then she'd be out of here. Then she could get on with her life.

She pulled the keys out of the ignition and reached over to grab her purse from the floor of the passenger seat. And when she sat back up, she snuck a quick peek in the mirror.

"Jesus," she said. Her long, dirty hair hung in her face in a tangle of loose curls. She hadn't bothered running a comb through it that morning when she woke up in the back seat of the car. It had been days since her last shower.

Lyla tied up her hair with a rubber band and slid on a dash of lipstick. And when she straightened the mirror back into place, she saw the mechanic was doing the same, coiffing. He tried, though unsuccessfully, to wipe the grease from his hands onto his coveralls. And just before she opened the car door, he quickly spat into his hands and smoothed back his blond hair. He then cupped his hands in front of his mouth and exhaled, smelling his breath. As if!

Yes, Lyla thought. *I will definitely have to lie. I have a fiancé. I have a fiancé. I have a fiancé,* she repeated to herself as she grabbed her purse and threw open the car door.

"My name's Hap." The attendant raced around the car and held the door open. "Here you go, ma'am."

Lyla held out her hand, but Hap quickly held up his hands like he was under arrest.

"Oh, I don't think you want to touch these greasy things. Not unless you want to be put to work."

"Oh, right." Lyla slung her purse over her shoulder and looked around for a telephone booth.

"Anyhow, welcome to Pine Bluffs."

"Oh. So that's what the *PB* stands for." Lyla laughed. "I thought it stood for peanut butter."

Hap stood in the hot sun, looking at her as though she were speaking Chinese. Lyla pointed to the plateau out beyond the service station. "You know, the big white letters over on the hillside. Peanut Butter, Wyoming?" she joked.

"Oh, yeah," he said. "They just put those stupid things up a couple of months ago. Still not used to them. Sort of an eyesore, if you ask me. Anyhow, let's have a look under the hood and see what's bothering her. Shall we?" Lyla followed Hap around to the front of the car, finding it strange he kept calling the car a *her*.

That her beat-up Chevrolet Impala might have actual feelings?

Or a vagina?

Hap lifted the hood and fitted the metal rod in place. He took the dirty rag out of his back pocket and slowly twisted the radiator cap. Lyla leaned over his shoulder as though she had a clue about engines. For all she knew, she could be looking inside a typewriter.

"Feel free to wait inside." He turned and smiled. "We have the AC on."

Standing this close to him, she could smell the Wintermint Certs on his breath.

"You wouldn't mind?" Lyla blew her bangs out of her eyes again. "I am a little overheated myself."

"No, ma'am. Go on, make yourself comfortable. I'll come in and get you when I figure out what's wrong with her."

There it was again, calling the car a her. As if only females needed fixing.

"Is there a bathroom I can use? I'm about to burst."

"Around back," he said, running his hand over the hot engine as if he were feeling for *her* problem.

"Okay, thanks. I'll be right back."

Around the far side of the garage sat a pile of junk heaped up against the wall—crumpled-up beer cans, bald tires, a rusted car door with the window broken out, a jumble of loose wires that looked like robot intestines, and a raft of gunked-up machine parts. Sitting at the top of the mess was an old *Playboy* magazine with Miss December on the cover. Lyla had seen this issue before. Al chronically left his magazines lying around in the bathrooms at home, dog-eared and well scoured, forever claiming the articles *were really well written. Good reads. Educational.*

There she was again, Miss December dressed in a terribly revealing Santa's helper outfit, her arms held overhead after having joyfully broken out of a large Christmas present. In a ballpoint pen, someone had scribbled, *Come and get me, big boy*, in a thought bubble next to her merry face. Lyla wondered if the artistic additions were Hap's doing.

"What a creep," Lyla said as she grabbed hold of the door handle with a fold of her shirt. She started to pull the door open when she noticed a note taped to the door. *Stop! Broken lock. Knock first!*

Lyla was fairly certain that nobody was in the bathroom—there wasn't another car in the lot—but she did as she was told. She rapped on the metal door with her car keys and waited, looking behind her to make sure that Hap character wasn't up to any funny business with the broken lock and all.

"Hello, anybody in there?" Lyla knocked a little louder, and when nobody emerged or told her to hold on, she hauled the door open and held her breath, half expecting the bathroom to smell like weeks-old urine, for there to be no toilet paper left on the roll, or to be greeted with lewd salutations written in the same ballpoint pen and phone numbers of where to call for a good time.

But when she flicked on the light, the bathroom was immaculate. The walls had been freshly painted a pale lilac color. There was even a fake silk flower in a vase beside the faucet handles and a scented candle on the back of the toilet. Lyla propped the trash can against the door, now wondering if perhaps Hap was married, if his wife was responsible for all this. But then, remembering the way Hap had checked his breath before she got out of the car, she was pretty sure Hap was no married man.

When she finished, Lyla washed up, splashed a little water on her face, and combed her hair. And this time she opened the door with her bare hand and walked back over to the garage.

"Well, California." He let the hood slam back in place and then wiped his upper lip with the blue bandana tied around his neck. "Looks like you'll be here for a bit." He reached into the icebox and grabbed two cold sodas, offering one to Lyla. "At least until I get the parts delivered."

Lyla took the cold soda can and pulled the tab off. "What kind of parts are we talking about?" she asked, twirling the aluminum ring tab around her finger, calculating the money left in her wallet and whether she'd need to call her grandmother and ask for a little advance to tide her over.

"First off, you'll need a new starter relay. That's a given. I'll have to get the boys to send one down from Cheyenne. But your fan belt is darn near fried. Won't be long until it starts hollering too. Anyhow, it shouldn't take long to fix them both once I get the parts. Until then, I called my sister, and she said you are welcome to sleep on the couch for a bit, if you'd like."

"She wouldn't mind?" Lyla took a sip of the soda. The cold fizz felt refreshing on such a hot, dusty day.

"Are you kidding? My sister's like Mother Teresa. If you give me a few minutes, I can drive you over myself. I'm just about to close up shop, anyhow."

Lyla looked at her watch. It was only three thirty p.m. in the afternoon, awfully early to close down, but what was she going to do? Haul her luggage down the highway?

Outside, the dried wheatgrass and pockets of bitterbrush were being beaten in the afternoon wind. And the heat? Lyla wasn't cut out for this kind of weather. She was used to wet fog pouring over the coastal mountains in the afternoons, sunshine that didn't cook like this. She was dirty and tired, and all she really wanted to do was take a long, cold shower.

"No funny business?" Lyla asked, probing Hap's eyes, searching for something that would give his intentions away. Anything strange, and she promised herself she'd call a cab or hitchhike her way out of there.

Hap held two dirty fingers up to his forehead. "Scout's honor."

"All right then." Lyla glanced back at the white letters on the rock face. "Show me the way to Pine Bluffs."

"With pleasure." Hap smiled, then stuck two fingers in his mouth and whistled. "Come on, Emma. We've got ourselves some company." A thick golden retriever bounded out of the garage and jumped her front legs up onto Hap's chest. Hap took Emma's paws into his hands and did a little two-step dance as he bent over and kissed his dog on her nose. "Oh, I love you too." He tossed Emma's paws to the ground and slapped the dog on her backside. "Come on, girl. Let's go."

Lyla stood awkwardly. She wasn't sure if he was talking to her or his dog.

Hap opened the door to his truck and turned to Lyla. "Don't worry. We don't bite."

When Hap pulled up to the front of his sister's house, Lyla was surprised to see a blue clapboard single-story house, simple and clearly well cared-for. There were terraced flower beds, a terra-cotta sun nailed by the front door, and an American flag hanging off the porch. The house seemed pleasant enough.

Definitely not the home of some psychopath, Lyla thought. Though what did she know about psychopaths? She had called her mother *psycho* plenty, mostly joking. But Lyla was on guard. Who knew if Hap even had a sister? What if he lived there alone and this was all a trap? She took in the house again; it looked like the home of a little old lady, not a psychotic car mechanic from the Cowboy State who was ready to cut out her kidneys.

Lyla unbuckled her lap belt and opened the car door. "It's nice," she said as she watched Emma run up the front steps. She got out of the truck.

Across the street was a more dilapidated house, with the paint peeling off the sides and the torn curtains flapping out of the dark living room window. And there, behind the chain-link fence, a little girl stood in the front yard, holding a dirty doll on her hip and talking gibberish as she paced the dead lawn. The barefoot girl couldn't have been more than seven years old; she looked like one of those Vietnamese refugees that Lyla had seen on the television in her motel room a couple nights ago. The girl's black hair was cut in blunt chops around the face, the rest hanging in uneven tangles, and she appeared to be wearing nothing more than an oversized men's T-shirt that read, *Just another beer drinker with a fishing problem.*

The girl stopped and eyed Lyla.

Lyla smiled and waved, but the girl didn't wave back. She stood there with the doll on her hip, taking stock of Lyla as if she were another social worker ready to take her away. Behind her was a plastic pool filled with a couple of inflatable toys that circled around. The hose that snaked its way from the side of the house was draped into the pool. Water was sloshing out.

"Clara Jean!" a voice yelled out from the inside of the dark house. "Turn off the hose and git in here now." Still, the girl didn't move. She watched Lyla with the hard, firm stare of somebody who was used to the smell of change.

Standing there, Lyla regretted her decision. What in the hell was she doing here? Why hadn't she just checked into a motel? Why did she so readily accept Hap's offer to stay at his sister's house?

She was about to walk over to the girl and ask if that was her mother at home. To tell her she needed a phone. But then there was Hap with his bright, wide smile as he took hold of her suitcase.

"Don't worry, California. We're good people. You don't have to worry."

As his hand brushed hers, Lyla wanted to believe she could feel his goodness, that he was just an honest man lending a hand.

"Sorry. I guess I'm just a little tired." Lyla looked at the pale scar running down Hap's neck and followed him inside the house, promising she'd call for a cab the minute things got weird. Hap bounded up the steps after Emma. He held the screen door open, and when Lyla looked back across the street, the girl was gone. The yard was empty except for a plastic grocery bag stuck in the cottonwood tree and the inflatable plastic dolphin swimming around in circles in the hot Wyoming wind.

That first year Lyla lived with Hap and Mary-Ellen, they went everywhere together—to parties, to the drive-ins, out to the lake. The three of them huddled up in the cab of Hap's truck like happy siblings with Emma sitting in the back; she rested her head over the front seat and blew hot dog breath in Lyla's ear. Lyla and Mary-Ellen would press their sweaty bare feet against the windshield of Hap's truck.

"God, California. You've got some damn ugly toes. Did you know that?" Hap said one November evening as he rolled onto the highway and headed out to the lake. Air rushed through the truck's open windows. It was unseasonably warm out, but a swim, as far as Lyla was concerned, was a no-go, despite what Hap had pressed for earlier.

"Seriously." Hap cracked open a beer. "Those may be the ugliest things I've ever seen."

Mary-Ellen reached over and slugged her brother on the shoulder. "You can just shut your mouth right now, you moron. I think Lyla's got lovely toes."

It was a lie, of course. Lyla's middle toes were a good inch longer than the others and crooked, each hooked toward the big toe as though they had been broken and not properly set.

"Oh, come off it, M.E. They look like antlers." Hap took his hands off the wheel and held his fat fingers over his head like a five-pronged elk. "Look at me. Watch me pull a rabbit out of my hat," he joked, sounding like Bullwinkle. They often watched *Rocky and Bullwinkle* together when they were too hungover to do much of anything else. He grabbed the steering wheel and righted it back into the lane.

"Shut up." Lyla grabbed his beer and took a sip.

"I mean really, how do you even find shoes that fit properly? What do you have to do, cut out a peephole for those things?"

"Albert Eugene!" Mary-Ellen shouted. "That is enough."

Lyla sprayed a mouthful of beer across the cab. "Albert Eugene?" She pulled her bare feet off the windshield and sat up straighter in the cab. "Wait, you are telling me that your given name is Albert Eugene? And you're making fun of my toes?"

Hap snatched the beer back and took a careful sip as he turned onto the bumpy forest service road. His high beams bounced off the thick, towering trunks of the ponderosa pines.

"Wow, you've got some nerve. Albert Eugene." Lyla repeated his name in a squeaky, high-pitched voice. "Albert Eugene, Albert Eugene, Al Gene. Get it? Algae."

Neither Hap nor Mary-Ellen laughed. They sat in the cab stone-cold as the truck jiggled down the washboard of the dirt road.

Lyla snagged the beer back and took another swig. "Thanks, Albert Eugene Richards."

Hap slammed the brakes. Because Lyla was not wearing a lap belt, she lurched forward and rammed up against the windshield. Beer sprayed everywhere. Emma flew against the driver's seat and yelped.

"What the hell was that for, Bert?" Lyla asked. This time she wasn't trying to be funny. She was mad, and her shoulder hurt. "Jesus. What the fuck?"

Hap didn't answer, so Lyla looked over at Mary-Ellen. "What's wrong with him?"

Hap's sister sat there, concentrating hard on the forest road ahead as though they were lost in a blizzard.

"Hello? Is anybody going to answer me? What's going on?"

Hap sat behind the wheel as the engine hummed, his eyes tracking the woods lit by his headlights.

"Is something out there?" Lyla asked. Goose bumps crawled up her neck. "What is it? What's wrong?"

Hap finally turned to her. "Nobody calls me by that name." His jaw tightened. "Nobody but my sister and Uncle Sam. Got it?"

"Aye, aye." Lyla saluted. It was the first time since she had moved to Wyoming that she had seen Hap anything but lighthearted. He was always popping off jokes like a toy gun.

Hap spat a long string of tobacco into the empty can wedged between his thighs. "I'll let that one slide, Lyla, but don't ever call me by that name again. Do you copy?" He gripped the steering wheel. "And second. Those are still the ugliest damn toes I've ever seen." Hap shifted the car back to drive and continued toward the lake, swerving around the deep potholes in the forest road.

Lyla pressed her feet back up against the windshield and wriggled them. "I have to admit, I hate my toes. My father had the same damn ugly feet. As a kid, I used to run to him every time I stubbed my toes, screaming, 'It's your fault,' wishing he could just cut them off as he sat me on the countertop and bandaged them. They are ugly; they're just awful." Suddenly embarrassed, Lyla tucked her feet underneath her, leaving a foggy impression of her toes on the glass—two unexpected *i*'s that faded away.

"Well, I think they're just beautiful." Mary-Ellen finally turned and smiled at Lyla.

And just like that, they returned to normal, Hap being the jokester and Mary-Ellen being the protector.

They were kin now.

They were *family.*

Sleeping on Hap and Mary-Ellen's couch that first week after her car had broken down, Lyla knew she wouldn't make it to Chicago, that week or the next. She had had no trouble calling her mother to tell her about a slight change in plans. She wasn't going to study psychology. She wasn't going to become a doctor. She had decided she was going to become a cowgirl. Maybe even work at a dude ranch.

"You mean you want to shovel shit?" her mother had asked, her exasperation traveling through the telephone lines that spanned across three states.

"I've been doing that all my life," Lyla had said, hanging up the phone before her mother could say anything else. To be honest, Lyla had never really wanted to go to college in the first place—that had been her mother and grandmother's grand plan. What Lyla had really wanted was to simply get out of California. To start something new. To breathe clean and deep for the very first time. The summer before she left, Lyla had read about the wide expanse of Wyoming's landscape, a sky that stretched on forever, jackrabbits the size of mules, and fishing for trout that could outweigh a small child. And the grizzlies! What she wouldn't do to see a grizzly bear or bighorn sheep! Let alone the ranch hands.

In the end, despite her blue jeans, boots, and newly purchased cowboy hat, Lyla didn't become a cowgirl or date a ranch hand. She became a waitress, earning $1.25 an hour, plus tips. And she was terribly happy. Hap and Mary-Ellen had welcomed her home.

Later that night at the lake, as Hap went off with Emma to take a pee in the woods, Mary-Ellen and Lyla lay side by side with a wool blanket over them. They shared a cigarette, taking long, deep drags under the clean light of the stars.

"Why didn't you ever carry on?" Mary-Ellen asked.

"Huh?"

"After Hap fixed your car. Why didn't you continue on to Chicago? Or go back home?"

The thought of going home zapped her like she'd touched a socket. "Simple." Lyla exhaled a thick smoke cloud. "The minute I stepped foot in your house, there was nowhere else I wanted to be."

"But isn't Pine Bluffs too small for a city girl like yourself?" Mary-Ellen propped herself up on her elbows and blew a stray hair out of her eyes. Mary-Ellen was far shorter than Lyla's five foot eleven. Mary-Ellen was a bit thick, had a flat pink face, curly hair, and small hands. She wasn't a classic beauty but strong as an anvil and had a huge heart. That was the kind of beauty Lyla admired.

"City girl? I'm not a city girl."

"Oh, you know what I mean. You had a chance to go to Chicago. God, what I wouldn't give to get the hell out of here sometimes, to go live in a city with all those people and drown myself in all that noise."

The lake was dark and calm; stars twinkled bright on its mirror. Lyla almost told Mary-Ellen about her father and what he did. To himself.

To her.

"I don't know." Lyla sighed. "I guess going to Chicago or going back home didn't seem right after seeing the magic of all this." Lyla took another drag on the cigarette. "Both carrying on or going back felt like wearing a too-tight coat. Neither option seemed to fit. Either the sleeves were too short or I was too fat, unable to button the damn thing up. You know what I mean?"

Mary-Ellen reached over and fiddled with the corkscrews in Lyla's hair. "You're funny, Lyla. 'A too-tight coat.' I'll have to remember that one."

Then, underneath the wide night sky and Hap taking a walkabout in the woods with Emma, Mary-Ellen told Lyla the story of how their parents died in a car accident when Hap was in his last year of high school. How their father, a terrible drunk, had slammed head-on into an elk. Mary-Ellen was only nineteen at the time. She had just graduated high school, and overnight she became Hap's legal guardian.

"Just like that." Mary-Ellen snapped, the sound echoing over the lake like a skipped rock over water. "I became his mother *and* his sister."

"Oh my God. Mary-El. I'm so sorry." Lyla knew her words rang terribly hollow. She'd always hated it when her parents' friends told Lyla they were *sorry* her father died. *Sorry for what?* Lyla would blurt out when she was younger. *You didn't put the rope around his neck, did you?* Lyla liked the *did you* part. She learned to throw that bit in when she was old enough to figure out how to get people to just shut up and leave her alone.

But now, with Mary-Ellen at her side and the collection of small twigs caught in her hair and tiny pebbles pushing up against her spine, those five letters of an apology seemed like all she had to offer.

"I'd just been accepted to a nursing school." Mary-Ellen took another drag off the cigarette; she held the smoke deep in her lungs before slowly letting it out. "I asked Hap to finish out high school in Casper with our uncle. 'Don't be such a baby,' I told him. But one look in Hap's eyes and I knew I had no choice. He needed me to stay. So I did. And—" Mary-Ellen blew a series of smoke rings in the air. She turned onto her side and began tracing a finger across Lyla's face, connecting the freckles along the bridge of her nose. "Well, here I am." She handed the nub of the cigarette to Lyla. "I mean, here we are. You, me, Emma, and good ol' Hapster. Happy as clams."

Lyla took one last drag, letting Mary-Ellen outline her facial features as she told the rest of her and Hap's sad story. Even before their parents died, Mary-Ellen was the one who watched over Hap. Their mother was useless. "She was just a mouse skittering along the baseboards of the house. And dear old dad was a mean drunk, always taking it out on poor Hap."

Mary-Ellen stopped touching Lyla's face.

"Dad used to sneak up on Hap and burn his back with cigarettes. Calling him a girl when Hap refused to fight back. 'What's the matter with you, Albert Eugene, you're nothing but a goddamned sissy? You too scared to fight, Albert Eugene?' He'd spit out Hap's legal name like wet tobacco. But Hap knew better. He always walked away. He'd go to his room and lock the door. I'd hear him through the heating vent, though, sobbing and punching his pillow. Screaming how he hated our father. Saying he wanted to kill him. That's when I started to stand on my desk and sing songs to him through the heating vent until he fell asleep. Sometimes I'd sing stupid church songs, but mostly I'd just hum for hours until I could hear him softly snoring."

Lyla snubbed out their cigarette in the dirt and tossed it aside, suddenly connecting the dots as to why Hap grew so cold earlier. "God, no wonder Hap doesn't like that name. No wonder he made such a fuss."

"Frankly, I'm surprised he never changed it, legally, I mean," Mary-Ellen said. "My father's name was Albert too. At some point, my brother began to only answer to Hap, which really pissed my father off. But then Hap started getting bigger and stronger than him. And dear old dad didn't like it one bit. Honestly, I think he was scared of Hap. And the more scared my dad got, the meaner he became."

Lyla had the whole picture in her mind: the layout of the house; Hap's father stumbling home late at night, slamming the screen door, the drywall beaten by the throw of the door; their mother hiding in the kitchen; Hap on the couch in his tank top and jeans, his biceps bulging like grapefruits. The yelling, the fighting. The crying. It was all there, clear as night.

"And once"—Mary-Ellen's voice suddenly, but quietly, broke the silence—"when things got really bad between them, I stepped in front of my brother when Dad was swinging a baseball bat around the living room, drunk as shit, trying to scare the piss out of Hap. I thought he'd knock it off. But he kept on swinging, telling me to get the hell out of the way. When I didn't move, he cracked that bat on my arm. Broke my wrist clean in two." Mary-Ellen held her arm overhead, the knob on her wrist poking out oddly, something Lyla only now noticed.

"God, he was such an asshole," Mary-Ellen concluded.

"Sounds like it might be a good thing he isn't around anymore?" Lyla was surprised she could say such a thing.

"It is. I'm glad he died. He wasn't worth shit." Mary-Ellen let out a long breath.

In the silence that fell afterward, Lyla rolled over and spooned Mary-El, marveling at the expanse of sky out here. It was so much bigger, bolder. Cleaner. In the midnight sky, Orion splayed above them. The constellation she'd loved as a child looked so much greater out here too.

Lyla took Mary-Ellen's small hand in hers and began tracing the belt on the huntsman's waist, his sword, his shield. "My dad and I used to sit under the stars like this," Lyla said, breaking the quiet space between them. "He told me how Zeus sent Orion up into the sky as a constellation, rising and setting with the sun to be used by those down here to reckon the time of night."

Mary-Ellen let Lyla guide her hands, her breath calm, her glassy eyes as still as the water across the lake.

"No matter where you are on Earth in the wintertime," Lyla said in the slow, steady voice of her father, "Orion will rise above your eastern horizon in the early evening and move westward until it stands directly above you in the middle of the night. And just before dawn, he will hang over your western horizon."

It is always the same, Lyla bird, her father had said so long ago. *So, if you ever lose your watch come winter, you can count the distance of Orion's journey to find your way to morning.*

Lyla had thought her father was just being silly. She wasn't going to get lost. Like Hap, her father was always fooling around. But now, under the wide November Wyoming sky, Lyla wondered how she'd ever doubted her father. The pattern in the night sky was so clear, so obvious. Lyla wrapped her arm around Mary-El's chest like a seat belt.

"Our dad wasn't always such a jerk; he could be fun sometimes," Mary-Ellen whispered. "But when Hap snuck into my room that night and we fell asleep in my bed, my arm in a cast, I swore I'd always look out for him. Hap's a good guy, Lyla. But he'll always need me. There's no getting around it."

Something in the way Mary-El confided in her made Lyla a little sick.

Behind them, they heard a whistle. And that was the last Mary-Ellen spoke of their upbringing. That night or ever. And Lyla knew, without ever having to ask, the scar running down Hap's neck was no accident.

"Hello, my lovely ladies." Hap returned from the truck with a second woolen blanket. He laid it over their bodies and crawled in between them, just wearing his jeans and boots. His naked chest felt stone-cold. He leaned over and kissed his sister first, then Lyla on the forehead, and together they fell asleep in the warmth of each other's arms with Emma keeping watch.

Lyla woke briefly later in the night and smiled at how Mary-Ellen rested her arm over Hap's naked chest, pulling him close to her, and how Hap leaned into the crook of his sister's neck, snoring softly like a child.

Overhead, Orion had tilted far to the west.

Lyla could no longer find his sword or his shield. Unknown constellations filled the near-dawn sky—black holes, burned-out stars, and probably faraway myths that her father had never spoken of, never had the time to teach her about before he left. She rolled back over and folded her body around the back of Hap's, stealing the heat of his bare skin as he stole the heat from his sister. Lyla drew in a deep breath. For the first time since moving to Wyoming, she knew she had found her way home. She was right where she was supposed to be. Under the big bright Wyoming sky, wearing a coat that finally fit just right.

CHAPTER FOURTEEN

CLEAR AS ICE—FEBRUARY 1967

W hen the snow fell in Laramie County, it dropped from the sky fast as salt or swirled around like small paper plates. Either way, it was cold. So cold Lyla's eyelashes froze shut the first winter she lived in the Cowboy State. It had barely registered above five degrees that December. January wasn't much better. There was no getting used to it, Lyla had come to believe, despite local assurances.

Even now, over a year later, with a closet filled with thick puffy jackets, scarves, woolen hats, and the warmth of Hap's arms since they had started dating, Lyla remained dumbfounded by the bitterness of a Wyoming winter. She wasn't cut out for this kind of cold. She was from California.

And recently, she'd started thinking about moving home.

"Ready, California?" He and Lyla lay side by side on the carpet, wrestling cross-legged while Mary-Ellen packed her suitcase. Hap's sister was headed to Denver for the weekend, her annual getaway with work friends, girlfriends who had become Lyla's friends too. Looking at the hoar frost gathering on the window, Lyla couldn't help but wish she could go along. She needed a girls' weekend. Plus, Denver had reached above freezing for five days in a row now. It was practically balmy over there.

"One, two!" Hap counted. Emma jumped off the bed, her tail wagging as she barked. On three, Hap and Lyla each hooked a leg around the other's, trying to force it to the ground. Hap won every time. At six foot three, he was four inches taller than Lyla, and cowboy strong. He could wrestle a steer to the ground with those thighs alone, Lyla knew, because he always gave her a good hold down with those thighs, especially whenever they messed around in bed.

"When will you be back again?" Lyla pushed Hap off of her and sat up, adjusting the skirt that had inched up her waist and the tights that had wormed sideways.

Emma lay down and rested her head across Hap's lap, and he, in turn, stroked her coat, rubbing his thumbs on the backs of her ears. He bent over to kiss her on the head. Lyla envied that kind of attention. Lately, Hap had seemed more in love with Emma than her.

"Monday," Mary-El said. "By dinnertime at the latest." Mary-Ellen held a spaghetti strap top up to the mirror. "What do you think?"

"A tank top?" Hap reached for the ashtray sitting on his sister's bed, holding Emma's head still in his lap. "You're not going to Florida. It's cold as shit in Denver too."

"Yeah. But it's not like I'm going skiing, you moron. They have heated movie theaters, restaurants, and museums."

"Museums? Spare me." Hap laughed. "You haven't stepped foot in a museum since the fourth-grade field trip to Cheyenne."

"Oh, hush it. You have no idea what we do on our girls' trips."

"I have a pretty good idea. And it ain't going to museums."

"Well, nobody asked for your opinion." Mary-El yanked off her T-shirt and slid on the tank top. She turned and modeled it. "Yes? No?"

"Definitely a yes." Lyla gave two thumbs up. "It looks fabulous." Lyla stood up and began fixing her own hair in the mirror. "Hey, what time is it, anyway?"

"Ten forty-five," Mary-El said.

"Oh shit." Lyla was due at work in fifteen minutes and couldn't afford to be late again. She had finally landed a full-time job as a bookkeeper at Shepard's Auto Body, Hap's old place of employment where he was fired a few months ago for pinching a twenty out of the drawer. Lyla had been hired just before his sticky-finger incident and was now under careful watch. She had already been reprimanded by the boss's wife for being late. "I gotta run," she said.

Hap leaned over and grabbed hold of Lyla's leg. Emma jumped up and barked.

"Come on," Hap pleaded. "One more round?"

"Nope. Can't." Lyla put on her heavy coat, wrapped a scarf around her neck, and tried to pull away. "We need the money, Hap. You know that."

But Hap didn't let go. He let Lyla try to drag him like a child across the floor. Emma bounced back and forth, barking with excitement.

"Come on. Three out of five? Winner takes all?" He looked up at her with those begging brown eyes, the ones his sister said he always used to get his way. Lyla used to do anything those eyes asked, but lately she was getting irritated with the way he constantly pestered her. They had only been dating for a few months, and that already seemed like an eon.

"Hap!" Mary-Ellen barked her little brother into the wide-eyed attention that only she could seem to draw out of him. "Lyla's got to go to work. You, of all people, should be able to appreciate that."

Hap let go and sat up. He grabbed Emma by the collar and brought her close. "Whatever." He then fished a cigarette out of his front pocket.

"I'll be home at five." Lyla bent over to kiss Hap on his forehead, but he refused to look up. Instead, he slouched forward, dropping his head between his raised knees. When he blew out his cigarette smoke, it rose from the sides of his legs like a venting volcano.

"Come on, let's go out tonight," Lyla said. "Just you and me. My treat."

Hap had blown through his unemployment check already, and she thought it'd be nice to do something special, just the two of them, with Mary-El leaving town and all. Plus, he'd been in such a funk after he lost his job. A night out, a real date, might just lift his spirits a bit. Hers too.

"Maybe." Hap sat up and took another drag, stroking Emma's back. "I'll see what I have going on."

"What do you mean, *maybe*? I'm offering you a night out on the town, buster. And all I get is a maybe?"

Maybe you can kiss my ass. Maybe, Lyla thought, *I should go out on my own.*

"You heard me." Hap took a deep drag on his cigarette and held it.

Mary-Ellen threw a hairbrush, hitting her brother square between the shoulder blades.

"Hey, what did you do that for?" He coughed the smoke out of his mouth.

"Because you're being an idiot, that's why. Lyla's offered to take you out, but all you can do is sit there and pout. What's gotten into you?"

"It's okay," Lyla said, putting her hair up in a loose bun.

"No, Lyla. It's not okay. My brother is being a total jerk." Mary-El walked over and kicked Hap hard in the rump. "Sit up," she ordered.

"All right, all right. I was just kidding around. But geez, just because Dad isn't here to beat up on me, you don't have to take up the slack."

"Do *not* even go there!" Mary-Ellen threw him a look that told her little brother that he knew better. "That isn't even close to funny. I'll throw you out of this house by your ear if you ever compare me to Dad again. Got it?"

Hap tapped the long ash from his cigarette into the tray. "Got it, chief."

"Now apologize."

"Okay." He snubbed out his cigarette and was smiling again. "Lyla, I'm sorry." His apology rang hollow, but it was a start at least. "What time?"

Lyla straightened her skirt and tucked a stray strand of hair behind her ears. "Six thirty?" she offered.

"Sure. I'll be waiting in the bar at Allister's."

They both knew he was pressing his luck. Allister's was for special occasions like weddings or anniversaries.

"Fat chance." Lyla blew a bubble and popped it. "I'm thinking more along the lines of Elaine's."

Hap shook his head. "Rabbit food."

"How about The Eagle's Nest then?"

"Deal. Don't be late." He slapped Lyla on the ass as she turned to walk out of the room. "I'll be real hungry by then."

Lyla didn't let him see her wide smile as she left the house, but it was there all right. Bright as the white snow falling outside. She had to admit, she liked when Hap slapped her ass like that, letting her know she was his.

Lyla did love Mary-El, but sometimes she felt stuck in a corner when it was the three of them all of the time. And if she was being honest, she slightly envied the way Hap loved and respected his sister. How he listened to her, relied on her. But sometimes their relationship puzzled Lyla too. It was a little odd, when she thought about it. Lyla couldn't ever really put a word to how she felt, but sometimes they acted like more than just siblings. Like how Mary-El changed her clothes in front of him, stripping right down to her underwear as though she were wearing a bathing suit, or how she'd sometimes curl up with Hap in his bed until he fell asleep, before Lyla became his gal. Or how Hap would reach into his underwear while standing in the kitchen making coffee and scratch his balls.

Or how they wore matching rings on their left hands.

It wasn't normal.

But then again, Lyla thought, *what do I know about normal?*

After dinner, Lyla and Hap sat in the cab of the truck and were fooling around for a bit, waiting for the heat to kick in. Hap pressed Lyla up against the cold glass. He unbuttoned the front of her coat and reached underneath her shirt.

"Come to Papa," he whispered. His hands were warm, but being pressed up against the door like this, Lyla felt icy air sneak down the back of her neck. It was the kind of cold that went straight to her bones. She pushed him away. "Stop it, Hap."

"What's wrong now?" He reached over and petted Emma on the head. Her dog breath filled the cab, fogging up the glass. Lyla didn't always love that Emma had to come with them on their dates. And she definitely didn't love Emma resting her chin over the front seat, watching the two of them while they messed around. It reminded her of the time she was caught with her high school boyfriend one afternoon when she thought her mom was out. Lyla had rolled over on her bed with Kyle's hands squarely up her shirt. Her mother stood in the doorway, watching them. Lyla had no idea how long she had been standing there, but Louise stared at them like she was witnessing a bullfight. She then simply turned away.

Without saying a word about it.

Ever.

Hap reached over and started to unzip Lyla's pants. "Come on, California. You were the one who wanted to go on a proper date."

Lyla moved his hand away. She was tired of having sex in the car. "I'm not a two-bit hooker, Hap." Lyla wanted to remind him of the way he first tended to her when they decided to tuck into this relationship. Like a proper girlfriend. Not some cheap floozy.

"Geez, you're no fun." Hap cracked open another beer—the one he'd polished off before dinner had rolled at his feet on the drive over. This fresh beer had started to freeze in the car, so Hap hit the top of the can with the butt of his hand, breaking up the layer of ice. He took a sip and wiped his mouth. "Want some?" He handed the beer can to Lyla, but she'd already had enough to drink. Three beers in and she could already feel the headache coming on.

"No, thanks." Lyla rubbed her arms and stomped her feet on the floorboard, trying to get the blood to flow. "I'm good."

They sat like that for a while with the engine running, staring at the fogged-up window waiting for the truck to heat up. Lyla drew her initials on the cold glass and then Hap's next to hers. She drew a heart around them and an arrow. Then wiped it away with the butt of her fist.

Hap took another long sip. "What's with you tonight?"

"Nothing," she said. Her breath was cold every time she exhaled. When she was a kid, she thought it was funny when she pretended to smoke a cigarette in front of her parents and blew the cold out of her mouth, acting like a real tart in a low-budget movie. "I'm just cold. That's all." She folded her arms across her chest, wishing they'd just go home and climb into bed. It wasn't turning out to be the date she'd hoped for after having gotten kicked out of the bar.

Hap put his beer on the dash and leaned over, starting at it again. "Well, hey, you're in luck. That's what I'm here for, California." Hap burped his sour beer breath into her ear. She turned her head away as he lifted up her shirt. Then he yanked down her bra. "I'll warm you up in a jiffy." He smiled.

"Hap! I said stop. Please."

She missed the old Hap, the *happy* drunk. The guy who could always make her smile. But ever since he lost his job and had to kiss ass at the unemployment office, he got what Mary-Ellen called *deaf* drunk. He never heard a word anybody else said.

When he leaned over and started in again, Lyla held his face in her hands, just the way he'd hold Emma's muzzle when he was about to kiss her wet nose. "Please, Hap. I'm not in the mood." She shooed him over to his side of the truck.

"What's the big deal? Nobody can see us."

"I know," Lyla admitted. Nobody could see them inside the cab, not with the windows fogged up. But still. She felt self-conscious, like she was on display. Sometimes with Hap, she felt like the whole world was watching them.

"I just wish we could go somewhere warm." With the sleeve of her coat, she rubbed circles on the inside of the passenger window, and for a moment—and really it was only the briefest of moments before the window clouded back up again—she could see the stars above. Without a moon, the stars looked so close; it was as if she could reach up and pull one out of the sky.

Lyla rolled down the window and reached into the darkness.

"What in the hell are you doing?" Hap reached over and rolled the window back up, almost pinning her arm. "Just a minute ago you were complaining about being too cold to fool around, and now you open the goddamn window? Jesus, girl, make up your mind."

"You're right." Lyla turned to him with a sad sort of smile, as though she were a child looking up to Hap. Hap once said he liked it when Lyla smiled at him like that. Made him feel older than her. Superior. "I was just thinking of how my dad used to say that if I reached high enough for the stars, someday I might just be able to grab one."

"Yeah, but your dad killed himself, remember?" Hap said.

The smile slid off Lyla's face. His words stung hot and hard. Lyla rarely talked about her dad anymore, but when she did, Hap was usually kind and gentle. He'd stroke her cheek and hold her in his arms as she resuscitated old memories. And once he'd licked the tears off her cheek, telling her he would swallow all her sadness if he could.

"Thanks a lot." Lyla wiped at the glass again, watching the stars reappear then flee in the fogged-up window.

"Well, it's true, isn't it?" Hap looked in the rearview mirror and checked his broken nose. He popped it back into place. "Sorry, babe, but it is what it is. I'm just being honest. That's all."

He untied the blue bandana around his neck and held it out to Lyla. "Here, put this on."

Lyla looked at him like he'd asked her to pet an alligator. "What do you mean, put it on?"

"You know, cover your eyes." That old eager, sweet smile in his eyes returned. "I've got a surprise for you. For us."

"What kind of surprise?" Lyla did not like surprises. She hated them. She held Hap's bandana out like a rotting pear.

"Come on, Lyla. Trust me. Here, turn around. I'll tie it on for you. I promise you're gonna love it." Seeing the sweetness back in his eyes, Lyla decided not to make a fuss. She let Hap take her by the shoulders and turn her around to tie the blindfold as if she were about to pin the tail on the donkey. When he caught a piece of her hair in the bandana, he kissed her neck and whispered, "Sorry, California, I didn't mean to hurt you."

He turned Lyla's face to his and kissed her hard and told her she was the sexiest thing in Pine Bluffs. "Hands down."

Even blindfolded, Lyla could taste the smile on his face. She wanted to kiss it. And maybe in a small way, she wanted to taste the old Hap, the one who had once come to her rescue and made her feel like there was nobody else on earth he'd ever want to be with.

Hap fastened her lap belt over her thick coat and stole the chance to kiss her again. "Ready?" he asked.

"Do I have a choice?" she teased, breathing in and out of her mouth, trying not to take in the smell of days-old sweat and cheap cologne caught in the bandana.

"Nope. Emma and I have something up our sleeves. Don't we, Emma?" Lyla could also smell Emma's dog breath as she rested her muzzle over the front seat.

Hap put the truck in drive and rolled out of the parking lot. In the darkness, Lyla felt the car turn right on the highway, then left, left again, and then pull into what Lyla assumed—hoped, really—was another huge empty parking lot, because he goosed the gas pedal and whooped the truck around in a series of figure eights.

The tires screeched along the pavement. Then the car slid along a patch of black ice.

"Hap?" Lyla fumbled for the handle above the car door to steady herself. "What are you doing?" She reached for the bandana to slip it from her eyes, but Hap held her hand still.

"Not so fast." Hap laughed and pulled back on the highway. "I was just trying to confuse you. Come on. Let's go have a good time, shall we?"

Lyla didn't know if they were heading north or south as the truck merged onto the highway and picked up speed. All she knew was they were on Route 215.

"So, are you going to give me a hint?" Lyla asked.

"No siree, Bob." Hap pressed down the gas pedal even harder. "But I promise you've never seen anything like it."

Lyla hated it when Hap drove fast like this, especially after having had so many drinks. "Hap, I don't want to do this," she said, even though she didn't know what *this* was. She reached behind her head and tried to undo the knot in the bandana. "I just want to go home."

"For fuck's sake, Lyla. Just relax, will you?" Hap grabbed her arm and squeezed it tight, awfully tight. Tighter than she was sure he'd meant to. She felt the car accelerate even faster. She was certain he was pushing a hundred miles per hour.

"Hap?" She tried to yank her arm out of his grip. "You're scaring me." Her stomach grew ice-cold and she tried to steady her trembling hands, trying to make sense of what was going on, why Hap was acting this way. He was drunk, she knew that much, but this? This felt like something else.

Hap didn't let go. He held onto her while he pressed down on the gas pedal, driving faster and faster along the highway.

"I told you, we are not going home yet." His voice was curt. "I said I have a surprise for you. Please. I am just asking you not to ruin it."

Lyla knew she should have ripped the bandana off right then and there. She should have looked him straight in the eyes and demanded he turn around and drive her back to the house. She should talk to him, reprimand him like Mary-El or jump out of the car at the next opportunity.

But she didn't. She just sat blindfolded in the cab and swallowed the dry fear growing in her mouth. She did as she was told.

After a stretch on the bumpy road, Hap asked in a voice that now sounded defeated, "Am I not good enough, Lyla?"

She had no idea what he was talking about—good enough? Good enough for what? She didn't need to see the frustration in Hap's eyes. She could feel it. It had started right when he threw his napkin on the table earlier that evening. When he had gotten up and walked up to the bar to confront a man who was apparently eyeing Lyla's backside as she put quarters in the jukebox.

"Got a problem?" The man had stood up, his Stetson tipped back on his head. He was a good head taller than Hap, but Hap threw the first punch. And the cowboy—being the good cowboy that he was—had thrown a few quick jabs, left, left, right, and had broken Hap's twice-broken nose yet again. Knocked him flat to the ground. The bouncer had picked him up and taken him out back before things got further out of hand.

"Come on back when you're sober, Hapster," he'd said, patting Hap on the back. He'd given him a stack of cocktail napkins to stop the bleeding.

Lyla had known better than to inflame the situation by telling Hap the cowboy had actually winked at her before turning back around, throwing his drink back and slamming the glass on the bar. Lyla had chased after Hap and the bouncer with their big heavy coats in her hands, wondering why their dates without Mary-Ellen often turned into train wrecks. She should have known better than to let Hap have that last Jack and soda. She had watched him stumble across the parking lot, holding his head back. He'd pressed the bridge of his nose and looked up at the stars, oblivious to the cold.

Lyla had stood under the awning and watched Hap crack his nose back in place, then lean back and howl to the moon. "Come on, California," he'd called. "Let's get out of this shithole."

Lyla had buttoned up her coat and chased after Hap, who stood by the driver's side door while simultaneously trying to free the keys from his pocket and pinching the bridge of his nose to keep the blood at bay. She knew she should have driven home. She knew Hap had had too much to drink, but in some strange way, she'd felt heat surge inside her body, knowing he'd thrown a punch for her and taken one too. Lyla had gotten in the passenger side and opened the door for him.

"Get in, silly. Before we both freeze to death."

Hap slammed the brake pedal. Still blindfolded, Lyla threw her hands against the windshield. The canvas lap belt burned into her hips. "Hap!" she screamed.

"Shit!" he yelled, and honked the horn while Emma let out a series of barks.

"What is it?" Lyla didn't even try removing the bandana. She could feel his mood veering south again.

"A huge buck. He jumped out into the road, and I damn near hit him. And now the lil' fucker's just standing there, staring me down. As though I'm the one doing something wrong. Come on, get out of here." Hap honked. "Go on, before I get out and shoot ya." And after a moment, he spat his chewing tobacco into an empty beer can. "That's right. Go on now."

Hap inched the car back along the road. He was driving slower now, which Lyla appreciated, and when they finally reached their destination, he threw the truck into park. He leaned over and whispered, "Give me a second and then you can take it off. Okay?" His voice was now quite sweet. He jumped out of the truck, but before he closed the door, he added, "I promise, no funny business. Trust me."

Lyla sat in the front seat, wishing he'd had the courtesy to keep the engine running. The cold began crawling up her pant legs like icy spiders.

"What's he doing out there?" Lyla asked Emma, as though the dog could be her eyes, as though Emma would rat him out. Lyla rubbed her legs and crossed her arms, and just when she'd had enough, Hap opened her car door, making her jump and Emma bark.

"God, Hap. You scared the shit out of me." Lyla's heart was beating faster than normal.

Hap didn't answer, so she called out to him again. "Hap? Where are you?" She heard a twig break right next to her, then his voice crept into her ear. The sweet smell of alcohol lingered on his breath. "Okay, you can take it off now."

Lyla untied the bandana and let her eyes adjust.

"Follow me."

Lyla let Hap take her hand and carefully lead her to the edge of the frozen lake, the same lake the three of them would come to in the summer. Lyla couldn't help but smile. It was all so beautiful. The stillness of the lake, the bonfire he'd lit, the blanket he had laid out. Hap got down on his knee and held a bouquet of dried reeds in his hands. He didn't say a word at first, and Lyla wasn't quite sure what to make of it.

Was he proposing? If so, what would she say?

Hap lit the tips of the reeds with his lighter. In the dark, the burning grasses glowed a bright orange. Hap had a big innocent smile on his face, like the smile of a child trying to please his mother. He no longer looked mad or drunk. He looked sincere and clear-eyed.

"Come on," he said, holding his burning bouquet and reaching for her hand. He walked her to the edge of the frozen lake.

"What are we doing?"

"We're going for a skate."

"A skate?" Lyla looked down at her tennis shoes.

"A pretend skate." Hap carefully led Lyla out onto the ice.

"Is it safe?" Lyla had pond-skated as a girl, back in the Sierra where the ice only thickened enough to skate for a couple of weeks each winter. Even then, she remembered the terrifying sound of the ice warbling underneath, like the call of whales and the pinging of a submarine radar.

"Trust me." Hap smiled. And in that moment, with the beautiful burning reeds, the blanket, and the fire, she did. She trusted him.

Lyla tiptoed out onto the ice and held her breath as if that made her lighter somehow, making the ice less likely to break. As she got farther away from shore, she looked down and gasped. She couldn't believe what she saw. It was like walking on clear glass. The stars shone bright in the reflection.

"Check this out." Hap brought the burning reeds onto the surface of the ice, and Lyla could see all the way to the bottom—to where round stones, like baseballs, were stuck in the mud.

"Oh my God, Hap, it's the most beautiful thing I have ever seen."

"See, I told you. It gets even better, come on."

Lyla let Hap glide her farther out into the middle, and she watched the lake floor give way, deeper and deeper still. Small rocks gave way to larger ones. Baseballs grew to bowling balls. Bowling balls became beach balls. Beach balls were replaced by Volkswagen Beetle–sized boulders that sat at the bottom of the lake.

"Erratics," Lyla cried. "Look at them."

"What?"

"Glacial erratics. Or at least, I think that's what my dad called them." Lyla looked up at the steep mountainside next to the lake. The slope was filled with massive rocks, precariously set and ready to let loose. "They're boulders glacially transported from their place of origin and left in an area of different bedrock compositions." She couldn't believe she remembered so clearly what her dad had said all those years ago.

"God, California. You make me so horny when you talk all smarty-pants like that." Hap slid right up behind Lyla and pressed into her. He wrapped his arms around her waist. "Come on, say something else."

"Oh, stop it." Lyla pushed away and skated around in loose figure eights in her tennis shoes, gaining more confidence with each loop. "This is so cool, Hap! How did you even think of this?" Lyla glided around in her sneakers, holding the stems of Hap's slow-burning reeds overhead like an Olympic torch.

She hadn't been out on a frozen lake in so long. Lyla's father used to take her skiing in the mountains when she was little, and on their way home, he would stop at this one particular pond on the side of the road and take her skating. The first time she stepped foot on the ice, she had never felt anything so terrifying in her life, all the what-ifs choking the fun out of it. What if the ice cracked open? What if she fell through, scrambling to hold onto the broken lake? What if she sank deeper in the cold water? What if her father couldn't get the rope out of the car in time? Her father always assured her she would be fine. He would tell her that she worried too much, when really, she thought years later, she didn't worry enough. She had those same questions, those same worries with Hap, but she tried to stuff them deep inside.

She twirled in tight circles and watched the smoldering embers trail in the dark. "Honestly, Hap. I don't think I've ever seen something this beautiful. Not in my entire life."

"Told you!" Hap yelled to her from the shore as he lit another bundle.

It felt so peaceful being out here with nobody else around. Not even Mary-El.

Out here on a sheet of glass, with nothing but the stars and the trees, and the rocks, and the ice.

And Hap.

Lyla no longer felt cold, no longer felt scared.

"Watch this," she called out as he threw his burning reeds into the bonfire. He watched her as he warmed his hands by the flames. She skated in wider and wider circles. She held the smoldering embers out at her side and twirled, the orange light following her like a comet. The farther and faster she skated, the longer the burning, glowing tail.

"I'm sorry for being such a party pooper earlier."

"It's okay." Hap was petting Emma's coat now, keeping her warm.

"No, Hap. It's not. I'm truly sorry." At that very moment, she couldn't believe she'd ever doubted Hap. He had known all along how special this would be, and she had almost ruined it when she asked him to drive her home.

Lyla continued to skate in figure eights, careful not to let the embers catch her hair. Why did she always have to make such a fuss? Why couldn't she have just let him take her where he wanted, no questions asked?

THE PALE FLESH OF WOOD

She let her sneakers zoom along the ice, satisfied in the silence and the beauty of it all. Stretched out along the glass sheet, the stars reflected on the surface as though she were skating through the universe itself. She skated farther into the night sky, along Orion's Belt and through his bow. She was giddy in all she saw.

And that was when she heard it. The ice below her made a terrible sound.

First, there was a deep rumble.

And then the eerie groan of an organ pipe that popped beneath her feet. Certain the ice was going to fail, Lyla slid to a stop.

"Hap?" she cried, taking tiny sips of air as if taking a deep breath would somehow make the ice fail.

Another groan warbled beneath her feet with a series of laser-like pinging sounds.

"Hap? Help me!" she cried, not wanting to move another inch. She felt stuck out there by herself, paralyzed with fear that the ice would break beneath her feet. She had seen it on television and in the movies—children falling through the ice into the bitter water below, helpless arms clinging to the broken edges, their cries as they were unable to pull themselves back up because their limbs were too cold, frozen, and no longer of use.

The sliding of bodies underneath the ice sheet.

The faces turning blue.

"Hap!" she cried again.

"It's okay, Lyla. It's frozen solid." Hap laughed as he held Emma in his lap. He had placed a wool blanket over the dog's back and was stroking her head. "The ice is just breathing. That's all. You're fine."

"Breathing? What in the hell do you mean, breathing?" Lyla screamed.

"Expanding and contracting. It does that. Nothing to worry about. I promise you nothing can happen, not with these temperatures."

The ice pinged and ponged and groaned again.

"Hap. Goddamn it. I need you!" she screamed in a guttural, animalistic way. She carefully got down on all fours. "The ice is going to

223

break wide open. I'm going to fall in." Lyla crawled a couple of inches along the surface, trying to steal her way back to shore, holding her gaze steady on the erratics below.

"It's not going to break, Lyla. Just walk back. You're gonna be fine."

Lyla looked up and was about to scream at him again, really scream. But he stood at the edge of the lake with another bright grassy torch in his hand, Emma at his side. If she weren't so damn scared, she would have thought it the most romantic thing she had ever seen. But every time she crawled farther along, the ice groaned, then shot beneath her. She swore she could even feel the ice move. "Oh my God, Hap. I'm going to fall in." She was crying now.

"You are not going to fall through, Lyla. Don't be such a chicken shit. Here, watch." Hap skirted out along the surface of the ice with two big bundles of burning reeds in his hands, twirling them around like a cheerleader. He threw one bundle up in the air and tried, unsuccessfully, to catch the unlit end with his hand as it floated back to the ground. The sparks flew high in the air, creating an explosion of light, like fireworks that rained down and almost got caught in his hair. "Oh shit," he said, laughing, patting the top of his head, "that was close."

And that was when they both heard it—not the deep grumbling of the ice below them but a high-pitched whine. A sharp clawing on glass. Emma had followed Hap out onto the ice. Her legs shook as terrible sounds shot beneath her.

"Emma." Hap threw his embers and ran over to his dog, who had her tail between her legs, her body flattened on the ice. Her whole body shook as she cried. "I'm coming, girl, hold on." Hap slid over on all fours and swept Emma up in his arms. "I've got you, sweetheart."

"Hap!" Lyla yelled, frozen in place. The ice contracted and boomed below her feet again. But Hap didn't turn around. He was carrying Emma back to shore. "Jesus Christ, Lyla. Just do it! You don't need my help," he yelled.

Lyla stared down through the ice, through the tears in her eyes. The erratics sitting at the bottom of the lake were no longer clear and round but blurred mounds. "Hap!" she screamed again, paralyzed while the ice shifted and groaned. "I said I need you."

But Hap wasn't coming to her rescue. He was sitting on the blanket next to the campfire with Emma in his lap, holding his dog like he would a lost child. Lyla watched him rub Emma's golden coat and speak to her in a low voice. Just the way Mary-El would rub Hap's back, talking the calm back into her brother whenever he'd slide off the rails.

Something Lyla never quite had the power to do.

In the bitter night air, Lyla could see everything with a clarity she hadn't quite understood or appreciated before this night.

She could see she wasn't Hap's gal. Never would be.

She could see it in her frozen breath.

And in the erratic's trapped in the ice below.

She could see she wasn't meant for this kind of cold.

She could see it all, clear as ice.

CHAPTER FIFTEEN

COLLECT CALL—FEBRUARY 1967

"Hello?" Her mother's voice crackled through the line. Lyla stood in a phone booth somewhere between Elko and Winnemucca with a blanket over her shoulders. She picked the sleep crumbs out of her eyes after having slept in her car the night before. By her calculations, she'd cross into California later that afternoon.

"Mom?"

"Hello?" her mother asked again.

A sixteen-wheeler whizzed past as Lyla held the phone to her ear, steeling herself for what to say. *You were right, Mom. I don't belong out there. It was all a mistake, just like you said.*

"Is anybody there?" Through the static, Lyla could hear Al ask Louise who it was and her mother, clearly with a hand over the receiver, say she didn't know, that it was a bad connection. "You'll have to speak up. I can't quite hear you."

Then Al, telling Lyla's mother to just hang up. That they were late; they had to go.

And Louise, saying more firmly, "Jesus, Al. Give me a minute. Please."

Then a *tap, tap, tap*. "Hello?"

And then Al telling her he'd be in the car.

Listening to the two of them bicker, Lyla slid her finger on the plunger and ended the call. She wasn't ready to go home yet.

She leaned against the glass, thumbed through her address book, and put her finger next to her uncle's number. She fished more dimes out of her purse and slid them into the coin slot. But the operator came on the line and told her she needed to deposit fifty more cents to place the call.

Lyla dug through her purse but could only find a couple of nickels.

"May I place a collect call?"

"Hold, please."

The coins dropped into the tray one at a time, tinkling like she had won a jackpot. She slid them into her pocket as the operator dialed.

Ring, ring, ring.

Lyla held her breath.

When her uncle answered and accepted the charges, Lyla burst into tears. Through sobs and apologies, she told her uncle that she was headed back to California but wasn't ready to go home quite yet.

"I just need a little time to think my shit through, David. To sort everything out. I just don't want to freak my mom out. You know, show up on her doorstep and 'Ta-da! I'm home!' Plus, she has Al, and I don't really want to move in and be a third wheel. They need their space too."

"Stay as long as you want, Lyla. I'd love your company. It'd do me good too," he said. "I'll make up the spare room."

―――――――――

The light was on when Lyla arrived later that evening. She parked underneath the twisted manzanita tree out front, and when she got out of the car, she put her suitcase down and immediately walked over to it. She ran her hands along the tree's rust-colored bark, smooth as a baseball bat. The small pale pink urn-shaped blossoms were just starting to color the tree.

"Welcome back, stranger." Uncle David bounded out of the house, smiling; he held his arms out wide and welcoming in the way he always had. He walked down the driveway and grabbed Lyla's suitcase. "You're just in time. I've got some dinner heating up." Her uncle slid his arm around her shoulders and walked her to the house.

"Nothing fancy, mind you. Just some bachelor food, canned soup and cheese sandwiches, but it'll do you some good."

"Sounds amazing," Lyla said. "I've been basically living on Ritz crackers and Pepsi for the past couple days, and I could definitely use a bit of a change."

"Change is good. Change, I can do. Come on, let's get you settled."

Lyla followed her uncle up the steps and stopped as he held the door open. She looked up at him, the man who had slowly, over the years, replaced her father. The man she called when she was feeling out of sorts or needed advice when she was negotiating the price for her car, jump-starting the battery, or even just exploring ways to invest her small bit of savings.

The man who had told her to put Hap on the line when she locked herself in the bathroom after the night on the lake, with Hap banging on the door, begging her to forgive him.

The man who had told Hap in no uncertain terms that if he ever laid a hand on his niece again, he would personally drive out to Wyoming and make sure his hands were rendered permanently unavailable.

Standing on the front stoop, Lyla tried not to find her father in her uncle's aged eyes, the graying at his temple, or in his neatly trimmed beard. She tried not to collect pieces of the person who was no longer alive but the man who stood before her now, holding the door open.

"I'm sorry, Uncle David," Lyla apologized. "I didn't know what else to do. I just wasn't ready to go home yet and face Mom."

"Nonsense, kiddo. I could use a little company now that Dianna has moved out. Keep this old guy from feeling sorry for himself, yeah?"

"But—"

"But nothing. It's good to have you back, plain and simple. Plus, if you don't mind me saying, you never struck me as the cowgirl type. Thought that was a bit of a wrong turn if you asked me."

"Yeah, you're right about that." Lyla paused for a moment. "Can I ask you something?

"Always."

"What do I strike you as? You know, when you think of me, what do you see?"

He stood there looking into Lyla's eyes, thought about that for a moment, then smiled.

"A kaleidoscope," he said.

"A what?"

"I've always marveled at your curiosity, your tenacity, Lyla—to examine something one way, tilt it, and under a different light, let the tiny reflective mirrors reorient themselves so that you always discover something a bit new. All the while, you've been looking through the same tiny hole. That part never changes, but what's inside does."

"Huh. A kaleidoscope. I like that. I thought you were going to say an accountant or something boring. I wasn't expecting something so artsy-fartsy from you of all people."

"Well, sometimes we don't really let on who we are. We are nothing if not full of surprises. I've been doing a little soul-searching myself. Reading a bit. Anyhow, come on, let's get you settled. You must be exhausted."

Lyla followed David into the house where half the living room furniture was missing. The space looked far more spacious and generous compared to when she was younger, when Lyla along with her cousins, the sofas, bookshelves, blankets, and childhood toys crowded the room.

Before shutting the front door, Lyla looked out at her green Chevy Impala parked under the yellow streetlight. She took a moment to gather herself, to take in the flowering manzanitas' thick scent of honey and the loamy, friable soil of home. Already, the dry, prickly landscape of the Wyoming sagebrush and bitterroot had begun to drift away like a long-ago dream.

BOOK III

(1981)

CHAPTER SIXTEEN

PAR AVION—SEPTEMBER 1981

If there was one thing Lyla and her cousins could agree upon, it was this: Caroline Hawkins wasn't a *real* grandmother. She didn't bake. Nor did she mend. And she would've never been caught dead reading a book about talking bunnies or singing narwhals to any one of them back when they were in elementary school.

As kids, they rarely questioned their grandmother's stiff bearing, her exacting nature; they just accepted it as part of everyday life, like toothpaste. But now, as they moved their grandmother into a nursing home and spent the weekend together packing up her things, they began to scrutinize who Caroline really was. What made her tick.

"What do you think?" Margaret waltzed into the living room, wearing one of Caroline's floor-length formal dresses and a silk shawl; her fingers were spread wide like a starfish, just as Caroline would do after she'd polished her nails. Margaret had their grandmother nailed to a T, except that she couldn't quite mimic the regal way Caroline seemed to float into a room.

There was something otherworldly about it.

About her.

Not angelic, exactly. Olympian.

"It's like she's Hera." Margaret tried to glide like her grandmother, but her feet kept tripping up on the carpet. "It's so weird. It's like her feet never really touch the ground. Have you guys ever noticed that before?"

Lyla looked up and shook her head. "Can't really say I have."

She took a sip of her beer and continued sorting through Caroline's old bank statements and bills, separating them into two stacks—one pile for Uncle David, the other to be thrown away. It was getting late, and Lyla wanted nothing more than for everybody to just go home so she could turn out the lights, take a long bath, and plop into bed. But they still had a lot of work to do.

"It's like—" Margaret squared her shoulders, again trying to affect the formality of their grandmother. "I don't know. It's like she has wheels for feet or something, even now." Margaret stopped and opened a beer from the six-pack sitting on the coffee table. She twirled around the living room, letting the long skirt billow like a parachute. "I just don't get it."

"What? You don't know?" Robert walked into the living room with a bunch of collapsed boxes under his arm and snagged Margaret's beer out of her hand. "It's because she's not actually human. That's how." He took a long sip and let out a loud belch.

"You're such a pig," Margaret said, whirling around and grabbing her beer back, "and that's not a very nice thing to say about her."

"Nice? Who said anything about being nice? I'm not here because I'm nice, or loving this, Mags. I'm just trying to get all her shit packed up or thrown away as fast as possible, so I can get back home to the things I really care about. And you playing dress-up isn't helping."

"I just needed a break. This is all so depressing." Margaret kicked off her grandmother's shoes and grabbed a couple of books off the coffee table. "We've been at it all day, and I don't feel like we even made a dent." She placed the books on top of her head and walked across the room, carefully balancing the stack just as she learned to do back in cotillion many years ago. "And what do you mean? She's not really human?"

"Like, maybe she's an android." Robert mimed a clunky robot walking around the room and with a mechanical tone said, "Ro-bert Char-les Haw-kins, act your age." Then in his normal voice, he added, "God, I don't know how Pops put up with it. Maybe she was an animal in the sack."

"Jesus, Robert!" Margaret came to a halt, sending the books toppling to the floor. "I definitely don't need *that* image in my head." Margaret picked the books up and placed them on her head again. "She's not all that bad. She's just complicated. Right, Lyla?"

"Sure. Whatever you say, Mags." But Lyla was only half listening. The mountain of paperwork was daunting and trying to make sense of her grandmother's finances, worse. How long before she ran out of money and the state would kick in?

"What would you know?" Robert grabbed a new beer from the six-pack and pulled off the tab. He took a long swallow, let out another belch, and smiled. "You were always her favorite. The one who could do no wrong."

"That is *not* true." Margaret turned around slowly to keep the books from falling again. "She loved us all the same. I just didn't try to push her buttons the way you guys did."

"Oh, come off it, Mags." Steven was sitting on the floor, boxing up Caroline's collection of art books from the Met, the Art Institute of Chicago, and a host of other museums she'd never once stepped foot into. "You're the only one she ever talks about in those stupid Christmas newsletters. 'Margaret graduated summa cum laude from Stanford. Margaret married a neurosurgeon. Margaret is due with her first child. Margaret this, Margaret that,'" Steven mocked. "And what did I ever get? 'Steven went to Woodstock.'"

"You're just jealous." Margaret lifted the books off her head and plopped down on the couch.

"Of course, I'm jealous. It wasn't like our dear old Caroline went out of her way to hide the fact that *you were* her darling and the rest of us were all—" Steven paused.

"Chopped liver," Robert filled in.

"Are," Margaret said.

"See! You admit it."

"No, not that," Margaret lectured. "*Are* her favorite, not *were* her favorite. Present tense. She's not dead yet."

"Whatever." Steven taped the box shut and wrote *USELESS ART BOOKS THAT WERE JUST FOR SHOW* on all four sides before hauling it to the top of the stack of boxes.

"Is that true, Lyla?" Margaret asked over her shoulder. "Is that how you feel too? That I was her favorite? I mean, you're the one she asked to move in here and be her roommate, not the rest of us."

"Well," Lyla responded. "I wasn't exactly on the A-list like you when we were growing up, that's for sure. But you all got married and started families and moved out of town, so that left only one person to move in and care for her. Lucky me."

Lyla pulled out an old airmail envelope stuffed in the back of the desk drawer. She held it under the desk lamp to get a better look. *Par Avion, Italia* was stamped on the front and dated *August 1955*—mailed the year before her father died.

Strange, Lyla thought. The letter was addressed to her father but was mailed here to her grandparents' house.

Lyla slid the thin sheet of notepaper out of the envelope and unfolded it. Paper-clipped to the letter was a black-and-white photograph of a young boy dressed in short pants, a white fisherman's sweater, and leather shoes. He stood on a cobblestone street, holding the handlebars of a bicycle that was far too big for him. Lyla held the picture closer to the light. There was something oddly familiar in the way he stared into the camera. The boy didn't look mad exactly, but he certainly didn't seem very happy to have his picture taken either.

Lyla put the picture down and began to read the letter.

My Dearest Charles, I hope this letter finds you well . . . The note opened with the most beautiful handwriting Lyla had ever seen. Each letter was evenly spaced, perfectly rounded, and bent slightly to the right. It was the handwriting of somebody who took penmanship seriously, something Lyla's grandmother would have certainly appreciated.

It has been many years since . . . Lyla continued reading, when Margaret snuck up and tapped her on the shoulder.

"Excuse me, Lyla May Hawkins, but what do you think you're doing, rifling through my private correspondence?"

Lyla slapped the letter face down over the photograph. "Oh God, Margaret. You startled me." She laughed, though she had no idea why she felt the need to hide the letter from her cousin. She hadn't the faintest clue who wrote it, but something felt strangely invasive in reading a letter to her father that was kept in her grandmother's drawer, like peeking into a neighbor's house at night when the shades had yet to be drawn, when you might glimpse things you weren't meant to see.

"And heavens to Betsy," Margaret continued, "how many times have I told you to sit up straight?" Margaret grabbed Lyla by the shoulders and jerked them back. "There. That's better." Margaret sat down on the edge of the desk, unknowingly on top of the letter. "Anyhow, you just have to go back there and check out her closet. It's absolutely stuffed with the most gorgeous things. I had no idea she was such a clotheshorse. Did you?"

"Clotheshorse?" Again, Lyla shook her head. Lyla eyed the corner of the envelope that peeked out from underneath Margaret's skirt. She was just about to slip it out when Margaret grabbed Lyla's hands and tried to pull her to her feet.

"Come on, you might as well see if there is anything in there that you want to keep. My brothers aren't going to want anything. They'll just throw everything away if we aren't careful. Plus, it's kind of fun to see all her different outfits; it's like a museum."

"Okay, okay." Lyla drained her beer and stood up. "But just promise me one thing."

"What's that?"

"When it's my turn to go, please take me out back and shoot me. I swear I won't be able to stand a day in one of those places.

They're just awful." Lyla held her pinky finger out to her cousin. "Promise?"

Margaret hooked her pinky around Lyla's. "I promise."

Lyla stalled for a moment, waiting for Margaret to stand up so that she could bring the letter with her to the back room and read it quietly, but her cousin stayed sitting on the edge of the desk, sweeping her hands at Lyla. "Go on. I swear you'll be amazed."

———

Inside the closet, Lyla pulled the chain to the overhead light. Along each wall were two long rows of clothes. Everything hung meticulously on identical wooden hangers and was oriented in the same direction. Each garment was protected in a plastic dry-cleaning bag—everything from Caroline's evening gowns to the clothes she wore to church. Even the clothes she wore to the grocery store were protected in a thin plastic sheet. On the shelves above were neatly stacked glove boxes, hat boxes, and shoeboxes, each labeled with a description and the corresponding season.

Spring, Cream Heels for Bridge.
Summer, Boat Shoes.
Winter, Black Suede Formal Parties.

Odd, Lyla thought as she wandered down the length of the closet and trailed her fingers along the plastic sheets, protecting the light cashmeres, the airy linens, the sturdy pressed cottons, the heavy winter coats. How in all these years had she not stepped foot into her grandmother's closet, not even in the months she'd been living here with Caroline to help her manage her affairs, household chores, and such? Caroline had remained steadfast in her determination to dress herself, even as her hands worked against her and buttoning became difficult. Even over at Arbor Vine, Caroline insisted on laying out her clothes the night before to prepare for the following day. Lyla had just chalked it up to another one of her grandmother's oddities.

Lyla pulled a hanger off the rack and slid the dry-cleaning bag over the yellow Easter skirt and pale blue blouse her grandmother had worn the day she let slip that the Easter Bunny wasn't real.

And Santa Claus.

The Tooth Fairy too.

Oh, come on, Lyla. You are far too old to believe in such things. Go on, tell her, Charles. Even all these years later, Lyla could feel the sting as she stared into her Easter basket of fake green grass and colorful eggs, then looked up to her father, who shrugged his shoulders and told Lyla her grandmother was right. None of it was real.

Lyla returned the outfit to the rack and continued wending her way through the seasons of her grandmother's clothing—from the itchy wool gabardine jackets of winter that gave way to the pastel oxfords of spring, to her sailor summer dresses, to the houndstooth jackets of fall.

"Oh, Caroline, you were something else," Lyla muttered when she came across the midnight-blue gown her grandmother wore when she took Lyla to see *The Nutcracker* in the city, remembering how hard Caroline scrubbed the dirt from Lyla's hands, making her nail beds bleed. Decades later, Lyla could recall that strangely sweet feeling of telling Caroline ballet wasn't her thing. Baseball was.

Amongst the familiar clothes were also many things Lyla didn't recognize: a khaki-colored pantsuit replete with safari loops at the shoulder, a floor-length fur coat, and a perfectly pressed tennis outfit. There was even a tight-fitting, zebra-striped dress that Lyla couldn't imagine Caroline wearing in a million years!

Near the back of the closet, Lyla came across the outfit she knew she would model for her cousins, Caroline's famous Christmas skirt made of silk brocade with ornamental silver and gold threading. That skirt, heavy as a bedspread, was as much a part of the holiday as the goose Caroline cooked for every Christmas dinner.

Lyla removed her clothes and slipped the skirt from the hanger. She opened the slim waist and stepped in, careful not to step on the hem, then zipped it up as far as it would go. Next, she slid on the matching silk blouse, which she left untucked so as to hide the wide yawn left in the unfastened skirt. Finally, she pulled the shoebox labeled *Winter, Christmas Heels*, off the shelf and slid them on her feet.

"Good enough for government work," she said, knowing she was not an exact replica of Caroline, but close enough to make her cousins spit with laughter. Lyla snapped off the light and lifted the skirt to keep the hem off the carpet as she walked over to the vanity.

Lyla sat down and took stock.

She had long, curly black hair as opposed to Caroline's shoulder-length, straight bone-white hair. Lyla's face was round, flattish even, and her skin was pale with a row of freckles spread across her nose and the beginnings of crow's feet around her eyes, while her grandmother still had amazing, unblemished skin with high cheekbones and remarkably few wrinkles even in her eighties. But the two things they did share were their height—both just brushing up against six feet—and the same wolf-blue eyes.

Lyla picked up the bottle of Jean Naté After Bath Splash and dabbed some onto her wrists, then fastened her grandmother's signature choker of pearls around her neck. She tried her best to tame her hair into one of her grandmother's low-slung ponytails, but that was useless. Her black corkscrew curls kept popping out, so she fastened them down with hair clips and blasted her hair with Aqua Net.

She then slid on her grandmother's red lipstick and rubbed her lips together. While not an exact resemblance, it was definitely good enough.

"Okay, Caroline," Lyla said, getting up, "let's do this thing."

When she emerged in the living room, Lyla cleared her throat just as Caroline would do when she had something to announce to the family. "What, pray on earth, are you kids doing?"

Beer sprayed from Steven's mouth. "Holy shit, Lyla!"

Lyla held out her hand. "Steven James. If I have told you once, I have told you a thousand times. There will be no using that kind of language in this house."

Steven wiped his mouth and smiled. "Yes, ma'am."

"And you!" Lyla pointed her finger at Robert, who sat on the couch wrapping the fireplace tools in a sheet of brown paper. "Did I give you permission to touch those? Did I? Did I? Answer me." Lyla slapped the back of Robert's head as she walked past. "Put it all back. Everything. Do you hear me?"

"Hey, Lyla!" Robert rubbed the crown of his head. "What the heck?"

Lyla stopped. "Lyla? Excuse me, young man? But you are mistaken. This is me, your grandmother, Caroline." Lyla held her chin up. With one hand resting on the mantel of the fireplace, she gestured up and down the length of her gown with the other. "Clearly. And," Lyla continued in her haughty tone, "the least you all could do is have the courtesy to wait to pack up my life until I've passed—which, mark my words, will not be for a very long time."

"We'll see about that," Robert muttered.

"What on earth did you say to me, Robert Charles Hawkins?"

"Just counting the days," he said, louder this time.

Could it really be days? Lyla stood at the mantel looking at a framed picture of her father taken the day he returned from the war. *No,* she convinced herself, *not days. But weeks? Months?*

Lyla fingered the choker of pearls around her neck. She felt a sudden sting of irritation at her father.

He was the one who was supposed to be here, making all these decisions about Caroline.

He was the one who was supposed to handle her finances.

He was the one who should be working with Uncle David.

Not Lyla and her cousins. This wasn't supposed to be their job.

And it wasn't supposed to be Lyla's responsibility to move in six months ago and be her grandmother's roommate!

Lyla picked up the frame. Dressed in his tan uniform, her father stood next to Caroline under the front eave, both of them looking stiff. Her father neither had a casual arm around his mother's waist nor was he smiling at the camera, which Lyla only now thought a bit strange. Her father had always smiled terribly bright for the camera.

She then realized her father wasn't even looking into the camera at all.

The photograph, grainy and yellowed with age, had been sitting on the mantel all Lyla's life. Lord, she must have seen it a thousand times. But this was the very first time she noticed something off in her father's eyes as he looked out into the distance, something that prevented him from giving his *Smile of God.*

"Jesus, this is such a huge waste of time." Steven broke her train of thought. "It's just a bunch of junk. I mean, none of us want any of this stuff, right?"

Holding the framed photograph, Lyla was beginning to think Steven was right. What was the point? She slid Caroline's silver heels off and put the framed photograph of her father and grandmother on the desk. It was the only thing she actually wanted to keep. The rest could go.

"I'm starting to agree. This is starting to feel like a colossal waste of everybody's time." Lyla sat at the desk. "Margaret, you have a young kid back at home, and I'm sure Roger would love you back. Robert, you have a family and work and coaching Tim's Little League team. And Steven has his PhD to finish up."

"Well, it's not going to just magically box itself up, now is it?" Margaret came out of the kitchen wearing Caroline's apron over her clothes and a pair of her yellow rubber dishwashing gloves. "And we can't leave it all to you just because you live here. We all have to do our part. It's just the way it is." Margaret had always been practical.

"But why are we spending all this time sorting through everything? She can't keep any of this stuff over at Arbor Vine, despite what she thinks," Lyla offered.

"Yeah, Mags," Robert piped in. "I could get a dumpster bin

delivered here tomorrow and have all this crap gone in a day. Boom. Done. And we can go back to our lives."

"Stop it. It's not that simple," Margaret argued. "We can't just up and throw her things away. This is what is left of her life. It's our job." Margaret took off her gloves and leaned against the wall. "We're all going to get old one day too, and we won't want our lives just thrown away in the garbage. Trust me."

"But that's where you are wrong, Margaret. I will be dead and won't care a lick about what is saved or thrown away." Then with a sort of half-annoyed, half-ironic smile, Robert said, "Trust me."

In a way, Lyla agreed. She was staring into the faraway eyes of her father who just up and left everything and everyone behind.

"Well, it means something to me. Caroline *means* something to me." Margaret was near tears now. "And I think going through her things is important. I think it helps us appreciate her more."

"Appreciate her?" Steven blurted out. "Are you kidding me? 'Boys, wash your hands. Boys, you're too loud. Boys, you weren't singing in church today. Boys, don't talk to your father like that. Boys, boys, boys . . .' That woman never appreciated Robert or me a day in her life."

Margaret blew a strand of hair out of her eyes. "Oh, come off it. Caroline was strict, I'll give you that, but she loves you guys."

"Easy for you to say," Robert said. "You're probably the only one who is in her will."

"Oh, please. Stop being so ridiculous."

"I'm being ridiculous? Excuse me, sis, but you're the one dressed in her clothes."

"Whatever. You know what I mean." Margaret waved her hands at her brothers. "I think you guys want to see the worst in her, like that somehow makes it easier for you." Then after a moment, she continued, "I honestly don't think you guys ever bothered to see Caroline for who she was and all she did for us. I think you just made up your own myths. Right, Lyla?"

But Lyla was only half listening. She was sitting at the desk, having a conversation with her father in her head for leaving her with this mess. *How could you?* She imagined sitting with him on the hood of his big yellow convertible at the Marin Headlands looking over the Golden Gate, the little turnout they used to drive to when the weather was nice. *Leaving us like that.*

"Not that bad?" Robert slapped his brother on the shoulder. "Oh, you just hold onto that thought, sis. Come on, Steven. Follow me."

Together, they ran off to Caroline's bedroom and shut the door.

Lyla put the framed photograph face down as she listened to Steven and Robert giggling in the back bedroom.

"I'm not making things up. She wasn't so bad, was she?" Margaret came over and sat on the desk. Her lipstick was now smeared.

"Bad? No. But she was always stuck in her ways, and she's going to give those folks at the home a run for their money, that's for darn sure. We'll be lucky if they don't kick her out."

"God. I feel so sorry for her." Margaret picked a piece of lint off Lyla's blouse. "I just hate seeing her stuck in a place like that."

"I know. It's—" Lyla paused as she looked up from the photograph in her hands. "I don't know. I guess it's just not what I pictured. I thought she'd just die in her sleep here at home. I thought when I moved in here, I'd be able to take care of her."

Lyla thought about that for a moment . . . what it would have been like to be the one to come into Caroline's bedroom one morning and find her grandmother, open-mouthed and cold. Would that have really been better? Would she have been able to handle such a thing?

Margaret picked up the airmail envelope sitting on the desk. She slid the letter out as well as the photograph. "Who's this?" she asked.

"I don't have the faintest clue. I found the envelope stuffed in the back of Caroline's desk."

Margaret inspected the front and back. "I didn't know your dad kept in touch with anybody after the war. Who's it from?"

"Some woman named Gessica, probably the wife of one of his war buddies or something, but—" Lyla paused.

"But what?"

"I don't know, something about it feels weird, like why the letter was mailed here but addressed to my dad. I mean, isn't that strange?"

"I can read it first if you want. If that would be easier."

Lyla closed her eyes. "I don't know. I feel—" Again, she stumbled over what she felt. Guilty? Mad? Tired?

"Or I can just throw it away."

Lyla drew a deep breath. She reached for Margaret's hand and squeezed. "No. Go ahead. Just do it."

As Margaret silently read the letter, Lyla stared at the boy in the photograph. He was lanky and had thick black hair, the same springy curls as Lyla. The same aquiline nose.

Lyla instinctively felt the bridge of her nose. Her stomach then tightened as she picked up the framed photograph of her father that she had placed face down earlier. She felt suddenly cold and nauseous.

Lyla flipped the photograph of the boy over. *Luca Charles Fiorentino, Age 11* was printed on the back.

"Oh my God, Margaret!" Lyla snatched the wastebasket from underneath the antique desk and threw up. She dry-heaved several times while Margaret rubbed her back. And when she was done, she started crying. "Holy shit."

"I know." Margaret's face was white as cotton. She handed Lyla the letter. "It's all in here."

Lyla took the letter and tried to concentrate on the words.

There is no easy way to go about this, but I wanted to share . . .
I wanted you to know . . .
Luca is a good boy.
He is tall and . . .

Blood rushed through her eardrums as she tried to make sense of the letter. Whoosh, *Luca enjoys . . .*

Whoosh, *Luca has a . . .*

The inside of her head felt like a washing machine. Everything swirling and tangling around the agitator. *Whoosh, whoosh, whoosh.*

Just then, Robert and Steven burst into the living room, arm in arm. They were dolled up in Caroline's clothes, each wearing a wide-brimmed summer hat, and they both had gobs of makeup on their faces.

Lyla stared at them, gobsmacked.

Whoosh.

"Well, don't just sit there, ladies. You need to get this all packed up. I must have my things over at Arbor Vine." Robert teetered across the living room with his feet half in and half out of Caroline's shoes. And because his shoulders were far too broad, the dress he was wearing was unzipped in the back.

Whoosh, whoosh. Lyla's head was getting dizzier.

"Guys," Margaret tried to interrupt.

But Steven chimed in, clapping his hands to get their attention. "Come now, ladies, we don't have all day, now do we?" Because there was no hope of Steven fitting in Caroline's clothes, he stood in his boxer shorts with one of her dresses tucked in his armpits. He looked like a gorilla with his mass of chest hair poking out of the top of the dress; his thick hairy legs stuck out below.

"You guys!" Margaret said a little louder.

Lyla threw her hands over her ears to steady the constant whooshing.

But Steven pursed his lips and rifled through the clutch dangling over his arm. He pulled out Caroline's lipstick and slathered it messily on his lips. "And who left the toilet seat up? Robert? Steven? Was that you? If I have told you once, I have told you . . ."

Lyla lowered her hands. The whooshing started to soften. She wanted to tell them to just shut up, but she was speechless and numb.

"And who tracked all that mud in the house? My house! All of you, get outside and don't come back until I ring the dinner bell. Do you hear me?"

"Robert!" Margaret shouted again to no avail.

Lyla sat wide-eyed looking at but not really seeing her cousins. She began to shiver as time slowed impossibly down. It felt like she was having a stroke and couldn't get a word out. She saw everything playing out in front of her, Steven and Robert's banter, their mocking of Caroline, and Margaret trying to take control, but her jaw wouldn't move.

"And turn off that television," Steven barked. "It'll ruin your eyes. Robert, why can't you pick up a book like your sister?"

Margaret finally stuck her fingers in her mouth and whistled like a lifeguard.

Just like that, Lyla's cousins stopped but only for an instant.

"Margaret Jane, that is no way for a young woman to act." Robert and Steven were on a roll now. "And you, Lyla May." Steven had his hands on his hips. "Get away from my desk. None of that is your business. Do you hear me?"

And she did.

Hearing her name, Lyla finally snapped out of it. Sense of time returned.

"Stop it!" she screamed. "Just stop it. I can't think." She started bawling.

"Holy shit, Lyla." Steven dropped his dress and ran over to Lyla in his boxer shorts and white crew socks. "What happened?"

Lyla didn't say a word. Couldn't. What could she say?

"Christ, Lyla, what is it?" Robert kicked off Caroline's shoes and ran over too. He knelt down and took her hands. "Are you hurt? What do you need?"

Lyla's hands shook as she handed the letter to Robert and the two photographs to Steven.

"This is why he did it," she finally mumbled. "I am sure of it. This is why he killed himself."

Eventually, the four of them moved to the couch and sat side by side, in various stages of their grandmother's clothing.

Wearing her jewelry.

Smelling of her perfume.

"I wonder if my mom knows?" Lyla finally asked, staring at the mantel where the photograph of her father and grandmother once sat. "I wonder if he ever told her."

Steven stared at the two pictures again and shook his head. "I doubt it. I bet you Caroline didn't even show this to your father. I bet she kept this all to herself." He handed the photographs back to Lyla. "That would be so like her."

Again, Lyla stared at the little boy and then to her father and his faraway eyes. "Still, I can't believe I have a brother out there somewhere." Lyla traced her finger along the handlebars of the boy's bicycle in the photograph. "I wonder what he's like. Is he married? Does he have kids?" Lyla picked up the envelope and looked at the return address. "What if I wrote a letter and sent it to this address, introducing myself? What if I—" Lyla paused.

Behind them, the sliding glass door opened.

"A little help here?" Lyla's uncle was balancing a stack of pizza boxes in one hand and a six-pack of beer in the other.

They all turned around, but nobody got up. They just watched him fumble the door shut with his foot.

"Thanks a lot, team." David walked into the living room where they sat on Caroline's couch. He kicked Steven's feet off the coffee table and put the pizza boxes down.

"Mind telling me why you're all sitting around dressed up in my mother's clothing?" He opened the first box and slid out a piece of pizza, catching a long string of cheese in his mouth. As he ate, he looked around. "Hello? Anybody home?"

Still, nobody said a word.

Lyla handed her uncle both the letter and the black-and-white photograph of her half-brother. She watched Uncle David frantically scan the contents.

"Where did you find this?"

The way he said it caught Lyla by surprise.

"You knew?" She wanted to tear the letter from her uncle's hands.

David put his pizza slice back down in the box and sat on the arm of the couch. He raked his hand through his thick hair and let out a long, deep breath. Then, after a long silence, he said, "Know? Not exactly."

"What do you mean, *not exactly*?" Lyla barked. "It's pretty simple. Either you knew or you didn't. Tell me." Lyla jumped to her feet, nearly tripping on the hem of her skirt. She ripped the picture from her uncle's hands.

"You did know. You knew all along, this is why Dad did it. Didn't you?"

Lyla's uncle leaned forward and reached for Lyla's hand, but she slapped him away.

"Didn't you? Tell me." Lyla demanded an answer. "You knew he'd had an affair. You knew he had another child. And you never said anything? All these years? How dare you!"

"Lyla!" Margaret held Lyla by the shoulders, trying to calm her, but Lyla shook her cousin off.

"Leave me alone. I want to hear your dad say it. What is it, exactly, you know?"

Again, David drew in a deep breath.

"He tried to tell me one night when he was drunk, but I shut him up. I told him I didn't want to hear anything about what he'd done over there, and I punched him. I hit him straight in the nose and knocked him to the ground. God, he lay there, just looking up at me. Like he was drowning. He looked at me with the saddest eyes I'd ever seen. 'David, please,' he begged. But I didn't want to hear him say anything more. So, I sat on him and punched him again." David began hitting his chest with his fist. "And again, and again. His nose began to bleed, his lips, and he just sat there and took it. I just remember wanting to hit the look off his face. I hated him in that moment, I really did. I hated him for what he did," David admitted as tears welled up in his eyes.

"Dad!" Margaret reached for her father's hands, trying to get him to calm down. "Stop. It's not your fault."

"I just wanted him to forget about what happened over there. I told him to let it go, that nothing good would come from talking about it. About the war. Or *her*. He just lay there beneath me and told me in the calmest voice that he could never forget any of it. So, I punched him again. I swear, I'd never punched my brother like that before. Sure, we play-fought plenty, but I'd never hauled off on him like that."

Lyla's uncle balled up his right fist and began rubbing it. His voice softened. "'Forget it, Charles,' I told him. 'Let it go.' And after that night, he never said a word about it again. Or her. But I swear, Lyla, I didn't know he'd fathered a son."

Lyla didn't know if she wanted to take her uncle's fist in her hands and kiss it or slap him. In the end, she reached over and blew warmth into his fist as he read the inscription on the back of the photograph.

"Luca Charles." He sighed. "All this time, I was trying my best to forget my time over there, but not your father." He looked at Lyla. "He was trying his best *not* to forget. God, he looks so much like him back when we were just boys. Where did you find it?"

"In the back of Caroline's desk drawer," Lyla said. "I almost threw it away, then I saw the envelope was addressed to Dad but mailed here. But now I wish I had."

"Had what?"

"Thrown it away," Lyla said, wondering if she really meant it. What if she had simply tossed the envelope in the trash?

Lyla took the letter and slowly read it out loud while the rest of them laid their heads back on the couch and stared at the ceiling. And when she finished, Lyla folded the letter and slipped it back in the envelope. She sat back too and stared at the acoustic ceiling tiles above, while the letter lay in her lap, weighing a thousand pounds. Maybe even more.

CHAPTER SEVENTEEN

MURMURATION

In the deep plum light, between twilight and night, we fly. Amongst a family of starlings, you and I. We murmur, we soar. Heroes welcomed home from a faraway war.

You have not told me how to do it. Or even when. We just do, because you and I, we are brothers. In the slow swell of our DNA, we lift and turn, whirl and swoop, high, then low. Systems poised on the brink, capable of near and instantaneous transitions. In our rough-housing, we are boyhood avalanches, billows of snow tumbling over unseen atmospheric precipices.

We build. We thin. We fall.

We stop.

Right by day, twisting, then falling into the dark of night.

Left, bereft.

We are starlings. We sing. We roar.

But we do not cry.

No, we mustn't do that. Remember how Mother used to remind us to never let our metal tears turn to rust? *You are Hawkins men. My little kings.* She stood firm in her resolve, even if we stood half a foot over her.

Mathematical analysis proves that each of our movements influences our neighbors. You read that to me by flashlight one night inside our blanket fort. You read a host of science journals back then, watched the films. And once you pulled over to the side of the road and pointed to us flying in the nearly dark sky. "For God's sake, take a good look at that." You whistled.

I looked up and, by God, there we were.

You swooped right. I did too.

Until I don't.

I decide to soar left instead of right alongside you.

I veer up, while you sail down. Isolated in those brief seconds, I am cold in my aloneness, until all of you fly back and bring me into the fold, trying to hide my mistakes.

Who I have become.

In the fold, you can easily camouflage my confusion.

Until, yet again, I stray.

Until one day, I decide to try again. You see, I rather like it out there. In a quiet sky where I do not have to think.

About the blood and the dirt. The torn limbs and the red upon soft new lips. Translucent microscopic hands. Faults built in a foreign land. He was just a baby. A boy.

Again, I wander.

Again, you swing me back.

Again, I fly.

Back into the fold.

Until I don't.

It's so quiet up there.

And I rather like it that way.

CHAPTER EIGHTEEN

FELLING, FALLING, FREE—

NOVEMBER 1981

When the tree fell, the ground shook hard and fast beneath Lyla's feet. Her teeth rattled. Pinching her eyes shut, she tried to deaden the sound of what had just happened—the tearing of bark as it ripped from the stump, the awful crackling of its limbs, the eerie *whump* when thousands of pounds slammed against the earth, then bounced up, and crashed down again. Perhaps even worse was the uneasy silence once the arborist's chain saw whined to a stop.

The hush was sickening.

But it was finally over.

The tree was down.

Lyla walked over and rested her hand on the fallen trunk as if she were feeling for a pulse. "I'm sorry," she whispered, "but I just couldn't look at you anymore. It was time." It had been twenty-five years since her father had hung himself in the tree, but sometimes it felt like yesterday.

"You were just too damned big," she said, more certain than ever she'd done the right thing despite what everyone else had argued over the years.

Taking the tree down won't solve a thing; it won't undo what happened out there. You have to figure out a way to live with it, they all told her in their various well-meaning ways, particularly Caroline, who for over a decade sat underneath the tree every morning with a cup of tea and stared up into the towering foliage as if she were waiting for a rare bird to land on its branches. *You have to learn to make peace with it, Lyla. I finally did.*

But Lyla wasn't so convinced she could ever find peace while it still stood tall.

Upright.

Alive.

Removing the tree would do her a world of good, especially given Caroline's recent announcement that she'd revised her will and was gifting Lyla the family home after she died. Lyla was equal parts touched and suspicious, as if Caroline was giving Lyla the house only so Lyla could find her own reconciliation with the tree, which Lyla knew was impossible.

Caroline was not dead. Yet.

So why not get a jump start? Why not just take the bull by the horns? Caroline wasn't ever coming back.

But now came the hard part. She'd have to call the family, one by one, and own up to the fact that she'd taken the tree down without the title, without Caroline's permission. She'd tell her cousins she did it on a whim, that she'd woken up one morning and before she even so much as made her first cup of coffee, flipped open the yellow pages to *A* and called the first arborist that she pointed her finger to: *Grizzly's Tree Service.*

"You're in luck," the man had said over the phone, his faint strange accent buzzing over the line. "I just had a cancellation. I could come first thing tomorrow."

And now, less than twenty-four hours later, the tree lay cold on its back. There was a certain resignation in how it stretched out upon the earth like Gulliver after having been toppled by the Lilliputians. The struggle was finally over.

"She's a real beauty." The arborist whistled. "Shame you had to take her down." There it was again. His accent. His consonants buzzed even more in person than they did over the phone.

Lyla popped to her feet. She hadn't realized he had been standing over her, listening to her apologize to the tree. But who was he to be whistling like that? Couldn't he see this was no whistling matter?

"Excuse me?" Lyla shielded her eyes. It was only nine in the morning, but the sun was already beating down. The whole town had been griping for weeks about how hot October had been; November was even worse. Yet Lyla knew soon enough winter would kick its way through the door, and everybody would start grumbling about how wet colds were far worse than dry ones.

People had such short memories.

"I said, she was a real beauty." The arborist took a step to the left to block the sun from Lyla's eyes. "Other than those couple of dead limbs, she looked healthy as an ox, if you asked me."

Over the phone, Lyla had told him the tree was diseased.

In a way, it was.

"Just look at her cross section, her pale insides." The arborist took a sip from his water jug and wiped his mouth on his sleeve. He offered a sip to Lyla, but she shook her head.

"And the way she smells. Will you get a load of that!" The arborist sniffed the air with a sort of excited, optimistic look in his eyes as he talked about the tree. It was like people who babbled about their dogs. Or worse, their kids.

"Golly, she's probably the biggest oak I've ever taken down. On my own, that is."

"That so?" Lyla said. The arborist smiled big and dopey, his blue eyes clear underneath his protective glasses. Adorable, she would admit if she was in the market.

But she wasn't. She was tired of dating.

She hated all the small talk over the phone.

Having to shave her legs before a date.

The awkward pauses over dinner, or worse, the clumsy hugs while standing on the doorstep at the end of the night. She despised all of it and had convinced herself she was meant to be single. She was better going it alone.

Plus, she rather liked her freedom, despite what her mother would say over and over again. *Don't bother with finding perfection, Lyla. Good enough is good enough.* Or Caroline, who insisted Lyla needed a man to get along in this world. Lyla would shake her head and tell them both she *wasn't Audrey Hepburn for God's sweet sakes* and if they didn't stop with all the needing a man mumbo jumbo, she'd start letting the hair grow in her armpits.

That would shut them both up in a jiffy.

"What I wouldn't do to have a beauty like that in my backyard," the arborist whistled again. "Such a shame."

Lyla stared down the length of the fallen tree, wishing he'd stop saying that.

It's a shame.

She is so beautiful.

None of it was true.

It was just an ugly tree.

But of course, that was a lie too. The tree was so much more than that. The kind of *more* nobody else could ever see or appreciate. The kind of *more* that hurts worse than stepping barefoot on rusted barbed wire or putting a hand through a windowpane.

For years, she'd tried to reduce the tree to its most basic parts, the way her family seemed to be able to do. *Just a bunch of roots, a trunk, branches, and foliage,* they'd tried to convince her. But unlike them, every time Lyla looked out at it, this is what she saw: her father's feet dangled in the air, his toes pointing to the ground, making small circles as his body slowly rotated around and around.

Some days, her father still had shoes on, his good leather ones that he only wore to church or the bank.

Other days, he wasn't wearing any shoes at all, only his black socks with the gold stripes on the toes and the thinning material at his heels.

Sometimes all she saw were his bare feet, pale and yellowed and warmed by the sun, the same bare feet she lay on when she was a little girl and he gave her airplane rides at the beach. The same bare feet that poked out of her parents' bright white sheets when they slept in on Saturday mornings.

And it never stopped there.

Every now and again, she saw her father's long arms, lifeless by his side. Arms that were no longer able to pick her up and fly her overhead as he ran through the house, yelling, "Mayday, Mayday, Mayday!" Arms that would never guide her down the aisle had she decided to get married. Hands that would never rest on the small of her back when they danced the first dance.

On the worst of days, she saw her father's broken neck, cocked to the side. His mouth open and wide. His black hair tousled by death.

And his eyes! When she got to his blank blue eyes, she couldn't help but be fixed with fear. She couldn't breathe. When he looked at her, through her, she could even feel the hairs of the rope tightening around her own neck, stealing *her* air.

But those days were rare. Somewhere along the line, she'd learned how to stop herself from seeing the worst of it.

Unless she was tired.

Then she saw it all.

Today, she was really, really tired.

"Well, you're all set for a few winters." The arborist took another sip from his water jug.

"Winter?" she asked, thankful he'd brought her back to the here and now.

"Sure. Live oak makes great firewood. Burns forever, but with less ash. It'll have to be seasoned, of course, but once that's done, you'll be able to heat your house for years."

"Seasoning?" Lyla let out a small laugh. What the hell did she know about seasoning? She barely knew how to cook.

"You know, let the wood dry out. You'll smoke yourself out if you try to burn the wood while it's still green. And you don't want that."

"No," Lyla said, "I suppose I wouldn't." She was up to speed now. But she could never do that.

Burn the wood.

Burn him.

"I don't have plans to burn it." She picked off a piece of the yellow wood, holding it in her fingertips like sliced pear.

"No?" The arborist looked at her as if she were the one with the peculiar accent. His big dopey smile was now gone.

"Nope. I don't have a place to burn it."

"Well, I don't mean to be rude, Mrs. Hawkins." The arborist was teasing her now as he pointed to the house. "But that brick structure sticking out of your rooftop—well, that, ma'am, is what we call a chimney, which runs down to your fireplace, and if—"

"Miss," Lyla interrupted him. She didn't know why she did it. She wasn't trying to advertise that she was unattached. Ma'am just felt old.

"Pardon me?" The tease in his eyes was gone.

"It's Miss Hawkins, not Mrs. I'm not married. And this isn't my house."

"What?" The arborist yanked the work order out of his pocket. His eyes scanned the crumpled yellow paper, searching for the name on the work order.

"This is my grandmother's house. But she doesn't live here

anymore." Lyla put her hand on top of his, intending to calm him, but instead she gave him an electric shock.

"Oh my gosh." She put her other hand on his, shocking him again. "Ack, I'm so sorry." She laughed and quickly lifted her hands off, holding them up in the air as if she'd been pulled over by the cops. "It must be the dry air."

"I'll say." His goofy smile returned. "They say we carry more electricity in our bodies here in the fall. Something to do with earthquake weather."

"They do?" Lyla was a fifth-generation Californian. She'd never heard that one before.

"No, I'm totally kidding." He laughed. "I have no idea. I'm just an arborist. What do I know?" He let out a big sigh, folded the work order, and stuffed it back in his pocket. "Anyhow, you gave me quite a scare there for a minute. I could have lost my insurance if I had taken down an unauthorized tree. Especially one as nice as this." He let out another long breath of relief. "Anyways, I'm sorry for your loss, Miss Lyla Hawkins."

"Loss?" Lyla didn't understand what he meant, especially given how he seemed to speak only from the front of his mouth. The consonants bunched up against one another like a car crash. Yet there was something soft and endearing about the way he spoke. About him.

"Your grandmother?" he offered with a polite look on his face. "Death can be so hard."

"Oh, no." Lyla waved at the air, careful not to touch him this time. "She's not dead. Not yet, at least." She laughed. "We just moved her to a nursing home a couple of months ago after she caught a piece of toast on fire. Could have burned down the whole house if I hadn't come home when I had." Lyla pointed to the blackened patch on the roof. "See?"

The arborist threw his hands over his eyes. "Oof, that could have been bad." The way he said *oof* made her smile. Like a puff of air escaping a piglet's mouth.

"A few weeks before that nifty bit, she'd forgotten to turn off the oven. Heated the house for days while I was away taking a little mini vacation. I came home and nearly fell over from heat exhaustion." She laughed. "And earlier last summer, the police called to say they had found her driving in the wrong lane across the Golden Gate Bridge. She said she was just going to the market and didn't know what the big fuss was about."

"Sounds like it was time. She's lucky to have you."

This puffed Lyla up. She enjoyed being needed by her grandmother. She liked how they had learned to forgive and start anew when Lyla had returned from Wyoming, how the two of them went right to the heart of a topic instead of nibbling around the corners like Lyla still had a habit of doing with her mother.

"Yep, but then we finally locked her away." Lyla rubbed her hands together like an evil cartoon character who had just announced plans to destroy the world. "Mwahahaha," she laughed a little too brazenly.

The arborist looked at Lyla with a sour, pinched expression. Lyla felt hot embarrassment flush through her.

"I'm totally kidding." Lyla swatted the air again, unsure why she was acting so weird. She would never see the arborist again.

"Anyhow, it's better this way," she lied again.

But this was only a partial lie. Putting Caroline into a home *had* been better for everybody, except for her grandmother. When they all sat Caroline down and told her the plan, she told them they ought to stay out of her *goddamn business*. She held her head high and waved them off, insisting she was *perfectly fine, thank you very much*.

But the bridge, Margaret had reminded her.

A simple mistake. It was nighttime.

Leaving the oven on for days? Lyla's uncle had held his mother's hand.

Anyone could have done the same. Caroline swatted David's hand away.

The toast? Lyla had asked.

Silence.

Her grandmother sat straight-backed in her chair and sipped her tea. Above, stars shone through the open patch in the roof.

"I'm not moving in with a bunch of old people who just sit around all day in their wheelchairs, wearing bibs and diapers. I'm fine right here. This is my house." Caroline got up and put her cup back in the cupboard without washing it, the tea bag still in the mug, her red lipstick marks stuck to the rim. When Margaret got up to retrieve the cup and wash it, Caroline pretended not to notice.

"Plus, Lyla's here," Caroline had said that night. "She'll take care of me. It's what we agreed upon." And with that, Caroline got up and went straight to her bedroom, leaving them all sitting around the kitchen table, staring at one another. But really, they were all watching Lyla.

There had been no such formal agreement. Lyla was in between jobs, and the particulars of how long she'd stay were all a bit fuzzy. Being her grandmother's full-time caregiver wasn't exactly what she had signed up for. Lyla looked up at the stars through the burnt-out gap in the roof. She was just filling a hole.

The day they finally moved Caroline into Arbor Vine Home for the Elderly, Lyla had stood aside watching her grandmother kick and scream at the entrance to the building. The sliding glass doors opened and closed, opened and closed as they stood on the sensor.

"You can't do this to me!" Caroline had barked when Lyla's uncle finally helped her down into a wheelchair. "I belong at home. I told you that!"

Caroline had tried to grab hold of Lyla's arm. "And you, of all people! I was counting on you, Lyla. You were supposed—"

Lyla stayed behind as her uncle wheeled his mother down the hallway. Supposed to what? She wasn't a nurse. She was a bookkeeper. She kept accounts. She tracked invoices and payments. She wasn't qualified to be a caregiver.

By the end of the month, however, her grandmother had somehow made peace with her new reality. Lyla figured it was the sedatives. And three weeks in, Caroline announced she had a boyfriend.

"His name is Eduardo," Caroline confided to Lyla in an unusually playful, girlish tone. "He's quite handsome. And so strong!" Caroline flexed the weak muscles in her arms and giggled again, kissing into the air.

Eduardo was not her boyfriend. Eduardo was a lovely Guatemalan nursing assistant who helped Caroline brush her teeth and go to the toilet at night. But her grandmother's giddiness almost got Lyla to change her mind—to pack up Caroline's things and take her back home, to learn the art of caregiving. But in the end, it was her cousin Robert who hugged Lyla and stopped her. "Hey, if Caroline's getting a little action, even if in her imagination, so be it. It's about time."

Lyla burst out laughing and found a way to let it all go.

Caroline was home.

"Anyhow, it's lucky I came back when I did or the whole house could have burnt to the ground." Lyla cracked her knuckles, one at a time. The arborist winced with each pop.

"Sorry," she said again, and shook out her hands. "I cut my trip short by a day. I just felt that I better come home, like it was irresponsible for me to be away for so long." Lyla was talking full speed now. *Nervous talk*, her therapist called it. She could go from zero to sixty in just a few seconds.

"I pulled into the driveway. Didn't even pop the trunk to unload my suitcase, when low and behold there was a plume of smoke blowing out the roof, just like you see in the movies. I half expected to see my grandmother behind the window, waving a hanky at me, yelling, 'Help me, help me!' But nope. I ran through the front door calling out for her. And guess where she was the whole darn time?"

The arborist shook his head as he glanced at his watch. "No idea." He wiped the sweat off his forehead.

"She was sitting in her bedroom, putting on her lipstick and pearl earrings. As if she had a date." Lyla twirled a finger next to her head and rolled her eyes. "Totally cuckoo."

That made the arborist chuckle. His eyes grew wide and agreeable like a big golden retriever ready to play fetch. And then he coughed nervously into his fist.

"Not too long ago we had to put my father in a home," he confided. His eyes were no longer wide, no longer agreeable. He looked as if he had swallowed a fig. His eyes began to water.

Oh, God, Lyla thought. *Not another crier.* Hap was a crier, especially when he was drunk. And so was the guy she had dated after moving home. That one cried a lot. Cried out patriotic songs. And sometimes, for no apparent reason, he'd just cry. But that was when he was a happy-turned-sad drunk. When he was happy-turned-mad drunk, he'd cry with his fists. Like Hap. After those two, Lyla had begun to wonder what it was about her that she attracted the *happy-turn-sappy-turn-mean* guys.

The arborist pressed his thumb against one nostril and blew. He did the same to the other nostril.

"It's horrible, isn't it? Those places and all." He wiped his hand on his jeans. "You never imagine you'd be the kind of person to do that to your family." He kicked dirt over the glob of mucus on the ground with the toe of his work boot. "But sometimes you just don't have a choice. Right?"

Lyla tried not to look at what he just blew from his nostrils. Tried not to look as aghast as she felt.

Instead, she looked into his begging blue eyes, knowing she'd worn that same pathetic smile herself when she shadowed the admissions director around Arbor Vine, checking out all they had to offer—the movie room, the bingo room, the dining hall, the library filled with Danielle Steel novels in large easy-to-read fonts. Because the director was a rather quick-paced woman, Lyla had to sort of jog alongside her to keep up. She felt like she once had as a kid, chasing her grandmother around the shopping mall.

"Yes," Lyla told the arborist, "getting old sucks. I keep telling my cousins to just take me behind the barn and shoot me." She laughed.

The arborist didn't. Which, if she cared a lick about what he thought, would have worried her.

He looked around—maybe looking for the barn.

"It's just a saying," she said.

"Oh." He smiled.

"So, now what?" Lyla asked. "Put it in a wood chipper and haul it away?"

The arborist looked at the fallen tree. "Are you sure you don't want to sell it? It's worth a lot of money. You know that, don't you? It's a shame to just chip her up, turn her to mulch."

Lyla shook her head. Sure, she could use a little extra spending money since being laid off, but not from the tree. "No, thanks. I don't have what it takes to—what did you call it?—season it? I just want it gone. Today if possible."

The arborist took out his handkerchief and wiped the sweat pooling in the depression above his upper lip. He carefully folded the handkerchief back up and slid it in his back pocket. "Mind if I ask you something?"

"Sure, go ahead. I'm an open book." Which wasn't true at all.

"Why'd you cut her down?"

Lyla didn't answer him at first. She'd become too focused on how he kept calling the tree a *she*, a *her*. Hap used to say the same about cars. For a short time after moving in with Hap, she had convinced herself it was kind of sweet when he talked like that, something protective in the way he took care of the cars that came through the shop, of her. But there was that night; he took her on the ice and left her to fend for herself while he cared for his dog. Then rattled her up with the back of his hand when she refused to talk to him on the drive home. Then she locked herself in the bathroom and called her uncle for help. Hap knocked over and over again on the door, crying, begging for her to come out and forgive him. But she didn't forgive him. Couldn't. She packed up her things when he was asleep that night and drove straight back to California.

On the long drive back, she reminded herself how she hated that sort of talk. Calling things *hers* and *shes*.

———————

"My dad hanged himself in it," Lyla finally answered the arborist in the matter-of-fact tone she had perfected over the years, as if she were reciting her grocery list.

The arborist reached out, she guessed on instinct as an act of comfort, but Lyla didn't take his big, calloused hand. "Oh Lord," he said, "I didn't know. I'm terribly sorry."

"Of course you didn't know. How could you?" Lyla barked. She hadn't meant to be rude, but she wished he'd just stop it with the constant apologies. "What? Were you supposed to know my family history before you took the job?"

When she could see he was about to apologize again, she held out her hand like a crossing guard. "I was ten when he did it. I'm over it."

Of course, that was another lie.

"Sorry."

"Please. Stop doing that." Irritation bubbled up inside her.

"What?" The arborist cocked his head to the side. "What did I do?"

"Apologizing like that. I don't even know you."

"I . . . I should . . . I didn't mean . . . I was only—" He looked back at his watch and then the tree. "I guess I should get back to work. I've got another job after this." He pulled his protective glasses over his eyes and didn't so much as look at Lyla when he walked back to his chain saw he'd left propped up against the stump.

Lyla could have, should have, stopped him. She knew that. She should have called him back and apologized for barking at him, but she wasn't in the business of apologizing to strangers. Hell, she barely ever apologized to her family, and she knew she had a doozy of an ask of forgiveness ahead of her when she called to tell them about what she'd done to the tree.

The arborist stuffed his orange earplugs back in his ears and turned on the motor.

It was a warped quirk of hers, she thought—to push people away like that.

She hadn't meant to be so blunt.

But she was hot.

And she was tired.

Plus, she just wanted him to get the job done. To get it over with so she could do what the rest of her family could so easily do: move on.

Lyla should have gone inside and washed up.

Come back out when it was all over.

But she didn't. She couldn't.

She stood in the hot sun and watched the arborist walk the length of the tree, measuring how many rounds to cut. She admired how confident and competent he was at that moment. How he worked his way from the crown of the tree to the back, slicing small grooves into the bark with his chain saw at equal intervals. When he walked back to the head of the tree, he turned off the motor for a bit, sussing out the best way to clear the mess of broken limbs and tangled foliage.

"You can take whatever you cut!" Lyla yelled out to him, waving her hands to grab his attention.

"What?" He took out one of his earplugs.

"I said, you can have the wood when you finish."

The arborist put down his chain saw and jogged over to her, as if nobody had ever offered him so much as a dime before, let alone this much wood. His shirt was thoroughly soaked with sweat.

"Really?"

Lyla liked the way his eyes lit up with her offer, as if she had made up for her rudeness before.

"Absolutely! Just get her out of here!"

She had never done that before.

The tree had always been a *he*.

Him.

Always her father.

"And thank you," Lyla said, "I really appreciate it. More than you can imagine."

"Well, geez. Thanks!" The arborist put his earplug back in and cranked the motor on his chain saw. "You'll need to back up!" he shouted, waving her off.

She took a few steps backward.

"A little farther." He waved at her again, still smiling. "Things are going to get a little messy."

That, of course, made Lyla laugh. "Honey, you don't have a clue about messy," she said under the roar of the chain saw. She stepped back and watched him dig his saw into the tree as he cut the first round. He took a few steps forward and dug in again. And then again. The fumes from the chain saw drifted downwind to where Lyla stood.

She had always liked the smell of gas.

Even as a kid.

It smelled like she was going somewhere.

It smelled productive.

Later, when the arborist came out of the bathroom, Lyla stood in the hallway, holding onto her checkbook. "So, who should I make the check to?"

"You can make it out to me." The arborist dried his hands on his jeans and reached out. "Here, give it to me, though. It's a devil of a name. Nobody ever gets it right."

"Try me." Lyla smiled, trying to make up for being such a crab earlier. "I'm a hell of a good speller. Went to the spelling bee state championship when I was a kid. Could have gone to nationals, but I got tripped up on *resuscitation* of all words. I choked and totally blanked when it came to that sneaky *c* in the word. I lost to some pimply-faced kid from Orange County." She laughed.

"Impressive." The arborist smiled. "But I doubt you'll get this, Miss Spelling Bee Champ." He winked. "Nobody gets it on the first try. Or the second. Or tenth for that matter."

"Well, you've never met anyone like me. Have you?" Lyla balanced the checkbook against her thigh. "Hit me."

"Okay. Grzegorz Grześkiewicz," he said slowly; the consonants buzzed out from his teeth.

Lyla hadn't even so much as gotten down the first *g* when she snorted like a horse. "What on earth did you do to your mother in the womb? Kick her like crazy?" She was laughing harder than she meant to.

The arborist just shrugged.

"Seriously, what kind of name is that?"

"My parents were from Poland. Came here just before Hitler took Krakow and named me after my mother's father who decided it was best to stay behind. Heck of a bad decision if you ask me."

"I'll say." Lyla snorted again. She thought he was still referring to his parents' decision to give him that crazy name. But seeing the shock in his eyes, she realized she'd made a mistake. "I'm sorry," she said. "I thought . . . Oh, never mind."

"It's okay." Again, he offered to write out the check, but Lyla waved him back.

"No, wait. Give me at least one go at it. Mr. Grzegorz Grześkiewicz." She fumbled his name around in her mouth, trying to get a purchase on it. But there were too many consonants, too many *g*'s and *r*'s and *z*'s. It was like talking with a fistful of sand in her mouth. She made one attempt and ripped up the check before she even showed him the mess she'd made. She handed him the pen and the checkbook. "You're right," she admitted. "Too much, even for this long-ago spelling bee champ."

When the arborist grabbed the pen, he accidentally shocked her this time.

"Wow, sorry 'bout that." He held onto her hand as if he were grounding a hot wire. "Must be the earthquake weather."

This time, Lyla didn't get angry at his apology. She rather liked the way he held onto her, secretly wishing he'd shock her again, so he could hold on a little longer. It had been some time since she had been touched like that.

They were good hands.

Capable hands.

Productive hands.

Even dirty and cracked, they were hands that could make her swear back into dating again.

Grzegorz bit the cap off the end of the pen and wrote his name on the check. Despite the accordion of consonants in his name, his signature was neat and tidy. *Grzegorz Grześkiewicz.*

"Anyhow, people just call me Griz." He ripped the check from the book and tucked it into his front pocket and tapped it. "It's a whole lot easier."

"Griz, yes, that is a bit more manageable." Lyla laughed. "And very Ursus Californicus of you."

Griz looked at her suspiciously.

"You know, the state flag." She held up her hands and growled, baring her teeth at him. But with that look on his face, she quickly dropped her hands and stuffed them into her pockets, feeling foolish. "I've been volunteering over at the Point Reyes Station Visitor Center. People are always asking about bears."

"Oh, right. The flag." He smiled. "I was raised in Wisconsin. Moved out here just a few years ago. The winters take a little getting used to here with the constant sunshine and no snow, but"—he laughed—"the women are a whole lot prettier. And a lot less hairy."

"Well, you know what they say about us?"

"What's that?"

Lyla held the pen out like a microphone and began singing the tune "California Girls," belting out how girls from the West coast are so blessed with sunshine and tans.

Griz snatched the pen from Lyla and picked up where she had left off. He closed his eyes and in his other hand waved an imaginary lighter in the air, as he rocked on about them Southern gals and the farmers' daughters and those ladies from the North, not seeming to mind one bit that he was singing the lyrics out of order.

When Lyla tried to snag the pen mic back, to take the next verse, Griz peeked one eye open, shook his head and closed his eye again as he carried on about having travelled the world and how nothing compared to the cutest girls of them all.

Lyla just stood there, watching this guy in her kitchen singing terribly off-key, admiring how it didn't seem to bother him in the least when he hit a wrong note. How he was really getting into it. Maybe he was tone deaf, she thought.

And when it was time for the famous chorus, Griz stepped back toward Lyla and held the pen out between them. Lyla leaned in and together they sang their hearts out, wishing they could all be from California. They sang the chorus over and over, until their voices finally trailed off.

And then silence.

Griz opened his eyes and smiled.

"Or something like that." he handed Lyla back her pen.

"Yeah," Lyla agreed, feeling the sudden heat flush in her cheeks. "Something like that," And put the cap back on the pen.

"Well, all righty, then. I guess I'll see you around." She put the check-book in her back pocket and walked Griz to the door. He stood there for a moment before opening it.

"Say." Griz nervously coughed again into his fist. "I was wondering if you might want to grab a cup of coffee with me sometime, or dinner? We could talk about putting our folks in a home. You know, share notes."

"My grandmother," Lyla corrected him, as if it really mattered.

"Come again?"

"My mother is still humming along. She's remarried and off seeing the country in an Airstream. She and Dad Number Two are trying to hit every state and all the national parks now that they're both retired."

"You don't like him? Your stepfather?"

"He's okay," Lyla said with a slight shrug. "Anyhow, my mom would be horrified if anyone mistook her for my grandmother. They never really got along all that well, especially after my dad died."

"Oh, sorry."

"Seriously, Griz, you don't need to keep doing that, you know." Lyla smiled at him this time.

"What?"

"Apologizing like that."

"Yes, well." He coughed again. "Old habits. You know what they say about them. Anyhow, what do you say?"

"Are you asking me on a date?" she asked, playfully. She kind of liked his willingness to acknowledge how hard things are to change.

"I suppose. Yes, ma'am, that is what I'm doing." He tipped his sweaty baseball cap. "I'm not really all that good at it. I haven't dated in a long time. Well, not since my wife died. It's been two years now."

Of course, he's been married, Lyla thought. Griz was not the kind of man destined to be alone for long. He was too busy being kind— blocking the sun out of people's eyes, offering the last of his water, apologizing for every last little thing—to have remained single all his life. Plus, he smiled a lot, perhaps a little too much. He was practically begging her to go on a date with those eyes.

And Lyla had sworn off needy men.

They drained her.

"That's kind of you, but"—Lyla reached over and opened the door—"I don't think that would be a good idea. I'm in a relationship already."

"Oh, I'm sorry. I didn't mean to be so . . . so . . ." he stammered.

"Griz." Lyla put her hand up, preventing him from uttering yet another apology. "Please."

"Okay, then. See you tomorrow."

Griz stepped off the porch and started down the driveway toward his truck; his heavy work boots clunked along the concrete.

She liked the sound.

It sounded sturdy.

Solid.

Lyla watched as Griz climbed into his truck and turned on the engine. Then it caught her. *Tomorrow? What did he mean tomorrow?* She hadn't agreed to such a thing. Wasn't he listening? She just told him that she wasn't available.

Lyla jogged down the driveway and flagged him down before he drove off.

Griz stopped and rolled down the window. "Forget something?" He left the engine running.

"You're coming back tomorrow? I thought—"

"To pick up the wood. You said I could have it. Right?"

"Oh, right," she said, relieved. "The wood. Yes, of course. I thought maybe . . ." She paused. She could feel her cheeks getting hot. She put her hand on the window, slightly wishing he'd reach out and shock her again. If he did, it would be a sign; she'd tell him that she had lied, that she wasn't dating anyone. That she could maybe get a cup of coffee. It would be good for her.

But Griz kept his hands planted on the steering wheel.

"Oh, never mind. Sorry." She hadn't a clue as to why she apologized. Maybe it was contagious. "Okay, then." She smiled and waved goodbye. "See you tomorrow."

Lyla still stood at the edge of the driveway as Griz pulled away, thankful at least he'd agreed to come back to haul the rounds off the next day, thankful that if she couldn't go on a date with the poor guy, at least she could feel good about giving him the firewood. Giving him the ability to heat his house for years.

Lyla walked back into the house and filled a glass of water, drained it, and filled it back again. Above her, a little black starling had flown into the kitchen and was thumping against the window. She slid the sill open, but still, the bird did not fly out. It continued to flutter and flail at its reflection.

"Go on." Lyla waved a dish towel at the bird, trying to shoo it outside. But the bird just kept fluttering around the kitchen, relentlessly hammering its beak at the window until it finally gave up and perched on the windowsill.

Lyla slid the window open a little farther, and still the bird didn't fly out. It hopped back and forth on its spindly orange legs, cocking its head to the side as if it were watching Lyla watching it.

Lyla filled her glass again and took a sip and stared beyond the bird, out the window to where the massive tree lay on its back, felled and sawed into equal parts like a CT scan. Lyla dumped the water down the sink, thankful she would never have to look at it again. Tomorrow, it would all be gone.

She turned on the faucet and began scrubbing the backsplash, the grout on the counter, the metal faucet handle. The empty cup. When she was finished, she rinsed her hands under the water and dried them on the dish towel, folded it, and laid it on the countertop as her grandmother would have done. The bird was still watching her with those longing black eyes.

Daddy? she nearly asked the bird.

But she knew she was being silly.

She was overheated.

And she could feel her gut sinking. Now was the hard part. She had to make the round of calls and tell them what she'd done. She'd call Margaret first. Mags wouldn't try to make her feel guilty, but Lyla would hear the disappointment in her inevitable sigh. Robert would tell her she'd just sunk the value of the house with that tree gone. Steven wouldn't care all that much. And her sweet uncle David, he would tell her what she needed to hear, even though she knew on some level he felt that tree was his too. He had a long history with it that predated Lyla's. But when it came time to tell Caroline, there would be hell to pay. There would be the inevitable screaming.

The *How could yous.*

The *That was my tree!*

The guilt.

None of it would be easy, and for a moment, Lyla wondered if she even had to say anything to Caroline at all. Maybe she could find a way to avoid that confrontation altogether.

Lyla removed the handset from the cradle and started dialing Margaret's number as the bird sat on the windowsill next to her, its head still cocked. The line began to ring.

One.

Two.

On three, Lyla slapped her finger on the switch and ended the call.

She looked out at the fallen tree that Griz believed was over three hundred years old, telling her it had lived through plenty of history over the centuries. "Can you imagine what that tree has seen? What it's lived through? Boy, if trees could talk, now that would be something."

That would be something indeed, Lyla thought as she wrapped the blue telephone cord around her finger. She watched it swell and turn deeper red, then purple. It started to throb, then grow numb. She was so tired of her whole body feeling that way too.

Lyla unwound the cord and let the blood flow freely. When her fingertip returned to normal, she flipped the phone book open.

I can do this, she said to herself as she punched each number, slow and sure. *What's the worst thing that could happen?*

The line on the other end rang and rang.

And the bird flew off.

Wait, she almost cried, as though she had just realized she might need company. But the bird had disappeared. And as the other end of the line rang, she wished she'd thought to have closed the window and kept it.

She could have fed the bird and loved it.

Given it a home.

Cared for it.

Distracted, Lyla was just about to place her finger on the switch again when the recorded voice on the machine answered.

"You've reached Grizzly's Tree Service. I am sorry that we are not here."

Lyla laughed at the soft, buzzing nature of Griz's voice. Even on the answering machine, he had an apology at the ready.

"Please leave your name, number, and the time you called."

And she did.

She left her number and hung up.

I am falling, she thought.

And now, maybe, just maybe, she was finally free.

CHAPTER NINETEEN

CEREMONIAL SONGS OF CHANGE—

NOVEMBER 1981

Beyond the sun-beaten gray fence sits the stump, two feet tall and four feet in diameter. The stump is, in a strange way, very old—nearly three hundred years or so—dating back to when the Miwoks held sway over this part of the Earth.

Yet the stump is also quite new. A week old to be precise.

The sweet smell of sawn wood was still fresh, the circle of annual growth rings pale and clean.

The stump had once been the base of a great magnificent California oak that had survived centuries of change. It had listened to the ceremonial songs of the native Miwoks as well as the distant jackhammering sounds of industry.

It outlasted an invasion of the Franciscan missionaries, the introduction of smallpox, a signed Declaration of Independence, and several wars, some considered great. Others not so much.

The tree lived through a time when stories were passed down through oral tradition, projected in silent movies, transmitted through radio waves, and broadcasted on televisions around the world.

The tree was alive at the advent of Atari and bore witness to the creation of glorious, gut-wrenching poetry—words that could move alike the souls of lovers and the most hardened criminals.

The tree survived the extinction of the passenger pigeon.

And a host of other lost species.

CHAPTER TWENTY

COST OF LIVING ADJUSTMENTS—

DECEMBER 1981

From where Lyla sits, she cannot see the stump. It's hidden by the height of the countertop, the backsplash, the corner of the kitchen cabinet. Out the window, she sees nothing but bright, fabulous sunshine, a terribly blue sky, and the green hills just beyond.

Sitting at the head of her grandmother's table, Lyla crumples up a draft of a letter. She tosses it across the tabletop, and it lands next to the other crumpled-up versions of what she wishes to say.

She pulls out another blank sheet of stationery from the box and starts anew.

Dear Gessica,
You don't know me. My name is Lyla Hawkins.

Lyla pauses. Her eyes are drawn to where the tree no longer stands tall. Sitting where her grandmother always sat, Lyla tries to pretend the tree had never been there at all. She attempts to fool herself into believing, even if just for a moment, she never climbed into the tree's arms.

Or hung the rope on the great, expansive branch.

Or sat on the rubber tire, pumping her legs as she swung over the sloping hill below.

Lyla stares into the emptiness, trying to erase all the times she sat underneath the tree's wide canopy with her father. The way she collected acorns and stuffed them in her mouth like a squirrel, making him laugh like it was the funniest thing he'd ever seen.

Making him laugh until he cried.

In the silence of her grandmother's home—the house that will eventually become hers—Lyla tries to flush the memory of the time her father told her about what it was like to shoot men in the tight spaces between their eyes.

How it nearly killed him to do it.

How he pressed his finger to her seven-year-old forehead and whispered, "*Bang!*"

How he seared his burden into her like a cow brand.

Gripping the barrel of the ballpoint pen, Lyla clicks the end button.

In. Out. In. Out.

She closes her eyes and attempts something spectacular in her eradication efforts. She tries to forget she ever had a father at all.

But of course, that is impossible, because when she opens her eyes, the new draft of the letter sits before her on the tabletop. She continues.

Dear Gessica,
You don't know me. My name is Lyla Hawkins. You knew
my father.

She reads these three sentences out loud and realizes it sounds too harsh. Too cold. She crumples this draft into a baseball-sized wad; she knuckles the imaginary seams. This time, she doesn't lob it to where the other drafts sit. This time, she chucks it clear across the room. She watches the curve of the paper ball before it hits the window and falls to the floor.

"Oh, forget it! This is stupid," she says, and stands up. She brings her dishes to the kitchen sink, convinced she does not know how to do any of this. Writing the letter and all the rest.

She turns on the tap and runs her dishes under the faucet. From there, she can see it all.

Every last bit of it—both the real and the imagined. The stump that sits beyond the slats of the fence like a stubborn rhino captive at the zoo. After watching endless numbers of nature shows with her stepfather, Lyla has come to learn that rhinos are not pacifists but dangerous beasts. She knows not to be fooled.

It is just a stump for heaven's sake. Lyla gives herself a quiet pep talk as she fishes the tea bag out of her mug. *Just a mass of woody tissue, bark and hidden roots. Nothing more.*

But of course, she knows that is not entirely true. It is so much more than that.

Because even when the stump is eventually ground down and hauled away in the back of Griz's truck, she knows everything will remain stuck inside her like sap.

The tree's joys. Its beauty. Its sadness. The questions and answers newly unearthed.

She drops the tea bag into the trash and chides herself for having been so naive. She is a grown woman for Pete's sake who knows, deep in her bones, things of this magnitude cannot disappear with the simple snap of a finger, a call to an arborist, the buzz of a chain saw.

The grinding of a stump into woodchips.

Things slowly erode over time, but the evidence will remain forever. And still.

Lyla sits back down and pushes the box of stationery aside. She removes the rubber band from the *Index-Tribune* newspaper and combs the headlines: the assassination of Anwar Sadat, a royal marriage, the end of the Iran hostage crisis, inflation rates, and changes to the cost-of-living index.

"Cost of living!" Lyla chortles as if costs of living could simply be reduced to a theoretical index that measures the differences in the price of goods and services, or allows for substitutions with other items as prices vary.

"Give me a big fat break," Lyla blurts out. She folds the newspaper and walks out back to where she could swear the cobalt-blue sky is brighter than she's ever witnessed before. Lyla cannot take everything in all at once.

Or even in little bitty pieces.

There are too many memories trapped inside, only to die when she does. Even then, who knows? Oral tradition has a long lineage in this country.

Just ask the Miwoks.

Looking beyond the fence, Lyla imagines how the story of what happened out there will be told for generations, like a spooky ghost tale shared around a campfire. The details will take on new shapes and shades of shadowy gray lore and will last long after Lyla's own ashes are thrown out to sea. As a little girl, Lyla had already endured mashed-up versions of what her father did. Whispered tales of her family's story were callously spread around the playground and shared by neighborhood kids—through tin cans connected by lines of string and telephone games at sleepovers. And once she walked past Betsy McGregor and Elsa Jacobs who were jumping double Dutch in the middle of the street one Saturday afternoon.

Not last night but the night before
The ghost of Old Man Hawkins came knocking at my door
I asked what he wanted
And this is what he said:
Spanish Dancer, do the splits
Spanish Dancer, do the twist
Spanish Dancer, turn around

Spanish Dancer, touch the ground
Spanish Dancer, pick up the slack
Spanish Dancer, take that rope off your neck
And never come back.

Standing on the cement porch, Lyla fortifies herself from the memories that outlasted her childhood. She glowers at the stump, almost as if challenging it. Who will blink first? The stump doesn't move or charge her. And why should it? It's not a rhino. It is just a stump, a once full and mature tree now cut off at the shins.

"Goddamn you, Daddy," she finally says. She is just so tired of it all.

Below the stump are things left unseen, such as the mass of tangled-up roots that forge deep into the earth. Lyla knows from her high school physical science class that root systems can take hundreds of years to fully decompose. And somewhere down there buried amongst the roots are the bones of poor old Washington and Jefferson and Lincoln, the Hawkins family dogs.

Those will take longer to decompose still.

But there is something else buried underneath there too, something Lyla had long ago tucked into the bed of the earth. Something that generations of pill bugs and worms and ants would have continued to crawl up and over and inch around for centuries. Something that would have remained down there forever had Lyla not stepped out on the patio just when she did.

Man-made items have a habit of sticking around long past their intended use. Like concrete war bunkers, they don't go anywhere for a very long time.

"Oh my God," Lyla says with a sudden cold, dry mouth, instantly remembering what she had laid to rest under the tree. She races to the garage and grabs a trowel from her grandfather's old workbench and rushes out back to the stump. She does not remember where she buried the doll. Just that she did.

Lyla sits down on the stump and begins inching her way around it like a sundial, digging small holes in the soil, soft after the first heavy rains. The December dirt makes her job easier. In the cracked, hard earth of July, this job, she knows, would have been nearly impossible. Her trowel clinks something. Not a rock. Something different. She taps again, more carefully this time, so as to not crack the object below.

Tap, tap, tap.

The pinging of the porcelain rings out of the dirt like a wind chime.

Lyla drops to her hands and knees and begins to rake the earth with her fingernails, moving the dirt carefully aside like a paleontologist until the doll's decapitated head is revealed. Lying in the dirt, the doll's innocent eyes stare up at Lyla, as if she were wondering how long she had been down there. How long had she been holding her breath, waiting for Lyla to come back and fetch her?

"Holy shit," Lyla gasps, trying to swallow the guilt she feels for having buried her grandmother's favorite doll, the only souvenir from her father's time overseas, and then for letting her cousin Steven take the blame. Lyla doesn't move at first. She can't. She's stuck, staring at the beheaded figurine with that same dumb smile plastered on her face. Lyla excavates the doll's head and holds her up in the air, like an idol. She's seen such apotheosizing before, not at church. Maybe in Hawaii. She was just there, vacationing on the Na' Pali coast, taking a break from it all: wading through the warm, turbulent Pacific waves, making sense of all the decisions her family has made. Her nose is still peeling from having fallen asleep in the midday sun, dreaming of a different life.

Lyla rests the doll's head on the stump. She looks terrible and strange, like a demented character in a horror movie. Lyla remembers that about the doll.

Her ghastly smile.

The slow batting of those horsehair eyelashes.

Lyla goes back to work and digs deeper. She is intent on finding the rest of the girl. The bodice. The Scottie dog that was once attached to the leash in the girl's gloved hand. It doesn't take Lyla long to find the remaining pieces. She had, after all, buried everything together, unknowingly right next to poor old Jefferson's left femur.

Lyla gets up and cradles the broken doll in the fold of her shirt and heads back to the kitchen. She turns on the faucet and runs her finger under the tap, making sure the water is just right, Goldilocks style. Not too hot. Not too cold. She holds the girl's head under the warm water, bathing her clean, just like how Lyla's mother used to care for her—when Louise would hum Irish lullabies and pick tiny pieces of asphalt out of Lyla's torn-up wrists and knees.

Lyla starts humming too, not a lullaby, exactly. Jethro Tull's "Bungle in the Jungle." It's not intentional. It's just the first song that pops into her head. She heard it recently on the radio after her drive back from visiting her grandmother and sharing the news of the tree, when Lyla conveniently waited until her grandmother's eyes were half-mast before she shared what she'd done.

Her grandmother had not said a word in return but simply sighed back to sleep.

Lyla removes one of her grandmother's dishrags from the drawer and gently washes the mud off the doll's cheeks. She then takes an oyster fork and combs the dirt from the doll's long brown hair. Lyla feels another sharp pang of guilt for having done this to her. The doll was never meant to be outside. She was never meant to get so dirty. The doll was made in Italy and should have never crossed the Atlantic Ocean in the first place. Maybe, Lyla decides as she cleans the mud off the porcelain, had the doll stayed in Italy like the news of Lyla's half brother, things would have turned out differently.

Lyla spends the better part of the night gluing the doll back together. Everything fits so nicely, except where a tiny piece of porcelain from the doll's bodice is missing, leaving a hole the size of a tomato seed, as though she's been shot in the clavicle.

Lyla riffles through the junk drawer, searching for her grandmother's sturdy red flashlight. She storms out back, swearing she'll find the missing piece, even if it takes her until morning. Climbing over the fence in the dark of night, Lyla knows she is being silly. Dramatic even. She knows it will be next to impossible to find.

The missing bit is far too small.

Yet there she is with the flashlight clenched between her teeth, sifting the dirt, long after the moon has risen and started to fall again, as if she's panning for gold like when she was on her fourth-grade field trip in the foothills, when Joe Daniels first kissed her on the cheek on the bus ride home. She could have slapped him for being so bold but hadn't. She liked Joe Daniels. She used to write her name on scraps of paper, Lyla Daniels, Mrs. Lyla Daniels, Mr. and Mrs. Joe Daniels, like she had when she first dated Hap.

Rooting around in the dark, Lyla wonders what ever happened to Joe after he came home from Vietnam. She heard he returned missing a leg and part of his brain. She heard he lives somewhere on the streets of San Francisco.

Lyla promises she will go searching for Joe and give him a great big hug and thank him for his service.

Like gifting the wood to Griz, Lyla feels energized by the thought of giving something back to Joe, even if a simple thank-you.

Occasionally, Lyla comes across a teensy pebble, holds it up to the light, examines it, and tosses it aside. For hours, she sifts the earth until her fingers are cold, waxy, and numb.

Eventually, Lyla becomes too tired. She is exhausted by it all.

She leans on the stump to help her up, the stump that is, in a strange way, very old, but is also quite new.

The stump that is now silver-white in the moonlight.

Lyla's hand rests on the collection of annual growth rings, the circles of scars in the pitch of pale meat. She traces her finger along the outermost ring, working her way inward. She used to do that, trace things in the dark, like the scar on her father's shoulder when he used to lie next to her in bed, telling Lyla stories of her mother, about how they met. How he fought for her to love him like he did her. Stories that used to make Lyla blush.

She even did that with Hap, walked her fingerprints like an itsy-bitsy spider down the length of his scar. Then she and Hap would do things that would make the older Lyla blush too.

Back in her grandmother's kitchen, Lyla gets to work. She spreads out the newspaper and glues the dog to its leash. She secures the leash to the doll's hand. She then holds the two sections together for a whole minute, letting the pieces bond. But when she tries to let go, she can't. She has accidentally superglued her fingers to the doll.

"Well, here's looking at you kid," Lyla says, dizzily swinging the doll around the kitchen, like the two of them are dancing.

Waltzing.

Doing the cha-cha.

The tango.

She knows she is being silly, but she feels deliciously delirious in being a little whackadoo.

Lyla doesn't want to let go. But when she boogie-woogies up to the table and sees the blank pieces of stationery and the crumpled-up paper balls heaped in a pile, she finally does.

She pries her fingers away, leaving bits of her skin stuck to the porcelain doll.

She turns out the light and goes to bed.

Lyla still sleeps in the guest bedroom even though the house is, for all intents and purposes, hers. At the nursing home, Caroline had broken her own news; she told Lyla she had willed the house to her. Not to any other of the grandchildren.

Not even Margaret, her favorite.

Not Uncle David.

But to Lyla and Lyla alone.

"It's yours. Take care of it. And it will take care of you."

In the dark, Lyla wonders if this is all a sick joke—living here after all that transpired. But Lyla didn't want to come across as if she was looking a gift horse in the mouth as she sat in the attorney's office reviewing Caroline's revised last will and testament. Plus, Lyla had grown tired of living alone in her small studio apartment where the landlord was slow to respond to broken appliances, leaky faucets, and all the rest.

As the silver-white moonlight slices through the guest bedroom window, Lyla thinks about the letter she's been having trouble writing. Underneath the sheets, she can feel the dried glue stuck to her forefinger. She rubs her thumb over the missing scraps of skin. It kind of hurts, but she can't help but to keep rubbing. It's the kind of pain she can deal with.

"I'll try writing again tomorrow," she says, and falls fast asleep.

In the morning, Lyla drives to Arbor Vine Home for the Elderly without so much as taking a shower or brushing her teeth. The doll is sitting beside her in the passenger seat. Lyla has even placed a lap belt across the doll.

Just to be funny.

Lyla almost wishes to be pulled over just so she could see the expression on a police officer's face. She thinks about pressing down on the gas pedal, swerving into the next lane, trying to garner attention. But of course, she doesn't.

She isn't really feeling all *that* humorous. She was, after all, up for most of the night digging in the dirt.

At the entrance to the nursing home, Lyla holds her breath and stands on the automatic sliding glass door sensor. The doors flash open, and she walks down the hall to her grandmother's room. Room 126A.

Lyla breathes through her mouth, trying her best to block out the scent of loose bowels and the rose-scented aerosol spray the cleaning crew uses to cover up the stink of those who can no longer care for themselves or those who have flatlined off the face of the Earth.

The smell makes Lyla gag every single time she pays a visit.

One Mississippi, two Mississippi, three Mississippi, four, she counts in her head and hooks left down the hall.

Her lungs want to explode as she rushes past the terribly old people slumped over in their wheelchairs with nightgowns slipping off their bony shoulders. As she turns the next corner, Lyla nearly runs into Harold Tomlinson from Room 149B, the white-haired man with bright red cheeks and milky eyes who roams the hallways, with yellow tennis balls stuck to the feet of his walker.

"Olive!" he cries after Lyla. "You're here. You've finally come!"

Lyla dodges past Mr. Tomlinson and turns into room 126, but he still follows her, still calling out, "Olive, Olive. Wait. It's me, Harold."

One afternoon, Lyla had sat with Harold and pretended to be his long-ago wife, believing it was a gift she could give. A lifeline to this man's past life. But today, Lyla's in no mood for pretend play after having played gravedigger for most of the night. She shuts the door on Harold mid-sentence as he is recalling their apparent long-ago trip to China, when he and Olive stood at the head of the Great Wall and then took a boat trip on the Yangtze. Lyla feels guilty when she hears the faint glimmer of hope in Harold's voice on the other side of the door, the voice that sinks into something darker.

"Olive?" His voice trembles. "Olive, what's wrong?"

Nothing and everything, Lyla wants to say behind the closed door. But she doesn't. She stands as still as she can until he walks away.

It is dark inside room 126. The curtains are drawn tight enough to block out the mid-morning sun.

"Caroline?" Lyla bends over and whispers. "You awake?" There is no answer, and seeing how still Caroline is, Lyla suddenly wonders if her grandmother has died in the middle of the night. Lyla places a hand on her grandmother's shoulder and gives her a gentle shake. "Caroline, it's me. Lyla."

Her grandmother exhales.

She is not dead.

She is just fast asleep while the woman in the next bed over watches *Wheel of Fortune* on full volume.

The other bed, the third one next to the window, is empty. The sheets are clean and tucked in tidy hospital corners. All the hand-drawn crayoned pictures from the past resident's great-grandchildren have been taken down from the wall. A piece of Scotch tape is all that is left. Lyla never knew the woman's name. She wasn't a resident there long enough.

"Caroline? It's me." Lyla again tries to rouse her grandmother, who is lying in bed without a pillow. Lyla does not like it one bit; she looks like she is in a coffin. Lyla bends over and searches the floor. She almost gets up to complain and ask for a new pillow, but she doesn't want to face Harold. So she sits back down on the chair beside her grandmother's bed, deciding she'll inform the nurse on the way out.

"She's still asleep!" the roommate yells over the sound of the television.

"Yes, I can see that. Thanks!" Lyla yells back, watching the sheets over her grandmother's chest rise and fall ever so slightly, almost floating. It's a mystery her grandmother can sleep through the television noise. She used to be such a light sleeper. But not anymore. Not with the sedatives. Even the whirling of the fortune wheel on the television and the audience wildly clapping fail to stir her.

"Sleeps like a log, that one," the roommate barks.

Lyla fights the urge to explain—this is new. It must be the medications. But she doesn't. There is no point. The woman will be deaf to what she has to say because the TV is on too damn loud.

Despite what she wishes, her eyes are drawn to the stupid game show.

"I'd like to buy a vowel," the contestant nervously says. "I'd like to buy an *E*."

"An *E*. Yes, there are two *E*'s," Pat Sajak enthusiastically says as if he were announcing a cure to the common cold has been found. "And with that you are dangerously close to winning *ten thousand dollars!*"

"Oh my goodness gracious, oh me oh my," the roommate says as she tries to turn up the sound with her remote control. But the volume is maxed out. "Oh, Lordy. What I wouldn't do with that kind of money." She sits up straighter, with not one, but two, pillows propped up behind her head.

Lyla wants to get up and rip her grandmother's pillow out from under the woman, but she decides to wait until the roommate is helped to the bathroom. Then Lyla will sneak over and grab it back.

The roommate begins shouting random answers like a child stabbing at a puzzle, clearly not thinking her answers through. "Christmas movies, Norman Rockwell!" she shouts, not realizing both answers only have one *E* apiece.

Lyla can't stand it anymore. She gets up and kisses her grandmother on the forehead. She tells her she is sorry.

"I'll come back later tonight. I'll even sneak you a gin fizz," Lyla promises, rubbing Caroline's bony shoulder, amazed at who her grandmother has become. Her grandmother is no tiny woman. But lying in the hospital bed, she looks smaller than Lyla wants to believe.

She is eroding, decomposing.

Her snow-white hair is matted to one side, and one stray eyebrow hair pokes out like an anglerfish. Lyla licks her finger and smooths it down. But true to form, her grandmother is wearing her lipstick, always her Rouge Dior lipstick. The nurse must have put it on her after breakfast. Lyla will remember to thank her for that on her way out.

Lyla takes one of her grandmother's hands and squeezes it, hoping Caroline's eyes will pop open, even if momentarily. But Caroline remains asleep, snoring even. Little gasps of breath wheeze through the saliva webbing in her mouth.

Lyla wonders if she is choking, but of course, she isn't.

She is just sleeping.

Like a log.

Before she leaves, Lyla pulls the porcelain doll out of her macramé handbag and places it on the bedside tray table next to her grandmother's plastic drinking cup and walks out. Lyla doesn't leave a note explaining what she's unearthed.

What she's glued back together.

Driving back to the house, Lyla suddenly wonders if this will kill her grandmother—the resurrection of the treasured doll that had been buried for nearly a quarter of a century. But Lyla doesn't turn around. She is too damn tired.

She pulls into the driveway of her grandmother's house, the house that is starting to feel more and more like hers with each passing day, especially after stripping off the fuddy-duddy wallpaper, repainting, and taping up her own prints on the walls.

Placing candles in the fireplace.

Last week, she even glued her name—L. Hawkins—on the mailbox.

Once inside, Lyla draws the curtains closed.

And takes a very long nap.

Later that evening, Lyla stands at the kitchen sink. She fills the kettle and lights the stove. Outside it's too dark to see anything, even the stump.

The stump that, in a strange way, feels very old but is also quite new.

The kettle hisses and Lyla pours a cup of mint tea. She sits back down at the head of the table and blows into her mug, wanting to believe the stump has been removed while she was asleep. Wanting to believe that Griz came by, ground the stump up, and hauled it away for her.

It's possible, she thinks. Lyla has become a heavy sleeper lately. With the one-two punch of meditation and medication, she too has begun to sleep like a log.

Sitting at the table, she leans into the hope that the tree and the stump are forever gone.

She closes her eyes and tries to meditate on the emptiness—the thought that nothing was ever there to begin with.

Not the enormous oak tree that has withstood Herculean earthquakes, the Great Depression, staggering droughts, and celebrated pennant victories.

Not the very old memory of her father, that at times, still feels quite new.

But of course, all of that is impossible, because she is not very good at meditation.

When she gets up to rinse her cup, drying it from the inside out, something new begins to eat at her, gnawing on her insides like a bark beetle. Tiny legs of guilt or shame crawl around her stomach. She even thinks she feels itty-bitty teeth sink into her.

"Oh, God. What have I done?" she gasps.

Lyla bites her thumbnail, tearing it to the quick as she second-guesses her decision to fell the tree. Deep down she knows she cannot simply chop everything down, grind it away, or plant anything else in its place.

Because real or imagined, standing or felled, the tree will always inhabit the bold black of night and the bright white of day. Rain, sun, clouds and all.

It will forever inhabit that almond-shaped structure inside her temporal lobe.

It will inhabit all that is her.

She knows there is no escaping it.

Later, she sits at the table, armed with a glass of wine, a fresh sheet of stationery, and her trusty ballpoint pen. She takes two deep, steady breaths.

"You got this, Lyla. I mean really, how hard can it be?" she says aloud. She clicks the end cap of the pen and begins again. A new collection of words flows fast and sure.

Dear Gessica,

I hope this letter finds you well. I don't believe you know of me, but you may recognize my name, Lyla Hawkins. I am thirty-five years old and the daughter of Charles Hawkins, an American soldier you met during the war. I only recently discovered a letter you wrote to my father, and I am sorry to be the bearer of bad news, but I felt you should know that my father passed not long after his return from overseas. He died in 1956, here in Northern California, one night by his own hand. While it has been a very long time since his death, I suspect I, or we, will never fully understand what happened. I wanted you to know, he was a loving and caring father, a man I admire and will love completely and forever. But he was also a man who, according to my grandmother, could never get over what happened to him during his time overseas. From what I gather in your letter and the enclosed photograph, I have a half-brother who is several years older than myself. He looks like my dad and in a way me, as well. I know this is all terribly awkward and likely reintroduces a host of painful memories, but I felt it was best you know what happened to him in the end.

I don't expect anything from you, but if you should ever wish to write back, I would enjoy hearing from you. You can write to me at the return address on the envelope.

Sincerely,

Lyla May Hawkins

Lyla folds the letter in half and slips it into an envelope without rereading it. She licks the envelope closed, settles back into her chair, and lets out a heavy breath as though she'd been holding it in for a thousand Mississippis. Her shoulders relax.

A certain weight is instantly gone.

She is proud of herself.

She found the strength.

But she found something else too.

A new hollowness boring inside her.

Sitting with the unaddressed envelope in her hand, Lyla suddenly remembers how her mother confided she had burned a lock of her hair alongside Charles's body when he was cremated.

Earth to earth. Ashes to ashes. Dust to dust.

Lyla does not recognize why this comes to her now, only that it does. Her face heats. She feels a small bite of anger within her. She almost crushes up the envelope, but she knows she's too old to have a tantrum. She is thirty-five, about the same age as her mother when she admitted what she had done. And in that very moment, Lyla decides she wants to do something similar, something meaningful. She doesn't want to burn a lock of her hair and watch it disintegrate. Instead, she wants a piece of her father to grow inside her like a tomato seed.

She feels one part crazy with the thought of what she's about to dare to do, and two parts exhilarated.

———

Lyla walks out to the garage, more confident and measured this time. She finds the chisel and a hammer hanging on the pegboard above her grandfather's workbench. The dimensions of the removed tools are traced in blue pen. It was a trick her grandfather used so he could tell, in an instant, where the missing tool belonged. The tracings look like the chalky outlines at a murder scene.

She gets down on her knees in front of the stump; the weight of each tool feels terribly satisfying in her grip.

As she runs her hands along the growth rings this time, she swears she can feel the tree's pulse. It is the most noticeable at the center, the one that marks the tree's birth.

She picks up the hammer and whacks the butt end of the chisel, sending the blade deep into the heart of the stump.

She thinks she hears it cry.

She stops and listens before she whacks it again. But there is nothing but the songs of a still night and the boars grunting somewhere out there in the hillsides.

She hits the chisel strategically again and again, sending the blade deeper into the tree's pith. The sound of each thwack echoes off into the hills of her youth, the places she explored and played hide-and-go-seek with her cousins.

And all by herself.

Lyla yanks the blade out and recenters it, working counterclockwise until she releases a small plug of wood out from the middle. Sitting on the stump, Lyla weighs it in her open palm.

Lighter than a large pink Mead eraser, heavier than an arrowhead.

She closes her eyes, slips the wedge of wood onto her tongue, and begins to suck the essence of oak like it's a piece of candy. In the dark, she remembers how her father once handed her a piece of bark and told her about how he could manufacture memories from the smell of the tree. Lyla remembers how, at the time, she couldn't quite smell what he meant by that, but she believed him all the same.

When she garners enough saliva to soften the wood, she begins to take tiny bites, until she has effectively become a beaver and nibbled it all. The fibers slide down her throat, past her esophagus, and into her stomach where the tree takes up temporary residence inside her.

Lyla tells herself that even though she could never smell the memories, good or bad, she can taste them now.

And it is there, sitting alone in the dark with a bit of tree inside her that Lyla accepts that his decision was his and his alone. That it had nothing to do with her.

She looks up at the night sky and settles on Orion overhead, savoring the woody taste of memories.

Of her father. Of all that he gave.

And all that he could be.

"I love you, Daddy," she says, sitting with the fibrous tissue of the tree's pith swimming around and beginning to dissolve in her stomach.

Sitting there, letting everything just be.

EPILOGUE

REGROWTH—DECEMBER 1982

Beyond the sun-beaten gray fence sits a stump, two feet tall and four feet in diameter—a stump that is a whole year older now. And yet, in a strange and mysterious way, a stump that still feels quite new.

The sweet smell of sawn wood is no longer fresh.

The circle of annual growth rings has been hardened and browned by the sun.

The stump is a remnant of a once great California live oak, outlasting the buzz of a chain saw, the thunder of a tree's near and total collapse, and a host of other things. It has withstood the signing of death certificates, last wills and testaments, floods of tears, one proposal, two declarations of love, and penned promises that had the power to move the souls of a serially monogamous lover and a once self-confirmed bachelorette alike.

The stump is, if nothing else, a witness to history.

And a survivor.

Lyla and Griz walk out back with coffee mugs, both wearing wool sweaters, jeans, and heavy work boots. Their dog runs circles around them, bouncing eagerly at their side. Together they stand in the field next to where the tree once stood, the expansive canopy forever gone. They do this every morning now. A ritual before they start their day.

"Go on." Griz chucks their dog's favorite yellow tennis ball out into the tall green grass. And in the time that Charlie darts off, searching for, retrieving, then dropping the slobbered-up ball at their feet—his puppy eyes begging for more, always more—Lyla blows into her mug and stares at the stump.

Not at the stump, exactly, but the bright green shoot growing out of the roughened bark, reaching skyward.

The shoot that measures roughly five inches tall and is the width of a pinky finger.

The shoot that takes on new weight.

Heavier than an ordinary No. 2 pencil, lighter than a memory.

ABOUT THE AUTHOR

Elizabeth A. Tucker is a fiction writer, poet, playwright, and sixth-generation Californian living and writing at 6,600 feet above sea level in the Sierra Nevada with her husband and two children. Her work, often rooted in the fault-prone landscape of Northern California, can be found in a host of national and international literary journals including *Transfer Magazine*, *Red River Review*, *Aroostook Review*, *Ponder Review*, *The Bangalore Review*, *SNReview*, *Tahoe Blues*, and *JuxtaProse Magazine*.

When not carving words to page, Elizabeth can usually be found anywhere outside or playing her upright bass with the Reno Pops Orchestra. She is a founding board member of Adventure Risk Challenge, a California-based nonprofit with a mission of empowering underserved youth through transformational literary, leadership, and outdoor wilderness experiences.

Author photo © Annie Robillard

Looking for your next great read?

We can help!

Visit www.shewritespress.com/next-read
or scan the QR code below for a list
of our recommended titles.

She Writes Press is an award-winning
independent publishing company founded to
serve women writers everywhere.